Gilly trusted him. He was Channing Sabre, the master, the protector. No one had ever been sold away from the Sabre family. In all her life Gilly had never heard of Mr. Channing handing one of his people over to a slave-trader.

But she had been a bad girl. And now here she was, her belongings in hand, riding toward Vendue Range . . . and every slave knew what went on there.

"I sorry, master. I don't do it no more. Please, master."

Channing drove on, his throat too full to speak. He knew where he was taking the girl, thought he knew what would happen to her, convincing himself that he was doing the right thing.

But the truth was, Channing knew very little about the buying and selling of beautiful black wenches. And what he didn't know, Gilly would all too soon find out. . . .

STORM OVER SABREHILL

by

Raymond Giles

FAWCETT GOLD MEDAL • NEW YORK

STORM OVER SABREHILL

Although some of the characters and incidents in the following narrative are drawn from history, their interpretation is that of the author.

ISBN: 0-449-14018-0

Printed in the United States of America

10 9 8 7 6 5 4 3 2 1

To
Henry Morrison

Prologue

The Night of the Fires

They didn't hear the shots, half a dozen pistol and rifle shots fired in the night, but they saw the flames long before they reached Redbird plantation. From the first illusion of false dawn in the east, they recognized the fire for what it was, yet they reined up their horses and watched the glowing sky over the dark treetops for a moment, almost as if afraid to admit to themselves what they were seeing.

"Niggers," Balbo Jeppson said bitterly. "Niggers at it again." His gravelly voice could rise to a lion's roar or descend to a deceptively mild purr. Now it shook with anger: "Goddamn niggers!"

"Can't be sure," said the younger man, P. V. Tucker. "Could be anything started it. And I know some white folks that don't take to Vachel Skeet any too kindly."

"I'm betting it's niggers," Jeppson insisted. "Last week they burned barns on the McClintock and Haining places. And last Sunday night a bunch of them caught those two white men and damn near beat them to death. And those ain't the only burnings and beatings lately. The goddamn niggers, it's getting so you can't hardly hold them down no more."

They watched the sky in silence for a moment, filled with that peculiar awe that only flames can inspire.

"Some say it's Adaba that's stirring them up," Tucker said.

"Agh!" Jeppson made a sound of deep disgust. "That's just crazy nigger talk."

"Maybe it is, but—"

"There ain't no Adaba!" Suddenly Jeppson's anger was rekindled. The name of Adaba—reputed outlier, slave-stealer, Underground Railroader—always did that to him: set off feelings of frustration and rage so deep that even he did not quite understand them. "There ain't no

8

such nigger as Adaba," he repeated vehemently, "and let's stop wasting time. Vachel's gonna need our help."

While the flames grew ever higher, they rode on toward Redbird, traveling faster than was safe, considering the darkness of the night and the badly rutted condition of the road. They had to be wary too of traps. If slaves were responsible for the fire at Redbird, they were probably now on the run, and they might have stretched ropes across the road to slow pursuit. More than one white man had broken his neck when his horse tripped and sent him flying.

By the time the Redbird big house was in sight, the place was almost totally a roaring inferno. And as Jeppson and Tucker got closer, they saw—or thought they saw— what had happened.

Vachel Skeet, the owner of Redbird plantation, "broke" rebellious slaves for their owners. Not far from his big house, which was now ablaze, he had a "nigger jail," a small brick building with unglazed, barred windows. The single door was also barred—double-barred from the outside—so that it was virtually impossible for the imprisoned slaves to break out. And yet apparently they had done just that. The door was open, the jail empty. And Jeppson knew for a fact that Vachel had lately been breaking at least six or eight bad-acting slaves, including his own Buckley, a runaway he had recently recaptured after a dozen years.

The big house and several outbuildings were burning, but no one was making any attempt to fight the fires—not even at the outbuildings that might have been saved. No one was even watching the fires. Vachel Skeet's slaves were either hiding in their quarters or had run off. The only people Jeppson and Tucker saw as they dismounted and walked across the courtyard were the dead.

The first one they came to was Shadrach, Vachel's chief driver, who had been shot in the side of the chest.

The next was Dinkin, Vachel's overseer. He had been shot through the heart.

"And there's Vachel," Tucker said softly. "Goddamn, there's Vachel."

Vachel Skeet had been shot several times and was

9

lying with his head on the lap of the lone survivor on the scene, a black who had been so brutally beaten that it was a wonder that he was still alive. The black seemed to be trying to say something to Vachel, but his mutterings were incoherent.

"Would you look at that boy," Tucker said, "babbling and bawling away like he don't even know Vachel's dead?"

"Like maybe he don't know he's just about dead too."

Jeppson stepped closer to get a better look at the black. "Well, I'll be damned. He ain't got much face left, but do you see who this here is?"

"Hell, yes," Tucker said, also looking closer. "That's Buckley Skeet. He musta had something to do with all this."

"You damn right he did."

Buckley Skeet. Said to be none other than the murderous outlier Black Buck. Black Buck, who ran with that other slave-stealing outlier—Adaba.

Adaba!

The name turned Jeppson's soul to brimstone.

Of course, there was no Adaba, but . . .

Jeppson forced himself to remain calm. He took out his flintlock pistol and drew back the cock. He pointed the pistol at Buckley's head. He squeezed the trigger and felt a sensual pleasure as the weapon bucked in his hand. Buckley fell back dead.

"Come on," Jeppson said, "we're gonna be right busy the next day or two. We got more niggers to kill."

The slave Ruff, hiding in the woods, heard the shots, and he thought he saw the very slightest lightening of the sky in the east. He wished he dared move closer in order to be certain. As the flames grew higher and redder, he very nearly cheered aloud. This was the signal: Redbird was burning. Some of the runaways, he knew, were already on their way to the meeting place on Sabrehill plantation.

He watched the glowing sky a few minutes longer, then started back toward the Jeppson plantation as fast as he could run. He stayed off the roads; the patrol was unlikely to be out tonight, a Saturday night just before Christmas, but he was taking no chances. Ruff knew the trail well, and within a very short time, the Jeppson big house would be burning too—burning, Ruff hoped, with Mr. Jeppson in it.

The slave quarters were in darkness when he got back, but there was a single light showing in the big house. Ruff didn't like that. He had hoped that Mr. Jeppson would be asleep by this hour.

When he entered the dark barrack that he shared with several other men, a couple of them immediately got out of bed. They were completely clothed. They didn't have to be told what to do, and no one said a word. They would go get the supplies they had stolen and hidden, and proceed to a meeting place a few hundred yards to the east. If anyone got separated from the others, he would go on to Sabrehill plantation.

From under his thin corn-shuck mattress, Ruff took a shingling hatchet. He left the bunkhouse and crossed the street of the quarters to the cabin where his brother, Latham, and Latham's wife, Beulah, lived. Two bad niggers, those, and Mr. Jeppson locked them up nightly. Now Ruff had to make some noise, but there was no help for it. He brought the poll of the hatchet sharply down on the latch and broke it with a single blow.

Latham and Beulah were ready. Ruff didn't have to tell them, any more than the others, what to do. Beulah took her bundle and headed east toward the meeting place. Latham started off for the hidden torches.

"Nigger, what you doing there!"

Both Ruff and Latham spun around. It was Sabin, Jeppson's meanest and most-trusted driver. But what was he doing out at this time of night?

It didn't matter. He was here, and that was the only important thing. Ruff kept his hatchet close to the side of his leg.

Sabin moved closer. "I say, what you doing out here, niggers! Now you answer me! I tell Mr. Jeppson—"

Ruff brought the hatchet up in an arc. The flat side popped sickeningly against Sabin's skull, and the driver dropped like a stone. For a moment Ruff thought he had

11

killed the man, but Sabin was still breathing when he dragged him into the shadows at the side of the cabin.

"Go on," he said to Latham, "git! Fetch them torches!"

While Latham ran to get the torches, Ruff very cautiously approached the big house to see what the situation was there. Actually, it wasn't a very big "big house," but a modest frame building with its kitchen built into it rather than in a separate house. It was in the kitchen that the light, a lamp or candle, burned. As Ruff watched from behind a tree, Miss Lady, the housekeeper, stepped out onto the little piazza and said, "Ruff, boy, you come here," as if she had been watching him all along. Ruff obediently went to the piazza.

Miss Lady stood a few steps above him, her arms crossed under her full, high breasts. She held her head cocked back, almost haughtily, in a way that had once made the other slaves hate her. Except for a slight frown, her face was inscrutable. It was an ageless face, a face that might have been a dozen years younger or a dozen years older than the thirty-odd years she was said to be. Under faintly slanted eyes, she had a thin prominent nose, slightly arched and delicate, a generous mouth with barely everted edges, and a round, slightly dimpled chin. In sunlight, her skin had a coppery tone, which caused some to say she had white blood, others to say she had Indian.

Whatever her ancestry, Miss Lady had long had the reputation of being the best-looking black woman for miles around. She herself never gave any sign of being aware of this, though she must have had some idea: plenty of men, both black and white, had been after her for about as long as Ruff could remember. But she had given in to none willingly, unless it was to Mr. Jeppson. Some said she was Jeppson's bed companion; some even claimed to have seen the two pleasuring each other. Ruff found this hard to believe, knowing how Mr. Jeppson felt about white and black bedding together. Still, no one, not even Mr. Jeppson's closest white friends, could temper his angers and his stern judgments the way Miss Lady could.

"What you up to, Ruff?" she now asked softly.

"You know what we up to, Miss Lady. Tonight we all

going north—north to freedom!" Whatever her relationship with Jeppson, Miss Lady was trusted by the black people. She knew of the plan, though not of its details.

"But you can't do that now," she said. "Mr. Skeet done caught Black Buck, you know that. Now you ain't got nobody to take you north—"

"Black Buck ain't in that jail house no more." Ruff thought of the shots and the flames. "He done got out, just like they say he going do. And Redbird burning—that's the signal! We all going north, and you best come with us!"

Miss Lady came down a step, as if to see Ruff more clearly. She looked at him searchingly. "You know what you talking 'bout, boy?"

"I know. I *seen* it burning."

"Mr. Jeppson catch you, he likely 'nough kill you."

"He ain't going catch me—less'n you call him."

"He ain't here. Him and Mr. Tucker, they ride to Redbird to talk to Mr. Skeet."

Ruff laughed. He felt both disappointed and relieved. He had hoped to see Jeppson burn in his own house, but at least his absence meant there would be no difficulty.

"They going get a big surprise, they get there," he said. "And Mr. Jeppson, he get a bigger one when he get back. You coming with us, Miss Lady?"

For a moment he thought Miss Lady was contemplating doing just that. But she shook her head. "No. No, you go on, be free. But I reckon I ain't going be no freer up north than I be right here. 'Sides . . ." She shrugged. "Mr. Jeppson, he need me, and the people need me. This here is my home."

"Ain't going be much home after tonight."

"What you mean?"

Ruff's heart thumped. "Going burn it."

Staring at him, Miss Lady went back up a step and away from him. "No," she said. "No, you ain't."

"Miss Lady—"

"You run off, you want. I ain't going try stop you. I even help you if I can. But you ain't going burn down this house I live in all these years."

"But Miss Lady—"

13

"No! This here is *my* house! This is where I had my sorrows, so many sorrows, and this is where I had my joy, the little the good Lord give me, and I ain't never going see it burn! It's mine!"

"Miss Lady, we got to burn it! Ain't only this house! Redbird burning and Kimbrough Hall and all them others, all up and down the river. Houses, barns, everything! That way they can't come after us, not till the fires is out! They so many of us running off tonight, they find us right off if we don't set the fires. Likely they shoot us all down like them people in that maroon camp while back. All them people, just shot 'em down like wild dogs!"

A chair stood on the piazza. Miss Lady wandered over to it. She sank down onto it, closed her eyes, and rested her forehead on her hand.

Ruff waited. He wondered how he could possibly burn the house if she denied him permission. He owed her so much. She had nursed him in illness, comforted him in sorrow, stood up for him to Mr. Jeppson.

"Miss Lady?" he said. "Miss Lady? . . ."

"Burn it," Miss Lady said softly. "Burn it."

Fire, up and down the river.

When Theron and Lize, two young slaves from Kimbrough Hall plantation, saw the flames rising in the sky, they didn't restrain their cheers. What did it matter if Mr. Skeet's guards heard them? Mr. Skeet was most likely dead by now.

They hurried back to Kimbrough Hall to give the good news to a slave named Hector. Hector at once gathered up an armload of torches. He lit one of them. He then went to the end of the big house where he thought he was least apt to be seen. One by one, he lit the remaining torches and hurled them up onto the roof. Then he gathered his followers and set off for Sabrehill plantation.

Theron and Lize, meanwhile, set fire to a nearby barn. Though they did not plan to join the runaways, they did all they could to help them. While Lize fired other outbuildings, Theron ran as fast as he could to Sabrehill, where he met a slave named Zagreus in the field quarters. Zagreus dispatched his younger brother, Paris, to the Dev-

14

ereau plantation, which was the next one down the river.

Paul Devereau was in his study when he heard the alarm bell ringing. Rushing out of the house, he found that a cluster of shops and sheds was on fire. As he tried to get a fire brigade organized, he happened to look back toward his big house—and saw flames through the windows.

Still farther down the river, the Buckridge big house was burning—the big house that had been rebuilt after having been burnt to the ground less than two years before. While his son and his overseer tried futilely to fight the fire, and his wife wept at his side, Owen Buckridge gazed stunned into the flames. This could not be happening to him again. But it was.

On that immediate stretch of the river there were fires on five plantations that night. Other greater and lesser fires were started on more distant plantations. There was none at Sabrehill, because the black overseer, Jeb Hayes, had agreed to let the runaways meet there in the woods near the field quarters, on the condition that Sabrehill be spared.

And so, as the plantations burned, the runaways moved swiftly through the night to Sabrehill. For weeks this march to freedom had been in preparation. At times it had seemed that it would never come to pass. But harsh repression by the masters and abuses by the slave patrols had driven them on—and Black Buck, the outlying slave-stealer, had given them leadership. Black Buck would lead them north to freedom.

But Black Buck lay dead at Redbird.

And yet the runaways did escape. With the exception of a handful who were found and killed almost by accident, they vanished as if they had never existed.

How? Jeppson asked himself. *How?*

How could such a large group get away without having the most-experienced kind of leadership? Even with such leadership, it was a virtually impossible feat. Then, how?

"Adaba," P. V. Tucker said, and Jeppson shut his eyes and gritted his teeth. "Adaba," Tucker repeated, "and don't tell me there ain't no Adaba."

They were sitting, legs stretched out before the fire-

15

place, in the little cabin that for the last week had been home for Jeppson and Sheba. As they talked, Sheba silently replenished their glasses with whiskey. Jeppson was weary. Except for Christmas, when he could get no followers, he had spent every day leading a posse in search of the runaways. It had seemed a simple matter at first. Get the men and the hounds and the guns and run them down. A day or two of blood sport.

But where had they gone?

Surely it was impossible for thirty-odd slaves simply to disappear off the face of the earth, but exactly that seemed to have happened. Starting from various plantations, the hounds all went to Sabrehill, to the woods near the field quarters. From there, the dogs headed north. But before long the trail became broken and erratic and often false. It followed streams, doubled back, became five or six different trails, thinned, disappeared. . . .

And the slaves were gone.

"I remember when I first heard of Adaba," Jeppson said softly. His eyes were still closed, his whiskey glass rested on his chest. "Musta been eight, ten years ago, before they even talked about any Underground Railroad. Stories about some outlying nigger that was stealing slaves and sending them north. But nobody ever claimed to *see* this here Adaba. And it was never around here he done his stealing—it was always someplace else. And what kind of a name is that—Adaba?"

"A nigger name," Tucker said. "Gullah talk for the Brown Dove."

"The Brown Dove," Jeppson sneered softly. "Don't that sound made-up? Some nigger that turns hisself into a brown dove and just flies away?"

"Hell," Tucker said indifferently, "it's just a plain old nigger 'basket name' like Cudjoe or Quashee. How come it burns your ass so much?"

"The Brown Dove," Jeppson sneered again. "And then a few years after Vachel Skeet's Buckley run off, there was stories that he was running with the Brown Dove—stories that he turned into a nigger-stealer called Black Buck. Now, does that sound likely?"

16

"Sounds as likely as thirty or forty slaves disappearing all at once."

Jeppson opened his eyes and found himself looking directly at Tucker. Tucker was in his mid-thirties. He was a tall lanky man with a narrow face, long dirty-blond hair, and a thin-lipped, fleshy mouth. His gray eyes were deeply sunk under a high, broad forehead. He seemed to have no cheekbones, and his nose hung almost straight down, so that his face appeared suspended beneath the jutting rock of forehead.

"You ever considered that the Sabres mighta had something to do with it?" Jeppson asked.

Tucker shrugged. "Like what?"

"I think they did. Otherwise, how come they only lost one slave that night? I lost three, and the Haining place lost six—and Sabrehill is bigger'n us put together. And how come the runaways all met at Sabrehill? And how come Sabrehill was the only place around here that didn't get burned? And you know the Sabres always had abolitionist leanings—that goddamn Justin Sabre most of all."

"All right," Tucker agreed, "maybe Justin does know something about it. But he sure as hell didn't make them niggers disappear, even if he knew how. You know damn good and well he was in bed at the time with busted ribs. And old scar-face Miss Lucy sure as hell didn't lead 'em off. I say the facts point to Adaba. It was Adaba stole away those niggers!"

Jeppson sighed. "Just 'cause you heard some tall tales—"

"No! Look at the facts. Would you look at the facts, Balbo?"

"I'm looking, P.V."

"Vachel catches his boy Buckley after all these years. They say Buckley is Black Buck, who conducts on the Underground Railroad with Adaba."

"That ain't facts, that's just talk."

"Listen to me, goddammit. How come old Buckley come back here? To get hisself caught? Hell, no, he come back here to steal some slaves and maybe take a shot at Vaych. Only Vaych got him first and locked him up. *And*

17

in spite of that, Buckley got out of that jail, and all them niggers disappeared!"

"But Buckley got hisself shot at Redbird."

"Bad luck, that's all. What I want to know is how he got out of that jail house."

"He broke out—"

"Christ, you know better than that," Tucker said angrily. "That jail house door is double-barred, and the only way to get through it is for somebody on the outside to *lift* up the bars and set 'em aside. The *only* way, Balbo."

"Anybody coulda done it."

"Yeah, and anybody coulda made all them niggers disappear. Like the earth swallowed 'em up. Like—like—"

"Like they went off 'on an underground road,' " Jeppson said softly.

"That's right! Balbo, I'm telling you that old Buckley didn't come back here alone. Him and somebody else come here and got them slaves organized to run away. Then Buckley got caught. But *somebody* got him out of the jail. And then Buckley got shot. But *somebody* led them slaves off. Because organized or not, they needed a leader who knew what he was doing. And I say that 'somebody' was Black Buck's old friend—Adaba!"

Tucker talked on, but Jeppson paid no attention. He waited until Tucker had finished his whiskey and left. Then he looked up at Sheba.

"What do you think, Sheba Lady? Is there really an Adaba?"

"Well, Mr. Jeppson, I do hear the tales. . . ." Smiling slightly, she bent down and kissed Jeppson's forehead. "But I reckon I don't know, no more than you do."

"P.V. is right about one thing, though. There was somebody that helped them niggers get away. And I reckon," he added bitterly, "that Adaba is as good a name for him as any."

"Yes, I reckon it don't really matter what you call him."

Jeppson stared into the flames in the fireplace. Tucker was also right about another thing: the name of Adaba did anger him beyond reason. Sometimes he felt that it haunted him, as if it were associated with ancient, forgotten memories. And having said it aloud just now, he found that it was still bitter in his mouth as a sip of wormwood.

He sipped at his whiskey to wash it away.

But the taste lingered on.

Adaba . . . Adaba . . .

PART ONE

ADABA

Slaves and Masters

One: February 1818

It all happened in a few violent, explosive seconds.

Adaba had not wanted it to happen, had not expected it to happen. But he could not have held himself back if he had wanted to. The moment the white man raised his hand against Gilly, the instant he brought that big hand smashing down on Gilly's face, all caution was forgotten. Whatever the danger to himself, there was only one thing he could do. . . .

They had been going about their business, joking and laughing together, harming no one—Adaba and his Gilly and their young white friend, Lew Sabre. The morning was brisk and sparkling, and Market Street was crowded. It was the Saturday before Race Week in Charleston, the gayest week of the "gay season," the high point of the year, and the city had been invaded by planters and their families and servants, by small farmers and poor whites and country blacks, by beggars and pickpockets and thieves. The gentry had come for their parties and balls, the po' buckra for a holiday of drinking and gambling and whoring.

The commercial streets of the city had become a crowded swirl of bright colors. Children, black and white, pursued by barking dogs, darted between the legs of adults. Carriages made their way slowly among the pedestrians. At the stands and shops of the City Market, the black merchants hawked their wares, fruits and vegetables brought up from food cellars, fish caught that very morning, rabbit, turkey, and partridge shot the day before, and terrapin still alive—a thousand and one delicious things to grace a Charleston table.

Except that it was livelier than usual, this morning was no different from many another and there was no reason to anticipate trouble. Gilly, though only sixteen, was trusted to do the household marketing, and Adaba and

22

Lew, as often before, accompanied her. Now, the marketing done, Gilly's basket filled and covered with a neatly tucked-in towel, they were returning to the Sabre house.

Afterward, Adaba could never remember what it was that had made Gilly laugh so hard. He could only remember watching her with delight as she turned around and took a few steps backward, almost skipping, still laughing.

Of course, she hadn't been watching where she was going. But all she did was bump into the white man, jostle him, make him stagger awkwardly. Perhaps her foot came down painfully on his ankle. Why else would he have reacted so violently?

Gilly gasped and looked around. "Oh, I sorry!" she said. "Oh, master, I sorry! I . . . I . . ."

She couldn't help herself: her words dissolved in another peal of laughter. Gilly held her hand out to the white man in apology.

Perhaps he thought she was laughing at him.

Adaba saw the insane anger on the white man's face. He saw the hand lift high. There was no time to call out to the laughing Gilly, no time to sweep her away. Adaba saw the hand come down, heard the blow, felt it as if it had burned across his own cheek. Then the man had Gilly by the shoulders and was shaking her, shaking her as hard as he could. He released one shoulder and raised his hand to give Gilly another blow.

The blow never landed.

Every warning Adaba had ever been given was swept out of his head. The sight of the white man abusing Gilly, *his Gilly,* the white fingers digging into her shoulder, the white hand lifting higher for the next blow, was all that filled his mind. Adaba roared.

He dragged Gilly away from the white man and shoved her aside.

The white man regarded Adaba with astonishment. He was a big craggy-faced, barrel-chested man in his middle thirties—about twice Adaba's age. He was so heavy boned and heavy muscled that he might have rolled over Adaba like a boulder. But Adaba was tall, hard, and long limbed, and he had the advantage of surprise.

"You don't do that," Adaba said between clinched

23

teeth, and grabbing the white man's shirtfront with his left hand, he put all of his strength behind a blow to the belly.

The blow brought a gag of pain. Somewhere behind Adaba, Gilly cried out—cried out again. Beneath its weathering, the white man's face was sickly pale, his eyes still full of disbelief, as he tried to speak: "You—you goddamn—"

Adaba's fist slammed into the man's middle again, bringing another strangled cry. He seemed to be acting in a dream: his anger made him a stranger to himself. "You bastard!" he heard himself say as he struck a third time. "You ignorant swamprat bastard, you touch her, I'll kill you! You hear me, you buckra bastard, I'll kill you!"

And that quickly it was over.

Adaba saw the gray-eyed blond youth coming at him from one side, the dark-eyed round-faced man from the other, and all the warnings came crowding back into his mind: *Don't you ever dare raise your hand against a white man, boy! Don't you ever raise your eyes to him unless he tells you to! Remember that you're black and stay in your place! Never mind if he humiliates you and abuses your woman! Keep your mouth shut and your hands to yourself and your eyes down! Because if you don't, boy . . .*

But the deed was done, and it could not be undone. The workhouse, he thought. It was only a few blocks away, on Magazine Street. The whipping post. Thirty-nine lashes. Perhaps worse, far worse. He didn't even have a pass. And he'd been heard to threaten murder. In this crowd, with all these white people, he might not even live to reach the workhouse.

There was only one thing he could do.

He still had the big white man by the shirtfront. He whirled the man around and, with the strength of desperation, hurled him at one of the oncoming men. The big man went sprawling in the dirty street, and the other was knocked staggering to one side.

Then he had Gilly by the hand, and he was running, running like hell, thrusting people aside, tearing his way through the crowd. He couldn't leave Gilly behind—

24

impossible to tell what this crowd might do to her. She might end up at the whipping post herself, and he couldn't have stood that.

There were shouts behind them. "There they go! . . . Goddamn, nigger, get out of the way! . . . Get 'em! . . . Hey, stop 'em! . . ." Adaba looked back and saw that Lew was still with them.

There was no time to plan an escape, and they ran almost blindly, more by instinct than by reason. Around a corner and up Meeting Street, through more crowds, around another corner. Blacks behind them seemed to be obstructing the chase, but the City Guard might join it at any moment. Church Street. More shouts behind them. Over to Meeting Street again, and on . . .

Then, miraculously, they were approaching Denmark Vesey's carpentry shop, and except for Lew, there was not a white face in sight, either ahead or behind them. Adaba flung Gilly through the door of the shop, flung himself after her. Denmark looked up in surprise from his workbench as they ran through the shop to the courtyard behind. They heard Lew, still out in the street, yelling: "Come on! They went up there, around the corner! Come on! Come on!"

Pretending to be one of the pursuers, misleading the others. If only it worked . . .

It should not have happened. Not to Balbo Jeppson. He was too big, too tough, too dangerous. The niggers knew it when they saw him on the street, knew it by the glint in his eye and the set of his jaw. Move over. Get out of the way. That is one mean white man coming along there. Bow your head, boy, and look somewhere else. Don't let that white man so much as see you looking at him.

Not that he was really mean. Of course not. Hell, nobody took better care of his niggers than Jeppson. Nobody was more thoughtful, nobody more fair and just. The fact was, Balbo Jeppson *liked* a good nigger. But to keep them good, you had to keep them in their place. They had to be disciplined. Any hint of insubordination

25

had to be stopped instantly and ruthlessly. They had to be kept constantly aware of two things: you were white and the master; they were black and the niggers. Whites ruled niggers. It was the natural order of things. And on this day, the natural order had been disrupted. . . .

Ahead of him, he saw P. V. Tucker and Rolly Joe Macon turning back, too soon. They came toward him slowly, panting and sweating.

"You let 'em get away."

"Didn't let 'em get away, Balbo," Macon said. "They was faster'n hell and got lost in the crowd. Likely they turned into some passage where we couldn't find 'em."

Jeppson and his friends found a grog shop where they were known and could get a drink even at this early hour. Sweat continued to pour down Jeppson's body, chilling him. He felt bruised, frustrated, outraged. He wasn't sure he could keep his whiskey down: he was close to vomiting.

"Tossed on his ass by a nigger boy!" Tucker said, laughing, as he settled back in his chair. "By God, Balbo, I never thought I'd live to see it. Gut-punched, cussed out, and tossed on your ass by a nigger boy."

"He was no more a boy than you," Jeppson said quietly. He stared into his glass on the table.

Tucker shook his head. "He was a big skinny boy that you outweighed by half again, and he still sure as hell tossed you on your ass."

"Did you see the look on old Balbo's face when that boy grabbed him up?" Macon shook with laughter. He was a round-faced young man with a heavy load of gut overhanging his belt. "Did you see that, P.V.?"

"I sure as hell did!"

"Balbo, you should have seen your face. You never looked so—so damn *stupid* in all your life!"

Jeppson looked up slowly from his drink. His heart, which had started to calm, was beating harder again. "So damn . . . what did you say?"

"So damn stupid. You shoulda seen your face—"

So slowly that Macon didn't realize what was about to happen, Jeppson reached across the table and grabbed his coat collar. He pulled Macon toward him.

26

"Rolly Joe," he said in little more than a whisper, "don't you ever call me stupid."

"Now, Balbo, I didn't say you *was* stupid, I just said—"

"Don't you ever call me stupid. Don't you ever say I look stupid. Not to my face or behind my back. Because if you ever do, Rolly Joe, I'm gonna give you what I shoulda given that nigger. What I *am* gonna give him if ever I get my hands on him."

He shoved Macon back into his chair.

It didn't do any good. Both Macon and Tucker were still grinning at him. Balbo Jeppson humiliated in public. By a pair of niggers.

It was wrong. It should not have happened. It took away a man's self-respect. Somehow Balbo Jeppson was going to have to put things right.

Denmark Vesey, seated on his workbench, his iron-hard arms crossed on his chest, listened with an amused smile as Adaba told his story.

". . . and, of course," Adaba concluded, "we've been hiding in the courtyard ever since, just waiting for Lew here to come back and say it was safe to come out again."

Denmark threw back his head and laughed. It was a big laugh, fit for the big man that he was. At fifty-one, he looked much older, a thick-bearded, grizzled old bull of a black man, but he had all the strength and enthusiasm of youth. He had been born either in Africa or in the Virgin Islands—he was unclear as to which—and had spent much of his early life as a servant aboard slave ships. He had been brought to Charleston at the age of sixteen. In 1800, at the age of thirty-three, he had won $1,500 in the East Bay lottery. He had purchased his freedom from his master, Captain Joseph Vesey, for $600, and with the remainder of his money, had opened a carpentry shop. Since then, he had prospered. He was a well-regarded craftsman and property owner with considerable savings. Gifted with a brilliant mind, familiar with several languages, he had educated himself by reading widely. But he had never forgotten the grim holds of the slave ships.

"So you stood up to that white man!" he said with delight.

"More'n that," Gilly said, "he sure don't leave that white man standing up. He send'm flying!"

Sliding down from the workbench, Denmark turned fierce eyes on Lew. "And you helped them get away, white boy."

"Might not have got away if it hadn't been for Lew," Adaba said.

"Why did you do that, white boy? Why did you help them get away?"

Denmark's tone was a mixture of amusement, contempt, and challenge, and Lew obviously did not know what to make of the man. Few white people did. Some called him a troublemaker, others found it convenient to dismiss him as just a little crazy. Why else would a man of color walk along the street glaring so fiercely that even white men stepped aside deferentially rather than risk trouble with him?

"I said, why did you help them get away, white boy? Don't you understand the question?"

"Now, Denmark . . ." Adaba knew what was coming. He had seen it often. And he was too fond of Lew to see the boy embarrassed, especially after what he had done today. "Denmark, Lew is our friend."

"But I only want to talk to the boy," Denmark insisted. "Unless, of course, he has no time for an old nigger man."

Lew flushed. "I don't mind talking to you." He looked very young and coltish under his mop of dark hair. Adaba sighed and shook his head.

"Very good. I asked, Master Lewis, why you helped these two to get away."

"Like Adaba says, we're friends."

Denmark's heavy brows lifted in mock surprise. "Oh, you're friends! You, a white boy, have black friends? How did you ever come about?"

"Well—Gilly belongs to us—"

"I see—Gilly is your slave, is she? Then you were just protecting your property, isn't that right? Friendship really has nothing to do with it."

"They're my friends," Lew said stubbornly. "They been my friends 'bout long as I remember."

"Well, I'm glad to hear that, Master Lewis. You don't

want some strange white man bothering your friends, do you!"

" 'Course not."

"I'll bet you even think your black friend did right in striking down that white man, don't you!"

"He did it for Gilly," Lew said defiantly.

"That's right, he did. A black slave man struck a white man for the sake of a black slave woman. And that's against the law, isn't it, white boy?"

"Reckon it is."

Denmark's eyes widened. "But don't you have respect for the law?"

Lew hesitated. "Not always."

"Not always! Ah, now our colloquy becomes interesting! You think there are occasions on which a black man is entitled to strike a white man in spite of the law? Occasions when one might say that any decent black man would be *required* to strike a white man in spite of the law?"

Lew was silent.

"No answer? But surely it is obvious. The law is a *white* law. It is simply a white man's device, like chains, for keeping the black man in captive servitude. And if a black man bends to that white law—if he acknowledges its moral force—then he deserves to be a slave, does he not?"

Lew shook his head. "I dunno. I don't understand all this—"

"If I say to you, 'White boy, you bow, you scrape, you lick my boots, you act in all respects like a slave'—and you say, 'Yassuh, massa! Yassuh, massa!' and proceed to do so—you deserve to be a slave, do you not? Do you not collaborate in your own subjugation? Do you not to an extent enslave yourself to me? Do you not give yourself away to me, spirit, soul, and body?"

"I dunno, I guess so."

"You guess so. Well, if you guess so, do you approve of your binding yourself over to me in such a manner? Would you willingly make yourself a slave to me?"

" 'Course not."

"Would you not fight any attempt I made to enslave you?"

"You goddamn bet!"

Denmark looked pleased. "You goddamn bet. And how can you have any respect for me—how can I have respect for myself—if I don't do the same?"

"Oh, what are you talking 'bout?" Lew looked disgusted. "I heard you won some money in a lottery and went and bought yourself. You never did any fighting to get yourself free, and now all you do is talk."

Denmark looked as if he had been hit in the face. He stared at Lew for a long moment, and Adaba decided his worries for Lew had been quite unnecessary.

Finally Denmark smiled. "You're right, boy," he said, with unexpected gentleness. "All I do is talk. But you see, it took me a long time to learn what I have come to know —the obligation of a man to assert his freedom. In my childhood, with all its miseries, I hardly knew what freedom was. And later, when Captain Vesey took me as a servant, few men ever had a kinder master. Better had he been harsh—I would have learned sooner. But having learned at last, I shall never forget the lesson." He laughed quietly. "Now you may run along home if you wish, Master Lewis, and tell your family that old Denmark is talking crazy again, and maybe they had better hang him and get it over with. And I thank you for helping my friends."

"They're *my* friends," Lew said impatiently. "We better go, Gilly. We're gonna get bawled out for being so late."

Adaba decided to stay in the shop a little longer. It would be better if the three of them were not seen together now, and he would have to be very careful in moving about Charleston for some time to come. As Gilly tucked the towel over the contents of her basket again, she gave Adaba a look that carried a very special message: *Tonight!* Adaba smiled and nodded his acknowledgment.

After watching Gilly and Lew disappear into the crowd, Adaba turned away from the doorway.

"You ought to be more careful, the things you say, Denmark."

"Why? You think that boy is going to cause trouble for me?"

30

"Not Lew, but there are others. One of these days you're going to go too far."

Denmark shook his head. "I'll tell you something. Another nigger whispers, 'Wish I was free,' and he gets whipped. Because that's incendiary. Got a goddamn troublemaker here, wishing he was free! Get the whip! Take him to the post! But *I* get into conversation with a white man, and I say, 'Look at the goddamn niggers, no wonder they're slaves. Now, a white man stands up for his rights —no wonder he's free, isn't that right?' And the white man says, of course that's right. And I say, 'Niggers around here don't know how to stand up for their rights the way white people do, no, sir. Maybe it is self-evident that all men are created equal, maybe they are all endowed by their Creator with certain unalienable Rights, but these niggers surely don't act like it, do they? Must be that some people aren't so equal after all, isn't that so?' And he says, that's certainly true. And I say, 'It certainly is. If only the goddamn nigger slaves *did* stand up for their rights, they'd *be* more equal, isn't that so?' At that point, the white gentleman gives me a sudden look of consternation. 'And,' I add, 'why, no honest white man wants to do an injustice to his equals, we all know that! The white man would feel *much* friendlier toward the nigger if only the nigger would stop acting so much like a slave, wouldn't he?' And by that time, that poor white man is so perplexed and outraged that he doesn't know what to say. *What strange kind of nigger is this!* He just wants to get away from me and be left alone."

Adaba and Denmark laughed, but Denmark looked discouraged. "But the boy was right. It's all talk, nothing but talk. And I can only hope that it will leave some kind of small mark."

Adaba thought of his attack on the white man and wondered if he would have been so quick to defend Gilly if it had not been for Denmark. *"Hold your head high,"* Denmark had always told him, *"and remember, no matter who calls you nigger or slave or boy, you are a man!"*

Adaba wanted to say, *"You have left your mark.*

You've left it on me." But there was no need. Surely Denmark already knew that.

Lew was troubled. He was troubled by his conversation, if it could be called that, with Denmark Vesey. He was troubled by what the white man had done to Gilly and by what Adaba had done to the white man.

A hundred thousand times he had heard it asserted that the worst sin a black man could commit was to attack a white man, but he had never given the matter any thought. He never thought of Adaba or Gilly or any of his family's people as being black, any more than he went around thinking, *I am white*. Lately he had become aware that some people seemed to do exactly that, and that was another thing that troubled him. And when he saw Adaba hit the white man—*not* when he saw the white man hit Gilly—he was suddenly aware of the color difference. *A black man had hit a white man!*

That was wrong.

Everybody said it was wrong.

Even Lew, somewhere in his guts, felt that it was wrong.

But *why* was it wrong? This was Adaba, not just any old nigger! And he was defending Gilly, *our* Gilly! If Lew had defended Gilly, it wouldn't have been wrong!

And was he supposed to feel bad just because he had helped Adaba and Gilly to get away?

When he stopped to think about it, he supposed that just about every white person he knew would say that he was a terrible, rotten kid for doing such a thing.

But if he hadn't done it . . . if they had caught Adaba and Gilly . . .

All right, he thought furiously, I'm a terrible, rotten goddamn kid! And I'm going to *go on* being a rotten kid for the rest of my life!

In this mood—and possibly seeking either sanction or condemnation for being a "rotten kid"—Lew brought up the morning's incident at the supper table. Pretending a calm he didn't feel, he related the story quickly and simply. Gilly had accidentally bumped into a white man, the white man had commenced to beat Gilly, and Abada had struck the white man several times. They had all run off, and Lew had misled the pursuers so that Adaba and Gilly could get away.

On Lew's right, his mother, Louella, continued to eat, showing no interest in the story. On his left, his father, Channing Sabre, listened attentively but calmly. Across the table, Lew's sister, Georgiana, grew pinch-faced and hard eyed, while her husband, Norvin Claiborne, shook his head disapprovingly.

"Do you mean to tell me," Georgiana said, "that that Nigra boy struck a white gentleman right here on the streets of Charleston, and you helped him get away!"

"Shouldn'ta done that, Lewis," Norvin said in his deep politician's voice. "Shouldn'ta done that."

"But I told you, he did it for Gilly! That's just the same as if he did it for you and me, ain't it? She's one of us, ain't she?"

"She's one of *ours,*" Georgiana said, "and that's a far cry from being one of *us.* She's just a—a silly little Nigra wench who can't watch where she's walking and causes trouble on the streets of Charleston."

A wonderful feeling of indignation flowered in Lew's bosom. When one was in the right, it was glorious being a rotten kid. "But she didn't do nothing bad! She just bumped into a man. If I'da bumped into him, he wouldn'ta hit *me!* He did, I'da kicked his goddamn leg off!"

"Lewis, watch your language," his mother said, "and please, no more 'ain'ts.' "

"Yes," Georgiana said, "you stop talking like one of your nigger friends at the supper table." She turned to her father. "You see? You see? This is what comes of letting him run around with trash like that nigger yardchild—"

"Adaba ain't no nigger yardchild!"

Channing Sabre's hand came crashing down on the table like a warning shot across the bow. Instantly the table fell silent. Even Norvin seemed to freeze, and only Lew's mother continued eating as if nothing had happened.

Channing, still calm, turned to Lew. "Are you sure you've told me the entire story," he asked dryly, "without partisan shading?"

"Sure, I'm sure."

"You didn't say where Adaba and Gilly hid."

Lew hesitated. "In Denmark Vesey's shop."

"Denmark Vesey," Georgiana said bitterly. "Daddy, you have got to stop employing that Nigra man around this house. He doesn't show proper respect."

Channing silenced her with a look and turned again to Lew. "Lewis, you tell Adaba that I'm grateful to him for looking after Gilly, but hereafter he had better look to his own hide."

"But that man might have killed Gilly!"

"I doubt that very much. But somebody is going to get killed if Adaba persists in knocking down white men. If you're his friend, Lewis, you had better remind him of that."

"Yes, sir." Lew looked at his sister. "But Adaba ain't —isn't no yardchild."

With visible effort, Georgiana managed to keep her voice down. "His momma, from what I have heard, was a coal-black nigger wench, born in Africa, and his daddy never married her. If that's not a nigger yardchild *slave*, I don't know what is!"

"Adaba may be black," Channing said patiently, "but he's a slave only because his mother was a slave. That's the law. He happens to be the *acknowledged* son of Marcus Guerard, and that makes him anything but a yardchild."

"Well!" Georgiana threw down her napkin. "Next you all will be telling me he ain't a nigger at all, is that it?"

"Georgiana," Channing sighed, "please—"

"Well, I tell you he's got a yaller daddy and a coalblack momma, and he even goes by a nigger name, and if that don't make him a nigger—"

"I don't care what you call him," Lew said. "He's been my friend since I was a little kid. He taught me to swim. He taught me to fish. He taught me—"

"He taught you to be a *niggah-lovah!* My own brother, a *niggah-lovah!*"

"Well, my dear," her mother said indifferently, between bites of food, "at least that's better than being a niggah-hatah."

34

Georgiana suddenly burst into tears and fled from the table.

Lew didn't understand Georgiana. He knew she wanted to be a lady of tone, but somehow, as she fitted herself to what she thought to be the proper attitudes, prejudices, and articles of faith, she merely became coarser. When she tried to express ladylike disdain, she ended up screeching *"niggah-lovah!"* And then, perhaps seeing herself for what she was, she burst into tears. But why did she have to be that way, why did she have to make herself and others unhappy? Lew wanted to love his sister, but she made it extremely difficult.

Well, to hell with her. Lew felt good again as he got ready for bed. Well, not exactly good. Good, bad, excited, guilty, miserable, and happy. But mostly guilty, excited, and good right now. His feelings had been so mixed and so changeable the last year or two that sometimes he thought he must be going crazy. When he had told Adaba, the older boy had merely laughed and said not to worry, it would pass; it went with the hair that was sprouting around his dong. Remembering Adaba saying that, Lew took a moment to examine his dong in the dark. It immediately sprang to life. That was another thing that worried Lew. It sometimes seemed to him that he was rapidly turning into one great big uncontrollable dong. Now, as he thought of Gilly, his dong got harder than ever.

Gilly! The full brown breasts, darkly nippled, the lean brown body . . . As he touched his hardened flesh, Lew felt as if he might faint. . . .

Enough! He wasn't going to do that, at least not yet. Some people said it would drive you crazy and make hair grow on the palms of your hands. Lew visualized himself as a great hairy, fanged beast, growling with rage and rattling the bars of his cage. He had asked Adaba if it was true that it could do that to you, but Adaba had said he'd never seen one of those crazy hairy people. Lew wondered if maybe it only happened to white people, and they were locked away and never spoken of again, because of the disgrace. Or maybe everybody else resisted temptation, and Lew would be the first of his kind.

But, oh, Gilly, Gilly, Gilly, Gilly . . . with her finely drawn features, her merry eyes, her flesh like dark copper, brightly burnished . . .

The fire was low in the grate, and the room was rapidly chilling. Without bothering to pull on a nightshirt, Lew wrapped a heavy blanket around his shoulders. He pulled a chair to a window and sat down, making a warm cocoon of the blanket. From this window, he could look down across the yard to the line of outbuildings that stood along the courtyard wall on the corner of the block. Gilly occupied a small dormered loft over a storeroom, and Lew noted with satisfaction that a light, dimly flickering, still showed in her window. He wouldn't be able to see much, but even so . . . maybe tonight . . .

He shouldn't be doing this. He knew he shouldn't. Shame soured his anticipation—while lessening it not one whit. What if Gilly knew he was a Peeping Tom? He knew all too well how she would react. She would laugh at him. She would taunt and tease him out of his mind, and he knew he would deserve it.

But he could not stop looking and hoping. His obsession dated from an evening a few weeks earlier when they had just arrived in the city from the plantation. Lew had come in off the street and was passing through the courtyard when a light in Gilly's window caught his eye. Looking up, he saw her standing bare breasted in her room. He was sure she hadn't seen him, but she had moved away from the window so quickly that he had hardly been able to credit his eyes.

Oh, Gilly, Gilly, Gilly. What wild imaginings she had inspired since that evening. What *shameful* imaginings! That his thoughts of her should be thus polluted! But what if he were to sneak out to the storeroom some night? What if he were to climb up the ladder into her loft with her? Might she not actually *welcome* him? And, oh, what sport might they enjoy then!

But was it possible that Gilly already had a lover? The thought of her actually *doing* it—and doing it with someone other than himself—inflamed his mind all the more and scorched him with jealousy. Such a possibility had not even occurred to Lew until his father, speaking to the cook, had inadvertently put the thought into his mind: *"Goddammit, I don't want that Gilly getting knocked up! I've got too many mouths to feed already! You see any young bucks following her home, you shoo 'em off right fast. . . ."*

His father had said that the day after Lew had seen Gilly's breasts, and immediately Lew began noticing how the young men—white as well as black—looked at Gilly. He also observed the pleasure she took in being looked at. He had soon come to the conclusion that she "knew what it was all about" and that she might even have had some experience at it.

Could she and Adaba have . . . ?

The notion hit him suddenly and with surprising force. He remembered the laughter that Gilly and Adaba shared, the looks that sometimes passed between them. Now their laughter and those looks seemed to bind them together, to separate them from him, and he found himself growing resentful toward them both. How dare they abandon him for each other! They had no right!

Never mind, it wasn't true. He refused to believe such a thing. Adaba and Gilly? There was nothing between them, no secret they kept from Lew. Adaba was like an older brother to him and Gilly both, and Gilly would be Lew's and Lew's alone.

Oh, Gilly, Gilly, Gilly . . .

Lew settled down in his chair, his eyes on Gilly's lighted window, and waited.

It was a game to Adaba, one he loved to play. First, the silent departure from the house, and then the gliding from shadow to shadow. He would stand utterly still beneath a tree, observing every window, every corner, every bit of shrubbery in the moonlight, and hearing every sound for a quarter of a mile around. Then, when he was sure it was safe, he would move on to the next shadow. The City Guard hardly gave him the slightest worry, and to make the game more exciting, he rarely bothered to carry the pass required of slaves. In all the years he had been going about Charleston without papers of any kind, he had been

37

caught and put into the workhouse only twice, and never whipped.

Tonight!

They hadn't even had to use words. The moment he had seen her this morning, he had known she was ready for him to come to her again. A look from her as they had parted in Denmark Vesey's shop had confirmed it—*Tonight!*

The wait seemed interminable—the whole livelong day after he and Gilly had parted, the supper hour, his father's departure for some kind of Saturday evening meeting, the wait for his father's return. He hadn't dared leave the house until he was sure that everyone else was in bed and asleep. The older children, Philip and Diantha, would have kept silent if they had known what Adaba was up to, but he could hardly expect that of little Rose and David. Sooner or later, they would be bound to say something, and Adaba knew how his father would regard his having a love affair with Gilly.

He stood across the road from the Channing Sabre house for long minutes. There was no light to be seen in either the house or the outbuildings. If Gilly had a lamp burning, he could not see it from where he stood.

As a cloud drifted over the moon, he hurried across to the carriage gate. It was not barred, and he opened it just enough so that he could ease through and close it behind him. If he made no sudden moves, it was unlikely that he would be seen in this darkness even if someone were looking from the house.

Slowly, Adaba moved toward the storeroom where Gilly had her loft.

He slipped through the door into the utter darkness of the storeroom. Then, looking up the ladder nailed to the wall, he saw a flicker of light from the loft above. Silently he climbed the ladder.

Under the sloping roof, Gilly was lying on her pallet, propped up on her elbows reading a book by the light of a lamp. The blankets were pulled up on her shoulders to protect her from the chill of the loft. Adaba watched her silently, his joy growing until it was almost painful. She had to be his forever—but how was he ever to get his

38

father's consent? He knew there was only one way. If Gilly were to have his child, his father would never disclaim it—not his own grandchild. He would buy Gilly and the child from Mr. Sabre, and it would be the same as if she had been freed. Her slavery, like Adaba's, would be little more than a legal fiction, and no one would ever be able to separate them.

"Gilly!"

At the sound of his voice, she gave a startled little squeal and nearly knocked over the lamp. Gilly crawled out of her pallet, while Adaba scrambled the rest of the way up the ladder and across the loft to her. Kneeling, they embraced, and he traced the lines of her body through her thin gown. "I been waiting," she whispered, "waiting, waiting, waiting!"

She gave another little cry as she realized that they might be seen through the dormer window: she had forgotten to drape something across it. Quickly she hung a bit of cloth from two nailheads.

As she turned back to Adaba, a smile slowly spread over her face. "What you come here for, boy?"

Adaba answered by taking her into his arms again.

The face haunted Jeppson. No matter how much he drank, he kept seeing it: a high forehead, finely molded; thick slanting brows; a strong Roman nose; full lips, tightly pursed; and the eyes—the fierce, angry eyes, outraged and outrageous, defiant and murderous. No nigger had a right to look like that—certainly not at a white man.

No matter how he tried, Jeppson could not wipe the incident from his mind. To be so humiliated . . . to be struck repeatedly in the belly by a nigger . . . to be tossed contemptuously into the street . . . in front of people who would carry the story back home: Balbo Jeppson made a fool of by a nigger boy . . .

"Are you sure you wouldn't like to go upstairs with one of the girls for a while, dearie?"

No, he wouldn't. It was one of the things he had come to Charleston for—he came once or twice a year, to rid himself of the need, if only for a little while—but now he

39

didn't want a woman at all. He hardly knew why he had come to this place.

"Here, let me pour you another drink, and you look the girls over. We've got some lovelies here, dearie, white and black and in-between. And it's Saturday night—you should treat yourself to a real good time!"

Jeppson watched with disgust as a white man left the room with a black woman. That was wrong, he thought. White man with a black woman. Almost as bad as a white woman with a nigger buck. Back home, he never bothered his black women. Never. Had no use for these goddamn gentry who talked so righteous, and all the time you saw their little black bastards running around the yard.

It was wrong.

Well, maybe by God he would do something about it.

"I'll tell you something, dearie." The woman lowered her voice confidentially. "If you ain't in the mood for female companionship, we just happen to have here the nicest, handsomest young nigger boy you ever met. And he certainly knows how to appreciate the company of a fine white gentleman like you, if you know what I mean—"

The woman screamed as Jeppson flung his arm at her, knocking her down. Within seconds two men jumped on him, and that by God was all right, because no black boy was going to toss his ass into the street this time. Jeppson welcomed them—with his fists. Battered them back, then picked up a chair and beat them down with it. Used the chair to smash out one window after another. Flung the chair across the room at a screaming woman. Turned just in time to dodge a knife and kick its owner in the balls.

That finished it. Only he remained on his feet. Balbo Jeppson strode out onto the piazza and through the piazza door onto the street without even hurrying. Let them come after him if they wished. If they dared.

All right, he thought, as he walked along the dark street, one day he would just find that nigger boy. Maybe he would find him before he left Charleston. One thing was certain. Balbo Jeppson would never forget him. Jeppson prided himself on never forgetting a nigger's face. "I know 'em all," he often bragged back home, "I know 'em the way Caesar knew his legions, each one by name. There ain't no better nigger-watcher in all Carolina than Balbo Jeppson."

Somewhere in Charleston tonight there was a nigger boy laughing at him and bragging to his friends about what he had done. *"Oh, if only you see that white massa's face! . . ."* But someday, sooner or later, that nigger might find lightning striking him when he least expected it! Whether he knew it or not, for the rest of his life he would live under the threat of again meeting Balbo Jeppson. And then . . .

Someday, boy . . .

Two

As their mouths met, Adaba began drawing up her gown, and their kiss broke only when she pulled the gown over her head. "Oh, what take you so long," Gilly whispered, rolling her body against him as he caressed her, "what take you so long?"

How many times had they made love? It began the previous spring, one festive Saturday evening, when she lured him to an empty cabin. He had loved her long before that, this little orphan girl, but until then he had been almost fearful of her. There had been other women, of course: he was a handsome lad, and there was no lack of older girls to teach him the ways of love. But Gilly? Did *he* have the right to teach *her*?

She gave him her own answer on that Saturday evening, an evening of music and singing and dancing that Adaba would never forget. Gilly had seemed determined to baffle and frustrate him. She had danced with the other young bucks, had flirted with them outrageously, until he was convinced that she must be angry with him. Then she led him on a chase through the darkness that ended in the empty cabin where a candle already burned, as if they

41

were expected. He looked at her standing by the bed and understood: the time had come.

His heart pounded, his throat was dry. His knees shook.

"We can't," he said, "not here. They—whoever lives here—they could come back."

"They ain't coming back," she whispered. "Not till we go. We got long as we want."

Again, he understood.

They undressed slowly, facing each other. When he looked at her naked for the first time, he could only marvel at her beauty: the loveliness of the high, well-spaced breasts, the undulating flow of belly and mound, the tapering of her legs. He was not even aroused until she stepped close to him, rested her forehead against his chest, and reached down to hold and gently knead his penis. Then he came up hard and strong, and he reached to hold her in the same way. As their mouths and bodies met, he felt her liquids flowing hot. They floated down upon the bed as gently as leaves in a soft spring breeze.

She had become his, entirely his, that night, and she had been his ever since—a kind of extension of his being, yet with a being of her own that had to be respected. She was a creature of his will only insofar as he was a creature of hers. But to have lost her would have been like losing a part of his own body.

When the Sabres moved to Charleston for the hot months of the year, Gilly and Adaba worried about how they could be together, but they were lucky. The girl who shared the loft with Gilly soon married a man from another plantation and was sold to his master. No one else took her place in the loft—except Adaba. He came to Gilly once, twice, three times a week, as often as he dared and as she would permit. They would make a family, they decided. And Adaba vowed that he would never permit them to be separated.

Now, once again he lay naked with her in her pallet, kissing her breasts, stroking her sex, making her croon with pleasure. The pleasure he gave her was as precious to him as the pleasure he took, and only when he sensed that she was on the verge of coming did he rise up over her. With a cry of near agony, she lifted knees and buttocks

42

and seized that hard shaft of flesh to fit it into place. As he slowly penetrated her, still stroking her where they joined, she cried out again, a long wail of final pleasure.

Oh, my baby, he thought, driving still deeper into her, *oh, my baby, ain't never going to lose you, ain't never, never, never. . .*

Lew sat perfectly still. He felt numbed by shock.

Someone was with Gilly in her loft.

He had been leaning against the window sill, half dozing in his chair, when suddenly something brought him wide awake. The light in Gilly's window changed, something suggested movement within the room, and Lew was certain that for an instant he had seen a shadowy figure— someone other than Gilly. A man.

No one should be with Gilly at this hour, and Lew could think of only one reason anyone would be. His wild imaginings were true. Gilly did indeed "know what 'it' was all about," she did indeed have a lover. She had entered that unknown territory where men and women did things that Lew could only vaguely imagine.

But that wasn't right.

At the plantation, the people were allowed more or less to choose their own mates and make their own family arrangements. But this was Gilly! And his father had specifically said that he wanted the young bucks shooed off. No doubt he had his reasons, and at least in part they were for Gilly's own good.

What should he do about it?

As he watched, he again got a glimpse of a figure that was surely not Gilly. Then Gilly appeared at the window, but only for an instant. The light abruptly disappeared.

She had put something over the window. To conceal the light. To conceal whoever was with her.

Goddamn! Shock dissolved, leaving a sick, sinking feeling of envy. *Goddamn Gilly!* What had been a game, a conjuring up of exciting possibilities, had become a reality, and he didn't like it at all. By now Gilly and her lover were probably naked together. Someone else was looking at those breasts Lew longed to see, someone else was handling that body he longed to touch, someone else. . . .

He was going to do something about it. His father

would expect to be told. Lew got up from his chair, tossed away his blanket, and started yanking his clothes on.

Again, as suddenly as before, his emotions shifted. How could he possibly tell his father? The very idea made him feel like a sneak and a tattletale. No matter what Gilly was doing out there in her loft, he felt close to her. He professed to be her friend. She should be able to feel that she could trust him with her secret even if she hadn't confided it to him. To go to his father would be a kind of betrayal.

And what if that were Adaba out there with Gilly?

But he didn't really believe that, didn't want to believe it, and he put the thought out of mind.

What should he do?

It took him a long time to decide, but in his heart he knew the answer all along. He should ignore his own feelings; they would only mislead him. Whatever he felt for Gilly right now, jealousy or loyalty, was irrelevant.

He finished putting his clothes on, hoping that Gilly's lover, whoever he might be, would depart before he was caught: Lew was giving him plenty of time. When he was dressed, he went out into the dark hall and tapped softly but steadily on his parents' door.

When his father called "Yes?" Lew peered into the darkness of the room and said, "I've got to tell you something."

"Won't it wait?"

"No. It's about—about Gilly."

That brought his father awake quickly enough. He said, "I'll be right out."

A moment later, still in his nightshirt, he appeared in the shadowed hall. "Now," he said, "what about Gilly?"

"I—I think I saw someone in her room. At her window."

"How did you happen to be looking at her window?"

The question surprised Lew. "Why—I just happened to look out *my* window, is all. I was restless and couldn't sleep, so when I looked out and saw, I pulled on my clothes and called you."

"What exactly did you see?"

"There was light in her window. Candlelight, I guess.

But somebody moved around in there and I don't think it was Gilly. I remembered what you said about how you didn't want her knocked up, so I thought I'd better call you."

His father gave him a hard, measuring look. "And all of this 'just happened,' you say."

"Yes, sir." Why did his father have to look at him like that? Lew began to wish he had kept his mouth shut and gone to bed.

"All right, you go downstairs to the back door and keep an eye on Gilly's window. Don't let yourself be seen. I'll be with you in a minute."

Lew went down the stairs slowly. Embarrassing though it might prove for himself, he still hoped that whoever was visiting Gilly would get away while he had the chance. The feeling that he had made a mistake in reporting to his father was growing stronger.

When his father appeared, he had a pistol in hand. Channing Sabre's stocky, powerful figure led the way across the brilliantly moonlit yard to the carriage house, where he took a short whip down from a peg on the wall. Outside the storehouse, he paused a moment to look up at the dormer window, but there was nothing to be seen.

Carefully, silently, his father eased the door open. He looked in—and up the ladder.

He appeared to be satisfied, in a grim sort of way, when he turned back to Lew. "You get yourself to bed," he said quietly. "I don't think there'll be trouble here, but if there is, I want you out of it."

He stepped into the darkness of the storehouse. Lew started back across the yard but after a half-dozen steps came to a halt. Somehow he felt that he would be diminished, that he would be less than a man if he didn't face the consequences of his act. He couldn't leave. He turned back toward the storehouse.

. . . *ain't never going to lose you, ain't never, never, never* . . .

With none of the others had it been like this. It was Gilly who had made a man of him—a man in ways that

45

neither Denmark Vesey nor his own father could have taught him. Ways that only love can teach.

There had been no love with the others—not even the illusion of love. There had often been a certain fondness, born of shared pleasure, but nothing more. He had wanted them for the same reason that they had wanted him, and afterward they had always been ready to part.

By the time Adaba was thirteen, the wenches were looking at him, a handsome boy, big for his age, and his father had warned him: "Stay away from them. They are not for you. I don't want to see the face of a Guerard on any slave child born on this plantation or on any other plantation around here. You will wait until the proper time and for the proper woman."

But there were too many girls only a few years older than he who presented irresistible temptations, and it was a simple matter for him to write out a pass, sign his father's name, and go anywhere about the countryside that he wished. And among the women folk, he found himself welcome anywhere he happened to go on a Saturday evening or a lazy Sunday afternoon. . . .

But meeting Gilly brought such adventures to an end.

He was sixteen the summer they met; she was not yet fifteen. He had driven out to Jessamine, the Sabre plantation, with Mr. Sabre and Lew. When they arrived, they learned that Gilly's parents had both just died of the summer fevers. In her grandmother's arms, Gilly wailed with the pain and horror of her loss. *I know,* Adaba wanted to tell her, *I know. I lost my momma, my stepmomma too. I know.* . . . If he had ever seen Gilly at Jessamine before, he didn't remember. But that day he felt as if she had planted a barb in his heart, and not another day passed that he didn't think of her with a peculiarly sweet pain. He knew he had to see her again . . . and again. . . .

Not long after that, her grandmother died. She was an orphan, the last of two dying lines, but the people of Jessamine had ways of taking care of their own, and she soon found "aunts" and "uncles." And, too, the Sabres recognized her superior intelligence and appearance. After her grandmother's death, they began to train her as a housemaid. She felt secure and cared for.

By Christmas, Adaba was in love with her.

The happiest moment he had ever experienced came when he realized that she returned his love. One night, he, Gilly, Lew, and Medora, another of the maids, were crowded into the loft of the storehouse. He was helping Gilly with her reading. For some reason, Lew and Medora left, and the moment they were gone, Gilly tossed aside her book and gave Adaba an excited, mischievous look. Neither said a word as they melted into each other's arms.

That moment led to the still-happier one in the empty cabin the next spring. By then, there were no other women in his life. There was only the happiness and the agony, the joy and the frustration, of knowing that Gilly was his —and not knowing what to do about it. Not knowing, that is, until he found himself alone and naked with her, and they floated down upon the bed. Afterward, as they lay together, she told him, "They warn me. They say you love many, many wenches." He laughed. "No, Gilly. I been naked with many, many wenches, but I don't love them. I love only Gilly."

And that moment led to another, happier still, if that were possible. It led to this one, now, in the loft of the storehouse, with Gilly naked beneath him, pulsing on him, gripping the manhood that was so deep within her, Gilly coming to life, Gilly beginning to heave and sigh as once again he drew back and thrust into her, drew back and thrust, Gilly lifting to meet the thrust, the draw and thrust, Gilly crying out again as the time they both arrived at that blinding, shattering, scalding moment.

And then peace.

Oh, Gilly, I do love you.

Peace—and then the hand with the pistol coming up into the loft.

"Christ," Channing Sabre said, his broad, strong-jawed face twisting with disgust. "My sweet Christ. I guess I should have known it was you, boy—the way you've been sniffing around her all this time."

Adaba rolled off of Gilly, sick with the humiliation of being caught in bed with her, but more sick for her than for himself. Afraid too, with the feeling that this moment might poison what they had between them.

Channing Sabre stood on the ladder, his head, shoulders, and arms above the level of the loft floor. He lowered the cock on the pistol and started the rest of the way up the ladder.

"Get up out of there, boy. Get your pants on and get down below."

Adaba got out of the pallet, thankful that the guttering candle had burned down. He had never felt so shamefully naked, so vulnerable in every way. He pushed the blankets further up over Gilly as if to protect her, but—no chance. Sabre shoved him roughly out of the way. Gilly cried out and rolled away from him onto her belly as, with one sweep of his hand, he pulled the blankets down. In spite of the low slanted roof, he managed to bring the whip sharply down across her butt, and she cried out again. Adaba instantly, instinctively, grabbed Channing Sabre's whip hand and held it.

The look in Sabre's blue eyes turned deadly. "You let go of my hand, boy," he said quietly.

Channing Sabre was no stranger attacking Adaba's Gilly, and his eyes weren't deadly merely because Adaba was black. On the contrary, Sabre thought of himself as Gilly's protector, and he probably regarded Adaba as having abused her. And in his naked vulnerability, his sudden irrational guilt, Adaba almost felt as if he had.

Perhaps Channing Sabre saw something of his misery, because his eyes softened. "Let go of my hand," he repeated.

"Mr. Sabre, sir, you don't understand—"

"I said, let go."

Adaba let go. He reached for his pants and hurriedly slipped them on.

"You can put the rest of your clothes on down below," Channing Sabre said. "Get down there and wait for me. And I don't want you running off. I'm going to get this whole thing squared away tonight once and for all."

Gathering up the rest of his clothes, Adaba started down the ladder. He paused to look at Gilly, wishing there were some word of love he dared to say to her in front of

48

Sabre, but he doubted that she would hear him. She lay rolled up in a ball, her eyes tightly closed, her face drawn as if she were in the most exquisite pain. It was a pain that had nothing at all to do with the whip.

When he was halfway down the ladder, Adaba heard the snap of that whip and Gilly's sharp outcry, and he nearly dropped his clothes and raced back up to the loft. But there was no further sound except Channing Sabre's low angry voice. Adaba continued on down.

In the darkness of the storehouse, he put on the rest of his clothes. To hell with the man's orders, he thought. He had had enough of Sabre, and as soon as he was dressed he would leave. The man wasn't going to hurt Gilly anymore, at least not with that whip. Adaba would leave now but come back later, maybe in an hour or two, and comfort Gilly.

But how had Channing Sabre found out about him and Gilly? How had their secret been discovered after all these months? They had always been so careful. It was late, and there had not been a light in the Sabre house or any other house nearby, and Sabre was certainly not the kind of person to go roaming around with a pistol in the middle of the night.

Adaba knew the answer the minute he stepped out of the storehouse into the brilliant moonlight. Knew it, but could not believe it.

Could not believe it, that is, until Lew, white faced in the moonlight, spoke: "I didn't know it was you! I thought—"

"You," Adaba said. "You had to go and tell him, didn't you!"

"But I never thought it was you!"

"Who else would it be," Adaba asked incredulously. "You knew how it was with Gilly and me."

Lew hesitated. "No!"

"Lew, you know anybody closer to Gilly than me? You mean to tell me it never crossed your mind how it must be with Gilly and me?"

Lew shook his head. "No!" But Adaba saw in his moon-glazed eyes that he was lying.

Lew had done this to him. Had done this to Gilly. Lew, their friend.

"Why?" Adaba asked, near tears. "I was always good to you—why you doing this to us, Lew? Watching out here so late at night?"

"I just happened—just happened to see—"

"Spying on us, Lew?"

Lew's voice shook. "I was not spying! I saw something in Gilly's window! And I thought there was maybe a strange nigger out here—maybe a strange nigger hurting her."

"I say you was spying, Lew, and you saw me, or something you knew might be me, and yet you—you—"

He could restrain himself no longer—neither his tears, nor his anger. He grabbed Lew with one hand, flailed out at him with the other. Grabbed him with both hands and shook him, shook him, then hit him again. Shook him and hit him, while Lew remained maddeningly silent. Shook him and hit him until Mr. Channing Sabre tore them apart and spun Adaba around.

Adaba's head exploded in lights far brighter than the moon.

The fight had gone out of him. He let himself be led home as docilely as a child. Though Channing Sabre's anger seemed to dissipate during the walk, it was no comfort to Adaba. His father still had to be faced.

After considerable pounding with the knocker, Marcus Guerard, in a dressing gown, opened the door, and Adaba found himself looking into his father's pale stern face: the deep-set eyes under the noble brow, the solid Roman nose that Adaba had inherited, the dark flowing hair, touched with gray only at the temples. A handsome man. All of the Guerards were exceptionally handsome, Adaba thought, except perhaps himself—all of the *white* Guerards. And they all seemed to be assembled to welcome him home: the older of his half-brothers and -sisters, Philip and Diantha, were in the hall, staring at him from behind his father, and the younger two, Rose and David, were peering down from the shadowed top of the stairs.

50

"I seem to have awakened the entire household, Marcus," Channing Sabre said. "I apologize."

"No need." Marcus Guerard's voice was deep and musical. He turned and waved his hand at the children, who promptly headed back to bed. "Won't you come in?"

"I've brought your wandering young buck home, Marcus."

"So I see." As they walked through the hall, his father said, "You may go to your room if you wish, John. I shall speak to you later."

Adaba had no intention of going to his room if he could help it. As his father led Channing Sabre into the parlor, Adaba stood near the door where he could hear what was being said without being seen.

After a few pleasantries and the clink of glasses, Sabre said, "It's late, Marcus, and I'll be brief. I've got a maid, a little orphan girl—pretty as a picture, to understate the case—and Adaba has been—"

"I would prefer that you use his Christian name—John," his father said stiffly.

"I'm sorry. Anyway, John has had his eye on her skirt for some time now, and tonight I caught them in bed together."

Adaba sensed his father's swift intake of breath. "Oh, now *I* am sorry. John knows better than that. I'll speak to him."

"Now, don't be too hard on the boy, Marcus. He's reached that age, you know, and my God, you should see this girl. Sixteen years old, and not to be vulgar, but if I were the kind that chases wenches! . . . Unbelievable, Marcus."

"Nonetheless . . ."

"Furthermore, she's bright as a penny, and a damned good housemaid, and she's turning into a good cook as well. To get to the point, she's not the kind of slave you sell pregnant, so I don't want her knocked up."

Sell!

His father couldn't hide his shock. "You plan to *sell* one of your people, Mr. Sabre?"

Sell . . . sell Gilly . . .

"Listen, Marcus, I am purely up to my ass in useless

51

black folk. They're eating me out of house and home! I'm trying to buy more land so I can put them to work and feed them, but I haven't had a hell of a lot of luck. Now, I had a housemaid that got hot for a buck on the Beaufield plantation—that was fine. I sold her cheap just so she could go live with him. The girl had a widow momma that wanted to be with her daughter—fine again. I practically gave her away. It was two less people for me to feed, and made everybody happy. Now, Gilly hasn't got any family at Jessamine, and if I find a decent place where I think she'll be happy, you're damn right I'll sell her! And after tonight, I don't think I'd better wait any longer."

"I'm sorry, Mr. Sabre. I didn't understand."

"It's nothing so terrible. Young people grow up and leave home to make their own way all the time."

"You're perfectly right, of course."

"And there's another thing. It's my boy, Lewis. Best to put temptation out of the way. I never thought about it when I brought Gilly to work in the house, but the boy is reaching the age when, if I don't watch him, he'll screw anything from a bitch to a bedpost. If he had it his way, he'd take your boy's place in Gilly's bed anytime."

So that was why you did it, Lew. . . .

"I understand your position," Adaba's father said. "And I'll speak to John most strongly about this matter. He tends to be rather headstrong and reckless, but I'll make it clear to him that he's to have nothing more to do with your—your Gilly."

"Fine. I thank you." Mr. Sabre hesitated. "Of course, if John is serious about the girl, Marcus . . . if you should care to buy her, a nominal sum . . ."

Yes! Yes!

"No," his father said flatly. "Absolutely not. I'm sure she's a fine girl, but I have plans for John."

"Good luck with them."

"By the way, Mr. Sabre, about this wench . . . I wonder . . ."

As his father lowered his voice, Adaba strained to hear, but no more than a murmur came from the other room. *What were they saying? saying about Gilly?* After a moment, Mr. Sabre seemed to be making sounds of agreement.

Sabre was coming back toward the hall, taking his leave, and Adaba moved quickly away from the doorway to a place behind the staircase where he couldn't be seen. As soon as the door was closed, his father said, "John, I wish to speak to you," without raising his voice or looking around, and went back into the parlor.

"I suppose you heard most of that," he said, as Adaba entered the room.

"Yassuh, massa. De niggahs, dey listen 'hind de doah all de time."

"Most amusing. John, you are not to see this wench again."

"She's not a wench, father, she's a young woman, a girl—"

"You are not to see her ever again!"

Adaba closed his eyes and, without asking for permission, sat down. Suddenly he felt weak. In all of his life, as son and slave, never until this moment had he felt so much at the mercy of exterior forces.

"Father," he said, "buy her for me."

"Don't be an ass," his father said harshly. "You've been sowing your oats. I suppose that was inevitable. But I am not going to let you make a mistake you'll regret for the rest of your life."

"But I love her, father."

"You think so now, but—"

"I love her!"

Adaba opened his eyes to find his father staring at him, as if trying to penetrate to the truth. After a moment, his father nodded. "All right. I'll accept that. You do love her."

"Then why not buy her, and—"

"John, you know perfectly well why not. In the eyes of the law, you are a slave. That girl is a slave. Your marriage wouldn't even have legal status, and your children, *my grandchildren,* would be slaves. After my death, you and they would all have to belong to one of your younger brothers. Is that what you want? to have your children slaves to your brother? and their children and their children's children slaves? a family of slaves, owning each other generation after generation?" His father shook his head. "It couldn't go on forever, and you know what would happen. Some, at least, of your own grandchildren, or their children, would end up being sold, separated, turned into the fields, used as beasts are used. Is that the future you want for our family, John?"

"But you used to say that slavery would die out, that it was just a matter of time."

"A lot of people *used* to say that—we were wrong. No, the institution of slavery is growing stronger in the South every year, John, and you should give thanks to God in heaven that you have a free man for a father."

"But someday Gilly and I will find a way to be free."

"Listen to me. Your Gilly will never be free, and neither will her children nor their children. But your children will be. You'll find a suitable white girl to marry, as I did, or if you can't do that, you will most certainly marry a *free* young woman of color, one with the lightest skin you can find. And your brothers and sisters will have little difficulty in marrying white, and your children and theirs will be free—"

"And bleached lily white by a few generations." Adaba could have wept.

"Yes," his father said, angered by his tone, "bleached white! No more niggers in this family! I'll have grandchildren who can take my wealth north or to England or anywhere in the world and forget they have a drop of black blood in them! Hell, they don't even have to know! They can even turn into nigger-haters for all I care—but they'll be safe, they'll be secure! They'll never know the bite of the whip or the scorn of mere goddamn white trash who are unworthy to lick their boots!"

"You mean," Adaba said, "they'll *be* white trash."

His father looked stung. "I mean nothing of the sort!"

"Father, they'll be just like the po' buckra nigger-haters that in truth *are* niggers by their own definitions. Hell, you've seen them—the country is full of them. White niggers who don't know what they are until they look into the mirror at that fair-skinned but kinky-haired image, and the sweat comes to the palms of their hands as the mirror stares back at them and suddenly shouts *'Nigger-r-r!'* Is that the future *you* want for your grandchildren, father?"

"I've told you what I want. I want them to be safe and secure. I want them to be free. And I want you to get a good education and forget all about this girl."

Adaba stood up. He looked at his father—the handsome European features, the pale skin so much in contrast to his own. But the contrast didn't end there.

"You think of yourself as a white man, don't you?" he said. "You think of yourself as a highly intelligent, well educated, generally superior white man who just happens to have a dram or two of black blood, don't you?"

His father smiled thinly and nodded. "That's exactly what I am."

"But because of that dram of two of black blood, you address Channing Sabre as Mr. Sabre, while he calls you Marcus. And if you're respected by men like Sabre, it's only as long as you bow your head like a nice old darky and step out of their path."

"That's very true."

"Well, I gwine tell you somet'ing, daddy. I'se a nigger—"

"Don't talk like that! You can speak perfectly good English."

"*I am a nigger*, father, and every day I bow my head a little less, and I step out of their path a little less, because I am turning into a goddamn *bad* nigger, father."

"I know. And I am frightened witless that it will get you killed."

"Maybe it will." It was no use talking, Adaba thought; talk accomplished nothing. He turned to the doorway. "May I go now?"

"As you wish. But remember what I've said. You are to see no more of that girl."

"Yes, sir." *But I will,* he thought. *Somehow I've got to get her away . . . carry her off before she's sold. . . . Why doesn't he understand?*

Adaba turned back toward the room. "Father, did you love my mother?"

His father's eyes darkened. "More than my soul."

"Then why . . . ?"

55

"I hadn't the right to love her. I made my son a black —and a slave."

"But this is *me*. This is the only *me* that could possibly be. If I'd had another mother, I wouldn't *be* me." He wasn't sure what he was trying to say. Perhaps he was trying to ask, *Do you love me less because I am what I am? What am I to you?*

His father said, "Go to bed, John."

Adaba nodded. He knew what he was. His father's oldest son.

The black one.

"Did you love my mother?" the boy had dared to ask. A drink in his hand, Marcus Guerard closed his eyes and settled back in his chair, remembering her, all those years back. *"Did you love . . . ?"*

Black wench seasoning. God, had she been black. And not long out of Africa. Maybe a year or two down in the islands. She had come with a parcel of a dozen slaves, half of them male, half of them female, because his father believed they would be happier that way. She caught his attention instantly and exclusively. A broad, round face, a flat nose, a full mouth. Large brown eyes that looked about, not fearfully like some of the others, but with a kind of fierce curiosity. When she caught him looking at her, she returned his stare without blinking.

She had a long neck and a slender body, which made her look taller than she was. More used to being naked than clothed, she wore her rags with a kind of careless disdain, letting her breasts show—breasts like perfectly round unripe fruit, a young girl's breasts.

Was it love or lust? In the end, there would be no difference. But then, in the beginning, watching her still shackled to the others in the barn, he knew only that there was a sudden shortness of his breath and a growing consciousness of his body—and that he wanted her. And she recognized that want and felt it too, as she told him months later. She knew then that she need not be a mere slave and the mate of a slave. And she was an extraordinarily ambitious young woman.

Hester: that was what his father called her. He didn't

know why, except that it might have approximated some unpronounceable African name. In any case, she accepted the name and even seemed to like it.

His father put Hester into the fields with the others, and Marcus, when he wasn't at his studies, often went out to oversee the work gangs. Somehow he always managed to wind up near Hester—Hester chopping cotton, Hester planting potatoes. She was disdained by many of the older hands as an "ignorant African" who preferred to work half-naked, with her dress dropped to her waist.

"Better put on your dress, Hester," he told her. "Better put on your hat. The sun will make you sick."

"Sun . . . mek . . . you seek," she repeated after him. "Sun . . . make . . . you . . . sick." She had mastered the dialect of the field hands in a few weeks, and he realized that she was now trying to speak as he did. "The sun . . . make you sick, master. Put on you' hat. Put on you' hat!"

Because of Hester, he didn't go to Charleston that summer. She became his pet. Her powers of concentration and the swiftness of her comprehension astonished him. When he told her the word for anything—mule, plow, gin house—she would repeat it a few times, and it would be hers forever. Syntax was more difficult, and she got angry at her mistakes, but she kept working at it, grindingly, day after day.

The only disturbing thing about their relationship was that they wanted each other and they both knew it, but he could do nothing about it. He was a free man and a good man, and such a man did not touch his slave women. He did not bring into this world children who would be slaves. That was the way he had been taught, that was his code.

But not hers. And she could be so open and explicit and determined about her wishes, that sometimes he literally had to fight her off.

"You no wanna?" she might ask, sounding hurt and forgetting proper English.

"Yes, only . . . only we . . . no, we don't. . . ."

"No wanna *fut* with Hester?"

Fut was a Gullah word meaning to go naked and, by

57

extension, to have sexual intercourse. Marcus was amused.

"No," he said, "no, don't say that word, Hester—"

"No wanna *fut* with me!" she said, more hurt than ever.

"Yes, I *do!*" he said. "I only meant you shouldn't use that word!"

"What is the white word?"

"Never mind the white word."

"Master don't wanna *fut* with me!"

But Hester got what she wanted at last.

One late August morning, Marcus awakened at dawn to a day that was already hot and steamy. His naked body was damp with sweat and he got out of bed to splash water over his face, shoulders, and chest. As he was toweling himself, he turned from the washstand to find Hester standing by the closed bedroom door.

He stood blinking at her as if she might be a dream. How she had entered the house and gotten all the way to his room unobserved, he had no idea, but here she was, in an old and torn shift, which she was at the moment pulling over her head.

Then she was as naked as he, and his eyes took in everything—those high round breasts, the narrowness of her waist, the plump female sex. Her thighs were long, hard, muscular thighs, and as he stared at them and at her sex, his own flesh reacted. Hester giggled. "White word is fuck," she said, pointing at his growing erection. "Master wanna fuck Hester."

"Hester," he said, "you get out of here!"

He dived for the bed and pulled the sheet up, but Hester was too fast for him. She ripped the sheet away and threw herself on top of him, straddling him. He tried to push her away, but she managed to grab his swollen member, and then it was too late. He couldn't have said whether she seduced him or raped him, but his struggles soon became as ineffectual as those of a willing maiden, and without too much difficulty, she guided him into place and slid down on him.

Marcus had her twice that morning—or she had him. After the first earth-shaking, mind-shattering time, Hester refused to let him go until, to his amazement, she aroused him again, and he threw her onto her back and brought them both to a second jolting conclusion. But that left him drained and upset with himself. Never again, he vowed repeatedly, never again.

And yet that afternoon he felt the urge to see her. Not for sex, he assured himself, but simply because she was his Hester, his pet. He was still her master and her teacher, and he would show her that she had no power over him.

When he approached the field where she was working, she uttered a screech and ran off as if frightened of him. He followed her into the woods—only to find her naked and waiting for him.

After having had her twice that morning, could one more time possibly matter?

One last time . . . and then another . . . and another . . . and another . . .

Before long he admitted his addiction—admitted it and accepted it. He ceased to swear "Never again!" each time he was with her. Instead, he looked forward to the next time, and hardly a day passed that he didn't find opportunities to be with her.

There was no way to keep their relationship a secret. His father was angry with him, his younger brother and sister contemptuous. Marcus didn't care. He gave Hester her own cabin and began spending his nights with her. Every day was a long painful wait until they could be alone together, their clothes shed, making the kind of love that—he was certain—only Hester in all the world knew how to make.

But Hester, much as she enjoyed their relationship, had other things in mind besides love. She had not asked to come to this strange new world so far from her home, but having been brought here, she was determined to seize control of her destiny. She had made herself the first and only wife of the prince of this tribe, and by learning the customs and the values of the tribe, she would wield power.

And by bearing a son for the prince.

When Marcus realized that she was pregnant, he learned anew how precious she had become to him. She was no longer merely a seductive concubine, but his woman, the woman who ruled his cabin. By then, even his father was beginning to recognize Hester, for the exceptional person she was. And though she was a slave, she could always be freed when his father got around to accepting her. His wife and his child would be as free as he was.

His son was born in the cabin they shared, a perfect baby but for a little mark like a pair of wings low on the left side of the chin. Marcus decided to name him John after his grandfather. When the baby was put into Hester's arms, she smiled. She happened to look out through the open doorway of the cabin, where she saw a dove on the ground. "Adaba," she said, giving the baby its basket name. "Adaba." The Brown Dove.

A few hours later, she was dead of the fever.

But I survived, he thought, sipping his drink, *I survived.*

His father had probably done the right thing by sending him to England at once. There he had met Eleanor Crockford, the daughter of a man who had wasted most of his fortune at the gaming tables. Lord Crockford had been quite happy to see his lovely blond daughter safely in the hands of this rich, slightly exotic yellow-skinned American who admitted to having the blood of savages in his aristocratic veins. And if Eleanor had married him primarily for security, certainly she had also brought love to the union. She had accepted and loved his black son and had given him four more lovely children. In all their dozen years together, his loyalty to her had forbidden any thoughts of Hester. But now sometimes he thought back. . . .

The trouble had come when he realized that Hester had never been freed, John had been born a slave and would remain one. According to the law of 1800, a master desiring to free a slave had to appear before a magistrate and five freeholders and guarantee the slave's character and his ability to earn his own living. While John was still a child, Marcus had appeared before such a board, pointing out to it that his son would one day be wealthy. But would he? the board had asked. Who

60

knew what the future would do the Marcus's fortunes? And who could tell at so early an age how John's character would turn out? Marcus had tried again, and only lately still again, but as always he had been put off. Bad reports about John's character . . . twice caught without a pass . . . twice put into the workhouse . . . best to wait and see . . .

Marcus had been forced to conclude that John would probably never be free.

He knew what was behind the board's attitude. It was sheer envy that he, *a nigger*, could be one of the wealthiest planters in the region. But that was not what concerned him—he was concerned about John. He saw the shape of the future: the day was coming when it would be impossible for any slave legally to gain his freedom. But if that was to be John's fate, it would not be the fate of John's children, Marcus swore. Never. Never. They would be as free as their grandfather.

But was he free?

He had always thought of himself as a white man who just happened to have a dram or two of black blood. But was that what he had felt like when he had appeared before the magistrate and freeholders?

The truth was, though he tried to deny it, the bastards had made him feel like a nigger. The good white folk of Carolina made him feel more like a nigger every day. And a nigger in Carolina was never really free. . . .

Marcus finished his drink, got up from his chair, and wearily went up the stairs to bed.

Three

Unless he did something about it, he was going to lose Gilly. She was going to be sold away and neither he nor Lew would ever see her again. Since the death of his step-

61

mother, Adaba had not had to face a real loss, and now the possibility overwhelmed him.

He could not let it happen.

He fell asleep that night, trying to think of a way to save Gilly from being sold. He dreamed all night long, alternately of having her torn from his arms and of the two of them fleeing, the hounds hot on their trail. He awakened in the morning, planning their flight together.

There had to be a way. It would take money. He had some and he could steal more. Denmark would help him. Passes and freedom papers presented no difficulty—he had forged them for years, and most of the time nobody had even asked to see them.

An overland route, then, traveling in the backcountry until they were out of the immediate region and their trail was cold. And then travel boldly? A roundabout route, perhaps heading north from a point further west and thus avoiding the swamps. Or would that be anticipated? Would it perhaps be better to go north by sea? Could Denmark perhaps find a Yankee captain with abolitionist sympathies? Or should they pretend to be free blacks, using papers he had forged and arranging their passage at the very last minute?

Actually, Adaba had no idea of what might be the best way to run away with Gilly. He only knew that somehow slaves did contrive to escape to freedom, and that was what he and Gilly had to do.

On Sunday afternoon he stood across the street from the Sabre house, hoping for a glimpse of Gilly, hoping for a chance to exchange a few words with her. She never appeared. Later, when it was dark, he crossed the street and tried the carriage gate, thinking that it still might be possible to sneak into the courtyard and see her. But the gate was barred from the inside.

Monday morning he went to the City Market. He knew it would be wise to avoid that part of Charleston for a few weeks, until the man he had knocked down had time to forget his face or had left the city. But he felt desperate and went, hoping that Gilly might appear to do the marketing.

He saw her nowhere.

62

Monday afternoon he swallowed his pride and went to the Sabre house. He would even make peace with Lew, the betrayer, if only he could see Gilly again. If Gilly were barred from him, perhaps Lew could arrange a meeting.

The moment he walked through the carriage gate into the courtyard, he encountered Mr. Sabre.

"I don't think you're supposed to be here, boy," the white man said, not unkindly.

"Mr. Sabre, sir, I just want to see Lew."

Mr. Sabre shook his head. "I'm sorry, John," he said, "but I know who you want to see, and you're not going to. Believe me, boy, it's for the best. You go on out of here, now, and you can see Lewis another time. You come see us after we get back to Jessamine."

The implication frightened Adaba: when next he went to Jessamine, Gilly would not be there. She would have been sold by then.

Adaba managed to talk to Lew the next evening.

He was again watching the house from across the street, when he saw the boy leave on an errand. He followed for a couple of blocks so that they would not be seen together, then ran to catch up and crossed the street. When Lew saw him, he stopped dead and looked frightened.

"Don't worry, you little bastard, I ain't gonna hit you."

Lew looked terribly pale in the evening darkness. "What you want with me?"

"Don't want nothing, never again. I just want to find out about Gilly."

"Adaba, I didn't mean to get you in trouble. I really didn't."

"Yeah, yeah—your old daddy told mine how if you had your way, you'd take my place in Gilly's bed anytime."

"But I wouldn't—I didn't—"

Adaba laughed mirthlessly. "You telling me you ain't got hair growing on your palms for thinking about Gilly, boy?"

Involuntarily, Lew glanced at his palms, and Adaba nearly hit him.

"Never mind that. Maybe I don't put a goddamn voodoo bad-mouth on you if you do something for me. You want to do something for me?"

"Yes, if I can."

"I got to talk to Gilly. You fix it so we can meet somewhere."

"But I can't do that, Adaba!"

"Listen, you! you've got to! I've got to talk to her, make plans, somehow get her away from here. Now, if you'd just come and tell me when she's going out to do marketing—"

"But she don't do that no more! My daddy says she's got to stay strictly in the house and in the yard. She can't go out *no* place now."

He should have expected that.

"No way I can sneak in at night? You could unbar the gate."

"Wouldn't do no good. He locks Gilly up in her loft at night. He put a big old lock on the door."

"Then you get the key—"

"Ain't no way I can get that key! Adaba, there just ain't no way you can get to see her!"

No way, and the time was growing shorter. Suddenly it occurred to Adaba that not only might he lose Gilly but he might not even see her again.

"I suppose you know what's happening is your fault," he said bitterly.

Lew shook his head. "Adaba, it'll be all right. My daddy is aggravated with you and Gilly right now, but he'll get over it. Then you can see her again, you can see her all you want to. And I ain't trying to get you out of her bed, honest. I just want us all to be together again and happy like we used to be."

"Ha!" Adaba looked contemptuously down at Lew. "Don't you even know what's happening, little boy? Don't you even know that on account of what you did, your old daddy is planning to sell Gilly?"

"No, he—"

"Yes, he is. Gonna sell her. Told my daddy that on account of you he figured he'd better sell her just as soon as possible."

Lew looked at Adaba uncomprehendingly for a moment.

Then he crumbled.

With a wail, he brought his knuckles to his mouth, and he slumped halfway to the ground. Tears poured from his eyes and saliva from his mouth, and he was no longer a thirteen-year-old boy but a child in pain, beating his feet against the ground.

"He ain't! He ain't gonna sell her, he ain't, he ain't, he ain't!"

Adaba's eyes stung. "I'm just saying what he told my daddy last Saturday night. He said she was an orphan without no family at Jessamine, and damn right he'd sell her, and he'd better not wait any longer."

"No-o-o-o!"

Lew turned and ran away, wailing in desolation.

For a moment, Adaba almost regretted having told him, especially in such a cruel way. Through blurred eyes, he watched Lew running back home.

Well . . . served the little bastard right.

Good God, Channing Sabre thought, anyone would think the world was coming to an end, just because of one little black girl. But the fact that Lewis had come back to the house hysterical, begging him not to sell her, was proof that he was absolutely right in doing so. It seemed that Lewis had run into that goddamn Adaba—John—and found out about his plan.

He told Lewis to keep his mouth shut, not to tell Gilly or any of the servants, as it would only upset them. But Dorinda, the cook, had overheard and now proceeded to give him hell.

"That gal belong here, Mr. Channing!"

"Dorinda, she hasn't got any family here, and I think it would be best—"

"What you mean, no family! She got me, she got my Lucas, we take care of her."

"You aren't kin."

"We *like* kin! How can you say we ain't kin, her Aunt Dorinda and Uncle Lucas!"

It was either yield or dig in his heels, and Channing

Sabre rarely yielded to anyone. "Dorinda, kindly be quiet. All I want to know from you is if you figure the girl is pregnant."

"Ain't likely. She just pass her time of month."

"Good. Now, don't you go talking to Gilly or anyone else about this. Gilly will have a good home."

"Yes, and who you going sell next? Lucas and me?"

"Dorinda!" Channing was shocked.

Dorinda burst into tears and rushed from the room.

Best to get the entire matter over with as quickly as possible, Channing decided. God knew, he had looked for an alternative. He could have hired the girl out, for instance, and put her into someone else's house, but that was not likely to put her at a safe distance from Lewis and keep her there. No, the best thing to do would be to sell her. Preferably to someone who lived a long way from Charleston and from Jessamine.

However, since he had had little experience in selling slaves, he didn't know of a dealer he could trust with Gilly. Dealers, by and large, were held in pretty low regard, but after a couple of days of inquiry, he had decided that a certain Ulysses P. Gore might be his man.

Gore's offices, appropriately enough, were at the east end of Queen Street, near Vendue Range, where the slave sheds stood. Channing met him there on Wednesday afternoon. Gore was a tall, thin, sallow man with curly gray hair. He had a bony face, sadly sincere eyes, a wide, thin-lipped mouth. Channing was skeptical of appearances, but Gore made a decent-enough impression that he thought the man could be trusted with Gilly.

"But of course we'll be happy to handle the wench's sale for you," he said. "Now, I find that business is poor during Race Week. People are much more concerned with their pleasures. But they'll be buying again next week, before departing for the country, and we plan an auction—"

"No," Channing said. "There will be no auctioning of this girl. Or rather she's not going to be put up in front of a crowd and auctioned off like a piece of livestock."

Gore looked slightly disconcerted. "Really, you'll get a much better price if you let us handle the matter our way."

"No," Channing repeated. "Price is not my primary concern. My concern is to find the girl a good home, and you'll handle the sale my way or not at all."

Sabre went on to state his conditions. There were a great many good families in Charleston during the races, and surely more than one of them would be interested in purchasing an absolutely first-rate young housemaid and assistant cook. Gore had such customers, didn't he? The *best* families? Indeed he did, Gore assured Sabre, and he knew how to get word out to them quickly that he had such a girl. Good. Gore was to invite them to come take a look at the girl, to talk to her, to make a bid if they wished. But the bids were to be sealed. Channing would return and examine them. He would talk to any purchaser he seriously considered. The girl would go, not necessarily to the highest bidder, but to the one Channing thought would give her the best home. In fact, he reserved the right not to sell at all until he found a home for the girl that satisfied him.

"Really," Gore said, "this is most irregular. I really do think—"

"You'll handle it my way," Channing said again, "or not at all."

Gore's eyes held a calculating glitter. "Well, under the circumstances, I must ask a higher commission."

"How much?"

"Fifty percent," Gore said quickly. "This is so unusual—"

"Twenty-five. Take it or leave it."

Channing's tone left no doubt that he meant what he said. Gore nodded slowly.

"I'll bring the girl in tomorrow morning. Can you get bids tomorrow afternoon?"

"Maybe a few. Most of them will come on Friday."

"Very well. I'll be back Saturday morning to review the bids and talk to anyone who's interested. Oh, and one other thing . . ." Channing remembered the promise he had made to Marcus Guerard on Saturday night just before leaving the Guerard house. "You are to tell absolutely no one who the girl is sold to. There's a young buck who's hot for her, and he'll be trying to find out. His father doesn't want him chasing after the girl."

"Of course, of course. That's always a problem."

Gore's eyes were suddenly wise, as if the riddle of this unusual sale had been solved, and Channing felt himself flush. He liked Ulysses P. Gore less every minute. Well, let the son of a bitch think what he wished; in a way, he would be right, even if Channing hadn't been referring to himself.

And what harm could the man do?

Later, Channing wondered how he could have done such a thing. Had he really been so insensitive and unimaginative that he hadn't known what it would be like? He didn't think of himself as a cruel man, he thought of himself as essentially kind and reasonable. Then why hadn't he known? Why had he been in such a damnable rush to have the girl out of the house? Couldn't he have taken more time, found a new home for the girl himself, without the help of a trader, found a way to make the transition easy for her? Shouldn't he at least have considered the possibility? But, no, he had got a wild hair up his ass and determined that the girl had to go *now*, with hardly a thought of what it would do to her and everyone else in the house—until it was too late. . . .

But that Thursday morning the wisdom of hindsight was still to come. He told Dorinda to inform Gilly that she was going on a little trip. Dorinda said he could just go tell her himself. He did so. "Be ready in half an hour."

"Where we go, master?" The girl had a puzzled half-smile.

"Never you mind, just be ready."

A clean break, Channing figured. One swift chop, and it would be over. Gilly might have a bad day or two, until she was sold, but then she would have a new home with good people, and she would quickly be caught up in a new life. After all, she was young. . . .

Gilly knew something was wrong. She felt it in Dorinda's silence. She saw it in Lucas's hollow eyes. Her own eyes grew frightened, and she clutched at her bundle as she stood by the cabriolet in the courtyard. "I don't wanna go," she mumbled, "I don't wanna go."

Dorinda disobeyed orders by ⸺ clutching at Gilly. Channing nea⸺ aloud. Didn't she know she was just ⸺ Gilly? He tore the two women apart.

"Get into the carriage, Gilly," he said b⸺ haven't got all day."

"We going to Jessamine, master?"

"We're just going for a little ride."

Wide-eyed, clinging to her bundle, the girl was silent as they rode out through the carriage gate and into the muddy street. She knew at once that she was not being taken to Jessamine, for they took the road heading for the east side of the city.

When she first guessed where she was being taken, he could not have said. The fact must have been too terrible for her to face immediately, and of course, she trusted him. He was Mr. Channing, the master, the protector. And *no* one had ever been sold away from the Sabre family who didn't want to be, *no* one had ever been sold except those few who wanted to live on other plantations with their husbands and wives. In all her life Gilly had never heard of Mr. Channing, master and protector, handing one of his people over to a slave-trader.

But she had been a bad girl. She hadn't thought she was being so terribly bad, but Mr. Channing had said so.

And here she was, with all her belongings in hand, riding along Queen Street toward Vendue Range.

And all the people knew about Queen and Bay and Vendue Range. . . .

Channing heard a sound at his side, a sound choked and small.

"I sorry, master, I sorry. . . ."

At first he didn't understand her. He dared not look around.

"I sorry, master. I don't do it no more. Please, master, I'se good girl, I don't do it no more, master."

"Now, now, Gilly . . ." Channing tried to think of a soothing word, a word of comfort.

"I'se good girl. Don't do this to your Gilly. Oh, please, master . . ."

Channing drove on, his throat too full to speak.

....ed.

.... was out of the carriage before he could stop her.
He leapt out after her, leaving the horse for someone
else to catch and hold. He would never have believed she
could be so fast, that fear and heartbreak could drive her
so, but she was running, dodging, twisting, darting through
the crowd like a terrorized rabbit. And when at last he
caught her, the sound she made was the scream of the rabbit when the owl drops down and seizes it in its deadly
claws.

The whole business, Channing thought, was disgusting.
He had often seen auctions being carried on, but had
hurried past them as if in fear of contamination. He had
thought that he had made cleaner, more satisfactory
arrangements.

Chasing the hysterical girl through the streets of
Charleston was bad enough, but then came the business,
after he had gotten her into Gore's office, of doping her—
of looking into her tear-swollen face and pressing the glass
of whiskey and laudanum to her teeth. "I should have
warned you yesterday," Gore said. "Some of them take on
like this, and you'd think it was the most important thing
in their lives. When you spot that kind, it helps to give
them a little laudanum first. But by God, sir, I can see already that you have a mighty handsome wench here. I
look forward to inspecting her."

"Inspecting her?" Channing was surprised. "What for?
You have my guarantee that she's sound."

"Oh, not that I doubt you, Mr. Sabre, but my customers must have *my* guarantee, my personal guarantee. I
have my professional reputation to protect. I have to inspect her for piles, hernia, determine if she's a virgin—"

"Mr. Gore, I'm not going to have you pawing over this
girl!"

Gore looked surprised. "Oh, I'm sorry! Did I lead you
to think that I personally would inspect the girl? Why, of
course not! I have women who do that for me, sir, women
who are quite expert. But I insist that you come and
watch. I wouldn't want you to think that the wench was
being in any way mistreated."

And so Channing watched the inspection. When the

70

drug had calmed Gilly, a middle-aged black woman named Ora led her upstairs. Channing and Gore had a couple of stiff drinks, which Channing badly needed, even if it was still morning. They went right to Channing's head, but he had a third one anyway.

By the time they got upstairs, Gilly was almost unconscious. She was laid out naked on a narrow bed, a thin blanket thrown over her. The black woman, Ora, was sitting in a chair watching her. The room was barren except for the bed and a couple of chairs, but Channing hardly noticed.

Gore went to the bed, swept the blanket away, and stared down at the unmoving Gilly. "Lord God Almighty!" he said in an awed tone after a moment. "Lord God Almighty!"

"Anything wrong?"

"Not a damn thing," Gore said, grinning. "In fact, Mr. Sabre, if your wench's tits are as good when she's on her feet as they are when she's on her back, you've got one of the goddamnedest fanciest of fancies I've ever seen in my life. You are going to make one hell of a lot of money on this wench!"

"Yes, well, let's get on with it."

Gore nodded at the woman, who did a fast, expert job of the inspection, starting at the head and working her way down to the ankles, looking for everything from bad teeth to hernias and piles to badly mended bones. In the process, she stuck a spit-moistened finger up the girl's vagina and announced, "She ain't no virgin." Channing thought he was going to throw up.

"She fine," the woman announced when she was finished. "Ain't nothing wrong with her."

"A real fancy," Gore said gloatingly. He was staring at Gilly's naked body as if he had forgotten Channing's presence. "By God, a cunt like that is going to bring in some real money—and sure going to pleasure somebody!"

Anger stirred in Channing's breast, and the liquor pulsed in his brain. He stepped over to the bed, picked up the blanket, and spread it over Gilly again. "Listen, Gore. Maybe I didn't make myself clear yesterday. I don't give a goddamn how fancy you find her, she's to be sold as a housemaid to a good family. I'm not going to have her ending up in a whorehouse or in some degenerate's private harem."

"Why, Mr. Sabre, I had nothing of the kind in mind!"

"And furthermore, not to insult you, Mr. Slave-Trader, but I don't want her abused by anybody while she's here, not by you and not by any of your customers. Do you understand me?"

"Certainly I understand you. Mr. Sabre, if I don't have your confidence, I would prefer that you went elsewhere. But *you* came to *me*—and with an excellent referral, I might add. I have a reputation to maintain—"

"I know, I know. No offense, Mr. Gore, but I just want to be very clear on this one point. I'll be talking to the girl later, you know."

"And when you do," Gore said agreeably, "you'll find her bright and alert and accepting of her new circumstances. Mr. Sabre, I've been in this profession for a long time, and believe me, I quite sympathize with your feelings about this wench. And I do want you to be satisfied and happy."

Channing nodded. It was hard for him to believe that he would be happy for quite some time to come.

"I think we understand each other, Mr. Gore. I'll leave you now. And return on Saturday morning about ten."

"Perfectly agreeable, sir."

Gore went back downstairs with Channing Sabre and stood in the doorway of his offices until the cabriolet was out of sight.

Goddamn hypocrite!

Just like all the chivalry, as they liked to call themselves, eager to buy all the slaves they could afford, willing to sell all they had to, but looking down on the trader they made use of, as if that kept their own hands clean. Hypocrites, all of them.

Not that he gave a damn. He had better things to think of.

That girl upstairs . . .

When he went back up, she was alone in the room, still lying on the bed. He closed the door. Ora would understand and keep out. The girl looked at him uncomprehendingly.

Sweetest damn fancy he had ever seen in his life.

He pulled the blanket off of her. He placed a hand on each breast, kneaded them for a moment, then drew his hands slowly down her body. She stirred and moaned protestingly as he touched her sex.

Sabre had warned him: *"I don't want her abused. . . . I'll be talking to the girl later."*

Gore laughed. As if he gave a damn.

You just go ahead and tell him, wench, he thought, as he unfastened his clothes. You think it'll keep him from selling you and taking the money? Hell, no. I wouldn't be surprised if it was him that spread you in the first place.

What else is a nigger wench like you meant for?

Lew couldn't sleep. Thoughts of Gilly and Adaba ran through his head, every kind of memory and regret, keeping him tense and wakeful, twisting and turning in his blankets. Finally he could stand it no longer. Not really knowing why he was doing it, he got out of his bed and, fumbling about in the darkness, pulled his clothes back on.

When he was dressed, he looked out his window across the courtyard to Gilly's window, which would be dark from now on. He could hardly believe it had actually happened. Lew had seen his father and Gilly leaving, had seen Dorinda weeping in Lucas's arms, and he had rushed down to the courtyard. But he had been too late.

Lew remembered Adaba's words: *"On account of what you done, your old daddy is planning to sell Gilly."*

But had it really been his fault? He had only tried to do the right thing. Then why had he felt so bad about it right from the beginning? Why did he wish he'd kept his mouth shut? Why did people feel rotten for doing the right thing—and good for doing other things that most people said were bad?

Lew could make no sense of it. Hoping to escape his thoughts, he left the window and went out into the dark hall. Quietly, he felt his way down the stairs and across the hall toward the piazza door.

"Lewis . . ."

Lew froze. His father was calling from the parlor. It had not occurred to him that someone else might be up, and certainly not that that someone might be sitting in the dark. But his father had been acting strangely all day, especially since his return to the house without Gilly.

"Lewis, come in here, boy."

His father didn't sound angry or even disturbed at finding Lew up in the middle of the night. He sounded sad. Lew went into the parlor. Channing Sabre, a dim figure in shirtsleeves, was sitting in a chair, a glass in his hand and a bottle at his elbow. He had been drinking all afternoon, something Lew had never seen him do before, and yet he did not appear to be drunk.

"What are you doing up, son?"

"I couldn't sleep. I was going for a walk."

"Going to look on for your friend Adaba?"

Lewis was surprised. Such an idea had not occurred to him. "No, sir. I guess we ain't—we aren't such good friends anymore."

"I'm sorry to hear that. I think I know why, and I don't really think you have anything to blame yourself for."

"Well . . ." Lew shrugged. He didn't really want to discuss the matter.

His father stirred in his chair, sipped his drink, put the glass down.

"Lewis, I want you to promise me something."

"Yes, sir."

"You know that Jessamine is going to be yours one day. This house and Jessamine and all the people who depend on Jessamine. You know that, don't you?"

"That's what you've always told me, daddy."

"Lewis, I want you to give me your solemn word that when you take charge, you'll do your damnedest to keep all the people together. Oh, I know there may be exceptions, but if you can possibly help it, don't ever sell anybody off the place that doesn't want to go. Don't sell anybody away from his family unless that's what he wants—to get married, maybe. Don't even sell away families together, because in a way they're all part of one family, all one community. It's awfully easy to forget that."

Lew said, "Yes, sir."

"So give me your word," his father went on, "and don't do it lightly. Hell, to keep your word on a matter like that could be your ruination. But I want you to try, Lewis. At least try."

"I'll try, daddy. I promise."

The voice in the darkness became bitter. "My God, this is the nineteenth century, not the Dark Ages. We've had an Enlightenment. We fought a revolution based on its principles. Your grandfather thought slavery would die a natural death. But it's not dying, because we cling to it. And no matter how well a man treats his people, Lewis, that's a hell of a thing for him to have to explain to his Maker."

"Yes, sir."

"Always remember they're people, not animals."

His father had expressed such sentiments before, sometimes in heated arguments with his friends, but Lew felt now that he was actually trying to say something else, something about Gilly.

Lew dared to ask, "You could get her back, couldn't you?"

"Gilly?" His father sighed and shook his head. "No. It's done. I'll admit that if I'd known how hard it was going to be, I don't think I could have done it. Maybe I could have found another solution. But I did it because I thought it was for the best, and I wouldn't want Gilly to go through a day like today for nothing. No, what's done is done."

"Where did you take her?" he asked, perhaps too casually.

"I took her . . ." His father shook his head again. "Never mind, Lewis. I know you'd like to see her. I suppose Adaba would like to see her too. But that would only make it more difficult for her. Believe me, I have every hope that by Saturday morning she'll be with a good family, one that will take the very best care of her and make her happy."

By Saturday morning . . .

Lew knew now what he had to do.

"You'd better go back up to bed, Lewis."

"Yes, sir."

He went back upstairs, undressed again in the dark, slipped back into his bed.

Tomorrow he would go looking for Adaba. Adaba would not want to see him, but that was not important. The important thing was not to let Gilly and Adaba be lost to each other forever. And that meant finding out who she was being sold to.

Somehow they would do it. Adaba would do it.

On that comforting thought, Lew slept.

It was a bad year, Balbo Jeppson told himself. The races were unexciting, the weather was sultry, the whores were unattractive. For the first time in years he found himself not even wanting a woman. He told himself that it had nothing to do with that nigger boy who had humiliated him, but the fact was that he spent most of his waking hours keeping his eyes open for the sight of him. By Friday morning Jeppson was about ready to say to hell with it and head back for his plantation.

Afterward he marveled at how close he had come to not seeing the girl. Balbo Jeppson was not much of a believer, but it was hard to think that the good Lord didn't have a hand in it somewhere.

His friend P. V. Tucker was the one who first heard about the girl.

"This fellow, Henry St. Julian, told me about her. He wouldn'ta told me, 'cause he wouldn't want me to put in a bid, but he was drunk. He saw her yesterday afternoon, and he said she was the fanciest goddamn wench he ever did see. He bid a thousand for her, all he could afford, but he said he ain't got a hope of getting her, 'cause she must be worth twice that."

"P.V., you know you can't afford to outbid a thousand for a wench."

"Hell, I don't want to buy her, I just want to see her. They show her all naked, Balbo, and any wench that fancy is worth looking at. Come on, you ain't got nothing better to do."

Every morning Jeppson had been going to the City Market in hope of encountering the nigger boy again, and they were standing on the corner of Market and Meeting Streets. It was only a few short blocks to the establishment of Mr. Ulysses P. Gore, so Jeppson agreed to walk over with Tucker.

But even then he would not have seen the girl if it hadn't been for Gore's behavior. Tucker's appearance was hardly that of a gentleman of fashion and wealth. Gore took one look at him, stepped to block the door of his offices, and shook his head.

"I don't care who sent you, St. Julian or anyone else. If you've got the kind of money it takes, boy, you bring it here and show me. But if you just want to get your gun off, you take your pennies and run around to old French Alley—"

He didn't get any further. Jeppson's big hand spread over the center of Gore's chest, pushing him back into his office. "My friend's 'pennies' are good as anybody else's, and so are mine," Jeppson said in a low hard voice. His hand turned into a fist, gathering up Gore's shirtfront. "Now, you are going to show us that fancy wench you got, Mr. Gore, or else."

Gore's sallow face turned pink. "Well, of course, I didn't realize that *you*, sir, were also interested in the wench."

"Now you know."

Several other more affluent-looking men were also in the office. Gore, trying to sound more cheerful than he looked, rattled off some business about sealed bids and about being interviewed tomorrow morning by the wench's present owner who wanted her sold as a domestic. "But you gentlemen will see that God in his goodness made this wench much too special ever to be a domestic. You are about to see a wet dream like you haven't had since you were youngsters—ha! ha!"

The viewing was like no other that Jeppson had ever witnessed. Of course, he had never considered buying a fancy wench. He and the others were led to an upstairs room that might almost have been someone's parlor. It was carpeted and had a dozen comfortable chairs and divans facing a dais, which was also carpeted. Drapes were drawn over the windows, and several mirrors reflected the light from the lamps. Jeppson figured it was all calculated to make the wenches look better than they were. He didn't bother to sit down.

"Now, gentlemen," Gore said, "you all know I have a reputation for fancies. I've had buyers come all the way from New Orleans, where I've supplied the very finest houses of joy. Usually I show you several wenches at a time, but with this one here——"

"Get on with it," Jeppson said. "I ain't got all day."

"Yessir, yessir, at once!"

Gore opened a door at the side of the dais, and two middle-aged black women led the girl through it.

She was almost entirely concealed by what appeared to be a sheet of white silk that she clutched about her. Head low and face averted, she was led up the steps onto the dais and to the front to face her audience.

"As you see, gentlemen," Gore said cheerfully, "our little black lady is a trifle shy, a trifle nervous, even a trifle frightened. This is her first time on the block. But you are about to see a true princess."

"Then let's see her, goddammit," Jeppson said, bored. "That's what we're here for."

"At once, sir!" Gore nodded at the two women. "May I present—Princess Gilly!"

The girl moaned softly as the women uncrossed her arms, obviously against her wishes. They held her arms straight out from her sides so that from head to toe her body was seen against a background of white silk. A moan from the men looking at her followed her own moan like an echo, and even Jeppson found himself staring. He had seen wenches before, handsome wenches, but never one like her. She was entirely naked except for a necklace and some silver bangles Gore had hung on her arms and legs, several on a delicate ankle, another high on a long thigh. Her breasts seemed to float on her chest, and her narrow waist swelled to her hips without any hint of an angle. Her rich brown skin was flawless, and from the notch at the base of her throat to the full lips of her sex, all was delicacy, all was perfection.

Jeppson found himself growing angry. A black wench

had no right to look like that. Most of them were ugly, in his opinion—God meant them to be that way.

He felt the excitement in the room. Most of the men stood up. The two women were still holding the girl's arms out, and she moved her legs, one knee before the other, as if trying to cover herself. Failing to do that effectively, she began to twist about, trying to escape the hands that held her. But there was no escape, and her struggles, together with her sobs, only produced more excitement and sounds of approval from the men. Jeppson looked at them with disgust, his anger growing. White men after black cunt.

Grinning, Gore stepped forward and raised his hands in a bid for attention. "Gentlemen, you who have been here before know that in selling fancies I usually just ask one gentleman to step forward and make a brief examination of the wench to verify my guarantee. But in this case, since there are so few of you here, I'm going to ask you *all* to step up and look at our little princess. Step up, gentlemen!"

The pack rushed up, led by Tucker. Only Jeppson remained behind. Hands reached for the girl. Jeppson saw them moving over her thighs, sliding over her belly, squeezing her breasts. The girl twisted desperately against the iron grip of the women, and her sobs grew louder.

"Take a good look, gentlemen, front and back. You have one minute more, and then—"

"She a virgin, Mr. Gore?" someone asked.

"Now, sir, if a wench like this one came to me a virgin, do you reckon I'd let her leave as one?"

Laughter.

"How was she, Mr. Gore?"

"She may be a little shy in a crowd yet, but in bed she's the hottest little piece I've ever known. And the best. You get this little wench heated up, and she'll twist the dong off a stallion."

"By God," Tucker panted, "by God! How 'bout letting us try her out!"

"No, no, my friend—"

"I'll pay you ten dollars—hell, make it twenty—you let me have her just for tonight!"

The girl's sobs became one long wail of despair. Hell,

Jeppson thought, not even a nigger wench deserved this. If she'd done anything wrong, he wouldn't have hesitated to cut off her tits himself. Nobody kept niggers in line the way Balbo Jeppson did. But *this!*

He charged to the front of the room.

He grabbed Tucker by the collar and yanked him away from the girl.

He drove his shoulder to one side and knocked two other men away from her.

Then he looked closely at her face.

In that instant he knew there was justice in the universe.

It was the girl. The girl who could lead him to that nigger boy. The light in the room was not good, and she had kept her face down or turned away most of the time; but now he was directly before her, and he saw her clearly. And in that same instant, as if to confirm his knowledge, she saw and recognized him.

The despair in her eyes turned to terror.

Four

In her fear, the girl's legs had given way, and she cringed on the dais, her body half covered by the white sheet.

"I know this wench," Jeppson said. "Less than a week ago, her and her buck gave me trouble. Got violent with me out on the street and ran away before I could punish them."

"Sir," Gore began, "that is no concern of—"

"It's the concern of every white man. But I reckon a white man that'd spread a nigger wouldn't see it that way."

There were murmurs of dissent among the other men, but on the whole they looked amused. Gore's eyes widened. "Sir!"

"All I want to know is who that buck was, that black bastard that put his hands on me."

80

"Then ask her," Gore said indignantly. "Ask her, god-dammit, and get it over with."

"You heard me," Jeppson said to the girl. "Who was that nigger boy with you last Saturday morning? I want to know, and I want to know now."

The girl strained away from Jeppson. "Don't know, master! Don't know! Never see that boy before!"

"You never seen him, and yet he tried to protect you? You're lying, you little black bitch. That boy belongs to your master, don't he? He's your buck, ain't he?"

"No, master, he ain't!" the girl said, shaking her head violently. "I don't know that boy! You ask my master! He ain't got no boy like that!"

"But you know him—"

"No, master, no! I never see him before! Please! Please, master!"

Jeppson put all the menace he was capable of into his voice. "Gal, you know what I'm gonna do to you if you don't tell me? I'm gonna buy you, you hear me? I'm gonna buy you and take you home with me, and then I'm gonna flay your black hide off. I'm gonna nail you up naked on a barn wall and make you scream and beg and plead to tell me. I'm gonna punish you like you never been punished before. I'm gonna—"

"Oh, master! Master, master!"

The girl rolled over, the sheet falling from her body, and tried to crawl away. Jeppson grabbed her ankle and pulled her back. Tucker whooped, and several others laughed. Even Gore found the spectacle amusing and allowed it to continue until Jeppson gave the girl a round-house slap that might have knocked her teeth loose. Then suddenly a small pistol appeared in Gore's hand.

"I think that will be about enough from you, sir," he said, grinning. "I appreciate your interest in the wench, but we can't have you damaging her. You are abusing another man's property without his permission, sir."

Jeppson stared at Gore. Gore's grin became strained.

"If you don't put away that dinky little pistol in about two seconds," Jeppson said softly, "I'm gonna take it away from you and shove it up your ass."

Gore's sallow face reddened, and his grin disappeared.

"You bull your way in here, you ruin my shirtfront, you push people around. You think you can do just about anything, don't you?"

"I can make you eat that pistol."

"You try, friend, and I am going to blow you to hell. I am defending property, sir, as any jury will agree. Now, you've talked to the wench, and if you've got anything further to say to her, you can put in a bid for her."

Jeppson looked around at the other men. Some of them, including Tucker, were smiling openly, just waiting to see what would happen next. All he was doing was providing amusement for them—once again, because of a nigger. The same nigger who had started the trouble a week earlier.

And there was not a thing he could do about it.

Without another word, Jeppson left the room.

But he couldn't leave it at that.

He walked the streets of Charleston without noticing where he was going. He kept seeing the wench as she stood on the dais, naked, too beautiful to be believed, terrified. It was wrong, what they had done to her—wrong, what they planned for her. She was just a pretty little nigger girl who had caused him some trouble. Perhaps, he had to admit, even accidentally.

But she had the answer to his question: who was that arrogant young buck who had cursed and struck him, who had humiliated him before his friends and the crowds of the City Market?

She knew. But the only way he would ever find out would be to buy her.

She would cost a lot, though. Tucker's friend St. Julian had said she was worth twice the thousand dollars he himself had bid. He could buy three prime field hands for that. Twelve hundred was about all he could afford to bid. Fifteen hundred at the most. But he was damned if he would bid so much lower then the others that it would bring a sneer to Mr. Ulysses P. Gore's face.

What had Gore said? Sealed bids. And something about an interview. A lot would depend on that. The wench's owner wanted to be sure that the girl got a good home.

She sure as hell wouldn't be getting a good home with any of that lot who had been looking her over. Jeppson figured he could give her as good a home as any of them. Better.

And he would find out about the buck. Sooner or later, he would find out.

When Gore saw Jeppson again, he dipped a hand into his pocket for the gun, but he stopped as Jeppson shook his head and waved him off. "You was right," Jeppson said. "I shouldn'ta let the little bitch make me lose my temper. I reckon you know better'n me how to handle that kind of nigger." He wasn't used to apologizing or flattering, but he didn't want Gore bad-mouthing him with the wench's owner.

Gore smiled and relaxed.

Jeppson asked for pen and paper. He wrote out his bid. He signed it, folded the paper, sealed it with wax. He handed it to Gore. It was done. His bid was made.

Two thousand dollars.

"Adaba . . ."

From the shaded interior of Monday Gell's harness shop, Adaba looked out at the bright street where Lew stood. He said nothing.

"Adaba," Lew said from the doorway, "I been looking all over for you. I got to talk to you. It's about Gilly."

Adaba had spent Wednesday and Thursday and most of Friday morning prowling the streets near the Channing Sabre house, but he hadn't so much as caught a glimpse of Gilly. If she had left the house in that time, he had missed seeing her, and he hungered for any word of her.

"All right," he said, "come in. Tell me."

Lew hesitated, and Adaba knew why. Monday Gell, working quietly at his bench, did not look menacing. He was a handsome Ibo from the lower Niger, completely trusted by his master and allowed a great deal of freedom. But Denmark Vesey, a fierce glare on his face, was also in the room, and so was Gullah Jack. Gullah Jack was a sorcerer from Angola—a small man with a bushy beard who looked even more fierce than Denmark. There were no other blacks in all of Charleston so capable of inspiring fear as Gullah Jack and Denmark Vesey.

83

Adaba was amused. "Come on in. They won't eat you up. Leastways, not till I tell 'em to."

Keeping his eyes on Adaba rather than on the others, Lew slowly came into the room.

"Now, what about Gilly?"

Lew lowered his voice as if he wanted only Adaba to hear. "My daddy took her away yesterday morning."

The words were like a blow to the heart. "What you mean, he took her away?"

"He took her *away!* He took her off in our cabriolet and came back later without her. He acted real upset all the rest of the day and wouldn't talk about it. Except that last night he made me promise never to sell any of our people if I could possibly help it."

All of Adaba's strength seemed to drain out of him. He slumped down into a chair. "He sold her. He really did sell her."

"But maybe she *ain't* sold yet!" Lew said. "My daddy told me he had every hope she would be with a good family by Saturday morning."

"You mean," Denmark said, "you think he took her to a dealer and he hopes to make a sale by Saturday?"

"I only know he took her somewhere," Lew said, "and he told me what I told you."

"Gilly is a mighty pretty gal," Monday Gell said. "Maybe your daddy mean to say he figure it take only a day or two to sell her. Could be she sold by now."

"But she might *not!*" Lew said. "And we got to find out where she is! Maybe then we can figure out a way to get her back!"

Denmark's laugh was sad. "Nobody is going to get that child back, boy. Get that idea out of your head. If she's been taken to a trader, she is gone."

"No," Adaba said, "that ain't so." He slowly sat up in his chair. He felt as if he were gathering his strength back by an act of sheer will. He couldn't fail Gilly by losing heart now.

"No," he said, "Lew is right. Maybe we can figure a way to get her back. I'll buy her back if I have to. I've got some money, and I can get more. I'll earn it, I'll steal it. But I'll get it."

Denmark shook his head. "A slave can't buy a slave, boy. And he can't buy anybody free anymore, not himself nor another."

"I can't buy her, no. But if I gave you the money, you could buy her, Denmark. She'd belong to you, and that would be almost as good as being free."

Denmark looked as if he couldn't believe what he was hearing. "Denmark Vesey own a slave? You must be having your little joke."

"She'd be no more slave than you made her. Far less a slave than she is now. I'm asking you, Denmark. Please."

Denmark hesitated, then nodded. "All right, if there's no other way. For you, boy, I'll do it."

Which, Adaba thought, was more than his own father would do for him. He turned to Lew.

"I suppose you asked your daddy where he took Gilly? He give you any idea at all?"

"I asked, but he said it was better if me and you didn't know. He said if we saw Gilly it would just make things harder for her."

"That means she must be around close someplace, someplace where we might see her. She might be almost close enough to touch right now."

"If she ain't been sold yet," Monday said.

"Don't say that. Denmark, you know more people, black and white, than just about anyone else I ever heard of. Do you suppose you could start your friends asking around about Gilly?"

"We'll need luck, boy, a great deal of luck."

Luck. Adaba turned to Gullah Jack. "Jack, you reckon you can make a spell to keep her from being sold until we find her?"

"Ha! *Ban!*" Gullah Jack made fierce noises that meant it was as good as done.

We'll find you, Gilly, Adaba vowed. *And when I have you back, I'll never let you be taken from me again.* . . .

Though Channing Sabre had told Ulysses P. Gore that he would return on Saturday morning at about ten, he arrived before nine, anxious to get the business of Gilly's sale concluded. Channing was the kind of man who found it very difficult to backtrack. When he sensed that he might be making a mistake, his tendency was not to change his course of action but to hasten it, as if that might in some way minimize any error.

Gore was surprised to see him so early. "None of the bidders are here yet. In another hour or so——"

"That's all right. While we wait for them, I can look over the bids. But first I want to see the girl."

"Of course, of course."

Once again they went upstairs, and Gore led the way. When the dealer opened the door, Channing was surprised to see that Gilly was in the bed asleep.

"You still have her drugged?"

"No, no—well, a little." Gore's smile was kindly. "She had a restless night, poor little thing. So early this morning one of my women gave her a little something to help her sleep. You've got to understand, Mr. Sabre, spending a whole day being looked at again and again by strangers— that can be mighty upsetting for a young wench like your Gilly."

"I'd hoped to speak to her."

"Well," Gore said reluctantly, "we can awaken her if you wish, but——"

"No, let her sleep." In a way, Channing was relieved. He would have liked to receive assurances from the girl that she was being decently treated, but he did not look forward to more tears and entreaties. He had no particular attachment to Gilly, but it gave him an odd feeling to think that he was seeing her for the last time.

"Now let's see those bids."

Gore closed the door and led the way back downstairs. He conducted Channing to a cubbyhole of an office where they would not be disturbed, and a moment later brought in the bids.

The first thing that struck Channing as he began to open them was how high they tended to run. Ordinarily, he paid little attention to the current prices of slaves, but recent inquiries had led him to believe that prime field hands were going for perhaps six or seven hundred dollars, and a prime young domestic like Gilly might fetch seven or eight hundred or even more. But Channing had soon opened several bids at twelve and fifteen hundred dollars.

"Impressive?" Gore asked, smiling.

"Yes, sir, I must admit it is."

Under the circumstances, Channing felt that he might put aside, at least for the moment, those bids of only a few hundred dollars. He told himself he was only being realistic: a good home for Gilly was the primary consideration, but aside from that, why should he sell her for six hundred dollars when he could get over a thousand? He had to look after his own best interests as well as Gilly's.

There were certain bids that virtually eliminated themselves.

"Mr. Gore, you've given me a bid from Mr. Henry St. Julian for a thousand dollars. Do you know anything about that young man?"

"Why, ah, I have heard some rather nice things—"

"He's a libertine, a wastrel, a moral degenerate. He calls himself a gentleman, but I wouldn't waste my powder on him. He is not the kind of person I wish to accept a bid from."

"Mr. Sabre, please understand that I merely send out word to various potential buyers—the *best* families, as you required—but I cannot control who all learn about the sale. All kinds of people come to my offices. I merely collect their bids, encouraging the highest possible, and hand them over to you. Until you open them, I don't even know anymore who those bids came from."

"Very well. But as far as I'm concerned, you might as well have torn it up, and I don't care how high it is."

"That privilege, sir, is entirely yours."

One bid sounded an alarm in Channing's mind.

Twenty-five hundred dollars.

Channing didn't care how good Gore was at eliciting high bids. Twenty-five hundred dollars was entirely too much.

Channing looked at the signature. Antoine Bellesorte. He showed the bid to Gore.

"Oh, yes, Mr. Bellesorte of New Orleans. A charming gentleman, quite wealthy, travels a great deal—New York, London, Paris. He always stops by to see me when he can, because of my reputation, and I have supplied a number of servants to him and his family."

"Does he always pay so much?"

"No, not always. But he does always pay high, because his requirements are quite special. The ladies in his family will accept only the most intelligent and attractive wenches for their servants."

"I see."

Channing was skeptical of the story, but he decided he would talk to Mr. Antoine Bellesorte. Twenty-five hundred dollars was, after all, twenty-five hundred dollars.

He continued to look through the bids. He was disappointed to find that there were few impressive names. Good, respectable names, he felt, would be a kind of guarantee of Gilly's future well-being. Gore might have invited the "best families" to this sale, but almost none had responded.

By nine-thirty Sabre was talking to the bidders, and he didn't like what he heard. He had one question which disconcerted almost everyone whom he asked it. "You've offered twelve hundred dollars for the girl. That's a lot of money. What makes you think she's worth it?"

One man reacted angrily, as if Channing were a hypocrite. "You know damn good and well why she's worth it. That's one fancy bitch. Gore says to tell you she'll get a good home—well, she will. I treat my niggers good. But I ain't gonna tell you I ain't buying that wench for bedding and breeding, 'cause I am, and you and me both know it."

Christ, Channing thought, was that what they were *all* here for? Was that why there were so many high bids? It had all seemed so easy before: get the name of a reliable dealer and tell him to sell the girl to a good family. Keep an eye on him so that you knew he was doing exactly that.

When he talked to Antoine Bellesorte, he saw through the man's pretensions at once. Bellesorte said his family had the most beautiful house servants in New Orleans. He meant that his houses had the fanciest whores.

Channing was tempted to give up the whole thing in disgust. Or at least to forget the rest of the high bids and go to the two or three decent names, however low their bids. But money was money, and there were a couple of

88

high bids left. He still hadn't talked to the man who had made the second highest bid of all.

Two thousand dollars.

Jeppson figured Gore had caught a glimpse of the figure he had written on his bid and had been impressed. That was encouraging. In any case, the slave-trader was much friendlier now. "Remember," he said confidentially, "this Mr. Sabre figures on selling the wench as a house servant. He says she's a good maid and she can cook. Of course, all he really wants is the money, but I advise you to say nothing about how fancy she is or how you saw her naked. Don't say anything that might give him the idea you want her for a bed wench or some such."

"I don't," Jeppson said flatly.

Gore's eyes widened with false innocence. "Why, of course not, Mr. Jeppson."

Jeppson disliked Channing Sabre the moment he laid eyes on him, and he saw that the feeling was mutual. Sabre's eyes were ice blue and flat, and his wide mouth had a slight twist of distaste; he looked harried, irritated, as if Jeppson were merely interrupting some more important business. He didn't bother to lift his stocky body out of his chair or even offer his hand as Jeppson entered the room. Jeppson withheld his own hand and dropped into a chair without being asked.

No, Jeppson thought, this man is not going to sell me the wench.

"Jeppson?"

"Mr. Jeppson."

The twisted corner of Channing Sabre's mouth ticked.

"Mr. Jeppson, you've offered two thousand for the girl. What makes you think she's worth it?"

"I doubt that she is," Jeppson answered without hesitation. "Can I get her for less?"

Sabre looked startled, then irritated, as if he didn't like having his time wasted. Goddamn gentry, Jeppson thought, snotty like all Sabres. Like the Sabres of Sabrehill plantation, right near his own place. Probably related.

"You offered two thousand dollars," Sabre repeated.

"Is a sixteen-year-old housemaid, an assistant cook, really worth that to you?"

Jeppson sighed. "Mr. Sabre, I was dragged in here yesterday by a friend who wanted to look at a fancy wench jaybird naked. I saw all them sonabitches pawing the wench, and it made me mad. I pulled 'em off and damn near beat up the lot of 'em." Jeppson figured a little exaggeration could not hurt. "Then I made a fool of myself by bidding more than I could afford, just hoping I could keep the wench away from them. But I don't care—Mr. Gore mentioned that the girl can cook and keep house. I got a cook already, but she could help, and God knows my house could be kept up better than it is. I'll stand by my offer, but she ain't worth any two thousand, and you know it."

Channing Sabre's face had darkened. "What the hell are you talking about? A fancy wench jaybird naked and somebody pawing her? Are you talking about *my* girl?"

Jeppson shrugged. "Princess Gilly, he called her. Jaybird naked but for some bangles he hung on her. Little wench was scared shitless."

Channing Sabre came out of his chair like a man on the attack. "If you're lying, Jeppson—"

"*Mister* Jeppson, and don't call me a liar, *Mister* Sabre, or I'll tear your goddamn tongue out."

The threat, delivered with casual viciousness, had the desired effect. Channing Sabre sank back down into his chair and looked at Jeppson as if he were seeing him in a new light. It was a moment before he spoke.

"My apologies, Mr. Jeppson. Mr. Gore can wait. If I understood you correctly, you said that my Gilly was being abused and you defended her."

"That's about right. That goddamn Gore even pulled a gun on me for doing it—ask him about that."

"I shall. Mr. Jeppson, I owe you my thanks."

"I ain't asking for thanks. I did what was right. You just tell me if you accept my bid or not, and I'll get out of here."

"If you feel your bid was too high, you may withdraw it."

Jeppson shook his head. "I made it, I stand by it."

90

Channing Sabre looked pleased. "Then possibly we have a basis for discussion. I won't waste your time. Gilly is a high-quality girl, exceptionally intelligent and well trained. Not to deceive you, she may be a little lax morally by white standards, but many black people keep to the African ways more than we like to believe."

"That's the truth."

"I intend to put her with good people, the kind that will appreciate and take care of her. For reasons of my own, I'd like to put her with a family that won't bring her to Charleston often, if at all—perhaps a family from Columbia or Savannah or Wilmington. You're married, I suppose? have a family?"

Jeppson considered lying, but thought better of it. He might shade the truth, but he hated to think he had to lie outright to get what he wanted.

"No," he said, "I live alone."

Disappointment briefly shadowed Channing Sabre's face. "I'm sorry to hear that. A girl like Gilly—well, Mr. Jeppson, put it this way. This is no reflection on you, but I don't think a girl like Gilly should be in a bachelor home. You've *seen* that girl and any man—"

"Mr. Sabre!" In an instant, anger boiled up white-hot in Jeppson. "Mr. Sabre, I sure as hell do take that as a reflection on me!"

"Please. I was only thinking of human nature."

"Human nature, hell! Mr. Sabre, when I want a wife, I'll get me a wife. When I want a whore, I'll get me a whore. But it'll be a white whore."

"Well, good for you," Sabre said calmly, smiling in his superior way.

"The only thing worse than a white man spreading a nigger wench, Mr. Sabre, is a white woman spreading for a buck. And I take it as an offense, sir, when you say that I'm the kind that does such a thing!"

"Then I apologize again," Sabre said, as calm as ever, "but you must understand my position, Mr. Jeppson. I don't really know you or anything about you except what you tell me. I don't know where you come from, I don't know your connections. . . ." Channing Sabre shrugged.

"Hell of a way to sell a nigger."

"Perhaps. But it's my way."

Jeppson knew he was being dismissed. And a kind of panic came over him, drowning his anger, as he realized that the wench was not going to be his.

"Anyway, thank you for your bid, Mr. Jeppson." Channing Sabre turned back to his desk and picked up another bid.

Jeppson shrugged and got up from his chair, feigning indifference. "My bid was too high anyway. Maybe I'm well out of it." He paused at the door. "By the way, Mr. Sabre, I'm curious about one thing."

"Yes, Mr. Jeppson?"

"You any relation to the Sabres of Sabrehill? Aaron and Joel?"

Channing Sabre looked up, interested. "Why, yes. We're cousins, though distant. Do you know Aaron and Joel by any chance?"

Jeppson allowed himself a faint smile. Suddenly he felt that he had the situation under control. "My neighbors, just down the river a way. I practically growed up with Aaron and Joel, or at least it seems that way." A lie? or just an exaggeration?

"Then you must know . . ."

"The Kimbroughs, the captain and Miss Adamina, just west of Sabrehill . . . the Devereaus, on the other side . . . the Buckridges, the Hainings . . . all neighbors of mine."

A weight seemed to have lifted off of Channing Sabre's sturdy body. Jeppson was speaking of an enclave of the Carolina elite, a stretch of river where an exceptional number of rich plantations existed in a comparatively limited area. Sabre might not know all the families, but he would know the names.

"Do you know the Skeets, by any chance, Mr. Jeppson?"

"Redbird plantation is right next to mine." Jeppson shook his head sadly. "Shame about the old man, though. He's been going downhill ever since his missus died. Built hisself a brick jail and took to breaking niggers to get extra hands. Reckon young Vachel will have to take over 'fore long. Real shame."

"It certainly is. And such a fine family in the old days. General Washington personally decorated the grandfather, you know."

"I know. I know."

Channing Sabre looked bemused. "I'm really surprised that we haven't met before, Mr. Jeppson, with all the mutual acquaintances we have."

Jeppson laughed. "Oh, I ain't much for socializing, Mr. Sabre. I stay on my own place as much as I can, spend all my time building it up for the nice lady that I hope will soon share it with me—don't even own a house here in the city. Figure I'll let my bride pick it out when the time comes."

"Oh, then you do plan to marry?"

"Well, you know how it is. I been too busy hardly to think about it till lately, but a man wants to pass the fruits of his labor along."

Jeppson reached for the doorknob. "Well, I do see your problem with your Gilly, Mr. Sabre, and I know you have a lot to do. So I'll leave you, but if you're ever out my way—"

"Ah—don't go yet, Mr. Jeppson. Please sit down. I'm sorry we got off on the wrong foot. . . ."

At noon on Saturday, less than twenty-four hours after he had talked to Lew, Adaba learned where Gilly had been taken. Peter Poyas, a ship-carpenter friend of Denmark Vesey, brought a ten-year-old boy to Denmark's shop.

"My Aunt Ora, she say her master sell a Gilly gal this morning."

"She was sold? Who bought her?"

"Don't know. Aunt Ora say this here man going take her today."

There was hope. "Then she ain't gone yet?"

"This here man, he there to get her right now."

"Where? Where was she sold? Who sold her?"

"Mr. Gore, he—"

Adaba didn't wait to hear more. He knew who Ulysses P. Gore was and where his offices were located, at the east end of Queen Street, and there was no time to waste. Adaba ran as he had not run for a week, since the day he and Gilly had eluded their pursuers.

There was no carriage standing in front of Gore's place —no carriage, no white man, no Gilly.

He paused for a moment to regain his breath, then stepped through the open doorway. Half a dozen white men were inside, standing and sitting, discussing the afternoon's races. Adaba saw Gore sitting at a desk: a sallow man, almost as tall as himself but thinner, and gray haired. Gore looked at him and asked, "What you want here, boy? Who told you to come in here?"

"Please, master—" Adaba thought fast. Arrogance wouldn't serve him here. "Please, master, my master send me. He want to know 'bout a wench he hear you sell."

"I sell a lot of wenches. But not now. I'm about to close up for the day." Gore turned back to his friends.

"He want to know 'bout a wench named Gilly," Adaba said quickly.

"Well, tell him he's too late. She's sold." Gore looked at Adaba again and frowned. "How did he know her name?"

"He know from Mr. Sabre he going sell her. Please—"

"Who is your master, boy?"

Adaba decided he should tell the truth. "Master is Mr. Guerard, sir."

Gore stared at him as if puzzling something out. When he had the answer, he winked at the other men, then grinned at Adaba. "Bet you're that rich nigger's boy, ain't you? Marcus Guerard's black bastard, ain't that right?"

Adaba stood perfectly still. He had to work to keep his hands at his sides, strain to keep them from turning into fists.

"Well, boy?"

"I am his son, sir," Adaba said clearly, dropping his darky pose.

"His black bastard," Gore repeated, still grinning. He held out his hand. "Show me your ticket, bastard."

Too late Adaba remembered that he hadn't bothered to write himself a pass. He made a show of touching his pockets. "My father forgot to give me one, Mr. Gore, sir. He sent me out in such a hurry—"

"Yes, I'll bet he did." Gore got to his feet and came to-

94

ward Adaba. "I was told about you, boy. Got a real hard-on for that girl. Well, your Gilly was sold, so you can just forget about her, and don't think you're going to get me to tell you who bought her. By the time you get out of the workhouse for being without a ticket, she's going to have forgotten you anyway. In fact," he looked at the others and winked again, "after the screwing I been giving her the last couple of nights, she's probably already—"

Gore went down on the floor, gagging horribly, almost before Adaba realized he had hit him. Then the others were on Adaba, pounding him, kicking him, beating him to his knees. Distantly he heard Gore's tortured voice: ". . . tried to kill me . . . five hundred lashes . . . workhouse . . . by God, he's never going to get out!"

Darkness closed in on him. *Gilly.* He had lost her. *Gilly, Gilly, Gilly . . .*

Five

Channing Sabre felt good. The business of selling Gilly was over, and he no longer had to deal with the nagging suspicion that he might be doing the wrong thing. He regretted the pain to which Gilly had been subjected, but within a few days she would be settled in her new home and would have the distraction of new friends. Life went on, and he could put the entire matter out of his mind once and for all.

Though the afternoon was slightly overcast, his mood made it seem bright to Channing. The Washington Race Course was crowded; bands played, the horses were paraded, bets were laid on the next race. Channing spotted his cousin Aaron Sabre of Sabrehill. Aaron, his hair rapidly going white though he was not yet forty, was a tall lean handsome figure, who stood out in any crowd. Excusing himself, and leaving Louella with Georgiana and her husband, Channing went over to speak to his cousin.

Aaron was not much of a socializer, and Channing saw little of him, even during racing season.

After the usual amenities, Channing said, "I met a friend of yours this morning. Sold one of my people to him, as a matter of fact."

"Oh?" Aaron's brow lifted slightly, questioningly.

Channing smiled. "Orphan girl, no family at all. Excellent housemaid, and in a way I hated to let her go, but I've got too many mouths to feed. Of course, I wouldn't sell just any of my people, Aaron."

"I'm sure you wouldn't."

"For that matter, I wouldn't sell *to* just anybody, and I had the very devil of a time finding someone suitable. I even turned down one twenty-five-hundred-dollar offer for the girl."

Aaron looked impressed. "Twenty-five hundred—who in the world would pay that much for a housemaid?"

"Not just a housemaid, I'm afraid. The girl happens to be a beauty, and the gentleman, if he can be called that, had other plans for her. So of course I had to turn him down."

Aaron understood at once. "Of course. But who is this friend of mine that you did sell the girl to?"

"A man named Jeppson. Balbo Jeppson. I understand that his plantation is just upriver a little way from yours."

For a moment, Aaron didn't react. He merely stared at Channing. Then the expression on his face became one of incredulity. "Balbo Jeppson?" he said, as if offended by the very sound of the name. "Balbo Jeppson, a friend of *mine?*"

Suddenly the bright day turned gray. Channing remembered Gilly's heartbreak at being sold. He remembered the "inspection" of the girl, he remembered Gore's enthusiasm for her "fanciness," he remembered all the exceptionally high bids. And what did he really know about Balbo Jeppson? All of his rationalizations faded to nothing, and Channing faced the truth.

He had made a terrible mistake.

By God, he had her. Balbo Jeppson hadn't experienced such elation in years. The wench was his, the prettiest little wench he had ever seen in his life, and why should he give a damn about the disappointments of the past week, about Charleston, about anything else? All that was wiped out, because he had showed 'em, he had, he had showed 'em all. Maybe he hadn't found that nigger boy yet, but he'd sure as hell taken the boy's wench away from him. Weep, you black bastard, weep.

Now all he wanted to do was to get back to his plantation with the wench, and he laughed when he thought of what his people would do when they saw her. Esme, the cook, might welcome the help, but Esme's daughter, Fenella, the slut who cleaned his house, would sense a rival and be madder than hell. The bucks, when they got a look at her, would all be after her. She wouldn't have any trouble finding a stud to pleasure her and make her forget all about the boy she'd lost. The thought brought a stirring to Jeppson's loins that he hadn't felt in over a week.

By the time he had driven past the Charleston Neck, it seemed to Jeppson that the wench was calm enough to understand what he was saying. The tears had ceased to run down her cheeks, and she sat perfectly still beside him, clutching at her bundle and staring straight ahead. Gore had hobbled her ankles with a length of rope, but Jeppson doubted that it was necessary. She seemed too weak to try to run away.

"Feeling a mite better now?" he asked, making his husky voice as gentle as possible. The girl looked as if she didn't know the meaning of his words.

"Why don't you eat some of them sweets I bought you? Maybe put a ribbon in your hair? Make you feel better."

Not much business was conducted in Charleston during Race Week, but Jeppson managed to get hold of some sweets and ribbons before picking her up from Gore's offices. When she first saw him again, she looked as if she would die of fright. Once again she wailed her despair and crumpled to the floor. Ordinarily Jeppson liked to have such a strong effect on a slave: it gave him a sense of power. But he saw that it was going to be impossible to talk to her until she calmed down, and he felt oddly sorry for her.

97

Now, as she refused the sweets, he felt sorry for her again.

"Listen to me, Gilly—Gillian, is it? Is that your name?"

She nodded.

"You listen to me, Gilly. I ain't gonna hurt you long as you are a good little gal. I know I talked awful mean to you yesterday, all that about buying you and flaying your hide and nailing you up. But that was just 'cause I was mad, and I wanted to scare you into telling me something. I don't have to do anything like that to get you to tell me something, do I?"

She shook her head again.

" 'Course not. Now, you remember what happened a week ago? You bumped into me and near knocked me down. 'Cause you was careless. You can't go pushing white people around like that, Gilly, even accidental. But I don't think you meant to be bad. It was that black boy that was bad, cussing me like that and hitting me and pushing me around. Now, don't you think you ought to tell me who that boy was, Gilly?"

"Don't know, master," Gilly said softly.

"Oh, now, Gilly," Jeppson laughed, "you teasing Mr. Jeppson."

"No, master. That boy, he just follow me 'long the street. I never see him—"

"Gilly, you 'fraid for that boy? Why, we're leaving Charleston—how'm I gonna hurt him? What he got to fear from me?"

"Don't know that boy, master."

"Well, we'll see. . . ."

For the first time, it occurred to Jeppson that perhaps the wench really didn't know who the boy was and that he had spent all that money for nothing. But even that thought failed to dampen his spirits.

The trip to Jeppson's plantation took a full two days, and they had started late; but fortunately the weather held and the roads were good, and they made good time. Even so, it was long after dark the first night before they arrived at the old inn called The Roost. In a few nights the inn would be crowded with people leaving Charleston, but

98

now Jeppson had no trouble getting a room. Though Jeppson asked that Gilly be given a pallet on the floor, the lard-faced proprietor leered at the girl and referred to her as a "bed wench," bringing himself closer to a beating than he could have guessed. Jeppson arranged to borrow a fresh horse in the morning and to be awakened at dawn, and after a cold meal, he took Gilly up to his room.

As they slid into their beds in the darkness, Jeppson became acutely aware of Gilly's physical presence. He remembered her standing naked on the dais in the lamplit, mirrored room, her arms held out, the white sheet behind her dark body. He remembered the silver bangles hanging from her arms and legs and the glittering necklace swaying between her bare breasts as she tried to evade the hands that slid over her belly and thighs.

He remembered—and he couldn't help what happened then. He had not had his customary whores in Charleston. He had been months without a woman.

Desire brought guilt. He had rarely felt any attraction to a black woman, and never like now. In fact, he had only contempt for those of his friends who were drawn toward black women. But surely there had never before been a black woman like Gilly.

"Little gal," he said softly, "Gilly gal, you asleep yet?"

"No, master," came her whisper through the darkness.

"Gilly, honey, I just want to tell you something. Your Mr. Jeppson, he is a mean, mean master—that's what I tell all my niggers. Ain't no master keeps his niggers in line the way I do. But keeping them in line, that means I ain't gonna let nobody hurt you, you understand that? Ain't nobody gonna hurt our Gilly."

"I understand, master."

"Ain't nobody gonna look at you all naked like they did at that slave-trader place, ain't nobody gonna touch you like that. Ain't nobody gonna do nothing to you that you don't want. You understand?"

"Yes, master."

Jeppson thought of Gore's slack mouth, his lubricious grin. He was almost afraid to ask: "That Mr. Gore . . . he do anything to you . . . force hisself on you?"

99

". . . Yes, master."

Anger helped purge desire. "I should kill him for that. Him holding you in trust—and doing a thing like that!"

Gilly made a sound. Jeppson couldn't tell if she were weeping or not.

"Well, don't you worry, Gilly, honey, you gonna forget. Niggers is lucky that way, they forget easy. You gonna forget all about that goddamn Mr. Gore and that boy of yours and everything else, and I'm gonna see to it that you are happy again. No reason why a good gal like you shouldn't be happy as anybody else. Now, ain't that right? Ain't it, Gilly?"

"Yes, master."

Jeppson had an inspiration. "And you know the first thing I'm gonna do to make you happy? Gilly?"

"No, sir, master."

"Gonna change your name. How you like that?"

Gilly was silent.

"You know what I'm gonna call you? Sheba! 'Cause, Gilly, you just as pretty as the queen of Sheba! Now, ain't that a grand name? Sheba?"

". . . Yes, master."

"Sheba . . ."

Feeling much better, Jeppson drifted off to sleep.

Gilly fought to control her sobs by clamping her teeth fiercely on a corner of the blanket. She felt herself constantly on the verge of slipping into madness. How could such terrible things be happening to her? to Gilly, who had always been so safe in the love of her parents, of her "aunts" and "uncles," of Adaba? safe in the affections of the Sabres? Since the day Mr. Sabre told her to collect her belongings and she realized that she was to be sold, she had been living in a nightmare, subjected to one degradation after another.

And now this. She knew that Mr. Jeppson meant well, that he was only trying to be kind, but she hated the name Sheba. How could she possibly be Sheba? She was Gilly, Adaba's Gilly, and she would always be Gilly, no matter what Mr. Jeppson might call her. And someday Adaba would find her, he would come and carry her away.

Adaba. Her Brown Dove.

But meanwhile, Mr. Jeppson was her protector. She soon realized that. In a world that had suddenly turned hostile, a world in which she could be drugged, stripped naked, handled, raped, and sold like an animal, he would do his best to see that no such thing ever happened to her again. Mr. Channing Sabre had betrayed her by selling her; Mr. Balbo Jeppson had, in a sense, saved her by buying her.

At dawn he lifted her from her pallet while trying to awaken her as little as possible. He seemed to realize that this was the first undrugged sleep she had had since being handed over to Mr. Gore. She had slept in her dress, and she sat in a daze while he put her shoes on her, then all but carried her down the stairs. She heard the proprietor objecting feebly as Mr. Jeppson sat her down at a table in the public room and coaxed her to eat her grits and bacon and clucked over her like a mother hen. Then he put her into the carriage, bundling her with shawls against the winter chill, and they were off on the road again, as she curled up against the side of his big warm body.

She slept or dozed a great deal of the day. In the early afternoon, Mr. Jeppson pulled off the road into some woods, and there they rested the horse and ate bread and smoked meat and drank from a clear-running stream. Gilly ate some of the sweets Mr. Jeppson had given her and offered some back to him. That pleased him so much that she had to smile, which pleased him all the more.

"I know it ain't easy being sold, Sheba," he said, as they sat together on a fallen tree by the stream, " 'specially a young gal like you, but you ain't gonna find my place so bad. I keep my people firm in their place and working hard. I use the biggest and meanest of them to work the rest. But I keep them fed and clothed proper, and they have good Saturday nights. Niggers got to have their fun if they're gonna work good, and oh, they do have fine Saturday nights, Sheba! Them banjos a-ringing, with the cornstalk fiddles and the shoestring bows, and the old jug being passed around!"

When she had first encountered Mr. Jeppson at the City Market, she had seen only a savage-eyed vengeful

101

monster who threatened to destroy her. Now, for the first time since that fearful moment, she really looked at him, and she saw something quite different. She saw a big, rather craggily handsome man with gentle green eyes. Even his low harsh voice, which had once been so terrifying, was now reassuring.

"Mr. Sabre told me you know how to read and figure."

"Yes, sir."

"I don't hold with educating niggers. Gives them ideas they shouldn't have. But with you the damage is done already, and I reckon the figuring will be handy. Do you like to read, Sheba?"

"Yes, sir."

"I know some people find books a great consolation. Could you read aloud to me?"

"Yes, sir."

"I'd like that. I read slow. I got Shakespeare and a Bible and not much else, but I reckon I could get you some more. Would you like that, Sheba?"

"Oh, yes, sir, Mr. Jeppson, I surely would like that."

"So, you *can* say something more than 'yes, sir.'" Laughing, Mr. Jeppson put an arm around her shoulders and gently patted her. "Oh, Sheba, I don't think you're gonna find it so bad on my plantation. I think we're gonna have us some good times together. And I ain't gonna let nothing bad happen to you ever again."

Her reception at the Jeppson plantation, however, was less than enthusiastic. Though they arrived well after dark, and Mr. Jeppson complained that it was "time for all good niggers to be in bed," there was still a light in the kitchen, and Esme, the cook, and Fenella, her daughter, were still up.

One look at Gilly, and Fenella made it clear that she was afraid of being displaced as housekeeper, and her mother obviously shared that fear. Their respective husbands, Abel and Nicodemus, soon appeared, bringing Fenella's younger brother, Remus, with them. Nicodemus looked at Gilly speculatively, Abel looked at her appreciatively, and Remus, a boy of about Adaba's age, looked at her downright hungrily. But Remus was not happy when Mr. Jeppson told him he was to move from the sleeping loft to the floor of his parent's cabin, leaving the loft to Gilly. Their complaints increased until Mr. Jeppson told them to shut up and get some hot food on the table or he'd take a whip to the lot of them. They did as they were told, but none of them seemed very worried by the threat, and Gilly began to suspect that Mr. Jeppson's bark was far worse than his bite. After all, in spite of the fear he had at first inspired in her, for the past two days he had treated her with nothing but kindness.

Esme soon had food on two plates: ham, gravy, and cold cornbread. Fenella screeched a jealous protest as Mr. Jeppson had Gilly sit down at the table with him, saying it wasn't proper. Mr. Jeppson told her to hold her tongue, there weren't any other white folks present, and Sheba was a mighty tired child. While they were eating, he sent Remus to see if Mr. Birnie were still awake, and if so, to fetch him.

Mr. Birnie, the overseer, soon arrived. He was a grizzled but thick-armed old white man whose eyes never stopped being mean, not even when he gaped at Gilly. There had been a time when Gilly had liked being looked at by men, had been amused and flattered by it, but that seemed like a different life. Now she never wanted to be looked at like that again.

When Mr. Birnie could tear his eyes away from Gilly, he sat down at the table and reported to Mr. Jeppson. "Got everything plowed and manured, but for the new land. Still got to grub some stumps there. Corn and cotton fields just about bedded up. Everything done just about how you figured."

"You didn't have no trouble at all?"

"Yeah, I had trouble." Mr. Birnie's mean eyes got smaller. "Obadiah again. But he's back."

Suddenly it seemed to Gilly that the room was very quiet. The only sound she heard for a long moment was the crackling in the fireplace.

Mr. Jeppson slowly put down his fork and looked up from his plate. He smiled and when he spoke his voice was gentle, but there was green fire in his eyes. "Why, that poor boy. He come in by hisself this time, or did he get caught?"

103

"Caught him this morning. He wasn't gone but a day and a night, but he surely did waste my time, running around with them hounds."

"How many times does that make he ran away, five or six?"

"At least that."

Mr. Jeppson shook his head. "That poor, poor boy. Well, I reckon that settles it, Mr. Birnie." He stood up from the table, and Mr. Birnie stood up with him. "We just gonna have to cure that poor boy of running away."

"Tonight, Mr. Jeppson?"

"Mr. Birnie, a nigger is like a dog. You want to teach him something, you got to punish him as close as you can to his wrongdoing. Let's do it now and get it over with."

Mr. Jeppson looked around the room. Since the mention of Obadiah's name, no one had moved. They all acted now as if they didn't want to be noticed.

"Nicodemus and Abel, you gonna help." Nicodemus looked up at Mr. Jeppson as if to protest, then thought better of it and lowered his head. "Remus, we gonna need another real strong man to handle that Obadiah. You run get Sabin. Tell him not to waste no time. All right, let's go."

The five men filed out of the room. Esme and Fenella didn't move.

"What is it?" Gilly asked. "What they going do?"

Neither woman answered.

Several minutes went by. Esme got up and quietly started cleaning up the kitchen. She didn't even tell Gilly to clean her own plate, as Gilly had expected.

The scream, somewhere outside of the house, came so suddenly that Gilly nearly cried out. There was no crack of a whip, no other sound but the scream.

More than a minute passed before the second scream. Esme hid her face in her hands. Fenella wrapped her arms around herself and squeezed as if she were in pain. Seconds later, Gilly heard someone wretching outside the kitchen, and Remus came stumbling and weeping through the door.

A third scream tore through the night. By now, Gilly

thought, everyone on the plantation must be awake. Surely everyone was hearing those screams.

A fourth scream. Gilly covered her ears.

A fifth scream.

Gilly waited. She didn't think she could bear to hear any more.

Boots thumped on the piazza. A door opened and closed. Mr. Jeppson walked into the room. He held out his open right hand. At first Gilly didn't understand what the bloody objects were that were staining his leathery palm.

"If that don't cure him," Mr. Jeppson said, "he's still got five more."

And he flung the toenails into the fireplace.

To find Gilly: that was his one purpose in life. He could not accept the idea that she was lost to him forever. But he knew that with every hour he spent in the workhouse Gilly was getting farther and farther away from him.

"John Guerard! John Guerard, get your ass out here!"

On Monday morning, Adaba stepped through an open doorway and looked at a skull-faced Warden Pickett. Another warden stood behind Pickett, grinning.

"Reckon you figure you can get away with just about anything, don't you, boy?" Pickett said, his voice filled with spite. "Ain't nobody don't know his place like a nigger with money."

Adaba didn't know what he was talking about.

"You got nothing to say, nigger boy?"

"No."

"No, *sir,* God damn you!" The heel of Pickett's hand caught Adaba under the chin and slammed him back against the wall. "No, sir, *master*—you hear me?"

Pickett was shorter, thinner, and lighter than Adaba. Adaba could have broken him like a twig. But he dared do nothing that would prolong his stay in the workhouse and make it harder to find Gilly. He merely said, "Yassuh, massa."

Pickett flushed, and the heel of his hand slammed Adaba's head back against the wall again. "I know you talk better than that. You getting smart with me?"

"Nossuh, massa, nossuh."

"What's the matter, no fight left in you?"

"Nossuh, massa. No fight in John."

"You here for hitting a white man. Was me had the say, you'd stay in the workhouse the rest of your life. I was really looking forward to whipping you, boy, but I reckon I'll get my chance yet."

Adaba understood then. He was being released. Gore had dropped the charges against him, and Pickett was trying to provoke him into a fight so that he could be further detained and whipped.

He smiled. "Ah gwine home, massa?"

"Next time you here, nigger, I kill you."

His father, grim faced, was waiting for him in a carriage. Adaba got in and took the reins from his hands.

"You seem determined," his father said, without a greeting, "to ruin any last chance there may be for me to get you free."

"I'm sorry, father. Did it cost you much to get me out?"

"Not as much as it might have. Fortunately, I am not without connections—Mr. Sabre was of considerable help —and Mr. Gore is a greedy man. A hundred dollars meant far more to him than seeing you whipped."

"I'll try to find a way to pay you back."

"Don't bother. You can pay me back by staying out of trouble from now on. And you might make up your differences with young Lewis Sabre too."

"To help maintain your friendship with Lew's father?"

"There are worse reasons."

Adaba was silent. He didn't think he could ever be a friend to Lew again.

His father seemed to have some idea of what he was thinking. "John," he said gently, "I know you blame Lewis, but the fact is that Mr. Sabre intended to sell the girl anyway."

"But it was because of what happened that night—because of Lewis—that he decided to sell her right away. Otherwise, Gilly and I would have had a chance."

His father shook his head hopelessly. "John, you must see that it would have been wrong, utterly wrong, for you to marry that girl."

106

What had right or wrong to do with it? He only knew that he loved her, and he couldn't bear to have her vanish from his life forever.

It was afternoon before he could discreetly slip out of the house and go looking for Denmark Vesey. He found his friend at work on a job in James Poyas's shipyard on South Bay Street.

"I've had people asking about your Gilly," Denmark said, "because I knew you'd want me to. But so far they haven't learned a thing."

"That woman Ora—"

"She doesn't know who Gilly was sold to—or she's afraid to say. None of Mr. Gore's people seems to know."

"She could be right here in the city!"

"Or she could be fifty miles away by now—on her way out of the state. I hate to discourage you, boy, but usually with these things, you find out fast or you don't find out at all. And I think you'd better accept that."

"What are you telling me?" Adaba asked desperately. "Are you saying I should just forget her?"

"No," Denmark said, "don't forget her. Remember her, and be angry. Stay angry the rest of your life. And one day there will be enough of us angry to change the world."

Adaba shook his head. "I'll stay angry all right. But I won't accept that I'll never see Gilly again. If I have to, I'll tear the world apart—but one way or another, I intend to find her!"

Six

Adaba, find me . . . Adaba, come take me away. . . . From morning to night, it was her constant prayer.

Gilly realized almost at once that she was in danger, and the source of that danger was not Mr. Jeppson but Fenella. Fenella, feeling threatened by Gilly's presence, had set her family against Gilly. She did her best to set everyone from Mr. Jeppson to the field hands against

Gilly. And it was to Fenella that Gilly was assigned as an assistant.

She didn't mind the work; to a degree, it helped relieve her misery. Many years before, her mother had told her, "When you feel your miseries worst, child, go scrub a floor," and that was what she did now. Fenella, for all her complaints that she had too much to do, did little beyond making up Mr. Jeppson's bed and dusting a few surfaces. Gilly found that dust lay thick under every piece of furniture, on every shelf, in every cabinet. Unused silver was tarnished, and beautiful china was thick with dirt. The rugs didn't seem ever to have been beaten, and the windows looked as if they hadn't been washed in years. Gilly set out to give the place the most thorough possible cleaning, while Fenella, when she realized what was happening, looked on with consternation.

The afternoon after Gilly had washed the parlor windows, she found them smeared with dirt. She washed them again.

The next morning she found that again they had been smeared. Again she washed them.

That afternoon she caught Fenella smearing the windows.

Her voice barely louder than her pounding heart, she asked, "Fenella, why you do that?"

Fenella, a tall thin woman of about twenty with a raw-boned face, angry eyes, and a mouth that expressed scorn and contempt better than anything else, lashed out: "I don't tell you to wash no windows!"

"I am going wash them windows again. And if I find them dirtied up, I'm going tell Mr. Jeppson."

"I tell him *you* dirty them up. Who you think he going believe?"

Gilly considered the question briefly. "I don't know, Fenella. Whyn't we go ask him right now and find out?"

Fenella stared at her for a moment. Then she picked up a handful of dust rags, threw them at Gilly's face, and marched out of the room.

The windows were not smeared again.

At first, Mr. Jeppson didn't notice what was happening to his house. Then one day he happened to come in early from the fields and wandered into the parlor where the bright sun now shined in through clear windows onto well-polished surfaces. "My God, my God," he said, looking about, "I don't hardly believe it! I forgot this used to be a mighty handsome room!"

"I ain't hardly done with it yet," Gilly said, pleased.

"It's beautiful! And that ain't a word I hardly use at all!"

"Well, the room may be beautiful," Fenella said in a hard voice from the doorway, "but she sure been neglecting her work. You always say everybody got to earn their keep in the fields, Mr. Jeppson, house people and all. But she ain't put in one day working outside since she got here."

"Don't you worry 'bout that. She'll do her outside chores when the time comes. Right now she gonna go right on doing like she been doing. You're doing fine, Sheba, just fine."

As soon as Mr. Jeppson had left, Fenella came into the room looking as if she would like to tear Gilly apart.

"You think I don't know what you up to?"

"I'm cleaning this here house."

"You trying to make Mr. Jeppson dissatisfied with me, that what you up to. Think you can get rid of me, and you got the house and Mr. Jeppson all to yourself!"

"No, Fenella—"

"Well, I tell you you ain't. And I make you pay, you don't know how I make you pay. You going wish you was dead, 'fore I done with you. Maybe you *be* dead!"

Adaba, come to me. . . .

Gilly avoided Fenella's family as much as possible. She was never awake more than a minute in the morning before she was out of the sleeping loft and into the house. She built up the fire in the kitchen for Esme and went right to her housework, pausing only to eat a hasty breakfast. She worked independently of Fenella, who really didn't know how to organize tasks or issue orders. Gilly ate her noon dinner alone and immediately went back to work. She gave herself a long, emotion- and mind-deadening day.

Supper was pleasant enough. She usually ate it alone on the piazza, though frequently Mr. Jeppson either joined her or called her into the kitchen with him. That meant she had to suffer Fenella's and Esme's spiteful tongues afterward as she helped clean up. Sometimes she escaped that job by reading to Mr. Jeppson—Shakespeare or the Bible—but that only delayed the women's tongue-lashings and made them worse.

The worst time of the day came at night when Gilly had to retire to the small, crowded cabin she now shared with Fenella's family. It wasn't much of a home—a fireplace, two beds, a pallet on the floor, a table, a couple of often-mended chairs—but it was *their* home, and she felt their antagonism as she entered it. She was the intruder, she was taking up precious space. "Well, look who here," Fenella might say as Gilly stepped through the door, "look at the queen of Sheba. Her that don't need no chamber pot, she so good." Gilly always scrambled up the ladder into the loft as quickly as possible, getting out of the family's way.

On Saturday evenings she was fortunate: she had the cabin to herself, for Fenella and her family always went out to the field quarters to visit their friends. Mr. Jeppson urged Gilly to do the same, to go out and get acquainted, but she was reluctant to do so; she was still frightened by the sudden drastic change in her life. Instead, she spent Saturday evenings reading to Mr. Jeppson until Mr. Tucker and Mr. Macon came by. Then she went to the empty cabin. In blessed silence, without any harsh words from Fenella or hard looks from Esme, she climbed up to the loft and settled into her blankets. She tried to imagine that this was the loft of the storage house back home and that the last few weeks had been only a bad dream. But on the third Saturday night Remus followed her up the ladder.

A whisper: "Sheba, you 'sleep? . . . Sheba, I know you ain't 'sleep."

She must have been sleeping, because she had heard no one entering the cabin and preparing for bed. Now she was instantly awake, and a few sighs and snores drifted up from down below.

"Well, if you 'sleep, Sheba, guess I just come up there with you."

"Don't you come up here!"

Gilly raised her head. By the light of the dying fire, she could make out the long triangle of Remus's bare upper torso. He had wide shoulders, a narrow waist, and hard, well-formed muscles on a lightweight frame. His round, boyish face was in shadow.

"See, you ain't 'sleep at all. Want me keep you company up here, Sheba?"

"No! You go 'way!"

"Now, don't you talk like that, Sheba! Plenty room up here for you and me both. And I'se cold out here 'thout no clothes on!"

"You go way, let me sleep!"

"Why you so unfriendly, Sheba? Me, I just friendly, is all."

"I ain't unfriendly. I just—just—"

Remus laughed softly. "Just too good for us Jeppson niggers, ain't that right?"

"No—"

"That what Fenella tell everybody. Tell everybody tonight, 'That Sheba, she say she too good for Jeppson niggers.' "

"That ain't so!"

"She say that why you don't talk to nobody, don't go out to the quarters Saturday nights. Just 'cause you 'bout the most handsomest wench anywhere 'round here, you figure ain't no nigger 'round here good enough for you."

"I do not."

"That what everybody saying now, Sheba. Say you too proud to spread for anybody but Mr. Jeppson. He spreading you, Sheba?"

"No! He don't hold with that!"

Remus made a disbelieving sound. "White masters say that, and then they spread the wenches any chance they get. Maybe Mr. Jeppson don't touch none here, but I reckon he get plenty in Charleston. Why he bring a wench like you back here he don't want to spread you?"

"He don't! He don't never do that!"

A grumbling sound from down below silenced Remus

111

for a moment, but no one seemed to have awakened. He took another step up the ladder.

"Sheba, let me come up."

"No."

"My daddy got my momma, and Fenella got Abel. You and me, we ain't got nobody. That ain't right."

"You got plenty. Fenella always saying you get all the wenches you want. Saying you get *any* wench you want."

"That surely the truth, 'cause I'se the best at pleasuring that is. But you the only one I want, Sheba. Ever since you come here."

Gilly shook her head.

"You got your eye on somebody else? Sabin? Wildon? Orlando?"

"No." Gilly wasn't even sure who they were.

"Didn't think so. They ain't nearly good as me. But they going be after you, they all want you. Even Abel, Abel want you too."

Gilly was well aware of that fact. "If he tries," she said, "I'll tell Fenella."

Remus laughed again. "He do it to you, *he'll* tell Fenella. Fenella say she *want* him to. Want to *see* him do it to you. Show you you ain't too good for him and me."

How Fenella must hate me, Gilly thought how she must hate me.

Remus took another step up the ladder. "Sheba, I come up. I show you I'se better'n all them others."

"You go 'way!" Gilly cried out in panic. "You go 'way!"

But Remus was coming yet another step up the ladder, and then another, and as he entered the loft and threw himself toward her, she saw that he was naked and in need, as much in need as Adaba had ever been, but she didn't think of Adaba now but of Mr. Gore. Mr. Gore on the second night, when she had not been drugged and he had turned every pleasure Adaba had ever given her into degradation and pain. Mr. Gore had taken care not to damage her, not to bruise her or draw blood where it would show, but hurting her, threatening her, terrifying her, until she allowed him into her body, allowed him to use her in any way he pleased.

112

Remus's hand was over her mouth before she could scream. "You ain't going do that," he said in a hoarse whisper, "you ain't going do that!" His other hand went to her throat and tightened.

For perhaps half a minute he held her like that, and she thought he was going to kill her. Then the one hand left her mouth and the other eased up on her throat. "Ain't going hurt you none," Remus whispered. "Just you don't make no noise."

He was straddling her, and she could smell the whiskey on his breath. He pulled the blankets down off of her, and she felt her shift being tugged up. He was much stronger than she, and she could think of only one thing to do.

She relaxed. She lifted her hips so that he could more easily pull her shift the rest of the way up over her breasts. His hand moved over her breasts and down her body. She fumbled in the darkness until she found his genitals and began stroking them. He sighed. "Ah, Sheba. Now you being good gal. Ah, Sheba, you know you like this. Ah, Sheba, Sheba . . ."

As he began lifting himself to get between her legs, his hand slipped from her throat. He lifted one knee from the floor, spreading his legs further.

She tightened her grip on his organ and with all her strength brought her thigh pounding up solidly against the tight sack. Remus screamed and tried to pull away, but Gilly held him. She brought her thigh up again, and at the same time her free hand went raking across his face. Remus fell howling away from her across the loft.

His howls brought the whole cabin to an uproar. Candles were lit, and the wailing Remus was helped down from the loft. Gilly, of course, was blamed—at least by Remus, Fenella, and Esme. If Abel had his doubts, he kept them to himself. Only Nicodemus cursed Remus for being a fool who was just asking for trouble with Mr. Jeppson.

Lying in the darkness alone again, Gilly suddenly found to her horror that her life at Jessamine and in Charleston no longer seemed real. It had grown strangely dreamlike, and the bad dream of the Jeppson plantation had become the reality. There was virtually nothing in this new life to connect it with the old—only a few scraps of clothing and some trinkets. At this moment, in this darkness, she could almost believe that this had always been her life and always would be. Adaba was still as real to her as Mr. Jeppson and Remus, but she had the terrible feeling that he too was on the verge of slipping away from her. *Come, Adaba, 'fore it too late. . . .*

Inevitably, Mr. Jeppson found out about the incident. Not only was Remus's face badly scratched, but it was difficult to move, let alone work, and Mr. Jeppson wanted to know why. Ask Sheba, squealed Fenella, that Sheba ought to be called Jezebel! A kind of trial was immediately held in the big house kitchen, and the evidence was overwhelmingly against Gilly.

"She out to cause trouble ever since she get here," Esme said. "Trouble for Remus, for Fenella, for all us."

"I hear her whispering to him, 'Come up, come up!' " Fenella said. " 'You come up here and keep me warm, Remus, I give you a fine time!' "

"Why, I don't know," Abel said in a tone of scrupulous honesty, "but I don't think Remus ever go up there, she don't tease him on." He gave Gilly a sympathetic look. "And, poor little gal, guess she just can't help teasing."

Only Nicodemus didn't "know nothing" about the previous night, but "I know that gal be trouble the minute my eyes light on her."

"I hear her," Fenella insisted. " 'Come up, come up! You come up here with me!' "

Mr. Jeppson didn't believe a word of it.

"You all listen to me and listen good. I brought Sheba here to work 'round the house, and that means with you. I don't know what the hell you got again' her except she works so hard she puts the rest of you to shame. Now, I don't want her touched again, you all hear me? Remus, I oughta whip the hide off you, but I reckon Sheba done punish you plenty already. But you touch her again, and I'm gonna put a knife in her hand and let her denut you herself, you understand me? *You all leave Sheba alone!*"

114

Fenella pursed her lips. "She gonna go out and do her outside chores like the rest of us?"

"Hell, no!" Jeppson roared. "She's too good a housekeeper! And if you wanta go on working in this here house, you better follow her example from now on—and do exactly like Sheba says!"

Fenella looked stricken. "She—*she in charge?*"

"Sheba is in charge of this here house!"

The dismay in Fenella's eyes turned to something else. She turned those eyes on Gilly, and Gilly read the message in them.

Adaba, help me. . . .

Something was going to happen to her. Gilly had no idea of what it might be, but she felt it. Sometimes when she went out into the yard, she would see a black man staring at her, staring hard, and she would remember the threat she had seen in Fenella's eyes.

The next few days went by easily enough. Mr. Jeppson only once questioned her about "that nigger boy," and then only jokingly, as if he no longer believed she knew who he was. Fenella stayed out of her way, did nothing to spoil her work, and actually helped to some extent. She was no longer greeted by venomous remarks when she returned to the cabin in the evenings; there was only a sullen silence, which she found easy to ignore. And the loft seemed more like hers now, more her private place, where she was safe even from Remus. Yet the threat remained in the air.

Fenella put it into words on Friday evening. They were alone together in the kitchen, cleaning up after supper. Both were silent, but Fenella seemed tense and excited as she banged about the pots and pans.

Suddenly she laughed. "Don't think you hear the last of what you done to Remus," she said.

Gilly was shocked by the abrupt statement. It was the first time anyone had even referred to the incident since the previous Sunday morning, when Mr. Jeppson had spoken to them about it.

"Don't you think you hear the last," Fenella went on when Gilly didn't respond. "By now, everybody know what you done to Remus. Not just here, everywhere 'round here. How you hurt him and make trouble for him and me with Mr. Jeppson."

Gilly stared at her. "Fenella, you been lying 'bout me again?"

"I don't lie 'bout you!" Fenella said angrily. "Oh, you think you so grand! But Remus don't need you—he got gals all the way from McClintock plantation to Sabrehill! The only reason he go up in that loft is you ask him! And then you get scared, and you think he ain't good 'nough for you."

Gilly shook her head. "Oh, Fenella, you such a fool."

"Don't you call me fool!" For an instant, Gilly thought Fenella was going to strike her, but anger gave way to cunning. "We see who the fool is 'round here. Everybody 'round here know all 'bout you now, and they say what a shame what you do to Remus. The men—they gonna get you for that! You just watch out, 'cause they gonna get—"

She broke off as they heard a door close and a boot come down outside the room.

What happened next was a complete surprise to Gilly and probably to Fenella too. Gilly could only attribute it to Fenella's volatile temper and lack of common sense.

Fenella's eyes flashed. She grinned. Grabbing a china soup tureen from a table, she raised it high in the air and threw it against the floor with all her strength. Pieces of tureen flew across the floor. Gilly stared.

For an instant, Fenella seemed stunned by her own te-merity. Then in a loud voice she called out, "Why, Sheba, you naughty thing! You done drop Mr. Jeppson's nice soup tureen! Almost like you *throw* it down! Why, Sheba —"

Jeppson stepped through the doorway of the kitchen.

The momentary bravery of anger turned to fear: Fe-nella's eyes glistened with it.

"She don't mean to drop it, Mr. Jeppson," she said. "Sheba don't mean to drop it, it just slip."

Jeppson looked at the pieces of china, most of them near Fenella's feet. He glanced at shock-faced Gilly, and then looked at Fenella again.

He took another step into the room.

116

"That was a good tureen," he said softly. "How you gonna pay for it, Fenella? I got to take it outa your hide?"

"No-o-o!" Fenella made the word a howl of rage. She pointed at Sheba. "Was her done it! Sheba done bust it!"

"Don't you lie to me, goddammit, you busted that bowl—"

"You don't believe me, you believe her just 'cause she a fancy-ass nigger bitch you bring back here! Charleston fancy ass, but I make her not so fancy, I make her not so—"

Gilly didn't see Fenella grab the knife. Fenella snatched it from some table or open drawer and came flying at her. A single leap, and Fenella seemed to be floating slowly through the air toward Gilly, and Gilly couldn't move.

"Goddamn!"

Jeppson caught her. He caught Fenella's wrist with one hand and her throat with the other and brought her up short.

"Now, drop that knife, bitch."

Fenella's hand only tightened on the knife, and she bared her teeth as she struggled in Jeppson's grip. His hand tightened on Fenella's throat. Panic came to her face, and she clawed at his fingers, tearing them away.

"I said, drop that knife!"

"I kill her! I kill her!"

"Oh, no—"

Still holding her knife hand, Jeppson slapped Fenella hard across the face, but the blow seemed to have no effect except perhaps to heighten her rage.

"I cut her up! I cut her face! I cut her, you ain't never going look at her again! Ain't nobody never going look at her! I cut her, cut her, cut her—"

"Why, you black slut!"

Something seemed to go out of control in Jeppson at that moment, and anger became madness. Seizing Fenella by the hair, he dragged her out of the kitchen and into the central passage of the house, while Gilly followed. A lamp burned near a mirror on the wall of the passage. Jeppson shoved Fenella toward the mirror and, standing behind her, made her face it. Grabbing her hair again, he pulled her head up and back. With no difficulty at all, he slipped his hand over Fenella's knife hand and brought the blade to her throat.

"You gonna cut somebody up, Fenella? You know who you gonna cut up?"

Fenella's face was ghastly with fear in the flickering lamplight.

"You gonna cut yourself up, Fenella, that's who! You gonna look in this here mirror and watch while you cut your own throat. You just watch, Fenella!"

Mr. Jeppson started a sawing motion across Fenella's throat.

Fenella screamed.

In the mirror, Gilly saw blood running down Fenella's neck.

Fenella kicked, twisted, lifted her feet from the floor, always screaming, but Jeppson had the strength of great anger—and madness. He easily kept her dangling from her hair and facing the mirror.

He drew on the knife, cutting deeper.

Gilly started screaming then, a prolonged scream of horror. She found herself beating on Jeppson's back and begging him to stop. She clutched at the arm that thrust and drew the knife. She screamed, screamed, screamed. . . .

Something happened to Jeppson's face in the mirror. The anger was still there, but the madness went out of it.

He took the knife from Fenella's hand. He pushed her away from him, and she fell into Gilly's arms. Both sank weeping to the floor.

Jeppson, panting, sweating, looked down at them. "Fenella," he said huskily, "you are goddamn lucky to be alive. You got Sheba to thank, nobody else. But, woman, you ain't gonna get another chance. Remember that. Next time I'm gonna dig a fresh grave."

He left the passage.

"It's all right," Gilly whispered to Fenella as they wept together. "It's all right now, he ain't going hurt you. I promise, Fenella, he ain't going hurt you no more . . . no more. . . ."

By God, Balbo Jeppson thought, he was coming up in
118

the world. It had been a long, hard scramble out of the Carolina sandhills, but he had good land and a growing population of blacks and the prospect of one day being among the richest planters in the state. He had all that, and to hell with the goddamn gentry who looked down on him. He had one thing that none of them had.

He had Sheba.

He had purchased some fine blacks in his day, but no other like her. Nobody else in the region had a female like Sheba—a handsome wench, who could read better than many a white man, who could cook and keep house and even sew, a little black angel who could do just about anything she set her mind to.

And what a beauty she was. When he had first seen her, he had resented that beauty, but now he found it hard to keep out of his mind: the slightly catlike eyes, the occasional shy smile on full lips, the little indentation in her chin. He couldn't spend a whole day in the fields but had to return to the house at least once a day to see if she was all right and if she needed anything—and to look at her. Balbo Jeppson was not a man to sentimentalize his blacks, but he had begun to think Channing Sabre had been a fool to sell her even for two thousand dollars. He would have liked the chance to tell the silly bastard as much.

On Saturday afternoon, in the village of Riverboro, where he went for supplies, he got his chance.

"May I buy you a drink, Mr. Jeppson?"

He had heard that Channing Sabre was visiting Sabrehill, but he hadn't expected to see him. They met by chance in the noisy, bustling Carstairs tavern. Aaron Sabre, of Sabrehill, sat at the same table with them, but looked coolly distant and said nothing.

"I trust you've found the housemaid I sold you satisfactory."

"Quite satisfactory." The tavernkeeper's daughter brought Jeppson his whiskey and disappeared back into the crowd.

"I'm glad to hear it. I must confess, Mr. Jeppson, I've had some pangs of conscience about that sale."

"Oh?" Jeppson thought Channing Sabre didn't look too

good. There was something drawn about his broad hand-some face.

"Two thousand dollars—your bid was really much too high."

"I told you why I made it."

"Yes, but I shouldn't have accepted it."

Jeppson shrugged. "Well, if you want to give me some of my money back . . ."

Channing Sabre looked startled. "That wasn't exactly what I had in mind."

"I didn't think it was."

"You see, Mr. Jeppson, I've had certain regrets since selling Gilly—"

"Sheba," Jeppson said.

". . . What?"

"Sheba. That's what I call her. Her name is Sheba now."

"Oh, I see. . . . Well, Sheba, Gilly . . . whatever you call her . . . I've had certain regrets about selling her. Frankly, I didn't realize how important she was to us —how important a member of our family, our black family . . ." Channing Sabre paused, then plunged ahead. "Mr. Jeppson, I am quite prepared to return your money in exchange for Gi—for Sheba, and I hope you'll consider—"

"No."

"If you'll just consider for a moment—"

"No."

Channing Sabre blinked. There was a certain hopeless-ness in his eyes, and Jeppson almost smiled.

"Mr. Jeppson, I realize that you will have been put to a certain inconvenience. I am willing to compensate you for it, quite generously. Say, a hundred dollars?"

"No," Jeppson said with pleasure, "and not two hun-dred and not five hundred. Mr. Sabre, Sheba is not for sale."

"Please, I'm trying to be reasonable—"

"So am I. I spent two thousand dollars on Sheba, figur-ing I was overpaying. It turned out I got the best goddamn housekeeper I could have hoped for. The smartest, the hardest-working, the handsomest—and she's only a girl with a lot of years to go yet. I need Sheba, Mr. Sabre, and she's worth more to me than you're likely to pay, I don't care how much you want her back. Besides," Jeppson grinned, "we got to look out for the welfare of our people, don't we, Mr. Sabre? Make sure they don't go to just any kind of trash?"

"Well, of course—"

"Of course. Even if I was willing to sell Sheba, I'd want to be sure she went to a good home."

Channing Sabre bridled. "Mr. Jeppson!"

"I'd want her to go where she'd be as good off as she is now. Where she'd be the housekeeper, Mr. Sabre, same as now. You willing to give her that?"

"Of course not. I already have an excellent housekeeper. However—"

"Don't reckon she'd want to go back to you, then, Mr. Sabre."

Channing Sabre looked at him blankly for a moment, as if considering. "Perhaps you're right. But why don't we ask her? I've always felt that whenever possible one's people should have some say as to where they are to live."

"As much say as you gave Sheba before you sold her to me, Mr. Sabre?"

The shot went home. Jeppson had the satisfaction of seeing Channing Sabre's face turn gray. So much for the goddamn gentry with their hypocritical pretensions.

Jeppson tossed down the last of his drink and stood up from the table.

"Perhaps I made a mistake," Channing Sabre's voice was shaking. "I really don't know now why I sold the girl."

"You sold her, Mr. Sabre," Jeppson said, "because you are a horse's ass."

There, he had said it. He turned his back on the fools and strode out of the tavern.

Saturday night. The banjos a-ringing, as Mr. Jeppson had said, with the cornstalk fiddles and the shoestring bows, and the old jug being passed around. Gilly expertly rolled the jug up on her shoulder, tilting it, and took a big swallow. The stars reeled in the heavens as if to help her celebrate, and she found herself staggering and laughing as she handed the jug back to Abel. Abel took a drink in turn and handed the jug on to Fenella.

Gilly knew she was drinking more than she should; never before had she had more than a few sips of whiskey at a time. But she didn't care. She had friends now, her isolation was over, and she felt as if she had emerged from a month in hell. "Now, you just come with me, gal," Fenella has said earlier in the evening. "You can't spend all your time moping 'round that big old house. I know you still sad 'bout being sold, but you got to have yourself some fun! You just let your Fenella take care of you." Fenella and Abel, Gilly thought, giggling and taking another drink, they would take care of her.

Everything was going to be all right. She knew it. One day soon Adaba would come, he would buy her back from Mr. Jeppson and take her home. Or if he couldn't do that, he would steal her away. There had to be a way for them to be together again, and Adaba would know what it was. And meanwhile, she had her new friends, and the long lonely days and nights were over.

"We all friends now, Fenella?"

"Why, 'course we is, Sheba!"

"We friends, Abel?"

"Why, sho', Sheba."

"Going be friends forever."

Not that Fenella didn't still feel some resentment toward Gilly. Gilly perceived that and understood it better than Fenella herself. She understood perfectly well that the habit of hatred was rarely wiped away by a single incident. But Fenella was trying not to hate her any longer, and that was what mattered.

"Oh, I love you all!"

Fenella laughed. "Sheba, you getting drunk!"

"Ain't getting! *Is!*"

It was still possible to listen to the music on Saturday nights, and now it beat and sang and throbbed throughout the quarters. It was still possible to go from cabin to cabin, as Gilly and Fenella and Abel were doing now, to meet people and to visit. Outside one of the cabins, half of the population of the quarters stood in a torchlit circle, watching half a dozen dancers. Gilly stopped to watch and found herself swept into the middle of the circle. It was still possible to dance and sing and pat juba and watch happy couples wander off into the darkness. It seemed to Gilly that all of Mr. Jeppson's people were out tonight to help her celebrate.

Why had she been so afraid before? Why had she felt that she had been transported to a world that held only enemies? Now, dancing and singing, she had no idea, she could no longer remember. She found herself reeling out of the circle and falling, laughing, into waiting arms.

"Bitch having herself fun tonight, ain't she?"

The new voice was low and metallic, and as Gilly looked up, a face came out of the darkness to loom over her like a black quarter-moon. It was a thin, bony face with slanted eyes under heavy brows that formed a V. Gilly had seen the face before but only at a distance.

"Now, you let her be, Sabin," Fenella said quickly, breathlessly. "You let Sheba be."

"Got something to say to her." His eyes glittered.

"What?" Gilly asked, wondering if she had done anything wrong. "What you got to say to me?"

"Sabin!"

Fenella tried to put herself between Gilly and Sabin, but Sabin thrust her out of the way. Abel was instantly between Sabin and the two women, shoving the other man back.

"You don't do that, Sabin. You don't touch Fenella ever."

For a moment the two men seemed poised to fight. Then Sabin shrugged.

"I got no quarrel with you, Abel, so don't you make one with me. But I got something to say to this little nigger, and she ask me what it is."

Abel nodded and stepped aside. "Then say it and git. We busy having us a time."

Sabin looked at Gilly. "All I say is this. Gal, you done wrong to Remus—"

"That ain't your affair!" Fenella snapped.

"We the drivers. Remus tell us, that make it our affair. You tell us, *that* make it our affair." Sabin's voice suddenly rose. He looked at Gilly again. "You done wrong to Remus, and you going put it right. Ain't no gal too good for any Jeppson nigger, and you going learn that."

"You ain't going touch her!" Fenella said, almost frantically. "You touch her, I tell Mr. Jeppson!"

Sabin smiled. His face was not meant for a smile. "Why, Fenella. You the one telling everybody she don't come out here to the quarters 'cause her ass too good for the likes of us. You the one tell she tease Remus on, how she kick his balls that way, how she make trouble for him. Now you say let her be?"

"You let her be, or I tell!"

Sabin's smile widened. He laughed silently. "We see," he said. "We see."

Nobody spoke as he disappeared back into the darkness.

Gilly felt sobered. She knew what Sabin was. He was a man with power who took pleasure in using it. He was a man who had been brutalized and would take any opportunity to brutalize others. That was his revenge on the world—the world that Mr. Jeppson made and ruled and held him captive in.

"What he going do?" she asked.

"Nothing!" Fenella said vehemently. "You ain't got nothing to make up with Remus no more, and he ain't going do nothing!"

No. Of course not.

And the banjos were still a-ringing, with the cornstalk fiddles and the shoestring bows, and the world and the heavens were once more whirling with the music. Nothing was going to spoil the gladness that had returned to Gilly's heart this evening. She took the jug from Abel and tilted it up once again.

Jeppson was uneasy.

After Tucker and Macon and the others who had stopped by the house had left, he continued to stand out in his yard. Looking toward the field quarters, he saw little light and heard no music. The social festivities of Saturday evening seemed to be over. There was nothing left of the night now but some pleasuring, perhaps, and then sleep.

But where was Sheba?

He had been glad to see her going out to the quarters to enjoy herself with the others. It meant that she was coming to accept her lot as one of his people. But he had expected her to stop by the big house before retiring to the cabin. Come tell me about it, he had said. Come tell me how you like it. She had not yet returned.

Maybe, he thought, she had forgotten about his request and had simply gone back to the cabin and climbed into her loft to sleep. Somehow the thought hurt him. This was the first evening in four weeks that they hadn't spent together.

He walked through the darkness to the cabin. There was no light from within, but the moment he rattled the door it opened, and he found himself facing Nicodemus.

"Where's Sheba?"

"Ain't here, Mr. Jeppson."

"Still out at the quarters?"

"Don't know, Mr. Jeppson. I reckon." Nicodemus kept his voice low.

"Everybody else here?"

Nicodemus shook his head. "Just Esme and me is all."

"Sheba was with Fenella and Abel, wasn't she?"

"Don't know. You worried 'bout her, Mr. Jeppson?"

"Should I worry?"

"No, sir. That a mighty pretty gal. She ain't going take long finding her a buck in the quarters. They all looking at her, Mr. Jeppson—all the single men and some that ain't so single. You ain't got no worry 'bout her, master."

Jeppson felt his face grow warm and stiff. Was there something mocking in Nicodemus's voice?

"I ain't worried."

"Why, she pro'bly having herself a time right now. That what settle her down here, Mr. Jeppson—when she find a buck she like to give her what she need—"

"I said, I ain't worried!"

Then why did it bother him to think of a buck giving Sheba service? That was the natural thing to happen, wasn't it? Why shouldn't she find herself a man, even on her first visit to the quarters? The sooner she found one and settled down with him, the better.

125

Jeppson walked slowly back toward the big house.

Ten minutes, he decided. If she wasn't back in ten minutes, he would go looking for her.

Or maybe not. He was damned if he was going to be one of those men who made a fool of himself over a black wench.

She was an innocent in a strange place. She thought she had found friendship and safety. Should she have suspected what they were up to? Was there any way in the world she could have guarded against what happened?

She was drunk. She had never been drunk in her life. Much of the evening had vanished from her memory, but she remembered being violently sick, yet continuing to drink afterward. She remembered the world spinning in great swooping arcs that threw her laughing back and forth between Fenella and Abel. She remembered strangling on the whiskey and spraying it all over herself and bursting out laughing again, laughing so hard that she had fallen to her knees and Fenella and Abel had had to help her up again.

But how had she got here?

The doorway was open, and behind it was light and laughter. "Single man barrack," Abel said. "We go in."

"Wanna go home." The world was tilting and spinning again, and Gilly thought she might fall asleep where she stood. "Wanna go home now."

"Not yet." Abel guided her through the doorway. "This here party for you, Sheba."

She realized vaguely that they were being greeted as they entered the barrack. There was not much light in the room, but what there was seemed strangely blinding to her drunken eyes. Looking about, she saw that there were two or three other women besides Fenella and herself, but mostly there were men—perhaps twice as many men as women crowded the room. Near the fireplace stood Remus and Sabin. Sabin grinned at her, and she turned quickly away.

"I so tired, Abel," she said. "Can't I go back to my loft now?"

"Oh, no, Sheba, you just rest awhile."

Gilly nodded. "Wanna rest."

"Why, 'course you rest. Hey, you people, Sheba going rest a little while."

A number of beds stood side by side along a barrack wall, and she felt herself being led to one of them. She sat down on the edge.

"Now, you just lay you'self back, Sheba," Fenella said, "and shut your eyes. Pretty soon you feel lot better."

"Eyes hurt."

"Just you shut them eyes and rest."

"Better take off that dress, Sheba," one of the women said. "You got whiskey all over it."

The suggestion shocked Gilly. She looked up through dim eyes to see a young woman she had met earlier in the evening, a bold-eyed, flirtatious wench not much older than herself. Gilly thought her name was Carilla.

The woman reached down to assist her with her dress. "Come on, honey-chile—"

"No!" Gilly pushed her away.

"But you can't sleep on a clean bed in that dirty old dress. Now, be good—"

"No!"

Carilla, if that was her name, sighed and straightened up. Everybody in the room seemed to be watching the two of them.

"Well, Sheba, I tell you what. . . ."

Before Gilly's eyes, Carilla began lifting her own skirt. There was an explosion of laughter, which quickly died. The skirt ascended higher, showing that Carilla wore drawers. She kicked off her shoes, then dropped both drawers and skirt at the same time. There was a groan of disappointment, but Carilla stepped out of the drawers and began slowly lifting her skirt again. Then suddenly, as it reached her hips, she pulled the dress over her head and stood utterly naked before Sheba. There was another, greater explosion of laughter, and half a dozen hands reached for Carilla, but she brushed them away. Smiling, she bent down toward Sheba.

"Come on, honey-chile. It true what they say? You better'n the rest of us?"

A jug was lifted to Sheba's lips.

She wasn't sure what happened after that.

At first she thought it was Adaba who was with her, or at least a dream of Adaba. She welcomed his touch, his arms, his long hard body.

"Oh, Sheba like it!"

"Oh-ho, she like it good!"

"Is my turn next!"

"Plenty to go 'round for everybody."

Then Adaba was gone from her, but not for long. She whimpered a plea to him and reached for him, and he entered her again.

"Oh, Adaba, Adaba . . ."

She managed to open her eyes.

It took her a moment to understand.

The first thing she saw was not Adaba, not the man who was taking her, but Abel and Carilla, standing nearby, naked in each other's arms, locked in a writhing embrace.

Her lover, the great dark weight over her and in her, hastened his pounding rhythm.

Then she saw the others—men and women, naked and half-naked, some embracing in the dim light, some watching her and awaiting their turn, some already exhausted. In a dark corner of the room a woman moaned her pleasure—it might have been Fenella. Remus sat on the next bed looking sated and half-asleep. Sabin was standing nearby. His eyes met hers, and he laughed.

Her taker, the great dark weight over her, uttered a choked cry, hesitated, and began to thrust furiously.

She began to scream.

Her assailant was taken by surprise. Pounding and clawing at his face and shoulders, kicking and twisting, she freed herself of him while he was still in his moment of release. Somehow she managed to slide from under him and off the bed, while he, still throbbing, howled and tried to get her back. Springing to her feet, she ran blindly. She heard cries to get her, to stop her, to shut her up. Hands grabbed her, grabbed arms, body, legs, holding her motionless. Once again a jug was brought to her mouth, and whiskey ran over her chin and down her bare body. And still she screamed.

She heard the door come crashing open.
Darkness.

She was being cradled and carried in thick arms
against a massive chest. She wanted only to sleep, to sleep
forever and never have to remember, but she heard the
harsh, rumbling voice. "Don't you worry, you ain't gonna
have to be out there with them ever again. Not ever again,
Sheba. From now on, you stay with me in the big house.
From now on, you gonna be safe, Sheba. Safe with
me . . ."

Seven

"You find out fast or you don't find out at all."
Denmark Vesey's words kept coming back to Adaba
as day after day he failed to find any clue to Gilly's
whereabouts. Denmark had not given up the search: he
had informants not only in the city but throughout the surrounding countryside, and he was after them unceasingly
to find the girl. But all efforts came to nothing.

Denmark seemed as bitter about what had happened
as Adaba. "Now you're learning, boy, as I have learned. I
know what it is to marry a woman and have her and my
children denied to me because I have displeased their
master. I know what it is to have my children brought up
as another man's slaves—to see my sons turned into cring-
ing, fawning sambos, 'Yassuh, massa, nossuh, massa,' and
my daughters turned into worse. Keep learning, boy, and
never forget."

Ten days after the end of Race Week, Marcus Guerard returned to his plantation and Adaba went with him.
He had despaired of finding Gilly in Charleston and had
decided to widen his search. Perhaps he could find out
what Denmark's informants could not.

In the next few weeks, he traveled to dozens of farms
and plantations, approaching the slaves discreetly and ask-

ing questions, but he learned nothing. Occasionally he had trouble with whites. They didn't always like a strange black boy passing the time of day with their people, even if he did have what appeared to be a perfectly genuine pass, and when they found out that he was "that rich nigger's boy," they usually liked him even less.

Near the end of March, he decided he must widen his search still farther.

So far, he had been staying away from the plantation only a night or two at a time. Sometimes he had passed through Charleston and had stayed at the house there. What would he need to travel farther? Not much, he decided, and no more than he could carry, since his father couldn't or wouldn't spare him a horse or mule. The nights were rapidly growing warmer, and he would need only a couple of blankets. Some food. Some money. Some writing material for forging passes as he needed them. And perhaps a pistol and ammunition. It was dangerous for a black to carry such a weapon, but it might be useful.

His father discovered him making up his blanket roll and knew at once what he was up to.

"You're leaving. . . ."

"Yes, sir."

"To look for her."

"Yes, sir."

"And I don't suppose there's a thing I can do to stop you."

"You might try putting this pistol to my head. It might make me hesitate."

His father sighed and sank into a chair. "What I regret is the waste. You won't find her, you know."

Honesty compelled Adaba to say the words, though speaking them was like tearing flesh out of his own throat: "I know."

His father looked up in surprise. "Then what in the world . . . ?"

He would make one attempt to explain. "Father, I know that if you and Mr. Sabre don't want me to find Gilly, it will be almost impossible for me to do it. There are a hundred towns and cities where she might be and a hundred thousand farms and villages and crossroads. I'm

130

terrified by the thought that I may already have passed her by—that I'll be up in Georgetown or down around Savannah, searching always farther away, when all the time she's someplace near here where I've already looked. I know that most likely something like that will happen. I know that really I haven't got a hope in the world of finding her."

"Then why . . . ?"

The words burst out like a cry of pain: "Because I am goddamn well *going* to find her if it takes me the rest of my life!"

His father stood up from his chair very slowly. He walked away like a very weary man, and Adaba noticed that the gray at his temples was thickening. At the doorway, he paused and looked around.

"You are mad."

"Very likely, father, but I suspect that that is a rather common condition among slaves. And I am a slave."

His father made a gesture of disgust, dismissing the thought.

"You deny that I am a slave?"

His father too was capable of pain and anger. Marcus Guerard charged back into the room. "You have no right to call yourself a slave! You haven't earned it! What the hell do you know about the holds of slave ships, about the auction block, about dawn-to-dusk labor under the whips of drivers and ignorant overseers? You have been offered more advantages than most white men dare dream of, and you would spit on them and throw them away and call yourself slave."

"But isn't that why Gilly was sent away? Isn't that why I can't have her?"

"No! You can't have her because my son, slave or free, isn't going to marry a slave nigger wench and bring slave children into this vile world!"

"I'm sorry, father," he said, meaning it.

His father nodded, almost as if he understood. But, Adaba wondered, how could his father ever understand how he felt?

Turning to leave again, his father paused in the doorway. "As I said, what I regret is the waste. You think I

131

regard myself as a white man and cut myself off from our people, and to a degree, that's true. But I've had dreams of your going abroad and getting the finest possible education and returning to become a leader of our people. I think you have the gift for it, Adaba—you have a feeling for black people, a way to their hearts, as I've never had. I think you could be a leader where I could never be. Now I know that that will never happen."

Adaba found himself touched. "You've never called me by my basket name before. I thought you hated it."

His father looked mildly surprised. "Hated it? I love it. Your mother gave it to you." His lips twisted ironically. "But of course it would never do for a leader of men. Much too niggerish for all dem white folk."

Adaba laughed softly. "Maybe I'll be a leader yet, father. But in my own way."

His father shrugged. His eyes were empty of belief. He left the room.

Adaba finished making up his blanket roll. In the morning before dawn he would be on his way. *And I'll find her*, he swore against all reason. *Somehow I'll find Gilly.*

None of the women ran away, but four men left that same night. Those were the ones he would punish, Jeppson swore, not only for running away but because he could be reasonably certain that they were the ones who had abused Sheba. Too bad three of them were drivers—Sabin, Wildon, and Orlando—that was inconvenient. But it was a good idea to remind drivers once in a while that they were still niggers and could be punished. The fourth one, that damned Remus, could use some reminding too. He didn't mind them having their pleasure on a Saturday night; in fact, he expected it. But this time they had gone too far. Sheba could tell him little of what had happened, but he could guess most and ferret out the rest.

That night he had Esme and another woman bathe Sheba and put her to bed. She slept most of the following day, even when food was brought to her. She was nauseated and her head throbbed, and she kept trying to fall back asleep rather than face the little she could remember

132

of the previous night. Of one thing she was certain: she never wanted to be with a man again.

In the evening, while Jeppson was still out chasing the runaways, Fenella came to see her. "I sorry," she wept, while sitting by Gilly's bed, "I sorry what they done. Never meant it to happen."

"But you told me night 'fore last," Gilly said dully, "you told me I ain't heard the last. Say that the men going get me for what I done to Remus."

"But that was *'fore,*" Fenella protested. "Last night we friends. You hear me tell Sabin let you be."

"Yes," Gilly said, "and then we drink and drink, and you take me to that place."

"But we don't mean nothing to happen!"

"Then why Remus and Abel both do it to me?"

She didn't know why she asked, but suddenly it seemed to her that the memory had sprung from the dark recesses of her mind. Yes. She remembered. All too vividly. They had both done it to her.

"Wasn't just to you, Sheba. It was a party. Everybody was drinking and pleasuring—"

"Not like they done to me. Me out of my head with whiskey, and them taking turns without me knowing or having a say. You know that, Fenella, or why you cry?"

Fenella shook her head and sobbed. "We never done nothing like that before, Abel and me—pleasuring with others. Leastwise not since we marry. Others do it, the young that ain't settled down yet, but not Abel and me. I don't know what happen."

You know, Fenella, Gilly thought, *you know.* Fenella probably believed her protestations to be quite sincere. But the fact was that even after the Friday night incident with Mr. Jeppson, a part of her had still hoped to see Gilly humiliated, "put in her place." Sometimes it seemed to Gilly that she understood people better than they understood themselves.

Jeppson figured he knew pretty well what had happened. Fenella swore up and down that she had tried to stop it, and he was inclined to believe her. After all, Sheba had saved her from getting her throat cut, and the two had seemed friendly afterward. Why would Fenella want to hurt Sheba? Remus, on the other hand, carried a pair of aching balls and a heavy grudge, and after Fenella had bad-mouthed Sheba for a month, it would be easy for him to sic the drivers on her. Remus, then, was chiefly responsible.

Thanks to the patrols and the cooperation of his neighbors, Jeppson had the four runaways back by Monday afternoon, and he soon got out of them the information that Abel had also raped Sheba. That made five to provide an example.

The whipping was administered that same day at sundown. It took place at the whipping post in the clearing in the middle of the slave quarters. Jeppson intended all of his people to see it, and he had P. V. Tucker and Rolly Joe Macon on hand to help keep them in line. Remus was first, tied naked to the post, and Jeppson didn't count the lashes. When it was over, Remus was staked out on the ground, faceup and still naked. A few buckets of water brought him back to consciousness. Then Birnie the overseer, Tucker, Macon, and Jeppson each whipped one of the remaining four, taking them one at a time. Jeppson finished with Abel. They weren't staked out, just revived with cold water and made to watch.

But Jeppson wasn't finished. Now he was going to teach these black bastards a lesson they would never forget. And when he was done, they would never again dare to touch his Sheba.

In her bedroom, Gilly could hear what was happening. The crack of the whip and the cries of pain floated through the evening air from the slave quarters all the way to her open window. It never occurred to her to be glad of what was happening, to relish the punishment that was being meted out on her behalf. To her, it was just more pain added to pain, pain that went on endlessly, and what good did it do? Tears came to her eyes, blinding her.

At last the whip sounds and the cries stopped. By that time, the sky outside her window had turned a deep scarlet.

Then there was a new sound from the quarters, a wail of terror. Remus's voice.

Almost at once, she heard Fenella: *"Sheba! Sheba-a-a!"*

134

Fenella kept on crying the name until she burst into the room. "You got to stop him, Sheba! Oh, please, Sheba, don't let him do that thing to Remus, you got to stop him, only you can stop him! Stop him like you stop him from killing me! Stop him, stop him!"

There was no time to dress, no time to ask questions. Gilly was out of bed and running barefoot in her shift, down the stairs and out of the house. She didn't feel the sharp stones underfoot as she ran through the falling night toward the quarters, toward that wail of terror.

The people, ranged around the whipping post, seemed transfixed with horror. No one was at the post now, but Gilly saw Remus staked out naked on the ground, his legs wide apart. A few yards away, charcoal glowed in a brazier as Mr. Birnie pumped a hand-bellows at it. An iron poker lying in the charcoal was a dull red at the tip. It was hot enough to cauterize a wound.

Mr. Jeppson approached Remus. Stood over him, the gelding knife in hand.

Esme, in Nicodemus's arms, sobbed. One of the drivers began to vomit.

Gilly forced herself to look and saw that the job had not yet been done.

Jeppson had begun to lean forward, but some instinct kept Gilly from rushing to him. She walked toward him as if she had all the time in the world. Remus had ceased to scream, but his breathing was a harsh rattle.

By the time Gilly reached Jeppson, he was gathering up Remus's scrotum between his fingers. She put a hand on his arm and said very softly, "No."

He looked at her in surprise, seeing her here for the first time. "You know what he done to you, don't you, Sheba?" he said after a moment, almost as softly as she.

"I know. Won't help, you cut him up."

Jeppson continued to hold Remus's flesh. "He deserves it. He earned it. He got to be made an example."

She shook her head. "He only a boy, Mr. Jeppson. I know you whip him good. Whip him more, you want. But not this."

Jeppson looked at the panting, terrified Remus. He looked at Gilly again.

135

"You really want me to let him go?"

"I truly thank you, Mr. Jeppson, you let him go."

"Well . . ."

Jeppson released Remus and straightened up, looking as if he were considering the matter.

"Well, Sheba . . ."

Perhaps if she had wept, begged, pleaded, he would have gone ahead. He would have felt bound to show that he was a master as implacable as an Old Testament god. He would have been unable to do anything else. Somehow, Gilly understood this.

Jeppson tossed the knife in his hand. He held it up for all to see. He looked about. "Sheba says Remus been punished enough," he said loudly, "so I'm letting him go. This time. But I want you all to know that if anything like this happens again . . ."

"Thank you, Mr. Jeppson," Gilly said quietly. "Thank you."

He wanted her. Whatever he might tell others, there was simply no way Jeppson could deny that to himself. Only shock and anger had kept him from wanting her the moment he had seen her standing naked on Gore's dais, and that sight had come back to haunt him a hundred times since. It had come to him that night at The Roost when, to his shame, he had grown hard with wanting, and it had continued to pursue him night and day.

He fought the hunger. It went against his deepest and most abiding belief—that the races must never be intermixed.

He tried to kill his hunger with hard work. In March and April, the cotton- and cornfields had to be furrowed, sowed, and harrowed. The vegetable gardens had to be planted. In May, it was time to start barring and chopping cotton. There were a hundred other tasks to be done, and Jeppson threw himself into them, working harder than any of his people.

It didn't help. Sometimes it seemed to Jeppson that hard work actually made the hunger worse.

He thought of visiting Charleston. He considered visiting this or that nearby widow woman who was said to be available. Bodies, in his experience, had a way of being interchangeable. But he dimly realized that his hunger was something more than a mere physical need that could be relieved by an act upon one body or another. He would come in from the fields in the evening and see Sheba waiting for him on the piazza, a slight smile on her face—a smile for him, a smile that grew as he got closer—and his heart seemed literally to ache. How could he even dream of doing a thing that would offend and sicken her? How could he degrade her so, even in the privacy of his imagination?

One of the most terrible things about sex, Jeppson was learning, was that quite against one's will it could lead to something else. Call it cherishing, call it respect, call it love. Love was a concept that frightened Balbo Jeppson —how could a decent white man possibly love a nigger? —but he had a great and growing respect for his Sheba. And with whatever remained of his withered heart, he cherished her.

She was giving him the happiest times of his life. One of his greatest pleasures was having her read to him in the evenings by lamplight. He was utterly amazed at how her speech suddenly changed, how she seemed to be herself and another person at the same time. Sometimes she actually frightened him with her readings. "Out, damned spot! Out, I say! One—two—why, then 'tis time to do't. Hell is murkey! Fie, my lord, fie! a soldier and afeard? What need we fear who knows it, when none can call our power to account? Yet who would have thought the old man to have had so much blood in him? . . ." She could even explain most of the baffling words and phrases. They had been explained to her when she was learning to read from a big volume of Shakespeare, and she never forgot a thing she was told. In any other black he would have found such intelligence offensive and threatening.

After she had stopped him from castrating Remus, she had become his surrogate with the other blacks. It was not to him or to Birnie that they turned when they wanted a dispute settled or a tool replaced or some special privilege conferred, but to his Sheba. They might be sitting on the piazza, enjoying an evening breeze, when a field hand

137

would approach and nervously indicate that he wished to speak to her. She would walk to the far end of the piazza where the hand waited, and arms crossed under her breasts, head up and tilted a little sideways, she would listen gravely. Then she would walk back to Jeppson, slowly, considering the merits of the case. She would tell him what was wanted and make her recommendation. More often than not, he agreed with her. Yes, give the man a new shirt. All right, I'll write him a pass to Riverboro. (Only she would write it for his signature: she wrote better than he.) He didn't object to this; he found it fitting. It seemed to add to his own dignity. And when she sat down beside him again, he might reach out and touch her arm. It was the only gesture of affection he permitted himself, and he would withdraw his hand quickly, as if it burned.

April, May, June. The days grew hotter, and the slow-moving streams turned green with slime. The wealthier white families of the region had left for the city or the pine villages or the North. Frequently, even the nights failed to give relief from the heat.

And Balbo Jeppson's torture grew worse.

There were moments when he hated Sheba. She had no right to do this to him. He remembered how she had looked the first time he had seen her—the lithe brown body, the high breasts, the lightly hirsute mound—and he would be sick with desire.

He couldn't go on this way. It had to be ended. Somehow.

It ended on a hot night in June. For hours the air had been oppressive with the promise of a storm that never came. Every window and door in the upstairs of the house was open to allow the air to move, but there wasn't a whisper of a breeze.

Jeppson's bedside lamp still burned. Stripped against the heat, damp with sweat, he sat sprawled on his bed, leaning back against pillows. He sipped a glass of whiskey and tepid water, and thought of Sheba as he had seen her a week earlier—naked in her bed.

Not tonight, he thought. *I won't look at her tonight.*

But he had seen her intimately several times since he

had brought her into the house, and the memory was like a fire that refused to burn out. The first time had been about a month earlier. He had always made a point of not so much as glancing at her door; but on that particular night, the door had been open, and without thinking, he had looked toward it. Her back to him, she had been removing her dress. He hadn't broken stride, he had looked quickly away, but he hadn't slept for hours afterward. Since then, he had continued to avoid looking toward her door.

Until last week.

He had stayed up late. When he had come up the stairs, lamp in hand, he had looked in her open doorway and had stood transfixed. She had been lying face down on her bed, long legs spread out, her shift up over her buttocks. He had stared at her for perhaps three minutes before going to his room and had returned several times before going to sleep.

The next night, it had happened again.

But that night, she had seen him first. He had come upstairs early and had been sitting naked on his bed, just as he was now, one knee up and one leg dangling to the floor. Just as now he had been sipping whiskey and water and thinking about Sheba, when she had appeared at his door and asked if there were anything more he wanted. No, he had said, there was not. She had not even appeared to notice his nakedness. Her face was expressionless, but her gaze rested momentarily on the thick, blue-veined flesh that arched, half-erect, from the crisp black hair, and she had turned away.

Much later that night, when, lamp in hand, he had gone to her door, she had been lying on her back completely naked. He had looked at her for long minutes before turning away, afraid the lamp would awaken her. A man in agony, he had returned half a dozen times.

He had sworn every night since then that never again would he do such a thing. But now . . .

Once again she was lying asleep in a bed only a few yards away from him. Only two walls and the dark upstairs passage separated them. The doors of both rooms were open, and in that sense they were not separated at

139

all. The same still air that touched his bare flesh touched hers, and if he listened carefully, he could sometimes hear her stir. And hearing her, in his mind's eye he could see. . . .

Quickly he arose from his bed and paced back and forth, trying to distract himself, trying to quell the erection he could feel coming on. For the third or fourth time, he stood before his washbowl and splashed water on his face and shoulders and chest and between his legs. As he toweled himself, he grabbed his glass and bolted down the rest of his whiskey. But he knew that nothing, not whiskey, not cold water, could completely relieve this longing—and in his heart he knew he didn't want it relieved.

All right, he would go look at Sheba. One more time. How could that hurt? She was beautiful. And he wished her no harm.

He quickly wrapped the towel around his waist, picked up the lamp, and left the room.

When he reached her door, he saw with a pang of disappointment that tonight she was wearing a shift. As he stared at her, she made a little sound and, rolling away from him, curled into a ball.

The little sound, a sob, was repeated.

". . . Sheba?"

She was silent.

"Sheba? You all right?"

He now had a pretext for entering the room. He carried the lamp to the bedside table and set it down. Sheba's back was to him, and he put a knee onto the bed, trying to look over her shoulder.

"Sheba? . . ."

As she rolled toward him, opening her eyes, the tears on her cheeks caught the lamplight.

"Hey, now," he said softly, "what you crying about?"

"Ain't nothing, Mr. Jeppson."

"Got to be something. I ain't done nothing to hurt you, have I?"

"No. You good to me, Mr. Jeppson."

"I try to be."

The knee on the bed shook unsteadily; hot though the

140

night was, he trembled. He knew he should leave the room now. He had no business being here at all. Yet he looked for something more to say, some way to prolong his visit.

"You sure I ain't done nothing wrong?"

She looked as if she were trying to smile, but her chin quivered, and two more tears formed in her eyes. She lifted a hand and brushed her fingertips lightly over his belly just above the towel.

It was more than he could stand. A tremor went through his entire body, went down through his loins, and his flesh came up hard and throbbing.

"Oh, Sheba!"

He had her in his arms almost before he knew what he was doing. His mouth moved across her face, under her eyes, over her cheeks. To her mouth.

He felt her mouth open. Felt the wet flicker of her tongue.

Felt the towel fall away from his waist. Felt her hand move far between his legs, almost to his back, then sweep forward again to grasp and draw at him.

Felt his own hand following the soft flesh up between her thighs to the hot, wet mouth.

"Oh, my God, Sheba . . ."

No woman of Charleston had ever been like this, none had ever tried to please him like this. He had never before heard such sounds of pleasure as were now coming from Sheba's throat.

He couldn't stop himself, couldn't stop her. He found himself being drawn up onto the bed until he was stretched out over her and between her spread legs. Her shift was up to her waist, and he ripped the fabric away from her breasts. Then he let himself be fitted into that opening cleft.

Even as he started to enter her, the thought came to him one last time: he must not. This was wrong, he should stop right now, he should withdraw from her, leave this room, never return.

She whimpered and pressed against his aching flesh, and he felt her opening up.

His will was shattered. He belonged to her. With a

141

groan that was more despair than pleasure, he drove his manhood all the rest of the way in.

She would never again weep for what could not be. She knew now that Adaba never would come to her, that there had never been a chance for them to be together again. If she was to go on living, she had to accept that fact, and to have this pleasure with another man was to do so.

At least she had Mr. Jeppson. He was a strange and cruel man, a man who tore the nails from slaves' feet and threatened them with the gelding knife. But he had never been anything but gentle and kind to her. He wanted nothing more than to protect her—and to lie in her arms.

And now she had the comfort of his body, and she gave herself up to that mind-dissolving pleasure. She had known for a long time that this was inevitable, had known long before those nights when he had stood in her doorway looking at her. A week ago, he had offered himself to her, whether he wished to admit it or not, and that same night she had offered herself in return. It had to be.

She no longer hated the name Sheba. She *was* Sheba now. Mr. Jeppson's Sheba.

Gilly no longer existed.

Gilly was dead.

He didn't know what had awakened him.

Perhaps it was the dream—a nightmare dream in which he had at last found Gilly, only to have her recede from him, despair in her eyes, into a darkness that meant death. He had heard his rapid breathing and his pounding heart—and then the noisy dawn-chatter of the birds.

Or perhaps it was the birds themselves that awakened him. Adaba lay there, facedown, unmoving, his breath and his heartbeat gradually slowing, and ever so slightly he opened his eyes to the faint dawn light.

Or perhaps it was something else—a footstep, the cracking of a twig, a human breath. A sense that he was not alone.

He was lying on a blanket spread over needles in a grove of pines. He waited for another sound.

142

It came: a low chuckle. And then a voice, very soft: "All right, he's awake now, boys." ·

Opening his eyes wider, he saw a booted foot. Very slowly, he raised his head and looked about.

There were three of them, a bearded white man flanked by two blacks. The white man was pointing a pistol at Adaba's head. When the man hunkered down, Adaba saw that it was his own pistol.

The white man was dressed in a dark broad-brimmed hat and buckskins. His eyes were blue, his curly beard gray. His face was weathered. He might have been anywhere from thirty-five to fifty years old, though to Adaba's young eyes he seemed ageless. The two blacks were younger, in their early thirties. All three men had hatchets hanging from their belts.

"Been going through your things," the white man said. "Hope you don't object. We didn't find no pass." He held out his hand.

Adaba moved slowly and no more than he had to. He pulled the pass from his pocket and handed it to the man. The man looked at it and grinned.

"This here pass says you're going from Charleston to Columbia, Adaba. That's a mighty long way to send a nigger by hisself."

"Yes, sir."

"And this ain't a good way to Columbia. You kinda strayed from your path, you know that?"

"No, sir."

"And we found writing material in your things here—paper that just matches this. Why didn't you write yourself a different pass, Adaba?"

"I—I didn't write—"

"And this pistol." The man waved the pistol. "A slave carrying a weapon like this could get hisself in bad trouble, Adaba. Hell, he could get hisself killed, don't you know that?"

Adaba said nothing. There was nothing to be said. He was still lying on his belly, he was now unarmed, and he didn't see a way in the world that he could escape. For months he had been traveling, asking questions, searching

143

for Gilly, without encountering serious trouble. But his luck had run out.

The white man grinned again. "Pens and paper, a forged pass, a pistol—boys, what we got here is a goddamn runaway. And you know what we do with them. . . ."

PART TWO

LEW

Death in Charleston

One

Though he had been awake only a few minutes, Adaba had never felt more alert. He had no idea of what kind of people he had fallen among—honest yeomen, nigger-haters, slave-stealers?—and he had to watch every word he said.

The bearded white man moved away from him and sat down on the carpet of needles with his back against the trunk of a longleaf pine. The two blacks had moved quietly to contain Adaba in a triangle.

"Now, you may find this a little hard to believe," the white man said, "but maybe we can be of help to you. First, though, we've got to know something about you. Like your name. Ain't likely you'd use your real name on a forged pass, is it? What's your real name?"

"It's Adaba, sir. And that pass ain't forged—"

"Now, we ain't gonna be able to help you if you don't tell us the truth."

"That is the truth, sir. My name is Adaba—"

"Ah, me. Well, boys. Ain't seen Charleston for a while, and this nigger is most likely from somewhere near there. Suppose we take him to Charleston and turn him over to the workhouse, and when he's claimed, we'll get the reward from his owner."

Adaba thought of Pickett, the guard in the Charleston workhouse. "Why not take me to my owner, sir?" he asked. "He's in Charleston this time of the year. Get your reward from him right away."

The white man stroked his beard and looked thoughtful. "Well, now. That's a mighty helpful suggestion. And you're a mighty well-spoken nigger, Adaba—or whatever your name is. Just who would your master be?"

"It's on the pass, sir. His name is Marcus Guerard."

146

The white man looked at the pass as if reassessing it. "Marcus Guerard, the planter?"

Adaba nodded. "Yes, sir."

"I've heard he's too damn strict with his niggers. Is that why you ran away?"

"He's strict only when he has to be," Adaba said. "If he wasn't, people would say he was too lax. You know how they say that about most black planters. He's a lot more concerned about the welfare of his people than most whites are." He was a little surprised to find himself defending his father, and the white man looked surprised too.

"Why, is that so? Don't sound like you got much to run away from, then."

"I don't."

"Then why you running? 'Cause I still got this funny idea you wrote this pass yourself, even if you did use the right names."

The man seemed kindly enough, and Adaba was beginning to feel more sure of himself. He figured that more of the truth couldn't hurt. "I'm *not* running away. I usually write my own passes to save my father the bother—"

"Your father?"

"Marcus Guerard is my father. Do you mind if I sit up, sir? This is getting uncomfortable."

The white man didn't answer. He stared at Adaba. After a moment, he laughed. "Boys, we not only got us a pass-forging runaway nigger slave, we got us a *rich* pass-forging runaway nigger slave!"

Adaba heard chuckles from the two blacks.

"Adaba is Gullah," the white man said. "You got another name, boy?"

"John, sir. John Guerard. But I've found out that a lot of people don't take to me when they find out that I'm that —that 'rich nigger kid, Marcus Guerard's bastard.' So I use Adaba unless somebody like you asks me."

"Smart. Adaba, I got an idea that you're real smart."

"What are you going to do with me, sir?"

"Well," the white man said, "I don't rightly know what

you *want* us to do with you. If you ain't running away, just what the hell are you doing out here in the woods?"

Adaba sat up facing the white man. "Traveling, sir. Looking for somebody."

"And who would that be?"

"A black girl, sir. Named Gilly. She was sold, more than three months ago."

Very briefly, he told the story. The white man looked sympathetic and concerned.

"Son, it don't sound to me like you're gonna find that girl ever."

"I've got to keep looking."

The white man looked at the pistol in his hand as if he had forgotten it was there. He seemed to have more on his mind than he was saying.

"If somehow you got lucky and found her, what would you do about it?"

"Get her back somehow."

"How?"

"Buy her."

"What if her owner wouldn't sell?"

Adaba was silent. There were some things you didn't say to a white man even if he were sympathetic.

"Come on, goddammit, what would you do?"

"What could I do?"

"Steal her. Take her north, take her out of the country. A bright young black like you could do it. Would you do something like that?"

Adaba's voice shook. "Sir, I shouldn't say it to you, a white man, but I'd do just about anything in the world to get Gilly back."

"You'd steal her? They hang for that, you know. Would you help others do the same? Steal niggers free?"

Adaba stared. The man seemed kindly, but that guaranteed nothing. The question could be a trap.

"Come on, boy," the man said impatiently, "you've practically said that you'd steal this girl to get her. If someone stole her for you, would you steal another nigger in return?"

Put that way, Adaba could only agree. "Yes. I would."

"Well, if that's the case . . ." The white man shoved

148

the pistol, together with the pass, across the ground toward Adaba. "If that's truly the case, maybe we can help you look for your girl."

They were slave-stealers of a sort, Adaba learned. The white man's name was Murdock, and his black companions, Thomas and William, were his slaves. "And if anybody asks," Gavin Murdock said, "you're my slave too. My slave John, or Adaba, if you want. Johnny Dove!"

Adaba had little idea of what he was getting into, and Murdock wasn't yet ready to volunteer information. Adaba only knew that he had failed thus far to find Gilly, and this white man offered a hope of sorts. All right, he would go along with Murdock and see where this trail led.

Adaba had no idea where he was being taken. The four of them traveled rapidly, pausing briefly every hour or so for a rest and in the heat of the day for a light meal. They talked little while on the move, but as they ate, it seemed to Adaba that Murdock was baiting him, perhaps testing him.

"I don't reckon you got much real objection to slavery, do you, Adaba? I mean, you ain't a *real* slave, and black sweat surely kept you comfortable all your life. You please your daddy, and I reckon he'll make you a rich man when he dies, ain't that right? Except for your Gilly, what do you give a damn? Hell, niggers sell niggers in Africa—it ain't just the Arab slavers. It's natural for some niggers to own others—just like it's natural for white men to own them. Ain't that so?"

Adaba, liking Gavin Murdock, grew bold. "Yes, sir. Just like it's natural for the English to own the worthless Scots and the Irish."

Murdock threw back his head and laughed.

They reached the maroon camp at dusk—a dozen or more cabins tucked away in a pine forest far from any road or visible trail. The cabins were more substantial than Adaba would have guessed, and children as well as adults greeted their little party. It was evident that Murdock was an important personage to these people.

There was little fear in the camp, or lights would not

have shown from cabin doors and windows. There was a smell of good food in the air.

"You know where you are, son?"

"I know what this is. I don't know where it is. I'm lost."

Murdock laughed. "Just as well for now. Let's get us something to eat. These people maybe ain't as rich as a Guerard nigger, but they live better than you might think."

They ate corn cakes and a kind of stew made from a variety of vegetables and perhaps half a dozen different meats. The woman who handed them the wooden bowls as they sat outside her cabin said it had been a long time cooking, and she could no longer remember what had gone into it. It was delicious.

Afterward, Adaba and Murdock sat elbow to elbow, their backs against a pine, and watched the wheeling stars. Gavin Murdock puffed his pipe.

"Son," he said after a long silence, "you got any idea what's happening in the world?"

"Lots of things happening, Mr. Murdock, sir. Alabama Territory formed last year. Nigger boy up in Boston blew up a ship, because they wouldn't let him in on the Election Day celebration. And there's the war with the Seminoles."

"That's right. War with the Seminoles. Ever hear of the Apalachicola River?"

Adaba had indeed heard of it. It was in northern Florida. A year or two earlier, a number of runaway slaves had taken over a fort on the river. Runaways were felt to be a menace to all slave-owners and, of course, especially to those who had plantations in southern Georgia. But the menace had quite easily been disposed of. A military force had been dispatched to blow up the fort—and everybody in it.

"Two hundred seventy blacks killed," Murdock said bitterly. "Men, women, and children who just wanted to be free and have a place to live in safety. I took a lot of them people down there myself."

So that was the kind of slave-stealer Gavin Murdock was. Adaba had already been pretty certain of it.

"I been taking runaways down to join the Seminoles
150

for years," Murdock went on, "but it looks like that's over now. At least for a long time to come."

Adaba had heard the story of the war against the Seminoles only from a white point of view. "The Seminoles killed a lot of white people," he said tentatively. "It ain't no wonder the white folks—"

"The whites keep taking over Indian land, driving the Indians off, then they wonder that the Indians fight back. Last year, a chief claimed some land near Fowltown and said he was damned if he'd give it up. What happened then? General Edward Gaines personally led an expedition to burn the town and kill all the Indians, men and women alike. So of course the Seminoles got revenge by killing about forty soldiers and maybe a dozen women and children."

Murdock shook his head sadly. "I don't hold with killing if it can be avoided, especially women and children. I don't blame the Indians, 'cause they've seen their families slaughtered ever since the white man landed. But look what it all led to. Calhoun, the secretary of war, sent General Andrew Jackson down to take charge. And if you want to see Indians die, all you got to do is send for Jackson.

"I fought Jackson back in 'thirteen. You heard of William Weatherford, ain't you?"

Adaba nodded. "Chief of the Creeks. They call him Red Eagle."

"I fought Jackson with Red Eagle—the bravest Indian that ever was. Even Jackson had to admit that."

"You fought with the Creeks?" Adaba was surprised. "But you're white."

"So's Weatherford, mostly, but we're both Indians. Me, I'm a Cherokee. Seven-eights white, mostly Scotch, and all Cherokee. My family's been Cherokee for a long, long time."

Adaba laughed. "A Scotch-Cherokee nigger-stealer."

"That's right." Murdock's pipe glowed in the darkness. "Anyway, the war with the Seminoles is over no   but there ain't gonna be no sending runaways down th   long time. That means we got to take them n   from here that's a long way. It ain't like just c

Ohio River. We got to find more resting places, we got to build up the maroon camps, we got to blaze more trails that nobody knows but us. There's a lot of work to be done."

"And you want me to help you."

"You help us, we'll help you look for your girl. Notice I ain't saying we'll *find* her for you—I don't want to give you false hopes. But it won't just be you looking."

"But how can I help you? I don't know about these things—about blazing secret trails—"

"I'll teach you." A note of excitement entered Gavin Murdock's voice as he sensed that he had a recruit. "I'll teach you all you need to know, all the Indian ways. I'll teach you how to survive in the swamps and the forests, how to get around the patrols, how to throw the hounds off the scent. I'll teach you where the maroon camps are and how to get from one to another. I'll teach you things like—like—" Murdock laughed. "Well, like that pistol you carry. You don't need a goddamn pistol. A rifle would make some sense, but what you really need is a hatchet. A hatchet or an axe will feed and clothe and shelter and protect you—and I'll teach you how to use it. But a pistol ain't good for much more than getting you into trouble. Now, how about it?"

The pistol was stuck in Adaba's belt. He took it out. He slapped the butt into Murdock's hand.

"Teach me."

Two: October 1818

He stood tall, with broad shoulders, and under his tattered wide-brimmed hat he had the narrow eyes of a man who lived in the open. He was unshaven: smooth-cheeked, but with a muzzle of thick black beard. He walked in long fast strides, almost at a lope, down the Charleston Neck, ignoring the grog shops and the gamblers and the fancy women who gave him inviting looks and calls as he passed.

If he was worried about the patrol, he didn't show it. He had the look of a black who had never learned his place and had forgotten all warnings. Bad nigger. But best leave him alone. Who wants to get hurt?

He had the look of a man with a mission.

By late afternoon he had passed Boundary Street and was well into Charleston proper. When he came to Denmark Vesey's shop, he stopped at last and stood across from it, watching. A few people, white and black, came and went. A couple of white gentlemen walking along indicated that he was blocking their way. He didn't seem to notice them. One started to chastise him, then thought better of it. It was a fine October afternoon. Why spoil it by messing with a nigger who was too ignorant to stand aside for a white man? Besides, this one had a look about him. . . .

Satisfied that Denmark was alone, he crossed the street and entered the shop. He had always loved the place—the smell of resin and glue, the benches with their clamps and vises, the whirling lathes, the hammers, mallets, adzes, chisels, rabbits, plows, saws, braces, bits: good tools, lovingly kept.

Denmark was at one of the benches adjusting a box vise. His visitor watched silently for almost a minute before the big grizzled black sensed that he was not alone and slowly turned around. For a few seconds his face showed no recognition. Then he held out his arms.

"Adaba!"

Laughing, the two men embraced.

"Son, just let me look at you!" Denmark held Adaba at arm's length and looked searchingly into his eyes. "Yes, it's you all right. But there's something changed about you, boy, and it's not just the whiskers. You've been gone from Charleston almost seven months, and somehow you look seven years older. You've been looking for her, haven't you?"

"I've been looking. I'm always looking. But I haven't found her. Yet."

"But where all have you been? Not just around your plantation, I know that. How did you get along?"

Adaba shrugged. "It wasn't hard. I made up reasons

153

for my traveling, like how my master was sending me to Columbia to work for a friend, and I had to hire my time to earn my way. I'd work a day or two here and there as a carpenter, using the things you taught me. And all the time I'd look around and ask questions."

Denmark was delighted. "A carpenter, eh?" He looked at what appeared to be a shingling hatchet in a sheath hanging from Adaba's belt. "I see you've been doing some shingling, son."

Adaba smiled. Suddenly the hatchet seemed to leap into his hand. His hand swung up and thrust out, and the hatchet shot through the air to thud solidly into the wall at the far end of the room.

It was one of the few times Adaba had ever seen Denmark Vesey look truly nonplussed. He looked at Adaba, at the hatchet, at Adaba again. He walked to the end of the room and, with some effort, pulled the hatchet from the wall.

"Son, you have surely been cutting *some*body's shingles, all right." He touched a thumb to the blade. "You could shave with it."

"You can do a lot of things with it. Snare a rabbit, make a fishing spear, build a shelter—even skin a deer, if you've a mind to."

Denmark walked back slowly, staring at the hatchet. He handed it to Adaba. "Son," he said, no longer smiling, "just what the hell have you been up to?"

"It's something you may not want to know about. A lot of black people wouldn't want to know about it. Men get hanged for knowing too much."

"To put it another way, you're placing your life in my hands if you tell me."

"That doesn't worry me at all."

"Good. I've been putting my own neck into the noose for years. I think you had better tell me."

". . . And then last June I met a man. . . ."

I met a man. That was all. For the time being, no names. Never any more details than were necessary. Denmark understood.

"Every year a few slaves manage to excape. We all
154

know that. But most runaways are soon caught, because they have no help. They don't know where to go or who to turn to. This man—these people—take care of that."

"How?"

"In different ways. For example, if a cook on a certain plantation near here were to learn of a slave who wanted to get away, she'd give him a bit of food and tell him to head up the creek on a Saturday night to a certain other plantation and talk to the head driver there. That driver would hide the man until the search had died down, then send him on to another place. And then a certain young nigger we both know might take him to a camp up in the sandhills. And someone else would take him on from there."

Denmark considered the idea. "You're talking about an organization. A kind of rescue organization."

"That's right. An organization of waystations and guides."

"If there were such a thing, I would have heard of it."

Adaba shook his head. "I'm told that a kind of organization has existed for years. But it's been so small and scattered that—you're right—it can hardly be called an organization at all. Now certain people are trying to build it up, make it more effective."

"Northern abolitionists?"

"I don't know. Maybe. But mostly it's got to be our own people, people down here."

Denmark paced the shop. Adaba settled back in a chair. Fortunately, they had not been interrupted by customers since he had come in the door.

Denmark stopped pacing. He looked troubled. "It won't work."

"Why not?"

"First of all, most successful escapes from around here have probably been to Florida. That possibility has been closed for the foreseeable future."

"We'll send our runaways north."

"It's too far. But I'll come back to that. Secondly, you could not hope to be successful without a great deal of help from . . ." Denmark looked as if he wanted to spit. "Without help from Southern whites."

"Maybe, maybe not. But we have some help, and we'll have more. I know how you feel about white people, Denmark, but there are more than you think who are willing to help a slave escape—if only by looking the other way. And some of them own slaves themselves." Adaba thought of Gavin Murdock. "And third?"

"Third, I suspect that most successful escapes have been made on an individual basis. That is, I suspect they have been successful because of individual ingenuity or luck or both. In part, they have succeeded because no two have been quite alike. There have been no established escape routes for the authorities to trace down. And an escape route all the way from Charleston to the free North —as I said, it's too far. It would be impossible to keep secure. No, son, please don't waste my time by arguing with me. The whole thing is quite impossible."

Adaba had a sinking feeling. He had come a long way to see Denmark. The carpenter's help would have been invaluable. His trade took him in and out of and all around the city, and he had innumerable friendships that would have been useful. He worked in the shipyards and aboard the ships, and he knew many of the captains; he would know those with enough sympathy to their cause to smuggle runaways north. Adaba had counted on him. But he knew what Denmark was like once he had made up his mind.

"I'm sorry you feel that way."

The grizzled old black smiled serenely. "That's all right. Now—what can I do to help?"

"Have you noticed who's outside?" Denmark asked.

Adaba felt mellow, as mellow as he had been in months. His legs were stretched out before him, he had a small whiskey in hand, and the chill autumn air made the shop smell better than ever. The soft afternoon sunlight in the street glowed beyond the dimness of the shop. At a time like this he could think that perhaps Gilly was safe, unhurt, not too badly off, and he didn't want his mood spoiled.

"Yes," he said, "I noticed."

"Boy must have come by a hundred times over the

156

summer. He doesn't come in much, because he's afraid of me. Mostly he just stands outside. But he's always looking for you."

"He can go right on looking."

"He once got up the nerve to ask me if I would intercede with you for him."

"What did you tell him?"

"I said that you didn't want anything to do with him. I asked him if he hadn't already caused you enough trouble. I told him he'd be doing you a great favor if he would leave you alone."

Adaba sipped his whiskey. "That's just about right."

"I also told him that if he had anything to say to you, he should do it himself."

Adaba shrugged.

"You know," Denmark said slowly, "I don't really think he meant to cause trouble for you and Gilly."

Adaba was silent.

"I don't think it ever in the world occurred to the boy that his daddy might sell Gilly. Or even that you were her sweetheart. He might have been jealous of somebody visiting her, but I don't think he knew it was you. And even if I'm wrong and he did know . . . a boy of thirteen can be mighty naive, mighty confused. Think back, Adaba."

"Sounds like you been talking to him."

"A little. When he got up the nerve. He's not a bad lad, that boy."

"I never knew you had a brief for white folks."

"I don't. I despise them. I've said so a thousand times. But white folks as such don't enter into this. I'm talking about the friend of my friend."

"Aw, Denmark . . ." Adaba shook his head helplessly. "Maybe it wasn't altogether Lew's fault. But it happened. And things can't ever be the same with Lew and me again."

"I'm not saying they can. I'm not saying they should be. There comes a time when the things of childhood must be ended. But they can be ended in a way that leaves a certain sweetness or one that leaves a bitterness forever. Adaba, there is more to manhood than just standing up for one's rights and kicking a white man in the ass from time to time!"

"This don't sound much like my fierce old friend."

"Then you don't know your fierce old friend very well."

Denmark was telling him to make some kind of peace with Lew. Adaba didn't really care if he never spoke to Lew again, but he didn't want to seem like less than a man. And he had to admit that perhaps Denmark was right.

"All right, guess I'll have to say howdy to Lew."

Denmark's pleased look turned to his customary scowl as he went to the front door of the shop.

"You, there! Master Lewis! You come here! . . . No, don't you back away from me, boy! When I call you, you come . . . !

"You've asked from time to time about your friend Adaba," Denmark said. "Well, as you can see, he's here now."

Lew, big eyed, stood silhouetted in the doorway. From outside, he had been unable to see Adaba in the dim interior. Now he looked as if he might turn and run, but he forced himself to take a few steps into the shop.

"Afternoon, Lew," Adaba said indifferently. "Denmark said you asked about me."

"Nobody knew where you was," Lew said. "Everybody was worried about you. Your daddy and your brothers and sisters—everybody."

"Well, take a good look. I'm here, and in one piece."

"I'm glad you're all right."

"I thank you."

Adaba finished his whiskey and stood up. Lew looked much the same—a coltish boy, a thin face under a great mop of dark hair—and yet he too seemed more than seven months older.

"Something a little different about you, Lew."

"I'm taller."

"Growing up."

"My daddy says I started early."

They stood facing each other in awkward silence. On

158

the bright outside, a wagon clattered by, a horse neighed, people called cheerfully back and forth.

"Reckon you been looking for Gilly."

Adaba didn't answer.

"I been wanting to tell you . . . I know it don't do no good to say this, but . . . I been wanting to tell you I'm sure sorry for all that happened." Lew's voice shook slightly and cracked. "I sure didn't mean to make trouble for you and Gilly. I sure didn't mean to get her sold away."

Adaba sighed. "Aw, hell, I know that, Lew. I reckon you was fond of Gilly just like I was."

"Then maybe . . . maybe we could be friends again? . . . sort of?"

"Yeah . . . sort of."

" 'Cause I sure missed you last summer. Missed all the things we used to do. You and me and. . . and Gilly."

"Missed you too." Saying it, Adaba realized that it wasn't altogether untrue.

"Well . . . anyway, I'm sure glad we're friends again."

Lew thrust his hand out vigorously. Adaba shook it slowly.

"I reckon I better be getting home now." Lew's voice was full of false cheer. "My daddy said he had some chores for me, so . . . I'll be seeing you."

"I'll be seeing you, Lew."

Lew marched toward the door.

"Oh, Lew . . ."

Lew paused in the doorway. "Yes?"

"Thanks for coming by."

A wide grin flashed over Lew's thin face. He waved.

Adaba was eager to get back out of the city and to rendezvous with Gavin Murdock, but there was one other place he had to go first.

Lew was right. His family had worried about him, and the children made plain their delight at seeing him. Handsome fifteen-year-old Philip, the scholar and dandy of the family, wanted to know all his adventures. Fourteen-year-old Diantha, the beauty with the heart-shaped face, inter-

159

rupted Philip repeatedly and flirted to get Adaba's attention. And Rose and David, eight and seven, fought for a place on his lap as if they were infants. Pleased as he was with the reception, Adaba was glad when his father arrived home and gave him a chance to escape.

"So you're back at last." His father's relief was obvious. "I kept expecting to get word that you were in the workhouse."

"I nearly ended up there a couple of times."

They were talking in the same parlor where his father had discussed Gilly with Mr. Sabre.

"You might not find it so amusing if it actually happened. It's bad enough when you're picked up here in the city, but some of the country patrols! They seem to think it's their duty to half kill a black man before turning him in. Great fun for all, teaching the scamp a lesson." His father paused, then smiled at him. "But you're looking fit —beard and all."

"Thank you, father. I feel fit."

"I hope you're home now to stay."

"No, father. I'm afraid not."

The smile faded. "But you haven't found that girl, have you? And you must realize by now that you never will." His father put a hand on his arm. "John, I do have some idea of how you feel, but I won't pretend I'm not glad you didn't find her. It's for the best. But you can't spend the rest of your life searching—"

"I'm not the only one searching for her now, father. I have friends helping me. And searching for Gilly isn't the only thing I'm doing."

"What do you mean?"

"You wanted me to be a leader of men. Of black men. Well, I'm becoming a leader of sorts. So you'd better lock up your people, father. Or there's no telling how many I may lead off."

His father understood at once and looked at him with dismay.

"John, you're asking to be hung."

"Maybe, but they've got to catch me first."

"They will. Slave-thieves are hung regularly."

"On the other hand, I've met outliers who have been helping others escape for years."

"But, John, there are other ways you can help our people. Most of them don't even want to run away."

"That's true. They don't want to run away, they just want to be free. Free right where they are, with their own families and friends, in their own homes, on their own soil. To hell with going north, they want to be free *right here* with what's rightfully theirs. But black people are still being whipped to death—'accidentally,' of course—and branded and having their ears cropped and their balls cut off, and no number of slave-protection laws will stop it. Those people need help. And while I'm looking for Gilly, I, goddammit, am going to help them."

His father made a gesture of hopelessness. "I don't suppose I can stop you. I'm not even sure I want to. Except that I don't want you hurt—and perhaps killed."

"Then I have your blessing?"

"Did you ever think you didn't?"

A week later, Adaba left Charleston again, with no idea of when he might be back. This time he left far better supplied. He had a sturdy mule. He had food, plenty of blankets to protect himself against the oncoming cold weather, and a kit of carpenter tools. Who could possibly doubt that he was a young itinerant carpenter looking for work?

The weather was good, and travel was easy. Though the first frost had yet to arrive, many people were already returning to their plantations after a summer and autumn away, and he had plenty of company, white and black. A couple of people even tried to hire him, and he had to beg off, saying his services were already expected elsewhere.

Nobody noticed when he left the main road to follow a swamp trail.

Three days after leaving Charleston, he met Gavin Murdock, Thomas, and William in the slave quarters of a large plantation whose owner had not the slightest idea that they were there.

"You talked to him?" Murdock asked.

"I did."

"And?"

"Denmark Vesey is one of us."

Three: August 1821

Charleston baked. Baked, steamed, broiled. In the heat of the day, the temperature rose well into the nineties, and when a thunderstorm broke, flooding the city, the relief lasted no time at all. Almost at once the mud-choked streets began to steam.

But the heat of Charleston was nothing compared to the fires that burned in Lew Sabre. What in God's name was happening to him? Surely other sixteen-year-old boys didn't suffer like this. He had started going insane three or four years earlier, and it had been getting worse ever since.

It was sex. Pure, devilish sex. From morning till night, he couldn't keep his mind off of it for ten minutes at a stretch, and it pursued him into his dreams. When he was out riding with his father, and the carriage rolled over a cobbled street, the vibrations did terrible things to him.

"Lewis," his father would say to him, "sit up straight, stop wallowing around, what in the world is the matter with you?" "Nothing, nothing!" he would answer in embarrassment, as he attempted to conceal his impudent member. Was it all his own fault, he would wonder, sneaking a look at his hands. Were all the lurid warnings he had heard true? Was there somewhere in Charleston an asylum filled with hairy-palmed madmen?

And yet, difficult though it was, life was good. Lew had a knack for book-learning, so school and lessons were not burdensome to him, but he gladly escaped them in the summer. Summer was a time for going up on the Neck and consorting with bad companions of all complexions. It was a time for pitching pennies with ne'er-do-wells and sharing

162

bottles of booze and smoking cigars and—was there no end to it?—lusting after girls.

Oh, the girls. All manner of girls—white and black and brown and olive and yellow and copper girls. Fat girls and skinny girls, young girls and old girls. *"Her? You wanna frig her? Why, she's old, boy! She must be thirty!"* It seemed to Lew that if only he could have a girl, the *right* girl, just once, if just once he could assuage this terrible hunger, this savage need, he would be saved. He would never again hunger so desperately. But why was it that he didn't seem able to meet the right girl—or *any* willing and attractive girl—in the entire city of Charleston?

Summer was a time to gather with half a dozen other boys in the dusty streets, a time to tell tall tales and brag.

"When I was in Columbia with my old daddy last week, I had the best piece of nookey in my whole life."

"You? You ain't never had *no* nookey in your whole life!"

"Who says I ain't never had no nookey in my whole life?"

"I says!"

"I had more'n you ever *gonna* have in your whole life, boy, and this was the best!"

"Ya-a-a, tellme, tellme, tellme!"

"Her name was Janine, and she was a parson's daughter, and she just couldn't get enough of it. But I sure burned her down, boy. Ain't a woman in the world I can't burn down."

"Aw, shoot, now you know he's lying, 'cause ain't no man can burn down a woman that likes it that much. He just said she couldn't get enough—"

"Till I finally burned her down!"

"What you got to burn her down *with,* boy?"

"Yeah, I seen what you got, boy, and you couldn't light a seegar with that, if you set it on fire!"

"Who says!"

"I says!"

"You calling me a liar? You saying I didn't never frig no fucking Janine—"

163

"You ain't got 'nough 'quipment to frig a fucking knothole, boy!"

"Who says!"

"*I* says!"

"Aw right, put em up! Come on, just put 'em up! Come on, boy! Gonna whip your ass!"

"Hey-y-y, look what's coming. . . ."

"One last chance, boy! Put 'em up!"

"Hey, yeah-h-h, ain't that nice. . . ."

"Oh, man wouldn't you like to have a piece of that. . . ."

"Oh, m-m-m-myr-r-r-rum-m-m-m!"

"Hey, *boy!* Last *chance!*"

"Aw, shut up."

". . . Aw, shit."

The previous summer, Lew had been wildly in love with Diantha Guerard. Oh, that lovely heart-shaped face with the curl in the center of her forehead! That small, full, so red mouth, made to be kissed! That swell of bosom, so infinitely promising! How could all the rest of the world not be in love with Diantha? His fantasy of sweeping her up in his arms and carrying her up the stairs to a bedroom had something sacred about it. He could almost hear organ music as he imagined that culminating moment of ecstacy.

His passion had been quite obvious and had led to a considerable amount of teasing from Diantha and Philip. But, alas, it was a doomed love. Diantha was already engaged to a young sea captain from Boston, the son of a wealthy merchant, who sailed one of his father's ships down the coast to the islands. When they were married in the spring, Lew's heart had ached with grief.

But not for long. Not when Diantha was in faraway Boston, and ever present were Rosanna and Kitty and Larentia and Glennis and Zenobia and a hundred others, to be seen on the streets of Charleston.

The prettiest of them all, in Lew's opinion, was Jovita. A glimpse of Jovita was what had drawn him to congregate with the other boys on this sun-baked August afternoon. When he saw her coming down the street, he tensed.

"Mm, would you look at that!"

"Ya-a-a! That's real honeypot stuff!"

"She can haul my ashes any old time. . . ."

Somehow such remarks irritated Lew when they were aimed at Jovita. There was something fragile, something vulnerable about the little brown girl that made him feel protective of her. She was, he thought, a little younger than he—he preferred to think so. But there was nothing unformed about the mobile, expressive face, with its softly dimpled cheeks and dark eyes and the mouth that seemed always on the verge of a smile. The top of her head came just to Lew's eyes, and when she was close to him, he had a terrible urge to draw her to him and gently kiss her forehead.

The half-dozen boys grew silent as Jovita, holding two little packages beneath her breasts, approached. For several weeks, her sister's husband had been working with Denmark Vesey. Each day one of the women brought a midday meal to the two men, and today was Jovita's turn. Now every eye was on her, and her own eyes were demurely on the ground ahead of her. She was less than fifty feet away, and Lew had to act quickly.

Denmark still scared him and probably always would, but Lew tried not to think about that. With all other eyes diverted to Jovita, Lew slipped away, crossed the street, and entered Denmark's shop. Denmark and Benjamin, the other carpenter, were at work together and didn't look up from their bench. Lew stood by the open door and waited.

Seconds later, Jovita entered and walked by him. Denmark and Benjamin turned away from their bench and greeted her cordially. She flashed a smile that Lew found dazzling, and handed each man a poke of food. She chattered and joked with them for a few minutes. But Lew heard not a word that was said. All he heard was the music of Jovita's voice.

Finally, the visit was over. Jovita said her byes and started toward the front door, the little half-smile on her face. Lew held his breath. Had she noticed him?

"Afternoon, Jovita," he said when she was nearly to him.

There! He had done it. While the others had merely gawked at her in silence, he had once again braved Denmark Vesey's den and spoken to her, almost in private. And he got his reward. Her smile widened, and she looked over at him. "Afternoon," she said softly.

And she was gone.

Gone, and he would have to wait another day, perhaps two or three or more, for another such exchange.

Bam! a hammer came down on a workbench, an angry blow. "Boy," Denmark Vesey raged, "what are you doing in my shop! Do you have business here? You know I don't allow you lazy no-good loafing rascals in my shop, you know I don't allow—"

In an instant Lew was out the door and across the street, as he would have been in any case, watching Jovita walking away. He wanted to follow her and talk with her. But others had tried it, and those she hadn't driven off, her brother-in-law had. Just the same, one of these days . . .

Oh, Jovita!

Oh, oh, the City Guard.

The goddamned, half-assed, incompetent, unbuttoned City Guard.

Adaba had one distinct handicap for a man in his chosen line of work. He was tall. He was big. Wherever he went, city or country, he stood out. He was noticed. He was rarely given trouble by the guardsmen or anyone else, but when several of them got together, as they had now, and when they had perhaps had a drink or two, they were apt to see him as easy pickin's. And Adaba was in a hurry to see Denmark.

"Boy!"

There it was—the upheld plump forefinger of a plump carrot-topped youth not much older than himself. The other two guardsmen looked familiar. One was older and skull faced; the other was Adaba's age and amiably moon faced.

"You, there! Boy!"

And yes, they were drunk. Carrot-top came lurching unsteadily toward him, and the other two followed, banging shoulders. That could make the situation worse or it could make it better. There was no way to tell.

Adaba started to walk away—testing.

"You, boy!"

"Yassuh, cap'n! Yassuh, cap'n! Good to see you 'gain, cap'n! Got to go now, cap'n, massa want me—"

"You, boy, you hold up there! Halt! Whoa! Slow down!"

Adaba sighed. Nearly to Denmark's, the street crowded with blacks they could have challenged, and they had to pick him. Well, since he had met Gavin Murdock and moved into his new line of endeavor, he had learned to maintain his sense of humor when these incidents occurred.

Adaba pointed down the street. "He go dat way, massa!"

"No! You! It's you we want to talk to!"

"Yassuh, cap'n, you talking. But him what *done* it went *dat* way!"

Carrot-top looked perplexed. "Done what?"

"I don't know, cap'n. You chasing him, he mus' done something."

"We was chasing *you*."

Adaba shook his head. "Massa, you mix me up with somebody else. You point at *him*, you point at dat *big* fella, and you say, 'Boy! You dere, boy!' and he run off, and I say, 'Massa, he go *dat* way,' and—"

Carrot-top swayed. "Anybody know what this crazy nigger is talking about? Did that really happen?"

"Aw, come on, Adaba," the moon-faced man said, grinning, "just show him your ticket and get it over with."

Recognition came to Adaba, and he sighed with relief. "Why, afternoon, Willy," he said. "Ain't seen you in a coon's age."

Carrot-top turned to Willy. "You know this here nigger?"

"Willy," Adaba said, "how come you stop me like this? You still sore 'cause I beat you pitching pennies out behind Madame Fifi's cathouse that time?"

"I *told* you I knew who he was," Willy said to Carrot-top. "I *told* you he was all right." He winked at Adaba.

"Why, thank you, Willy."

"Tha's *Massa* Willy to you, nigger!" Carrot-top said sternly.

167

"Dat sho' is," Adaba said genially, "an' I sho' glad to meet any friend ob Willy!"

Carrot-top blinked. "I ain't—I mean, you ain't—"

The eyes of the skull-faced man widened. "I remember this nigger now! I had him in the workhouse about three years ago! For hitting a white man!"

"Oh, not for hitting him, Massa Pickett, sir!" Adaba shook his head firmly. "For beating the shit out of him, you mean, begging your pardon, sir."

"Jesus!" Carrot-top looked at Adaba as if he couldn't believe what he was hearing.

"Le's take'm back to the guardhouse!" Pickett said. "Le's beat the shit outa *him!*"

"Don't be crazy," Willy said with great patience. "His old daddy got more money and pays more taxes and gives more to the guard and the fire brigade and everything else around here than all ours put together. His old daddy may be a nigger, but he's got more white in him that a lot of folks that pass for white. And you get him mad, he'll just buy your ass and grind it up for fertilizer. You know who his old daddy *is?*"

Eyes wide with consternation, Carrot-top leaned toward Willy. *"Who* his old daddy?"

"Ain't you never heard of . . . Mar . . . cus . . . Guerard?"

"Oh, Christ!" Carrot-top slapped a hand over his eyes.

"I say, throw'm inna workhouse," Pickett said to no one in particular.

"Listen, gen'mens," Adaba said, taking out his pass, "to err is human, to forgive divine."

"So move your ass and pass the wine!" Willy snapped his fingers and did a happy little jig.

"Oh, Christ," Carrot-top said, waving away the pass without looking at it.

Adaba gave Willy two bits and said to buy everybody a drink on him. As he walked away, Carrot-top was still wandering blindly about, and Pickett was fighting furiously with some invisible opponent.

"Insurrection," Denmark said. "What do you think when I say that word?"

Perhaps it was inevitable that he should say it. For years he had been preaching: *"Stand up like a man. Don't cringe, don't fawn. If you behave like a slave, you deserve to be a slave."* He had refused not only to bow down to the white man, he had aided in the escape of slaves. But this was the first time Adaba had ever heard him speak the word: *"Insurrection."*

Adaba sank down into a chair. He put his elbows on his knees, his face in his hands.

"Well, son," Denmark said, "I asked you: what do you think when I say that one word? Insurrection."

"Denmark, when you say insurrection to me, I remember when I was sixteen years old. A man up in Virginia, George Boxley, was going to free the slaves. I don't know how. He was betrayed by a slave. Somehow he got away, but six slaves were hanged."

"I have something quite different in mind."

Adaba ignored him. "And then about a month later six were hung for conspiracy in Camden. And thirty-six hung after Gabriel Prosser's rebellion. And in Louisiana . . ." He shook his head. There was no need to say more. Denmark knew the history of conspiracy and death as well as Adaba did. In Louisiana in 1811, more than sixty rebels had had their heads cut off and hung from trees across the countryside as a warning to blacks. "Don't talk to me about insurrection, Denmark."

"What if I told you I had in mind something bigger than anything you've mentioned? Something far bigger?"

Adaba raised his head. "I'd say you were dreaming."

"I am dreaming. I am dreaming of freedom. You see that boy out there?"

Adaba nodded. Denmark was pointing out the front door into the street, where a half-dozen boys were congregated. Among them was Lew.

"More than three years ago, that boy told me that all I did was talk about freedom, that I had never fought to be free. I shall always be grateful to him for that. Because he was right. And I think it was because of that conversation that I decided to *do* something to achieve freedom for our people."

169

"But you *do* do something. You are helping black people to freedom—"

"No." Denmark shook his head vigorously. "Adaba, how long have I been working with you, smuggling runaways out of Charleston?"

"It's almost three years now."

"And in those three years, how many have I taken out?"

"I don't know. Dozens—"

"A few dozen. Sometimes none for months. Adaba, there are over twelve thousand slaves in Charleston alone —far more slaves than whites. How many slaves are *born* in Charleston each month? How many more are born than we manage to free?"

The answer was obvious, but Adaba didn't like it. "We do the best we can."

"And the best we can do is help a desperate few. And no matter how many we send to freedom, the number of slaves keeps growing. Adaba, you must see that we'll never defeat slavery by stealing a few thousand black people. Slavery is growing more massive each year, it is becoming more entrenched, it has become the very soul and body of this land that the white man sucks dry!"

Adaba knew that they were alone—Benjamin had left earlier—yet he looked furtively about and kept his voice lowered. Words, mere words, he knew, could be suicidal.

"And your answer is insurrection."

"Insurrection is inevitable. As inevitable as it was in Santo Domingo."

"But most insurrections fail. And black people die. No matter how many whites die first."

Denmark smiled grimly. "It's not only in insurrections that they die. You were speaking of when you were sixteen. In that year, Major General Youngblood led his troops into the Carolina swamps, looking for maroon camps—the camps you and your friends use to move slaves. He found them. He bragged that he captured or killed every single outlying slave in them."

"But we're still here—"

"For how long? You keep on the way you're going, and

sooner or later they're going to shoot or hang you. Now, I ask you this. If you must die, isn't it better to die for the millions who are in bondage rather than for a mere hand-ful?"

Adaba stood up from his chair. All at once the shop seemed oppressive, stifling. He sucked at the warm humid air, trying to draw more into his lungs than they would hold.

"Well, Adaba?"

"First of all, Denmark, I don't intend to get killed."

"You may not have any say in it."

"All right, maybe they will get me sooner or later. But that'll just be me. Me and maybe a few others. But if you're talking about an insurrection of thousands—if any-thing like that actually happened—"

"The city—the entire district—even the state—"

"It's impossible! They've got the patrols, and the city guards, and the militia. They've got the guns."

"Suppose they don't have the guns. Or suppose we have more. Suppose we get the guns first."

Adaba shook his head as if to clear it. All right, sup-pose. In all fairness, try to envision such a thing. The black majority of the city armed and rising up. Almost thirteen thousand slaves and another fifteen hundred free colored against twelve thousand whites. They might ac-tually succeed in seizing the city.

But then what? . . . All Adaba saw was slaughter. And ultimately, loss. He had only the vaguest idea of what Denmark had in mind, but surely it wasn't another Santo Domingo. Impossible.

He shook his head again. "Denmark, I'm trying to keep people alive. I can't free every slave, but I can free some who are in deep trouble. I may not live long doing it, but that's what I plan to keep on doing. For the rest of my life."

Denmark looked at him steadily, unblinkingly, as if searching for some chink, some flaw, in his defenses. Fi-nally he shrugged and smiled. "Well, I'm not going to give up on you, son. Some of us meet now and then and talk about it. I want you to meet with us."

171

"An insurrection cannot succeed."

"Maybe you're right. Maybe it can't. I've thought about it for a long time, but in working with you and your friends I've come to realize how little I know about such things. Now, you could help—"

"I don't know any more than you do."

"Oh, I think you do. More than you realize. You know how to organize in the safest way—"

"Denmark, I'm sorry. I will have nothing to do with any insurrection."

Denmark nodded agreeably. "Because you think it can't be successful."

"Exactly."

"Then show us why it can't be successful. Discuss the matter with us before we do something foolish and get ourselves hanged. Surely that's the least you can do for old friends—persuade them not to die needlessly."

That was true enough. If Denmark were serious about this, perhaps Adaba could keep someone from getting killed.

"All right," he said. "I'll talk with you and your friends."

The street was just beginning to fall into afternoon shadow when Lew saw Adaba come out of the shop. He called "Hey, boy!" and Adaba raised a hand and smiled and said "Hey, boy, yourself!" and kept going. One of the others kids asked, "Who's that smart-ass nigger?" and another said, "That's John Guerard, the richest nigger boy in town," and Lew said, "He's a good old boy. I knowed him all my life."

Smiling to himself, he watched the tall young black man disappear down the street. Lew had grown bored with the other kids and had been about to leave when he had seen Adaba entering the shop. He had waited for him to reappear. They didn't meet often anymore and seldom exchanged more than a greeting in passing, but Lew liked to feel that they were still friends.

He didn't even notice when the other boys disappeared. He was still just standing there, staring down the street, a

172

silly smile on his face (like a fool, he thought), when he realized that he was alone.

With Denmark Vesey glaring at him from the door of his shop.

Denmark stood with his arms crossed on his big chest. Slowly he raised his right arm and made a peremptory beckoning gesture to Lew.

Christ, what now, he thought. Just because he had stepped in the door of the goddamn shop? His first impulse was to walk away, but he had an idea that Denmark would interpret that as a retreat—which it would be. In the end, he simply walked across the street to the door of Denmark's shop.

His arms again crossed on his chest, Denmark backed through the doorway, and Lew followed him into the room. From his height, Denmark looked down on him, inspecting him from head to toe and back again. Well, Lew thought, I ain't gonna take no shit.

"Master Lewis," Denmark said, "I plan to work a little late here this evening. When will you have finished your supper?"

"I don't know," Lew said, surprised. "Six-thirty or seven. Maybe a little later."

Denmark nodded as if that would work out quite well.

"Good. As soon as you have finished, even if it's late, I want you to come back here. I'll be waiting."

"Well, I—I don't know if I can."

"Why not?"

Because it was Saturday, and he had planned to go up on the Neck and raise a little hell, that was why. And what in the world was Denmark Vesey doing ordering *him* to come back here to his shop on a Saturday evening? or any other time?

"Well—I don't know."

"Then I'll be expecting you."

"Is it important?"

The thick grizzled eyebrows over the fierce brown eyes raised in surprise. "Of course it's important. Or I wouldn't be asking you, would I? Please be here, Master Lewis. As early as possible, but no matter how late."

173

"Well . . ." Lew wondered why he was agreeing. "All right, I guess."

A faint smile came to Denmark's face, and somehow his eyes were not quite as fierce as they had been.

"How old are you now, Master Lewis? Seventeen?"

"Going *on* seventeen."

The eyes saddened. "So soon. You've grown into quite a likely lad, Master Lewis. For a white boy."

Praise from Denmark Vesey, if that was what it was, was the last thing Lew would have expected, and he was uncertain how to respond to it.

"Well . . . I think I better be going now."

"Yes, you do that. And Lewis . . ."

"Yes?"

"All things considered, perhaps you would be wise not to mention our meeting to anyone. Let it be our secret."

Lew reluctantly agreed—and left hurriedly.

He was angry with himself. Why had he allowed himself to be talked into returning to Denmark's shop? Why should he give up any part of his precious Saturday evening to the old carpenter? And what could Denmark possibly want from him? He didn't owe Denmark anything. And besides, the black man made him nervous—crazy old coot, glaring at the world and shaking his hammer in a raised fist. He was a class leader at the African Methodist Episcopal Church up in Hampstead, and who knew what went on there when the whites weren't watching? Some of the kids said they kidnapped children, both white and black, and *ate* them in weird voodoo rituals. Maybe Denmark was luring him off to be a victim!

Lew was strongly tempted to forget his promise and not return to the shop, but of course he did nothing of the sort. As the last of dusk faded into darkness, he found himself following at the heels of Denmark Vesey through a part of Charleston that was unfamiliar to him. A light or two glimmered in almost every house along the street. Laughter and music came from some of the houses, and voices called and chattered from window

174

to window, Saturday night sounds floating on the warm August air.

They were walking west on the north side of the street. The little wooden "single houses," in the Charleston fashion, faced west, the piazza and front door of each one facing the back of the next. The "ends" of the houses were to the street, doors giving admittance to the piazzas and small fenced-off yards. Denmark came to a sudden halt.

"I'm going next door," he said. "I have a wife there. Her master hates me for the gospel I preach, and he took her away from me. I don't get to see her often, just when he's away." It was unlike Denmark to make such explanations, but the controlled anger in his voice told why he made one now. "I hope, Master Lewis, that your parents don't expect you home early."

"On Saturday night?" Lew was incredulous. " 'Course not! Besides, my daddy lets me do pretty much what I please, and my momma died a couple of years ago."

"Oh, yes, of course. I'm sorry, I had forgotten. Then it will be quite some time before you're missed, won't it?"

Alarms went off in Lew's breast. "Denmark, what do you *want* from me!"

"Not a thing."

Denmark turned to the piazza door before which they stood and gave it a loud thump. It opened almost at once, but Lew could see nothing in the darkness beyond it. Before he could resist, Denmark had pushed him up the few steps and into that darkness, and a slim female figure came into view.

"I don't know what you see in him," Denmark grumbled somewhere behind him, "but for what he's worth, here he is."

Lew heard Denmark close the piazza door. He leaned forward to look into that familiar face—the softly dimpled cheeks, the alert eyes, the mouth that seemed always on the verge of a smile.

"Evening, Mr. Lewis," she said.

"Oh, lord!" he said. "Oh, balls o' fire! I mean—good evening, Jovita!"

Four

Denmark was right, Adaba thought: escape took only a few to freedom; the growing number were left behind, and there was no sign that slavery in the South was approaching its end. Instead the shackles grew heavier.

But insurrection? Could it possibly accomplish anything?

He asked his father that evening as they sat on the piazza drinking coffee after an early supper: "If it's true that the South will never give up slavery, do you see any hope at all—even the slightest hope—in insurrection?"

The light was fading rapidly. The coral vine was in bloom, and the Guerard garden had the rich smell of damp earth and late-summer greenery. Light shone from the house next door, and an occasional face passed by a window, though the neighbors, mindful of their "north-side manners," never intruded by looking out into the garden. It was not the time nor the place for thoughts of violence.

His father turned his head very slowly toward Adaba. His eyes were large. His cup rattled on its cup plate, as he set it aside on the little table that stood between them.

"Any hope in—my God, boy, don't let me hear you even say that word!"

"White people use it all the time. Insurrection and malaria must take up at least half of their thoughts."

"But you're not white. When you use it, you're asking for trouble. John, you're not . . . not involved in anything—"

"No, sir."

His father was relieved that he had been spending more time in Charleston lately. Of course, he had no idea of how Adaba spent his time.

"No, I'm not involved in any insurrection, and I don't plan to be. But I suppose some black people give as

176

much thought to the possibility as the whites do. What if there were an insurrection, Father? A big one, let's say, that inescapably touched you. What would you do?"

"I'd fight it," his father said fiercely. "I'd do my damnedest to help smash it and see the leaders hanged. I'd put the rope around their necks myself."

"But why? You don't believe in slavery—"

"I, my father, his father before him, worked all our lives for what we have. An insurrection could threaten all of that. Not only for us, but for our people. We have over two hundred people, an entire village, who live far better than most blacks in South Carolina. Even better than a great many whites. There's no way they'll ever be free except insofar as they're free within the little plantation world we've built for them, but at least they have that."

"But some of those people hate you."

"I know that. They hate my guts because they see beyond the confines of that private little world and blame me for being their master. But nonetheless I care for them. They're *my* people. And I intend that there shall always be a Guerard here to look after them as long as slavery lasts. In the next generation it will be Philip or, if something happens to him, David. The rest of you—I'll fill your pockets and Rose's with all the money I can, and you can get out of this godforsaken country."

"But I love this godforsaken country," Adaba said sadly.

"That's the hell of it. So do I."

Faces passed the windows on the other side of the garden, bright blond faces, like faces on gold coins—faces that smiled at the Guerards on the street but never looked into their private garden.

Adaba finished his coffee and stood up.

"You're going out?" his father asked.

"Just for a little while. To walk off my supper."

"Don't stay out too late," his father cautioned automatically. "Keep an eye out for the guard, and be back before the curfew—"

"Oh, father!" Adaba laughed again. "Don't you know that half of the guards work in grogshops? You buy a

177

drink in the right shops from time to time, they know enough to let you alone. Picking you up is bad for business!"

His father shook his head. "Our incorruptible city guard . . . "

No doubt his father was right. No insurrection would ever result in the freeing of the slaves. Emancipation was inevitable, but the Southern white would fight it until the last possible moment.

But black people were not fools—they knew perfectly well that the world was changing and leaving the South behind. They read between the lines of the imperfectly censored newspapers. Pamphlets from the North were secretly read, exchanged, and read again until they fell apart. The better informed, and there were many of them, endlessly discussed the slave-uprising in Santo Domingo, the Congressional debates over the question of slavery in Missouri—that "fire bell in the night," as Jefferson called it—and the speeches of Senator Rufus King, "the black man's friend." With such ferment beneath the surface, weren't insurrection attempts inevitable?

Lost in his thoughts, Adaba had had no idea of where his feet were taking him, until he realized that for long minutes he had been standing across the street from the dark offices of Mr. Ulysses P. Gore. It was not the first time he had found himself here. Queen Street was quiet now and almost deserted. The nearest person was a middle-aged black woman who leaned against Mr. Gore's wall, taking the evening air.

What had it been like for Gilly to arrive here, Adaba wondered. When had she been informed that she was to be sold? At some point she would have to know, and then she would most certainly be terrified. By the time she was in Mr. Ulysses P. Gore's offices, she would guess her fate, and then . . .

"Don't you cry, boy."

Adaba looked at the middle-aged black woman in surprise. He hadn't noticed her crossing the street.

"Why, I ain't crying, Auntie."

"Yes, you is. Think I don't know 'bout you, Adaba?"

Adaba smiled. "Think I don't know 'bout you, Aunt Ora?"

They both laughed.

"Him ain't here. Him you want to kill."

"Why, I don't want to kill nobody, Auntie. I never wanted to kill nobody in my life."

Again they laughed, soft laughter in the darkness, and the woman touched Adaba's arm.

"Don't you worry. Him die."

"Don't we all, Auntie, don't we all."

The woman shook her head. "No. Him die soon."

"Oh?" Adaba looked at her with new interest.

"Him waste away slow in great pain. Doctor say cancer." The woman sneered at the doctor's ignorance. "Cancer!"

"Ain't cancer, Auntie?"

Suddenly in the dark street the woman's eyes were bright with hatred. Her nostrils flared. Her lips drew far back on her teeth.

"Momma Brigitte!"

A tremor of irrational fear swept through Adaba and slowly subsided. So Aunt Ora, the conjurewoman, had put a voodoo curse on Mr. Gore, and he was dying. Adaba could almost believe that the cancer was brought on by the curse. Why not?

"You good boy, Adaba. Many make spells for you find your Gilly. But . . ."

The woman shrugged. Adaba understood. The gods were often capricious, and they always demanded payment in full. Their prices were often high.

"I thank you again, Aunt Ora."

Adaba bent forward to kiss her forehead. Her face was blank again. She turned from him and walked slowly back across the street.

Adaba continued on his way.

Denmark opened the door and stood framed in the light. "Welcome, Adaba," he said, "welcome!"

The impossible was happening. After all this time, after all these months, these years, of looking and hoping and dreaming, here he was—*in bed jaybird naked with a girl!*

"You *sure* your sister and her husband ain't coming back soon?"

"Delia and Benjamin, they like to go visiting Saturday night, 'cept when they have a party here. Sometime they don't come back all night long."

"Goddamn!"

The trouble was that he didn't really know where to start. After half an hour of sitting together on the piazza, they had somehow managed to get up here to Jovita's bedroom. Another two minutes, and they had managed to get their clothes off and bounce onto the bed. But what now? What should he do first? Oh, God, the possibilities! Lew had hardly got started nuzzling one pretty nipple while tickling the other, when he had an irresistible urge to switch and nuzzle the second while tickling the first. And he had hardly got started doing that, when he had an irresistible urge to grab Jovita's ass.

Jovita giggled. "You *sure* you done this before?"

"Oh, sure. Hundreds of times!"

"You ain't hardly old enough to done it hundreds of times."

"Well, dozens, I mean."

Ah, the sweet explorations. He had had a fair idea of how girls were put together, but he hadn't seen one in her birthday suit for at least five years. And those he had seen before had been *little* girls, and he had been, at best, an evil little boy. Jovita was a *big* girl, and he was now an evil *big* boy.

No. Not evil at all. He cared for Jovita and felt that she genuinely cared for him too, and this was ever so much better than his fantasies. How could he possibly feel evil? But with this feast spread out before him—oh, God!— *what should he do next?*

"Now, Lewis, honey," Jovita said at one point, when his eagerness threatened to be self-defeating, "you just compose yourself for a time and let your Jovita pleasure you."

And pleasure him she did, in ways he had never imagined, tickling and stroking and scratching him. "Oh, Jo-

180

vita," he moaned as she nibbled away at his happy flesh, "how did you ever learn such things!"

"From my sister. She say mostly you got to take turns. And mostly a man like what you like, and you like what he like. And you got to take your time, 'cause haste make waste."

"Oh, Jov*i-i-ita-a-a!*"

And so they took turns, giving each other what they themselves liked, and taking their time. Lew had a strong suspicion that, thanks to her sister, Jovita knew far more about this kind of thing than he did, but he would never have admitted it. Instead, he paid close attention and tried like hell to learn. Fast.

At one point, he was surprised. He found that it was not as he had been led to expect. Fearing he might be revealing his ignorance, he nevertheless said, "I thought you told me you never done it before."

"I never. But Delia, she say I should fool 'round with it and get rid of it slow and easy, or it hurt something awful the first time, and that ain't no fun. You don't want that, do you?"

"No, course not."

"So I do like she say. And 'sides, she say I do that, and I can put in some sponge she give me with voodoo medicine. Ain't so likely to make a baby."

Lew had been carefully avoiding the thought of baby-making, and though he had little faith in voodoo medicine, he found this information heartening.

"God," he said cheerfully, "I can't get over it! How we can lie here naked together, both of us rarin' to go, and yet discuss all these interesting things so calmly!"

But even the most interesting intellectual discussions had to have an end, and so did this one. Lew was certain he could endure these pleasures no longer. His heart raced, his brain dissolved. He and Jovita, summer slippery with sweat, slithered against each other like eels one last time. He found himself shoving her knees apart and rising up over her on his own. His engorged six inches threatened to burst, as she drew them to her.

And then, in an instant of sheer terror, it hit him.

181

He was supposed to put it in *that!*
His . . . *in hers!*
All the way in!
He couldn't. He simply couldn't do it.
And his li'l ol' pecker jes' curled up and died.

It was a small, cluttered parlor, furnished with old scarred, often-repaired furniture discarded by the master: a few chairs, a sofa, a thread-bare carpet. Tattered curtains at the open east windows moved slightly in the breeze from the neighboring yard. It was a fairly typical servants' house in the city, less pleasant than some, but clean and habitable. If Denmark's wife, or anyone else, was in the house, she kept discreetly out of the way.

Adaba found four men waiting for him: Denmark, Peter Poyas, and two others he didn't know. "Two of Governor Bennett's people," Denmark said, "Rolla and Ned Bennett. This is Adaba Guerard."

The man called Rolla Bennett frowned. He was a big man who sat back in his chair, very self-possessed, as if he owned the house; a man who required explanations. "Marcus Guerard's boy?" he asked Denmark.

"The same."

"I would have guessed," Ned Bennett said, "that he was not one of us." Smaller than Rolla, Ned sat quite erect yet relaxed, a man in complete control of himself. The stern expression of his face never changed.

"I'm not," Adaba said. "I'm not one of you."

"But he will be," Denmark said quickly.

Rolla's frown deepened. "If he's not one of us, what's he doing here?"

"I hope," Denmark said, "he will be persuaded to join us. Meanwhile, I believe he may have some useful things to teach us."

"He can be trusted," Peter Poyas said, speaking for the first time. Poyas was a ship carpenter, a work-hardened bald bull of a man, stoic and impassive in his manner. "I know him. And if Denmark asked him here, he has good reason."

"But what has he got to teach us?" Rolla asked.

"Listen," Denmark said, "and learn."

182

An insurrection. A slave uprising not only in Charleston but throughout the lowcountry and maybe the upcountry as well. A great march from the plantations and farms that would converge on Charleston—and perhaps even inspire other such uprisings throughout the South. As he heard the immense scope of Denmark's dream, Adaba found it difficult to believe that such an insurrection could take place, let alone be successful, and yet he found himself caught up in the planning.

"We'll divide into three, or four, or five regiments," Denmark said, "depending on our final plan. Each regiment will be divided into companies, and each regiment and company will have specific tasks to accomplish."

"Will the leaders of the regiments know each other's tasks?" Adaba asked.

Denmark shook his head. "No. As we move toward a final plan, you'll find me telling you less and less. Because the less each of you knows about what the others are to do, the safer we'll be."

Adaba disagreed. "Each of your regimental leaders must know the entire plan. That way, even if you and most of them are killed or captured, there will still be somebody left to take over and lead. But the leaders of Ned's companies, to give an example, need not know what the leaders of Rolla's companies are to do. The leaders of Ned's companies only need to know each other's tasks, so that they can take over. . . ."

He was drawing on his knowledge of maroon life and the escape trails: never tell more than you have to, yet at the same time always try to leave someone who can take over for you. Finally, the others were beginning to understand what he was here for.

"You'll need weapons," Adaba said. "Where are you going to get them?"

"One of the first things we must do," Denmark said, "is break into the arsenal. There are more arms there than anywhere else in the state."

"But that's right by the guardhouse," Ned objected.

"Exactly. We seize the arms and kill the greater part of the City Guard at the same time. And there are other sources of arms. The Neck company of the militia stores several hundred muskets on King Street Road, and Duquercron's store has several hundred more. Then there are the gunsmiths' shops. And of course almost every household has some arms which the servants can seize if they're with us and act quickly enough."

"But the whites will still have more guns than we do," Rolla said. "It will be impossible for us to get anything like half of the guns in the city."

"That's true," Adaba said, "but you forget that if your plans succeed at all, you'll have the advantage of surprise and organization." He was startled to hear himself encouraging their enterprise.

"The bigger the insurrection, the more chance that it will be betrayed to the whites," Adaba said. "You'll have to watch them. You'll want to know what, if anything, they've learned about your plans."

"Governor Bennett trusts Ned and me completely," Rolla said. "I'm in charge of protecting his family when he's away. We'll know if he has heard anything about our plans."

"What about the intendant?"

"There's nobody in the intendant's house we can trust," Peter said. "Nobody at all."

"However," Denmark said, "his house is just two blocks to the east of mine, as the governor's is two blocks to the west. It should be possible to observe any unusual activity there. And of course we'll be able to see any unusual activity back and forth between the two houses even if Rolla and Ned have no opportunity to tell us about it."

As Adaba listened, he could not help but imagine what it would be like if Denmark actually succeeded. . . .

" 'And they utterly destroyed all that was in the city,' " Denmark quoted Joshua 6:21, " 'both man and woman, young and old, and ox, and sheep, and ass, with the edge of the sword.' "

Never before in his life had he been so humiliated. "I swear to God it never happened to me before!"

"Oh, that all right," Jovita said comfortingly. "Delia, she tell me it happen lots the first time."

"But this *ain't* my first time! I swear to God, I musta
184

done it a hundred times, and nothing like this happened to me!"

What was he supposed to do now? Get dressed and leave? Leave Jovita here thinking he was no kind of man at all? That this was his first time ever, for Christ's sake, and he was just a dumb kid, too scared to do anything?

What could he do, then, what, what, what . . . ?

Oddly enough, he did the intelligent thing and simply went to sleep.

And then the miracle happened.

How long he had slept, he had no idea, but suddenly he was aware of three things: the total darkness behind his eyelids, the kiss on his chest, and the hand that touched his newly aroused flesh. In that moment there was no thought, only sensation.

Oh, marvelous . . . !

He lay perfectly still, feigning sleep, afraid to move and perhaps break the spell. Ain't nothing to be scared of, he thought, smiling in the darkness. Nothing to be scared of at all.

"Lewis?" Jovita whispered, and he wanted to laugh, but he kept silent. "Oh, sweet Lewis . . . "

Then her kiss was moving over his chest, teeth catching at his nipple, and the liquid sounds that came from her throat excited him almost as much as her caresses. Before long he could lie still no longer. Crying out, he opened his eyes and reached for Jovita.

Blindly, he reached for her, but she slipped through his hands. Suddenly she was over and straddling him. Moonlight painted Jovita's body, accenting each bright curve and bowl and plane that emerged from the darkness. Her mouth was open wide, her eyes closed, her head thrown back, as she brought him to touch her where she most liked to be touched. She gasped, whimpered, as she moved against him.

There was no panic now. Instead, he felt oddly calm. Her head fell forward, her face shadowed, and she joined her body to his. . . .

So this was what it was like. . . .

Grateful, he slid his hands up her body to cup her hard-nippled breasts. She leaned into his hands and began

185

moving against him, slowly, rhythmically, and he pressed back. That, he realized, was all he need do: sense her wishes, her needs, and respond to them.

Time lost meaning. Images of Jovita as he had seen her earlier floated through his mind, mingling with images yet to be seen. "Oh, Jovita," he heard himself murmur, "I do love you."

It was as if he had given her a signal. She pressed closer to him and ground her mouth hungrily, bruisingly, against his. Then abruptly she stopped. The night seemed to stand still.

He pressed up against her.

She cried out, and as suddenly as she had stopped, she began again, rapidly, savagely, with all her strength. And she took him with her. He had no choice and didn't want one. He was lost, consumed, in that final fire.

A miracle.

"'Behold, the day of the Lord cometh,'" Denmark Vesey quoted Zechariah 14:1-3, "'and thy spoil shall be divided in the midst of thee. For I will gather all nations against Jerusalem to battle; and the city shall be taken, and the houses rifled, and the women ravished; and half of the city shall go forth into captivity. . . . Then shall the Lord go forth, and fight against those nations, as when he fought in the day of battle.'"

Five

Something was wrong. Adaba felt it the moment he stepped into Monday Gell's shop. He hadn't seen Monday in over two months, not since the last time he had been in Charleston, but the harnessmaker was looking at him resentfully, almost angrily.

"You ain't very happy to see me, Monday."

"I suppose to be?"

186

"I just come to wish you a Happy New Year. Hope your Christmas was nice—"

"What you want, Adaba? Just tell me what you want and be on your way."

Adaba looked at his friend in surprise. Ordinarily Monday was the most amiable of men, and he had never before given Adaba so much as a cross word. Now the lamplight made his face a stern black mask.

"Hey, that any way to greet an old friend?"

Monday returned to mending a worn bridle on his workbench, his hands moving agitatedly. "Denmark send you 'round to talk to me some more?"

"Monday, what you talking about? I ain't even seen Denmark since October."

"Yes, well, I see him this morning. And he say Ned and Rolla Bennett is in it and Jack Purcell and Peter Poyas. And he say you gonna be in it too."

So Denmark was still talking insurrection. Damned old fool, Adaba thought. Going to get himself hanged yet, if anyone takes him seriously.

After the meeting in August, the only meeting he had attended, Adaba had felt something between disappointment and relief. Denmark had grand dreams, but having heard them, Adaba simply couldn't believe the old carpenter could make them come true. They required a great deal of time and long-range planning, and the chances were that the enthusiasm of his followers would wane long before the dreams were realized. Furthermore, it had seemed to Adaba that there was considerable vagueness as to just how an insurrection could be used to obtain permanent freedom. Once Charleston was seized—what then?

Adaba dropped into a chair. "Monday, if you talking about what I think, I ain't gonna be in nothing."

Monday shot him a disbelieving look.

"In nothing, Monday. And what's more, I love old Denmark, but I don't like him using my name. I ain't about to get myself strung up for a bad nigger. Just what did Denmark say to you?"

Monday threw the bridle down on his workbench. "He come here this morning. Say he want to talk to me. He say he is trying to gather the blacks to see what we can do to overcome the whites. He ask me to join, so I ask if he got a plan. We talk for a time, and he tell me he got a plan for a big uprising. We take over the city, maybe the whole state." Monday took a big breath. "And we kill them all."

"What?"

"Kill all the whites. Every man, every woman, every child. I say, 'Denmark, you crazy? I'se good Christian man. Maybe I kill a white man I must, but I can't kill no woman, no child!' But he say it got to be, they all got to die. Don't the whites kill all them black woman and child in Florida? Don't General Jackson kill all them red woman and child? The black and the red, the whites kill them like animals. 'But a child,' I say, 'I can't kill no child!' And he say, 'What's the sense of killing the louse and leaving the nit?'"

Adaba was shocked. He knew Denmark's ferocity sprang from his concern for his own people, but he had never heard the carpenter sound so cold-blooded. He could understand Monday's being deeply upset.

"He got to be just talking."

"No, he ain't just talking! Him and some others, they planning it! He say it be the biggest insurrection since in New York, back in 'forty-one, eighty years ago. Only *much* bigger than that. And this one succeed!"

"Monday," Adaba said, "I don't care what Denmark told you, I ain't part of no plan to kill women and children, and I ain't gonna be."

"But you closer to Denmark than anyone. You like his own son."

"I don't care. I know him and some others been talking about this for a while—"

"You know Denmark been hinting 'round 'bout it for two, three years now?"

"But in all that time, what happened? Nothing. And it don't sound to me like nothing happened since he talked to me about it last summer. It's still just Denmark and a few of his friends. And he's gonna keep on talking to people like you and me, and we're gonna keep on saying no, and he's gonna have to give up."

Monday shook his head. "You wrong. Denmark been thinking 'bout this a long time. Now he made up his mind.

188

He going do it no matter what. He going to get followers —he preach at them, cuss them, josh them, even lie to them, but he get them. He going to make plenty people, black and white, die—unless somebody stop him!"

No, Adaba thought, not him—you. You're the threat, Monday, not Denmark.

"How do you plan to stop him?"

Avoiding Adaba's eyes, Monday picked at the bridle on his workbench. "I don't know."

"But you do know if you talk to your master about this —if you talk to any white people—Denmark could get hung. And those others too."

Monday shrugged. "Oh, maybe not—"

"Maybe not! I say, you tell anybody, and you put Denmark on the gallows! You say otherwise, you're lying to yourself and to me too. You're gonna get Denmark killed!"

Monday seemed to be holding his breath. He held it for a long time. Then, slowly, he seemed to collapse.

"I don't know what to do."

"Then do nothing."

Monday raised his head. He nodded. "I ain't going say nothing to Mr. Gell nor any other. But *you* got to stop Denmark. Anybody can, you can."

Adaba wasn't at all sure he could stop Denmark from doing anything. But he said, "All right. I'll try. And you remember your promise."

Monday nodded again. "I remember my promise. And you remember yours."

The city seemed to twinkle in the crisp evening air, as nightfall hid soot, grime, and mud. As Adaba hurried along the familiar streets for the first time in months, window after window lit up, making Charleston seem gay with the spirit of the holidays. He felt almost as if the city were welcoming him personally, but his pleasure was diminished by his worries about Denmark.

The lower level of the house at 20 Bull Street was lit up when he got there. He used the knocker a couple of times, and a moment later Denmark opened the door and admitted him to the piazza. The carpenter seemed happy and excited. He clapped Adaba's shoulders.

"You've been away too long, boy."

"I was way north this time. I came back to see my family for Christmas. And to see you."

"Welcome. Come on inside and join the others."

A burst of laughter came through the thin wall of the house. Adaba glanced through the window. There were at least half a dozen men in the parlor, including Ned and Rolla Bennett, Peter Poyas, and Gullah Jack. So Gullah Jack had joined the conspiracy.

"You holding a meeting, Denmark?"

"Yes. Our plans are now developing rapidly."

"Then I don't want to go in there. I went to one of your meetings, and that was enough."

Denmark laughed. "Yes, and I recall that you found yourself quite enjoying it. You'll join us sooner or later."

"I don't think so." Adaba shook his head worriedly. "Denmark, you ought to know that even if the worst you do is just talk about insurrection, you're taking the most god-awful chances."

"'Just talk'? You really don't think we're going to do anything, do you, Adaba?"

Adaba didn't care to offend his friend by throwing a "no" in his face. Instead, he said, "I don't see how you can. How many followers did you have when you asked me to that meeting last August?"

"Four. The three you saw and Jack Purcell."

"And how many do you have now?"

"Seven—not including Monday Gell and, of course, you."

"In four months only three people have joined you?"

"In four months only three people *out of the five I have asked* have joined me," Denmark said, as if he knew exactly what Adaba was trying to prove and saw the fallacy. "And the other two, you and Monday Gell, will join me sooner or later."

"And even if we do, that will give you a total of how many followers? Nine. That's a long way from the four or five regiments you were talking about."

"Six," Denmark said. He leaned forward in the darkness and put a hand on Adaba's shoulder. "Listen to me. I've spent over three years questioning our people, until I was morally certain they would follow me and my lieutenants when the time came. I've spent the last several months gathering those lieutenants together and working out a plan of action. We are now refining our plans and selecting our secondary leaders—Batteau Bennett, Mingo Harth, others. Preparation is all. Months, even years of preparation. Then a few weeks of gathering our troops— and we strike!"

"When do you expect to do that?"

"In the spring, or next summer at the latest."

"And how many followers do you expect to have?"

Denmark's smile was almost sweet. "Now, how can I tell you that? If each of ten men recruits another nine men, that is a hundred men. And if each of the hundred recruits nine more, that is one thousand and ten men, far more than we need to strike. But once we are marching in the streets, even if we are only a few hundred strong, don't you know that thousands more will join us?" Denmark grew more animated and his eyes brighter.

He's mad, Adaba thought.

But he could not believe there was madness in Denmark Vesey. He had known the man too well for too long, and there was a terrible plausibility in what Denmark was saying. And the vision was tempting . . . until he remembered his conversation with Monday Gell.

"On the march," he said, "and killing every white who stands in the way. And even those that don't. Even the most innocent."

Something happened to Denmark's face. It seemed to darken. The eyes held terrible visions, and he turned away into the shadows of the piazza as if to hide them.

"You've spoken to Monday Gell."

"I was on my way here from your shop. I was looking for you."

Denmark paced the piazza and returned to the light of the window. "I have thought of holding hostages, and perhaps we shall do that. But when the killing starts, I don't think I shall be able to stop it. And I don't think I should even try. When generations of black anger are unleashed

191

in this country, blood is bound to flow. And we know that if it comes to a pitched battle between us and the whites —as it may at some point—the whites won't have the slightest compunction about killing our children."

"Oh, I think some will."

"History shows otherwise." Denmark laughed sadly and shook his head. "Strange, isn't it? When the white man kills even the weakest and most innocent African or Indian, he justifies it by saying that the black and the red are, after all, only savages. And when the black or the red retaliates by doing the same thing to the white, the white calls it *proof* that the colored races are savages. . . . Very well, we shall be savage. As savage as the whites."

Adaba shook his head. "Then I can't be with you. Because I don't think I could ever kill anyone. I'm in the business of saving lives, not taking them."

"So am I—saving black lives. But that means taking white lives."

"I just don't think I could do it. I don't have it in me."

"When the time comes, you will have no choice. 'He that is not with me, is against me.' Do you really think you can stand aside? The whites too will say you are either loyal to them or against them. There will be no neutrality when blood is running in the streets."

Adaba saw now that there was no chance of fulfilling his promise to Monday. Nothing he could possibly say would stop Denmark. Nevertheless he said, "Denmark, it's not going to happen. You'll be betrayed before it happens."

"Perhaps. I shall do my best to prevent that."

"When Monday realizes I haven't been able to stop you, he'll tell Mr. Gell, and—"

"No, he won't, any more than you will." Denmark laughed. He sounded supremely confident. "I know Monday better than he knows himself. He's a good man, a kindly man. He will agonize long. But in the end he will be with us. As you will be, whether you know it or not."

Adaba shook his head. "If not Monday, then someone else. And they'll kill you, Denmark."

"I must take that chance. I shall die a happy man, if only I can see my people marching through the streets of

192

Charleston . . . and know that they are standing up before the world like free men and saying, *I shall be a slave no longer!*"

Lew's fear was not merely of missing her but of losing her. It had been bad enough, being separated from Jovita over the Christmas and New Year holiday season; the two months to come seemed unending. Would she have forgotten him, would she have found another, before he returned to Charleston? The fact that it was once again the Saturday evening before Race Week—the same evening he had caused the separation of Adaba and Gilly four years earlier—was surely an ill omen.

But Lew found Jovita's house full of warmth and brightness and laughter when he arrived that evening. Delia and Benjamin were entertaining. Lew was a familiar figure to the dozen or so guests, accepted with a certain fond amusement as "Jovita's boy," and it was difficult for him and Jovita to slip away, up the stairs to her room. But once there, they immediately fell into each other's arms, pulled clothing away, and with hardly a word, spent the next half hour making love—a task to which Lew brought a special, troubled intensity. Then, temporarily exhausted, they lay together in the rumpled bed, half-asleep, for another quarter hour, until Jovita said, "Lewis, what you fretting 'bout?"

"I got to go away again," he said miserably. He had been trying to avoid the thought. "I got to go away again, and this time I reckon I won't get back till early May. That's more'n two months!"

Jovita lay over him, her rich brown breasts soft on his white chest, and traced the aureole of his nipple with a fingertip. "Why?" she asked. "Why you go 'way?"

"That goddamn Georgiana, my sister. Ever since she found out about us from one of her housemaids last fall, she been after my daddy and me. After my daddy to take me back to Jessamine. 'Disgraceful!' she says." Lew mockingly imitated his sister. "'Mah own brothah, chasin' aftah little colahed doxies lahk common trash! Oh, mah Lawd, mah Lawd, whear will it all ee-yend!'"

Jovita giggled.

"It ain't so funny as I make it sound. I say I got to stay in school here, but she says I can go to the academy near Jessamine. I say our daddy got to stay here for city council meetings, but she says he can always come into the city for important meetings, same as others on the council. Just got to save my soul, that woman. Says I stay away two months, and you gonna have some other young buck in your bed." He paused, feeling the pain of the thought. What if it were true? "You ain't gonna have another, are you, Jovita?"

"No," Jovita said softly. "Ain't going have none but you, Lewis, long as you wants me."

"Ain't never gonna want anyone but you, Jovita."

Jovita smiled, but her eyes were sad in the lamplight. "Oh, yes," she said.

"It's true. Ain't never gonna want anyone else. You're the only one in the world for me."

"Till some nice white girl come along."

"No! I mean it!"

"But you only a boy, Lewis. How you know what you mean?"

"I love you, Jovita! And I'm gonna keep you mine! I'm gonna—I'm gonna marry you!" There, he had said it.

Jovita cocked her head at him and smiled, sweetly chiding. "*You?* marry a *black* gal?"

"Hell, I won't be the first white man with a black wife. You know that."

"But you take a black wife, your white friends, they ain't going talk to you never again."

"I don't give a shit. I'll have my own plantation and my own people, and they're all I care about. Taking good care of them, like I promised my daddy. And being with you."

"All right." Jovita traced more circles on his chest.

"You believe me?"

"I believe you."

But he had a feeling that her belief was qualified. She would not be surprised if the belief proved wrong. As if to convince her, he drew her more tightly to him, kissing her about the eyes. Her mouth went to his throat, and his hand slid down her spine, and for some reason he felt close to weeping.

194

"Goddamn," he said miserably, "how was I to know I'd fall so goddamn hard in love with the very first gal I ever . . ." Too late he caught himself, and he felt the sudden tension in Jovita's body.

She lifted her head to look into his eyes. "The first, Lewis? I was your first?"

He struggled to find some way to take back or modify what he had said, but he knew she would see through him.

"Aw, shoot, Jovita . . ."

"Whyn't you tell me I was your first?"

". . . Didn't want you to think I was a dumb kid."

"But I wouldn't think that, no matter what." Jovita put her lips firmly to his and held them there for a moment. It struck him that her kisses were much more a woman's kisses than they had been on their first night together. "I wouldn't never think that, Lewis," she repeated after a moment. "I'se glad I was the first for you."

"Aw, you ain't glad. . . ."

"Yes, I is. I *am*. Don't rightly know why, but I am."

"Well, then . . . I'm glad it slipped out. I'd ruther be honest with you, Jo. I don't like lying and watching my tongue. And it ain't right to lie to someone you love. I'd like us to be honest with each other always."

The tension he had felt a few moments before seemed to return to Jovita's body. Then, slowly, she sat up on the bed. Crossing her legs, she faced Lew. The fire was low, but she didn't seem to notice the chilliness of the room.

"You feel like that . . . reckon I better tell you something."

Lew felt a wave of apprehension.

"I lied to you, Lewis. You was *not* the first one for me."

Lew put a forearm over his eyes, trying not to appear upset.

"You had lots of fellows?"

"No. Just one."

"When?"

" 'Bout a year 'fore you."

"You like him?"

"Some. He was always after me, and he got me all bothered, and Delia say she figure I'se 'bout ready for some fun, so finally I let him."

"Here?"

"No. In a livery stable near Denmark's shop."

That was some consolation, though not much. This room was still theirs and theirs alone. Lew asked the hard question.

"Did you like doing it with him?"

"*No!*" The answer was sharp and immediate. Lew removed his forearm from his eyes and looked at Jovita in surprise.

"You didn't?"

"He *hurt* me! He hurt me so bad, that boy! And it didn't seem to matter to him at all. He was so het up, he just wanted to do it again right away, no matter *how* much it hurt me. And then I know all he care about is his li'l ol' cock—he don't care 'bout me at all!"

Lew felt a pang of guilt. Sometimes it seemed to him that all *he* cared about was *his* li'l ol' cock, that that wayward implement ruled him. But still he did love Jovita, and guilt was overcome by a rising wave of elation.

"And you didn't like it *at all?*"

"It was awful! I didn't even want to look at a boy for more'n a year after that. I was scared they was all going hurt me. You was the first one I even look at after that."

"But *I* don't hurt you."

She smiled slightly. She looked down at that shared toy, lifted it, and began bringing it back to life. "No," she said, "you sure 'nough don't."

He sighed with pleasure. "So in a way I *was* your first."

She didn't have to answer. Uncrossing her legs, she laid one across his chest and pulled his hand up between them.

Much later, but before they had finished, he held her tightly, impaled under him, his mouth roving over her face, and said, "There ain't gonna be no one else while I'm away, is there, Jovita?"

"No. Never nobody but you."

"Nobody for me neither. Nobody till I get back to you. Ain't never gonna let you go. Never, never, never . . ."

Arriving at the maroon camp at sunset one April day, Adaba observed with satisfaction that the corn and the vegetables had been planted. It was amazing how much good living could be scratched out of little patches of land abandoned as useless by all but a few outlying blacks. And the blacks took as much pride and pleasure in the results of their labor as any wealthy planter did in his crops.

It felt good to be back; as good as it felt, after a few weeks or months in the hills, to return to the city. Gavin Murdock helped Adaba unload his mule, curry it, and clean its hooves, and by the time they were done, Adaba's stomach was begging to be fed. The smell of the stew pot over the open fire made his hunger almost painful.

"Must be a lot of happy black people in Charleston," Murdock said, as they finished their meal sitting out under a tree. "You didn't bring nobody with you."

"Denmark didn't have nobody for me, Mr. Murdock."

"He ain't had nobody—for a long time."

"Well . . . you know what he's been thinking about these days." Adaba set his plate aside. "You know, I think he's gonna try it."

"You used to figure it was mostly talk." The moonlight made Murdock's beard look whiter than ever.

"It ain't just talk now. Not anymore. He ain't doing hardly any carpentering, he's spending all his time traveling around the countryside recruiting followers. And he's finding them too—it ain't just a handful of friends anymore. I've seen two and three dozen men in his house at the same time. And he holds big meetings at maybe half a dozen other places. I don't know how he does it without the whites finding out what's going on, but they don't. Denmark says that as far as they're concerned the meetings are just a bunch of goddamn niggers getting together for a sociable."

Murdock laughed. "He set a date yet?"

"Not yet. But it won't be long. He's collecting weapons. He's having his blacksmith friends make pike heads and bayonets to mount on poles, and the poles are being cut and hidden. Bacchus Hammet and Lot Forrester are getting some explosives for him. And he's even having some wigs made from white men's hair. He figures that with wigs, and in the dark, some of them can pass for white, and that'll make it easier to kill the guards at the guardhouse and the arsenal."

"Sounds like Denmark's got just about everything figured."

"I don't know." Adaba shook his head. "Some of it sounds crazy to me. Gullah Jack is collecting crab claws. He's going to tell his men to eat nothing but parched corn and ground nuts on the morning before the attack and to put the crab claws in their mouths, and that way they can't be wounded."

"Makes sense," Murdock said, to Adaba's surprise. Murdock saw the look on his face. "Well, he's a sorcerer, ain't he? a conjureman? and his followers believe in him, don't they?"

"Ain't no doubt some do. Most, maybe."

"If a man feels protected, he's more likely to act bold. And if he acts bold, he's more likely to survive than if he's running scared all the time. And survive or not, he's more likely to do what is expected of him. Your friend Gullah Jack knows what he's about."

They sat in silence for a time, enjoying the night air and watching the few clouds that scudded across the moon. But Adaba could not forget the one question that disturbed his peace, and he finally brought it up.

"Mr. Murdock, Denmark keeps saying I'm going to join him. And I keep saying I'm not. But I'm beginning to think he's right."

"Thought you said you couldn't kill nobody, except maybe to defend yourself."

"I don't think I can. But maybe I can help in some way. Maybe I can defend Denmark."

"No," Murdock said flatly.

"I feel I should. I'm beginning to feel I got to. Mr. Murdock, I owe Denmark so much. My old daddy is in many ways a good man, and he never wanted nothing but the best for me. But no matter how much white blood he's got in him, he always had to remember that to white people he was a nigger first and a nigger most, and he had damn well better not forget it if he wanted to keep what was his—including, maybe, his life. And whether he wanted to or not, that was what he taught me. But Denmark taught me different. Denmark taught me that a man is first of all a man and only after that a black or a white or a redskin. From

198

the time I was a little boy and he first brought his tools to our house to make repairs, I wanted to be like him. Tall and proud and fierce in his determination to bow down to no man. . . . Mr. Murdock, he wants me with him, he thinks he needs me, and I just don't think I can let him down."

"And if his insurrection fails?"

"Well . . . I guess I'll just get shot, hung, or skinned alive like the others."

"And the others that live?"

Adaba didn't understand. He looked questioningly at Murdock.

"If Denmark fails, it's gonna be harder than ever for the black man, son. And he's gonna need us more than ever. That's why I didn't want us to be drawn into recruiting for Denmark. I don't want to take no chances on his plans leading the whites to us. We got our own line of work, so to speak, and we got to stay with it. You steer clear of Denmark and his plans, son."

Adaba shook his head. "I don't know. I just don't know. . . ."

Six

Did she still love him? Had she found another? Had he faded in her memory?

Was Georgiana right in saying that Jovita would forget about him in a week? If only he had heard more from Jovita—but she wasn't much for letter writing, any more than he was, and there had been only two painfully written notes from her in the first weeks, and then nothing.

Lew and his father had arrived in Charleston very late the night before, and he had not dared to sneak out of the house to see Jovita—not when his father had expressly said that he didn't give a damn if it *was* Saturday night, they'd both had a long day, and Lew was to get his rest. But now it was Sunday morning and hot for April, and he was hurrying through the quiet streets toward Jovita's house.

They had returned a couple of weeks sooner than originally planned, but none too soon for Lew. Once his father had announced that business was taking them back to the city and that they might as well stay there for the summer, it seemed to him that he could not have waited a day longer.

Lew had to admit to himself that he was jealous—irrationally so. Of course, Georgiana had poisoned his mind. She and Norvin had come out to Jessamine for a weekend at the beginning of April, and she had lost no time in informing Lew that Jovita already had a new "friend," a black boy. She said she had heard about it through a housemaid. "Now, wasn't I right, Lewis? Those Nigra wenches are just animals. They don't have any more idea of love or faithfulness or—or even true friendship than a barnyard critter. Isn't that true, Norvin? Lewis, I know you just been sowing wild oats, but you're better off forgetting her. You're going to meet a nice decent white girl one of these days. . . ."

Lew had been certain that Georgiana was lying, but the more he told himself so, the more his jealous imagination was inflamed. After all, within a few days of leaving the city, hadn't he been almost *crazy* to have a girl? It was as if, having at last tasted of those joys, his body was unable to live without them. It was fortunate that it had been drummed into him that one never messed around with one's own black women, because there were two or three comely wenches at Jessamine who appeared not unwilling. With the forces now at play in his maturing body, could he have resisted temptation if he had found himself alone with one of those girls? In all honesty, he doubted it very much. How, then, could he expect Jovita to be faithful, when he knew she was every bit as lusty as he? And with plenty of eager bucks panting at her skirt. There had been nights when he had pounded his bed with his fists in angry certainty that at that very moment Jovita was pleasuring with another man.

Well, he would soon find out. He would know when he saw her.

He hurried along the streets under palmettos and magnolias and live oaks. Some azaleas were still in bloom, as were the spring camellias and the yellow bignonias. The hot, perfumed air reminded him of the scent of Jovita's body.

Having rushed to it, it seemed to him that he arrived at her house too soon. What was in those rooms that he did not wish to find? The street was empty and Sunday-morning silent. Moving closer to the house, he looked up through oak leaves toward Jovita's bedroom. How many Saturday nights had they lain awake there, before sleeping late the next morning? He wanted to believe that the room was empty now, that Jovita was safely away at church with Benjamin and Delia. Somehow he had the feeling that she was not.

He stood for a moment outside the piazza door. He could hear no sound within the house. He started to knock, then tried the door instead. It was not locked.

He hesitated only briefly. Stifling a feeling of shame at what he was doing, he opened the door and stepped silently onto the piazza. Still he heard nothing. It was possible that everyone within the house was still asleep.

He looked in through the parlor window. No one was there.

He tried the house door. It too was unlocked. It would be a simple matter to enter the house, go quietly up the stairs, look into Jovita's room . . . and if she were not alone . . .

He opened the door. He stepped into the hall and quietly closed the door behind him. He listened.

Silence.

And then he saw her.

She was sitting in the dining room, stitching away at some folds of cloth that lay across her lap. Her face was serene. Her lips, as always on the verge of a smile, pressed together slightly, as if for a kiss, as she worked the needle through the thick cloth. She hummed a barely audible phrase of a song. She had no idea he was there until he murmured her name. Startled, she looked up.

How could he have doubted her love? He had never before heard such a cry of happiness, never before seen such a look of delight on any face. The sewing was flung aside. Jovita seemed to float from her chair, she was wafted to him, and her arms opened to take him.

It was far better than any of his boyish fantasies, when he picked her up, cradled in his arms. "Yes, I'm back," he said, as he carried her up the stairs, "and I ain't never going away from you again!"

Monday was right. Denmark was not going to give up his plans, and there was going to be an insurrection.

And Denmark was right. The good and kindly Monday might agonize long, but in the end he would be with Denmark. More than that, he would be one of the leaders, taking an active part in recruitment.

"I thought about it hard," he said, on greeting Adaba at Denmark's door. "Plenty going die now, black and white both, but there's still a million black babies to be born. And I owe them, Adaba. We all owe them, or we ain't men at all."

Adaba knew what the decision must have cost the gentle Monday.

Denmark had asked Adaba to the meeting this Sunday late in May, and he had been unable to resist the temptation to attend, for he sensed that it was to be very special. As he entered the house, he found more than a dozen men crowded into the little parlor. He had come to know most of them. Peter, Ned, Rolla, Monday, Jack Purcell, and Gullah Jack: Denmark's principle lieutenants. William Garner, the head of his cavalry. And lesser leaders, all involved in recruitment: Batteau Bennett, Bacchus Hammet, Mingo Harth, Charles Drayton, and three or four others.

Adaba had been more or less accepted by most of them in recent months, though he had consistently disclaimed being part of the conspiracy. At first this had worried some of them. If he was not one of them, why was he there? "If he is in Charleston when the hour comes," Denmark had said, "he will join us." "But *he* don't say that," some had objected, and Denmark had angrily asserted, "This young man was helping us formulate our plans before most of you had any idea of them. And he has saved more black lives than most of you will kill whites!"

Adaba wished Denmark had not said all that. It was quite enough that some of those present knew he had a mysterious way of disappearing from Charleston for long periods of time. Still, these black men had shown a remarkable ability to keep their mouths shut, and he didn't feel particularly endangered.

The tension in the room increased as Denmark went to the middle of the crowd, held up his hands for silence, and called the meeting to order.

"I don't have to tell you why we're here," he said. "You've all met at one time or another at our meetings, but this is the first time you've all been in the same room at once. You are the men who are going to change history. You are the men who are going to lead our people to freedom."

An excited murmur went through the room.

"For months," Denmark went on, "we've been working and planning and arousing our people for action. And now we are almost ready. In a few weeks we shall strike. Our people shall rise up as they did in Santo Domingo. They shall rise up like a vast black tide—an African tide, Ibos, Angolans, Mandingos, people of all tribes—and wash across the land, cleansing it of the whites and taking all that has been denied us, taking the freedom and justice that is our right!"

"Hallelujah!" Charles Drayton said.

"Amen!" said Mingo Harth.

"And the world shall know that we endure our captivity no longer. Our bonds are burst. The age of slavery, after thousands of years, is at last at an end. The white man preaches freedom, but it is the black man who will achieve it for one and all. 'And the children of Israel sighed by reason of the bondage, and they cried, and their cry came up unto God by reason of the bondage. *And God heard their groaning, and God remembered his covenant with Abraham, with Isaac, and with Jacob!'* "

"Praise the Lord!"

"Glory be to God!"

"If I die tomorrow, my friends, I shall die happy—

knowing that our people shall soon rise up and the
bondage be ended. Only your failure to lead our people to
freedom could break my heart. But you have pledged to
take my place—"

"Nothing going stop us, Denmark!"

"Charleston going be ours!"

"When?" Charles Drayton asked excitedly "When we
rise up?"

"In seven weeks—at the latest. At midnight of July
14th. The anniversary of the storming of the Bastille. The
beginning of the French Revolution."

The chattering died away. Charles Drayton was a
small, volatile man who had been recruited by Monday
Gell. His face showed sudden disappointment.

"We got to wait *that* long?"

"Denmark smiled. "You will find that the time passes
very quickly."

There were other sounds of disappointment in the
room.

"But seven weeks—"

"Listen to Denmark," Peter Poyas said. "He has reasons for everything he does. You all listen to him!"

"Thank you, Peter . . ."

The room quieted again.

"We can move sooner if necessary," Denmark said. "In
fact, we could strike within the week if we wished to. But
there are reasons for waiting. First of all, the city is now
full of white people who have come in from the country,
as they do every spring. But now the whites are moving
out again, going up north to Virginia and New York and
Rhode Island to escape the heat. By July most of those
who are going to go will be gone—and the fewer there are
of them and the more of us, the better."

Adaba felt the enthusiasm of Denmark's followers
surging again. "July 14th," someone said. "What day of
the week is that?"

"It's a Sunday, the day when everybody expects to see
black people from the country in Charleston. And on that
Sunday they will pour into the city as never before. One
reason I picked it is that it falls in the dark of the moon,
which will help conceal our activities. As I said, we shall

204

strike at midnight—just as the watchman in the steeple of St. Michael's church is crying out that all is well."

The last statement brought a round of laughter, and Charles Drayton looked happier.

"Now," Denmark said, "each of you knows what you are to do when the hour comes. But few of you know our entire plan. There is no need for you to know every detail, but you should know the broad outlines so that you all can coordinate your actions—and, of course, take over command, should others of us fall. I am now going to show you a large map of the city. And I am going to ask each leader to point out to the rest of us where he and his men will be and what they will be doing."

The map was produced and laid out in the middle of the floor where all could gather round it. "And now," Denmark said, "on the night of July 14th . . ."

As each of the leaders outlined his part in the insurrection, Adaba was struck by the sheer genius of Denmark's planning. While Rolla Bennett and his men were killing the governor and the intendant, thus depriving the city of its most important leaders. William Garner's men would seize the stables and set up mounted patrols, making communication between the other whites almost impossible. At the same time, Peter Poyas, Gullah Jack, and Ned Bennett would seize the principle stores of arms in the city and begin the distribution of weapons. Then forces led by Denmark, Peter, Jack Purcell, and others would sweep through the city, devastating it completely in a matter of hours. It was a beautiful plan, essentially simple and quite logical, and Adaba could well believe that it would put Charleston into Denmark's hands.

But what then, he wondered. What then. . . ?

"One thing more," Peter Poyas said. "We intend to keep right on recruiting for the time we have left. But the more people we have with us, the greater the chance of betrayal. So I want you to warn your people again. Tell them to stay away from drunks and babblers. Tell them to stay away from those house servants, those asslickers who will do anything for an old coat from their masters, or they'll betray us. I know that many of us here are house servants, and there are other servants we can trust. But you all tell your people to say nothing to them without talking to us first. Tell them to let *us* speak to the house servants."

But the warning had been repeated too late.

The betrayal had already occurred.

Apprehension growing in his breast, Channing Sabre read the letter again. ". . . an emergency meeting of the city council at five o'clock this afternoon . . ." That was in less than an hour. ". . . don't wish to alarm you . . . an event that may be of extraordinary importance . . . urge you to attend if at all possible." The letter was dated May 30 and signed by James Hamilton, Jr., the intendant of Charleston.

"All right," Channing told the boy who had delivered the letter. "You tell Mr. Hamilton that I'll be there."

Seven

When Channing arrived at City Hall shortly before five o'clock, a number of the council had preceded him and were standing about the front of the Hall and on its two sets of front steps. Diagonally across Meeting and Broad Streets, the guardhouse seemed quiet enough, and St. Michael's Church and the courthouse on the other two corners were serene in the late afternoon sunlight. Nothing in the clamor and clatter of traffic and trade suggested an emergency. It was a peaceful afternoon in Charleston.

No one seemed to know what Intendant Hamilton's "emergency" was all about, but at five o'clock the wardens, or councilmen, moved as one into the Hall and up the stairs to their meeting chamber, with its life-size, full-length portraits of Washington and Monroe. Hamilton was already there, as were Thomas Bennett, the governor of South Carolina, and Captain Dove of the City Guard.

"Thank you for coming, gentlemen," Hamilton said,

as the wardens took their seats. "We don't have the entire council here, I see, but we do have a quorum." The thirty-six-year-old James Hamilton was short and slightly chubby, a handsome, dapper man with thick, wavy hair. He was a gallant—gay and witty and popular with men and women alike. He was also dangerous, in more ways than one: a man of extraordinary determination in every endeavor.

"What's your emergency, Jimmy?" one of the wardens asked, his skepticism evident. "It's a little late in the day to start new business."

Hamilton's grin held no resentment. "Gentlemen, I apologize for any touch of melodrama that may have crept into my letter—it was composed in a hurry. I wanted to impress you with the possible importance of this matter without alarming you unnecessarily, and I didn't want to specify its nature. But with all respect to your various servants and their undoubted discretion, letters that fall into certain hands do have a way occasionally of coming unsealed and their contents whispered about."

It was now past five o'clock, and Hamilton's audience was restive. *Oh, come on, Jimmy*, Channing thought, *if it's a matter of "possible importance," let's have it.*

"Gentlemen," Hamilton said, "there is some reason to believe that we may be faced with an insurrection conspiracy."

Great God! Channing thought.

If Hamilton had been aiming to produce an effect, he got it. Half of the council were on their feet, talking to each other and calling out questions to Hamilton. He held up his hands for silence but didn't get it quickly.

"Jimmy, that's not a thing to say lightly!"

This time there was metal in Hamilton's voice. "Beau, I wasn't aware of saying anything lightly. I didn't ask you gentlemen to come here at the end of the day to be frivolous. But I want to keep this matter in its proper proportions. We *may* have a nasty situation on our hands, but a little loose talk among a few discontented blacks does not necessarily constitute a conspiracy. I want you gentlemen to hear what I've heard and make up your own minds."

"Just what have you heard, Jimmy?" Channing asked.

"I'm going to let you hear that from the source." Hamilton turned to his clerk. "Would you ask Colonel Prioleau and his man in here, please?"

Colonel John C. Prioleau, a respected citizen known to many members of the council, came in. He was followed by a thin, middle-aged black man. The black man was clearly nervous, and the colonel was polite, almost deferential, to him. This was his man Peter, the colonel said, ". . . and I want to emphasize that I trust him completely. Peter is an intelligent, kindly, and honest man who never went out of his way to make trouble for anybody. He came to me voluntarily earlier today and told me the whole story, which he then repeated only two hours ago to Intendant Hamilton." He turned to his servant. "Now, why don't you just sit down here, Peter—if that's all right with the Council?—and tell these gentlemen the story just as you told it to the intendant and me. They will be mighty grateful."

Peter lowered himself carefully into the chair offered to him, as if expecting an objection at any instant. He looked nervously about the chamber and cleared his throat.

"Well, sir, it was last Saturday afternoon. . . ." And Peter told about meeting a younger black man named William Paul down at Fitzsimmons Wharf. William chatted with him for a time, but Peter hardly paid attention to his conversation, even when William said, "You heard what going on, ain't you?"

"No, I ain't heard. . . ."

"Ain't going take it no longer, Peter. Time us all doing something 'bout it, ain't that right?"

His attention finally caught, Peter asked William what he was talking about.

"Why, we ain't going stay slave no longer! They ain't got no right to hold us, say you black, you a slave! No more, Peter! Soon we *all* be free!"

Peter listened with astonishment. "Now, how you going to do that?"

"We got our plans. We all join together, so many us black people, they can't stop us. I tell you, Peter, you best join with us. You come with me, I show you a man who got a list of names. He take your name down, and then you be one of us. And soon we be free, Peter! You and me and all us! Ain't going be no more slavery, no slavery in Charleston nor no place else. You join us, Peter!"

Astonishment turned to horror as Peter realized what he was hearing. Words of rebellion, words of insurrection. Deadly words, hanging words, and William was still speaking them, talking on and on as if he had no real understanding of the implications of what he was saying.

It was a moment or two before Peter could collect himself sufficiently to tell William he would have nothing to do with this business, that he was grateful to his master for his kindness, and that he wished for no change. He made an excuse and hastened to get away.

"Now, don't you tell nobody 'bout this!" William called after him as he left the wharf. "You be in bad trouble with us, you tell 'bout this! You be in bad trouble!"

Peter arrived back at the colonel's house. What should he do? William Paul's warning rang in his head; the man had sounded as if he meant it. But a few days later, on the advice of a friend, Peter decided to tell his master, and that was what brought them here together.

"And I, of course, sent for you gentlemen at once," said James Hamilton, Jr., after Peter Prioleau had been dismissed. "Are there any comments?"

"No doubt about it," Captain Dove of the guard said. "We've got an insurrection on our hands." He sounded almost pleased by the prospect.

"I think it's a bit early to reach such a conclusion," Governor Bennett said dryly. "What we have here may be no more than a rumor of a rumor, one servant's misrepresentation of another servant's daydream. I think we should talk to this—what was his name?—William Paul, and see if we can't learn more."

"I quite agree," said Hamilton, "and I'm pleased to say that we have him here. He was arrested within minutes after the colonel told us about him. May we have William Paul, please."

The council questioned William Paul intensively and at length, but the frightened young black flatly denied that he knew anything at all about the conversation reported by Peter Prioleau. Channing thought it possible that Peter's vivid imagination had heightened and distorted the conversation, but for William to deny that anything remotely like it had taken place did seem to suggest guilt.

William was taken under guard from the room.

"We still don't really have anything," Governor Bennett said, "but I can't say I like the way he acts. Perhaps it would be unwise to discharge him as yet."

"Point taken," Hamilton said. "I suggest that we put him in the guardhouse for the night, and in the morning we'll give him a little time in the black hole of the workhouse. That won't hurt him, but if he really knows anything, it'll probably loosen his tongue."

"Just give him to me for the night," Captain Dove said, hard-eyed, strong-jawed, "and I'll guarantee to loosen his tongue."

"Now, captain," Hamilton said sharply, "I don't want my orders exceeded. I want that boy locked up and left alone and nothing more, and I trust you understand me."

The captain's cheeks colored at the rebuke.

"One last thing before we adjourn," the governor said. "I'm sure we all understand that even if there is no insurrection conspiracy, we have here a rather volatile situation. The mere hint, a mere rumor of a conspiracy would cause panic. And therefore I want to suggest that we say nothing, absolutely nothing, about this situation to anyone until it is completely cleared up. I see no reason why we should even worry our own families with it."

"So be it," said the intendant, and his words had the force of an order. "Let us all keep complete silence about this matter."

Jimmy Hamilton was angry. Channing saw it the moment he entered the intendant's office at noon the next day.

"William Paul has confessed," he told Channing.

The statement made Channing feel sick, as he thought of what lay ahead. "Then there is a conspiracy."

"How the hell would I know?"

210

"But if William has confessed—"

"He's confessed what Dove wanted him to confess," Hamilton said disgustedly. "Dove came to me this morning, pleased as punch, and told me that *he* had succeeded in 'loosening William's tongue.' What happened, of course, is that Dove scared hell out of the boy, so that he would repeat back anything he was told. Now we'll never know if William would have told the same story without prompting."

"Did he give any information that Peter didn't give us?"

"Yes, Chan, he did—William told Dove he had learned of the plot from James Poyas's man Peter and William Harth's Mingo."

"Well, at least that's something, Jimmy. I think our next move is to investigate Peter Poyas and Mingo."

"You got up late this morning, Chan. Mr. Wesner and Mr. Condy have already done that. They reported back to me just a little while ago."

"And?" Channing asked, though from Hamilton's tone he could guess the gist of the answer.

"They told me you couldn't meet any less-concerned slaves in the world. They treated the whole matter as a joke and were completely cooperative. Now, Chan, if you dangle a noose in front of a couple of guilty bucks, they aren't likely to joke. They're going to be scared, Chan, scared as hell. But those two apparently just didn't give a damn."

"Their quarters were searched?"

"And not one piece of incriminating evidence was found. No lists, nothing."

"Then you're going to let William Paul go?"

"No," Hamilton said slowly, "I can't do that—thanks to Dove. We're just going to have to keep him in the workhouse a few more days, scare the poor bastard some more, and see if he comes up with something substantial. I hate to do it, but I don't see that I have a choice. And if Dove gets near the workhouse, I'll kill him!"

"Somebody has been talking."

It was one of the few times Adaba had seen a breach

in Peter Poyas's stoic manner. His eyes flashed, his nostrils flared.

"What are you talking about?" Denmark asked. "And hold your voice down. Someone could come into the shop at any moment."

Peter rubbed his hands over his big bald head and took a deep breath, as if to calm himself. "This morning," he said. "Two men from the city council. They searched my room and questioned me. How long had it been going on, who were the leaders, what did I know about William Paul? Of course, I pretended I didn't know what they were talking about, but . . ."

"William Paul," Denmark said musingly. "The City Guard picked him up right outside here yesterday afternoon."

"Then that's the answer," Peter said. "William Paul has informed on us."

Denmark didn't seem unduly excited or alarmed by Peter's news, but Adaba knew how calm he could be in an emergency.

"We can't be certain of that. What does William Paul know?"

"Not much. A few names, but not many details."

"Then all they've got is a sullen young nigger who doesn't know his place and is trying to make trouble. That's common enough."

Peter shook his head. "I don't know, Denmark. I'm not sure it's that simple. I talked to Mingo before I came here. They questioned him and searched his room, too."

"But obviously they didn't find anything."

"Of course not. Nothing important."

"And they let you go. Didn't even take you or Mingo to the workhouse for further questioning. As far as we know, William Paul is all they've got—and that's almost nothing."

Denmark smiled, and Peter seemed to grow calmer.

"You really think we're safe?"

"We've never been completely safe, and we'd be foolish to ignore what's happened. I think it's time to take certain precautions."

212

"Burn our records," Peter said fervently. "I want to get rid of them."

"Exactly. They're the strongest evidence against us, and we don't really need them anymore. And there is to be no more recruiting, and we'll meet only as necessary."

"And the date? Do we have to wait so long?"

"We'll move the date up. The plan will remain exactly the same, but we'll strike at midnight on Sunday, June 15th."

"Only two more weeks," Peter said, as if to himself. "I can hardly believe it. Two more weeks, and we're going to do it—if only they don't find out."

"They won't, Peter. They won't."

Despite the high ceiling and the draft and the hour of the morning, the chamber was quite warm, and heat, boredom, and the droning of voices brought unseemly yawns to Channing's face. This wasn't a regular meeting of the council, and there wasn't even a quorum present. He might not even have attended the meeting, except that John Wilson had offered his services through Channing, and Channing could hardly turn him down. And so he and Wilson had come down to City Hall this morning.

And to this boredom.

There were, after all, Channing thought, other things in life besides slave conspiracies that failed to materialize. He had done his duty as a member of the city council and kept himself informed on this business. But William Paul had been in solitary confinement for over a week now without revealing anything more that was substantial—or insubstantial, for that matter—and investigation had brought nothing to light. Hamilton had ordered that Peter Poyas and Mingo Harth be watched, but nothing in the least incriminating had been observed. They had simply gone about their daily business in the most ordinary and innocent way.

". . . a spy, gentleman. Our man in their midst."

Channing had drifted. The man speaking was Major John Wilson. He had heard about the alleged plot—it was

213

impossible to keep the matter completely secret—and had come to Channing, as a friend, last night.

"I think we all know that the African Methodist Episcopal Church is one of the great sources of discontent in our city. It has been ever since it started several years ago. We've done our best to discourage it, but it persists —persists, *I* say, as a hotbed of potential insurrection. If we are going to learn anything about this plot, we shall learn it through the African Church. And my man George is the one to ferret out the truth."

"If your man George is the one to ferret out the truth, why hasn't he done so before?" the governor asked, and Channing noted with satisfaction that he too was suppressing yawns. "What makes you think that any conspirators in the African Church will be willing to confide in him?"

"Governor, my man has an excellent reputation with both races, and he wants to keep it. For that reason, he's shunned any hints of troublemaking. But if we ask him to investigate this matter for us, I know he'll be willing."

"I don't see any harm in it, Jimmy," the governor said, turning to the intendant. "Why not?"

"Wha'? Oh. Why not, indeed," Hamilton said, pulling himself awake. "Major Wilson, we'll be more than grateful for any help you and your man George can give us. And I'm sure that all of us here are grateful to you for coming to us this morning. A concerned citizenry . . ."

Drone, drone, drone . . .

The meeting adjourned. The dozen or so men who had been present broke into little groups and drifted down the stairs and out of the building. The heat of the day was building up. Channing wondered vaguely if he had time for a round of golf before dinner or if he should take his sloop out onto the river and catch a little breeze. He could ask Jimmy and the governor to come along.

"Intendant! Intendant Hamilton, sir!"

It was one of the wardens from the workhouse breaking in on Channing's thoughts.

"Yes, Dabney?" Hamilton said.

"It's that goddamn William Paul, sir. He's just plain going all to pieces! Screaming and yelling and crying, and
214

begging for you to come—says he wants to tell you all about it. He's ready to tell you everything!"

William Paul slid from his chair to the floor of the dark fetid little room in the workhouse. "Please, master . . . I ain't done nothing . . . say anything you want . . . but don't hang me, please don't hang me!"

For most of his adult life, Channing Sabre had thought of himself as an educated man with a liberated mind, a humane, enlightened, sensitive man, a man who understood. Somehow after the experience with Gilly several years ago, he had lost that view of himself. He now thought of himself as a rather dull and insensitive man, a man who had learned too little and too late. Now, looking at this weeping, slobbering wreck of a young black on the floor, he wondered if any of them here could even begin to comprehend what the slave was going through—any more than he had understood what Gilly was going through. The thought made him angry with himself and all the rest of the world.

William Paul was unable to stand at all, and his body reeked of terror and excrement. Surely it had taken more than the black hole to do this to him. It had taken threats of the noose.

"Pick him up," Hamilton said.

Two workhouse wardens lifted William Paul from the floor and sat him on the chair again. The intendant, the governor, Channing, and a couple other members of the city council confronted him.

"Calm down, William," Hamilton said. "Nobody is going to hang you. We just want you to tell us everything you know. Everything! Now, let's try again. How long have you known about this plot?"

"I don't know," William sobbed. "A month, maybe a month."

"Is that when it started? A month ago?"

William shook his head. "No. Long before. I think. Long time ago."

"And who is the leader?"

"I don't know. Mingo Harth say Denmark Vesey. Mingo take me to a meeting. . . ."

"Who was the leader at the meeting?"

"Don't know his name."

"Did you see him? What did he look like?"

"Think it was the little man . . . little man with big beard . . . had a charm 'round his neck so nobody kill him."

"Voodoo charm?"

William nodded.

"Where was the meeting? Where did it take place?"

"Don't know. Mingo take me there. Never there b'fore nor after."

"Who else was there? Who else was at the meeting?"

William shook his head.

"Oh, come now. You must have known some of them. Who were they?"

"Mingo. Peter Poyas."

"You've told us about them before. Who else? William, you're going to stay here until you tell us everything. Now, who else was there?"

"Quash Harleston," William said in a whisper.

"Which Harleston does he belong to?"

"He free. Like Denmark."

Hamilton looked skeptical. "You mean there are *free* blacks in on this? I don't believe it."

William whimpered something about not knowing.

"Who else, William?"

"Agrippa, belong Mrs. Perry. Scipio, belong Mr. Sims. George, belong Mr. Samuel Parker . . ."

"Yes, go on."

William gave the governor a quick frightened look. "Ned," he said softly. "Ned Bennett."

The governor exploded. "Why, that's ridiculous! My Ned wouldn't have anything to do with a conspiracy in a thousand years. There is no more faithful servant in South Carolina. Either this man is lying—or there is no conspiracy!"

"Or he's confused, governor," Channing said. "There's more than one Ned in the city, after all."

The questioning went on, but aside from a few names, it seemed clear that William knew nothing specific—if there really was a conspiracy. Even the names were

216

suspect, because he seemed willing to say anything that might save his neck.

"Are you going to let him go?" Channing asked the intendant as they returned to the harsh sunlight that filled Magazine Street.

Hamilton shrugged helplessly. "I was considering it—but now I can't. First we've got to investigate the few names he's given us."

"You mean," Channing said, "that because he's tried to cooperate with us, he must suffer a little longer."

"Well," Hamilton said uncomfortably, "if there is a conspiracy, he damned well deserves to suffer."

"Despite his cooperation." Channing shook his head. "Well, at least let's remember, Jimmy, that you promised him he wouldn't hang."

Hamilton looked surprised. "If it comes to that, it's up to a court."

"No, Jimmy. In effect, you promised him that if he would cooperate, nobody was going to hang him. Now you and I are going to do our damnedest to see that that promise is kept."

Hamilton shrugged.

Three days later, on Tuesday, June 11, Ned Bennett appeared before the intendant and said that he had heard that his name had been mentioned in connection with some kind of conspiracy that was being investigated. He apologized for taking up the intendant's time, but said that he would appreciate it if he could be interrogated about the matter so that it could be cleared up once and for all and his good reputation be preserved.

That finished the matter. Ned was questioned, as he had requested, and of course nothing in the slightest incriminating came to light. And questioning the others mentioned by William Paul had led to nothing.

"The governor was right," Hamilton told Channing. "What did he call it? A rumor of a rumor? I'm letting William Paul go. There is no insurrection conspiracy."

Charleston needed little excuse for a round of parties, and there was nothing to draw attention to the light and chatter and music that came from Denmark Vesey's house that night. Wednesday night divided the week, and that was as good a reason as any to celebrate; half a dozen houses along the street contributed gaiety to the sultry evening. As he entered Denmark's house, Adaba wondered how many of the guests knew the real reason for the celebration.

Denmark, towering over most of his guests, at once threw an arm around Adaba's shoulders and pressed a glass into his hands. "You've heard?"

"Peter told me earlier."

"The one crisis we've had, and we're safely past it."

Denmark had learned that William Paul's arrest had come about because of his talking to Peter Prioleau. He had also learned that William had been released from the workhouse and was now at home recuperating from his ordeal. That could only mean that the authorities were convinced that Peter was wrong about there being a conspiracy. Ned, having spoken to the intendant and to his master, was able to confirm this. As far as the authorities were concerned, there was no insurrection conspiracy.

Denmark guided Adaba past other guests to a corner where Peter and Ned were standing. Ned's usual stern look had quite disappeared, and Peter was grinning as Adaba had never seen him grin before.

"To the invisible insurrection!" Denmark said in a lowered voice. "May it soon become visible! My friends, to us —in all our endeavors!" The others laughed and raised their glasses. They were sober men who rarely drank, but this night was an exception.

"I'll tell you the truth now," Denmark said when they had drunk. "I feared that our white masters would come much closer than this to discovering our plans. I was ready to see half a dozen of us picked up at various times, though I was sure we could cope with it. But it has only happened once! We have been betrayed only once, and that was by an outsider. Our plans are perfected, we have troops aplenty, we have explosives, pikes, daggers—" He broke off and turned to a man who stood chatting with others nearby and drew him closer for the moment.

218

"Peirault," he said, "how many daggers do you now have for us?"

"Four hundred," the man said. Peirault Strohecker had been an experienced warrior in Africa before he was brought to the United States. "Four hundred, and may every one of them cut a hundred white throats."

Denmark laughed, and Peirault turned away.

"And now what do you think of our plans, my young friend?" Denmark asked Adaba.

"Right now I ain't ever been happier that I ain't white."

"You'll be happier still on Sunday night."

"If that's possible."

Denmark's smile faded, and he moved closer to Adaba, "One thing I would advise. On Sunday, do your best to persuade your family to leave Charleston. Telling them nothing of what's to come, of course."

"Maybe I should tell them to leave right away."

"No. Frankly, I don't trust your father. And the city council would take him much more seriously than any Peter Prioleau. Wait until Sunday afternoon or even early evening. Then get them out of the city as quickly as possible. Your father might pass for black at night, but your sister and brothers never would. And if they stay in Charleston, something very bad is likely to happen to them."

And to Lew, Adaba thought with sudden unhappiness, though he and Lew had hardly been intimate for years. Something very bad was likely to happen to Lew and to some other whites he didn't particularly want to see hurt. Well, if he stayed in Charleston, maybe he could help them.

"Can you do that?" Denmark asked. "Can you get them out?"

"I must. I will."

Ned laughed to himself, and they turned back toward him. "Poor William Paul," he said, shaking his head. "Guess they treated him mighty bad."

"Poor William Paul!" Peter was scornful. "First he didn't follow my orders about not talking to house servants, and then it didn't take him long to inform on Mingo and me. He deserved anything they did to him."

"Well, they didn't find out much," Denmark said. "And what they did find out wasn't any use to them."

"But maybe you should move the date," Adaba suggested. "Give yourself an extra month."

Denmark shook his head. "No. We're ready now. Our people have been told that we're about to strike, and we can't put them off any longer. We strike next Sunday at midnight."

"Four more days," Ned said. "Just four more days, and then . . ."

On Friday evening, Channing was enjoying an after-dinner stroll when he encountered Major Wilson. The man was obviously perturbed. As Channing started to greet him, he interrupted.

"I'm on my way to the intendant's house, Chan, and I think you'd better go with me."

"What is it, John? What's happened?"

"You remember William Paul? He was telling the truth all along."

Channing had so put the matter out of mind that for a moment, he could not think what Wilson might be talking about.

"An insurrection, Chan! An insurrection so damn big I can hardly believe it—and we've only got forty-eight hours!"

Eight

The intendant's house was the brightest on the street. At nine o'clock Governor Bennett arrived, and by ten the house was filled with city council members, city officials, and the commanding officers of various military and quasi-military units.

George Wilson was the center of attention. He was a big-framed, handsome, brawny mulatto blacksmith, intelligent and literate, and completely trusted by his white masters. Channing, like the intendant and the governor and virtually everyone else, had all but forgotten Major Wilson's offer to use George as a spy. At the time, it had hardly seemed a promising strategy.

As more people arrived, George was asked to repeat his story, or parts of it.

"I'm a class leader at our church. Last Saturday, Major Wilson told me the city council thought something bad was going on with the black folks. He asked me to listen to them and perhaps ask a few questions and try to find out about it, and so I did. And late today a friend of mine named Adam, a very good friend who is in my church class, came to me, very disturbed. He said he knew of a great trouble about to take place. He said many black folks were planning to rise up and take over the city and kill all the white people, even the women and children, and that white wenches would be abused just as black wenches had been abused. He told me that he had been trusted by the conspirators with their secret and had been asked to join them. He didn't know what to do. He is a man who hates to betray a trust. So at first he appeared to give consent to their plans. Now he regrets that and he came to me. I told him he must tell his master at once, and I told Major Wilson and came here with him and Mr. Sabre."

"Have we heard yet from this Adam's master?" asked Captain Dove, who had just arrived.

"Not yet," Hamilton said. "He may not have taken the matter seriously."

"Did your friend say when this uprising was to take place?" the captain asked George.

"In two days, he said. At midnight on Sunday."

"Did this friend of yours mention any names?"

"He said he thought Mrs. Perry's Agrippa consented to the uprising. He said that Mungo Poyas was part of it. And—and—" George looked uneasily at the governor. "Ned and Rolla from the governor's house, he said they were a part of it."

"Good Lord," the governor said sadly, "Ned again, and Rolla too . . ."

George mentioned several other names, as well as "a

221

little man with a great beard who makes charms. A sorcerer."

"Had this friend of yours talked to William Paul?" the captain asked.

"Oh, no, sir. He hardly knows William Paul and hasn't seen him in more than two weeks. Hardly anyone has since—since—"

"Since my men picked him up." The captain looked at the intendant and the governor. "Well, that means we've got independent testimony. George, what does your friend know about the plans for the uprising?"

"Not much. He said he had heard that there were a great many involved from the country, and that Mungo Poyas was to bring four thousand men from James Island—"

"*Four thousand!*" Captain Dove's military facade broke. For once he looked shocked. "Four thousand men from out James Island way alone?"

"You see, captain," Hamilton said, "we have here an affair of some dimension. If four thousand men are coming from James Island, how many more are coming from other points, and how many are already in the city?"

"What do you think we should do, Jimmy?" the governor asked. "We have a few more names now. Should we arrest them all? Question Peter Poyas and Mingo Harth all over again?"

Hamilton considered the suggestion and decided against it. "No. If this insurrection is as big as it sounds—and it still may be nothing but loose talk—our first consideration must be to stop it. Arresting a few people who may have little to do with it isn't going to do anything but alert the insurrectionists. If they intend violence, I imagine you can protect yourself from Ned and Rolla until Monday morning, can't you, Tom?"

The governor colored. "I can. I hate it, but I'm not going to trust anyone in my household until this matter is cleared up."

"Very wise. We'll all have to do that. We'll keep a close silent watch on the Negroes of the city, and on Sunday night the insurrectionists will be confronted by an overwhelming, trained, and ready military force."

"I just hope they do revolt, sir," Captain Dove said. "I'm ready for it. I'd just love the chance to cut down some of those black bastards."

"I'm sure you would, captain," Hamilton said wearily.

"I don't suppose there's anything more we can do to-night," the governor said.

"No, we might as well adjourn now. We have a lot to do before Sunday night, but I know damn good and well we can do it, so . . . gentlemen! let's have a drink!"

Channing watched it all, participated in it all. The governor, the intendant, and the civil and military officials planned swiftly and surely and with no sense of panic. Let ten thousand blacks rise up, let twenty thousand, and they would be ready for them.

Saturday, Captain Dove was ordered to take as many of the City Guard off duty as possible, without letting it be too obvious, to allow them to rest. He had three sergeants and a hundred men, and on Sunday evening he wanted to have every last one of them available.

Light-infantry militia, hussars, Neck Rangers—all military and quasi-military units were to be organized into a single regiment which would muster at ten o'clock on Sunday evening under the command of Colonel Robert Y. Hayne. A sandy-haired, rosy-cheeked, boyish-looking man, Hayne was nevertheless one of the most dynamic leaders in the state.

George Wilson had indicated that much of the black force was to come from outside the city. It was impossible to notify most of the rest of the state what was happening, but riders from the military would have to be dispatched to inform farmers and overseers for at least a few miles around. On Sunday, the whites were to tell their slaves that there was going to be no "trouble" in Charleston and that they were forbidden under any circumstances to leave home. And the whites were to have their weapons ready to enforce this order and to protect their own lives.

On Saturday afternoon, Denmark's house seemed to shake with excitement. Lieutenants and sublieutenants in the conspiracy came and went. Details were checked and

223

confirmed and the latest information was reported and evaluated. What was the commotion at the intendant's house last night? Was the meeting at City Hall today significant? There were always at least half a dozen men present, besides Denmark, breaking into small groups and talking in low voices and laughing hushed, expectant laughs. Adaba knew he shouldn't be there. He had told himself time and again that Gavin Murdock was right, that he should have nothing to do with Denmark's plans, and yet he found himself drawn irresistibly to them. And so he had spent most of the day with Denmark.

When he arrived at Denmark's house, Frank Ferguson was as excited as everybody else. "First chance I get to see you since the master and me come back to the city today," he said. "Denmark, I got slaves from four more plantations want to join us. Ferguson plantation and three others. *Four plantations!* That's more'n a hundred slaves! They going walk all twenty-five miles to be here tomorrow night, and they bring slaves from all the big plantations and little farms 'long the way. How you like that?"

"Frank, that's wonderful! You're doing fine work!"

"That's a good ten-hour walk," Peter said. "If they start in the early afternoon, they should be just in time to join Jack Purcell's men on the Neck."

"And by the time they get here, recruiting as they come," Ned said, "they should be several hundred strong. There shouldn't be any trouble with patrols—especially not on a Sunday."

"Only thing is," Frank said, "we got to tell them. They ain't coming 'less they know it really starting. So we got to send a man tomorrow."

"Can't you go?" Denmark asked.

"Denmark!" Frank held up his hands as if to plead for mercy. "I just get here, all this way. And my master ain't going let me go no place tomorrow. I'se lucky I get to see you now!"

Denmark turned to a man so light-skinned that he was sometimes mistaken for a white. "Then you're going to go out to the Ferguson plantation tomorrow, Jesse."

Jesse Blackwood's eyes widened. "I ain't going walk no fifty mile in a day!"

224

"No, you're not. I'm going to give you two dollars to hire a horse, and you're going to ride out there early in the morning and carry that poor horse back here on your back in the afternoon. Then you're going to go to bed and sleep through the revolution."

The room was filled with laughter.

Later, while Denmark was talking to Peter and Ned, Adaba caught his eye, raised a hand in farewell, and left the parlor. He was hardly out on the piazza when Denmark joined him.

"You're going? You're welcome to stay for supper."

"No, I told my father I'd be home."

"Adaba . . ." Denmark hesitated, frowning. "I've changed my mind. Don't wait until the last minute to tell your family to leave the city. Tell them to leave as soon as possible. And go with them."

The unexpected advice startled Adaba. "Why?"

Denmark glanced into the house and lowered his voice. "I don't know why. I haven't told the others, I don't want to worry them, but . . ." He seemed to find the words hard to say. "I have the feeling that maybe . . . just maybe . . . something . . . may have gone wrong."

"Do you mean that meeting at the intendant's house last night?"

"Perhaps that's it. It's little things. I happened to see the governor go by here on his way to the intendant's house last night as if a swarm of bees was on his tail. Not at all on his gubernatorial dignity. And a maid told Ned that his bedroom door was locked this morning, the first time ever." Denmark smiled briefly. "Now, aren't those silly things to set a man worrying?"

"I don't know—"

"And yet it does worry me. And I don't like those meetings at City Hall today either. There were military men present. Why should these things be happening *now?*"

"But if we . . . if you had been betrayed again, they would have arrested somebody. Or at least questioned them. And we would know about it."

"Not necessarily. They might think an investigation premature. Or perhaps . . ." Denmark smiled again and shrugged. "Or perhaps I am worrying over nothing. Nevertheless, tell your family to leave the city, and do it soon. And you go with them. Your plantation people are loyal —I happen to know."

"I'll speak to my father," Adaba said, but he had no intention of leaving the city.

Could Denmark be right? Throughout the day, Adaba had had no sense of any difficulties, but now, as he walked through the streets of Charleston, it did seem to him that something was subtly wrong. The city was too quiet for a Saturday evening. Too few people were to be seen on the streets. But he told himself that that was nonsense. The sun was within an hour of setting, filling the streets with the rose and gold of evening, and the supper hour was coming on. Of course the streets were quiet. . . .

No one was to be seen on the street as he approached his family's house, and the silence was almost eerie. For a moment he had the feeling that all the surrounding houses were empty, that he was the last person in a deserted city.

The piazza door was unlocked. There was no sound from within the house, and no lamp was yet lit when he entered. He stood in the hall for a moment, listening, hearing nothing.

He called out: "Phil, David, Rose!"

"Oh, Mr. John!"

Adaba nearly jumped at the sound of the voice, but it was only Miss Livia, the elderly housekeeper.

"Where is everybody, Miss Livia?"

The old lady looked bewildered. "They gone, Mr. John—"

"Gone! Gone to the plantation?"

"Yes, sir. Gone this afternoon. Your daddy was real upset you wasn't here to go too. He say tell you hire a horse and carriage—"

"But why? Why did they leave?"

"I don't *know*, Mr. John! Mr. Channing Sabre come by at dinner time, say he on his way back to the City Hall and just stop by. Then him and your daddy go into the parlor and talk, and next I know, they is packing up to leave. He say Titus and me can come with you if we want, but he don't think we have to be scared to stay here. Mr. John, we ain't *never* scared here! Why we have to be scared?"

226

" . . . maybe . . . just maybe . . . something . . .
may have gone wrong. . . ."

"No reason, Miss Livia. I don't know why he said
that," Adaba forced a smile, "except that maybe he thinks
you and Titus are getting a little old to be alone here and
might not like it. But I'll get a horse and carriage for you
tomorrow."

"You coming with us, ain't you?"

"No, I'm staying here. What do we have for supper,
Miss Livia? . . ."

"It's the little things. . . ."

If Channing Sabre knew something about the insurrection, it would only be natural for him to warn Adaba's
father that he had best take his family out of the city until
the crisis was past. *If.* The incident might have nothing to
do with the insurrection. Still, he had to tell Denmark. Tonight.

Adaba slept long and hard and late Sunday and awakened feeling groggy and yet in a vague state of alarm. He
had returned to Denmark's house last night and told him
about Sabre's visit and the Guerard family's departure
from Charleston. Denmark had listened impassively, and
Adaba had been unable to tell if the story had added to
his alarm or not.

" 'Bout time you up!"

"You should have wakened me, Miss Livia."

"You think I don't try? You sleep like you was dead.
I get you some breakfast."

"Fine. And then I'll go get a horse and carriage for you
and Titus—"

"No! You stay here, we got to stay and take care of
you!" Miss Livia's eyes became troubled. "Mr. John,
what happening in this here old town? I was out early,
and something wrong, I swear. . . ."

When he went out onto the streets, Adaba soon saw for
himself that it was not the usual Sunday morning in late
spring. On the surface all was calm and peaceful, all was
quiet as if in deference to the day, and the sound of hymns
drifted out of the churches. But there were a number of
uniforms in the streets—not many, but enough to call at-

tention to the fact. The soldiers were not drilling or parading or patrolling—they would hardly be doing that on a Sunday morning—but merely standing about and chatting with one another and with civilian friends, as if waiting for something to happen. On Broad Street, near St. Finbar's, Adaba spotted straw-haired, round-faced Hadden Hargrave, a young lieutenant in the Charleston Riflemen, whom he had known all his life.

"I don't know what it's all about," Hadden said. "Yesterday afternoon the captain sends word that we all got to fall out today in uniform, and no excuses. But ain't nothing happening yet. I figure they're just gonna work out something special for the Fourth of July, since that ain't but two, three weeks off."

Maybe. But surely that wasn't sufficient to explain those meetings at City Hall yesterday. And the long meeting at the intendant's house on Friday night.

By four o'clock in the afternoon, the streets were filled with troops, and the number seemed to be increasing hourly. In Denmark's parlor, everyone fell silent as they heard a squad going by counting cadence. Adaba, Peter, Ned, and Monday had just returned from scouting the city, and they had seen strangely few black faces out on the streets. Adaba had had the odd feeling that many of the whites, especially the women, had looked at him with a kind of alarm and then hurried away.

The cadence-counting squad faded away, and still the five men in the room remained silent.

"You all do realize, don't you," Denmark said very slowly after a long moment, "that they know about us."

"Don't know for sure 'bout that," Monday said, looking for hope.

"They know," Denmark repeated. "They have heard something, someone has talked. It's no coincidence that the city is filling up with soldiers on the very day we chose for our uprising. Now we can be certain about the meeting at the intendant's house on Friday night. Now we know why there were meetings with the military at the City Hall yesterday."

"It doesn't matter," Peter said. "It's too late to stop us

228

now. Our people are ready, and when they strike, every black in this city is going to follow them, man, woman, and child, slave and free. And all those who are coming in from the country, all those thousands—"

"Thousands?" Denmark said with a faint smile. "I know of thirty who arrived by canoe today. Aside from them, none of the plantation leaders have reported to us."

"They hiding, Denmark," Monday said, "because of the soldiers!"

No one moved when they heard footsteps out on the piazza or answered when there was a banging at the door. The banging was repeated, and someone came into the hall, paused, and entered the parlor.

"What are you doing here?" Ned asked in surprise.

"Now, don't you go blaming me!" Jesse Blackwood said. He looked hot, dirty, and exhausted. "I done my best! I been out there for hours trying to get past them patrols!" Since there was no chair for him, he slumped against a wall, then slid slowly to the floor.

"What happened, Jesse?" Denmark still wore the faint smile.

"This morning I get the horse, just like you say. I head up King Street for the Neck, keep right on going. And I don't come to one patrol, I come to *three!* First say they ain't s'pose to let no niggers come in nor go out of Charleston even if they got a pass, but I beg and plead, and they let me go past. Then I come to the second patrol, but they don't pay me no 'tention, 'cause they think I'se white. But the last patrol, they send me back. Then I look for some ways to get 'round the patrols, and seems like everywhere there's a white man tellin' me, 'You best get you ass back, nigger, we going string you up!' Denmark, we *caught* here in Charleston!"

Jesse looked from one man to another, but they didn't move. Denmark stared at the floor, the little smile on his face, as if his thoughts were a thousand miles away.

"Ain't letting nobody in nor out," Monday said dully.

"They can't stop those that come by water," Ned said.

"They won't be enough," Peter said. "We were counting on two things—surprise and support from the coun-

229

try. Now we don't have either of them. What are we going to do, Denmark?"

Denmark raised his head and looked about at his men. He took a deep breath, held it, and let it out in a rush.

"What are we going to do? Why, we shall do exactly what we did when William Paul talked and you and Mingo were questioned, Peter. We are going to keep heart. We are going to reconsider our plans. We are going to look for alternatives. We may have to wait for a day or two. We shall carefully watch all developments and bide our time.

"Now!" Denmark stood up, and suddenly he seemed to be recharged with energy. "You people have work to do! The whites will no doubt try to enforce the curfew tonight, so you mustn't lose any time. You must get word to all the other leaders and their lieutenants, and they to their followers, that they are not to muster for a strike until they get orders. Make that absolutely clear. Nobody is to do anything—*anything*—until he gets the order from me. But assure them," Denmark brought his palms together explosively, "that when the right moment comes, they *will* get their orders—*and we shall strike!*"

One by one the men left the house until only Denmark and Adaba were left. Denmark went to the window where he could look out onto the street.

"Tell me the truth, Denmark," Adaba said softly. "Is it over?"

For a moment he thought Denmark had not heard him. Then the big grizzled man turned from the window and his eyes were shining.

"Why, no, son," he said, "it isn't over. We still have a chance. Never stop believing that. We still have a chance."

By now, everybody knew what was happening, and it seemed to Lew, as he went through the streets, that the city had never been more vibrant with life. Windows everywhere were lit up, chatter flowed from the piazzas, mothers called to children allowed up hours past their customary bedtime. A great number of civilians were keeping watch in the streets, and for the past half hour soldiers had marched by the company and by the squad, and military orders had echoed through the city. Only the small houses of the blacks were silent and dark, as if crouching in the night, hoping to go unnoticed.

Georgiana had been almost hysterical when she caught him about to leave the house. "You are not going out there with all those savages running loose!"

"There ain't no savages running loose, Georgiana. I don't reckon there's a safer place in Carolina tonight than the streets of Charleston."

"It isn't bad enough that my own daddy is out there somewhere, you are not leaving us here unprotected!"

"Georgiana, half of the neighborhood is in this house tonight!"

"Norvin, you stop him!"

Norvin had just come into the passage. One of Channing Sabre's pistols was stuck in his belt, and his soft, dewlapped face had an uncustomary grimness.

"You'd better stay right here, Lewis."

"Well, I ain't gonna!"

"You just wait till morning. Those niggers threatening to kill our women and children—we'll see what they've got to say when we go out and stretch a few of their necks." Norvin's face seemed to redden in the lamplight, and his grin was ugly. "Maybe that pretty little nigger whore of yours will find out how she likes it at the end of a rope."

After that, nothing in the world could have kept Lew away from Jovita. He had snatched the pistol from Norvin's belt, tucked it into his own, and charged out of the house.

No light showed in Jovita's house, but the piazza door was ajar, and Lew pushed it open. He was on the piazza before he saw Benjamin and Delia sitting in the darkness.

"Well, look who come visit us," Benjamin murmured. "Look who come on our piazza without a by-your-leave."

Lew was startled by the hostility in his voice. "Ain't I welcome, Benjamin?"

"Ain't for me to say. Why you here tonight? Why ain't you home hiding 'neath your bed?"

"I want to be sure Jovita is all right."

"Ain't that sweet, Delia? He want to be sure Jovita is all right."

"That surely is sweet, Benjamin."

"Where is she?" Lew asked.

"Jovita is inside. Go on in, you want. But don't you stay if she don't want you."

Lew tried to see Benjamin, tried to penetrate the darkness. For God's sake, he wanted to say, we're friends, we been friends for a long time. Don't you know I wouldn't do a goddamn thing to hurt you? Instead, he stepped into the house.

"Jo . . ."

She was in his arms at once, pliant against him, molded to him in the darkness. Her mouth sought his, found it, kissed him hungrily.

"Jovita," he whispered, "I was scared for you."

"I'se all right."

"I know you are now. But the white folks are angry, Jo. They think the black folks are going to try to kill us all, and maybe they're crazy, but there ain't no telling what they'll do."

"Is that why you come here?"

"Yes. I ain't gonna leave here till I know you're safe. I'm gonna take care of you, Jo. I told you I would. Always, I'm going take care of you. . . ."

At midnight, the sentry cried out that all was well.

No one seized the stables of the city. No black troops gathered on the Neck or at Gadsden's Wharf or on South Bay. No black armies gathered at Bulkley's Farm or at Boundary and King Streets or on Bull Street at Denmark Vesey's house to sweep through the city.

Only Denmark and Adaba remained in Denmark's dimly lit parlor. No matter what Denmark had said, the insurrection was over for now—and for a long time to come.

No one had spoken for many minutes when Adaba asked, "What if they hadn't found out? I've never really understood. After seizing Charleston, what did you plan to do?"

232

Denmark, slumped in his chair like a wrecked giant, closed his eyes.

"I know you spoke sometimes of commandeering ships for those who wanted to leave the country, but you couldn't have transported everybody . . . not that everybody would have wanted to go."

Denmark slowly shook his head. Adaba, looking about, found a bottle and poured himself a small whiskey.

"I remember too there was some talk about getting foreign help, maybe from England. But that doesn't seem very likely to me. Maybe you could have made some kind of treaty with the white people, but with the kind of killing you were talking about, it seems more likely that they would have sent troops. A lot more troops than are here tonight. I figure they'd probably send General Jackson, and what would you have done then?"

"Why, we would have died, of course."

The words were said so simply that for an instant Adaba didn't comprehend them. And when he did, he felt paralyzed.

"Why, we would have died, of course."

He knew that Denmark meant precisely what he said.

Suddenly he understood why there was a certain vagueness about the last phases of Denmark's plans. Denmark, Peter, Ned, the other leaders—they were intelligent men. They had known exactly what they faced—the difficulties, the possibilities, the risks. No doubt they had hoped with all their hearts to triumph in their crusade. They had thought they had a chance to triumph. But they had been willing, if neccessary, to die. Some of them—Denmark, Peter, Ned—had expected to die. Had from the very beginning known that they were almost certainly doomed. Had accepted their deaths and marched toward them unflinchingly.

"Why, Denmark?" Adaba asked softly. "Why?"

Denmark's eyes opened. "We had no intention of dying if we could possibly avoid it. But consider, Adaba, consider the hundreds of thousands who have died in slavery in the past, the millions who have died throughout history. Now at last the world is beginning to turn against slavery—but not here in the South. Here the coffles grow

233

longer, the chains heavier. Consider the thousands in the South, the hundreds of thousands, who may yet die in bondage. What is our small number compared with those?

"It was my dream to lead my people to freedom. For that, I would gladly die on the gallows, but what good has that kind of death done in the past?

"No, I decided, it would take much more than that. It would take hundreds, it would take thousands, willing to stand up and *take* their freedom—or die. That was what we would do. And if we failed, if we were slaughtered in Charleston, it would be such a slaughter as to make the whole world cry out in horror. Then the world would force this bondage to be ended, and black and white would at last be free to learn to be brothers.

"It seemed like a small price to pay. Do you understand?"

Denmark's dream.

It was a bloody dream, a terrible dream, to some even an evil dream. And yet it was also a noble dream, and Adaba listened to it with grief and horror and pride.

"Yes," he said, "I understand."

Nine

The City Council, Intendant James Hamilton, Jr., presiding, convened early.

"Gentlemen," said the intendant, "we have had a long night. Many of us have been completely without rest, and we have a great deal of hard work ahead of us. Therefore, at this time I shall be brief.

"Our first concern, gentlemen, must be for public order and safety, and to that end I am going to suggest that militia continue to be maintained in the city. After all, we don't yet know the degree to which this insurrection plot has been foiled. I, personally, happen to think that the vast majority of blacks are faithful and loyal to their masters. But some of these savages could turn on us yet.

234

"Secondly, I wish to appoint some of you gentlemen to a committee to assist me in investigating this plot and bringing the guilty to justice. Before this day ends, I want the committee to be at work, interrogating those whose names we already have, finding other witnesses and suspects, and arresting the guilty. Within two days I want to be able to present a court with evidence that a conspiracy exists and trials are justified, together with a calendar of the accused.

"Gentlemen, we all know that swift punishment is the most effective way of maintaining order among rebellious blacks. And the blacks of Charleston, by all that's holy, are about to feel our wrath!"

By Tuesday, Adaba wondered if this was what a war-torn city was like—the soldiers like an occupying army, the general air of mistrust, the feeling that normal life had been suspended for the indefinite future. He had the feeling of being watched and suspected wherever he went. He walked about the city like a man on guard, expecting to be attacked, caught, accused at any moment.

But it was necessary. Denmark had to know what was going on.

He first encountered the cordon as he came down the west side of King Street and started to cross Market. Suddenly the soldier who stood on the southwest corner brought his rifle to port.

"Hey, you! Back, nigger!"

"What—"

"I said *back*, goddammit, *back!*"

The soldier was sweeping the muzzle of his rifle toward Adaba and bringing the butt to his shoulder. Adaba backed away.

"Please, massa," he said, "jes' wanna walk down de street."

"You just stay on the other side of the street, then. You don't go past this line 'less you got business at the work-house. Ain't nobody, even white, gets by here 'less he live here or work or got business."

Adaba saw then: there was a line of soldiers along the west side of King Street extending south, and another

235

along the south side of Market Street extending west. He was willing to bet that when he reached Broad Street he would find a line of soldiers there too.

He walked down the east side of King Street. He was right. There was a line of soldiers extending to the west on Broad Street. Evidently there was a cordon of soldiers around the workhouse at a distance of two blocks.

There had to be a reason.

Looking around, he saw Lew Sabre coming from the City Hall a block to the east, and he raised an arm and hailed him. He hadn't laid eyes on Lew in weeks, had hardly spoken to him in months, and it suddenly struck him that his old friend was leaving boyhood behind. He was now as old as Adaba had been when he had first taken up with Gilly. Gone was the round face and the full cheeks and the eyes that were too big for his head. Now he was tall, lean, and sinewy, hard chinned and hollow cheeked, with sunken dark eyes of a peculiar intensity. Only the big mop of black hair was the same, and Adaba had to restrain an impulse to muss it as he had when Lew was much younger.

"You're the man I want to see," he said, "you or your daddy. I want to thank your daddy for warning mine away from the city."

Lew shrugged the matter off. "They been friends a long time. He couldn't do nothing else."

Adaba indicated the cordon. "What's all them soldier boys doing there, you got any idea?"

"That's to keep the niggers away from the workhouse and the jail, so they can't rescue the prisoners."

"Prisoners?"

"The intendant appointed a committee to investigate the insurrection. I heard all about it, 'cause he put my daddy on it. They started investigating last night, and this morning they had the guard arrest about five or six blacks."

Adaba felt faint. "Do we know any of them?"

"There's some Poyas people—I guess you know Peter. And there's some of Governor Bennett's people, but I don't know any of them at all."

Ned . . . Rolla . . . Batteau . . .

236

"What do you think they'll do to them, Lew?"

"Hang them, if they're guilty. That's what my daddy says. And I reckon some of them are guilty all right."

Adaba had difficulty keeping his voice steady. "Do they know who the leader is?"

Lew looked down and kicked at a pebble in the street. He seemed to be avoiding Adaba's eyes. "I was just now talking to my daddy, and he says they have a pretty good idea. He says they'll have him before the day is over."

"Who, Lew? Who do they think it is?"

"Well, I ain't supposed to say, but . . . a friend of yours. Denmark Vesey."

"Denmark . . . Thank you, Lew."

"Jeez, I'm sorry, Adaba. . . ."

He had to get away from Lew, had to get away fast. He had to get to Denmark. They could be arresting him at this very moment.

The ten or so blocks to Denmark's house had never seemed so long. He wanted to run, but didn't dare. He felt as if every eye was upon him.

He found Denmark in his parlor, and he wasted no time. "You've got to get away from here. Right now. I talked to Lew Sabre, and from what he says, you could be arrested at any minute. You've got to hide—"

"Wait. Calm yourself. Tell me exactly what you've learned."

Adaba told him about the cordon of soldiers around the workhouse area, the investigating committee, and the arrests.

"The governor's people," Denmark said thoughtfully. "We must assume that that means Ned, Rolla, Batteau, and Mathias. Mathias knows little, and I don't think the others will talk. Poyas means Peter, who will never talk, Abraham, who knows little, and possibly Dr. Poyas's Mungo, whom I'm not sure of."

"Denmark!" Adaba cried desperately. "You've got to hide *now!*"

"Listen to me," Denmark said as calmly as before. "As matters turned out, you were wise to dissociate yourself from our plans. They'll find it perhaps a little difficult to hang you. But you've been so close to me that your name is certain to be mentioned by someone. I think you should leave the city, go off somewhere with your friend Mr. Murdock, and wait until calm and reason return to Charleston. Promise me you'll do that."

"No, I'll help you hide out. I can take you out of the city right now."

"The patrols are probably being notified about me, and the guard is on its way here. But I have my plans."

"Won't you tell me—"

"No."

Denmark took Adaba's shoulders in his big hands. He looked into the younger man's eyes for a moment.

"I taught you a few things worth knowing, didn't I, boy?" he said.

"Oh, Christ . . ."

Denmark drew Adaba to him. Embraced him. Thrust him away.

"Now, go, Adaba. *Go!*"

As quickly as that they parted, after all those years. And Adaba left the house wondering when—if ever—he would see Denmark again.

Where was Denmark Vesey?

He had utterly disappeared. "He wasn't at his house when we got there yesterday morning," Captain Dove reported to the committee at City Hall, "and nobody admits having seen him since. We talked to his neighbors, and they couldn't—or wouldn't—tell us a thing. We've searched his shop and all the shipyards where he worked and the houses of his wives and children, but he's nowhere to be found. And nobody seems to have the slightest idea of where he might be."

"Isn't it possible that he's left the city?" Channing asked.

"It's possible that he got past the patrols," the captain conceded, "and we're having the countryside searched. We're covering the ships on the waterfront too, for that matter. But actually there are a lot more places to hide right in the heart of the city."

"Then seek those places out and search them, captain," Hamilton said insistently. "Vesey has got to be found. It's

238

become quite plain to this committee that he was almost certainly at the head of the conspiracy. He preached it, he inspired it, he planned it in every detail. In a sense, he's responsible for all those Negroes that are going to be hanged, and it would be the height of injustice if he didn't hang with them. I've got just one order for you, Captain. *Find Denmark Vesey!*"

The court was convened at noon, Lionel H. Kennedy and Thomas Parker, presiding, in a small, crowded room in the workhouse, where the prisoners were being held. The oath was administered by the justices to each other and then to the five freeholders who composed the remainder of the court. The intendant related how the insurrection conspiracy had been discovered, and presented to the court a calendar of the accused, the charges, and the witnesses.

After acting as its own grand jury and examining the testimony the committee had collected, the court laid down certain special rules. In the main, these seemed fair enough to Channing, as they had to do with such things as adequate counsel for the accused and the right to cross-examine, but one rule worried him. It stated that the witnesses should be faced with the accused in every case *except* when testimony was given under a solemn pledge that the names of the witnesses should not be divulged.

"I must object," Channing said. "You're telling us that the principles of common law and the settled rules of evidence don't apply here—even when a man is on trial for his life."

Kennedy knew a troublemaker when he saw one. "Now, goddammit," he said angrily, "for the most part, they don't! Chan, you know perfectly well that this court has been organized under a statute intended for the government of a distinct class of persons—namely, the blacks. We don't have to confront witnesses or administer oaths or any of that. We don't even have to worry about a default in form."

"In other words," said one of the freeholders, a beefy, red-faced man, who looked at Channing with distaste, "this here is *our* court, and we all are going to run it as we damn well please."

By midafternoon, the dim, poorly ventilated little room stank with the heat of the day and the presence of thirty or more closely packed bodies. Some of the wardens dozed, others looked close to fainting, and Channing, seated against a back wall, found himself blinded by the sweat that ran down into his eyes.

The public in general, the court determined, was not to be admitted to the trials. Only the accused, the witnesses, their owners, and counsel were to be admitted. The same permission was extended to the intendant and the wardens of Charleston—with a nervous glance in Channing's direction.

That decided, the court turned to the first trial—that of Rolla, a Negro man, the slave of His Excellency, Governor Bennett—Jacob Axson, Esq., attending as counsel for the owner.

The first witness was George Wilson's friend, Adam. He was led to the improvised bench, a long table at one end of the room, and asked to face his judges. He was a young man with a look of fear on his face, and Kennedy tried to put him at ease by announcing kindly that Adam had come forward voluntarily, asking only that his name not be divulged, that he might avoid the conspirators' vengeance. The court was promising to conceal his name, and all present were admonished not to reveal it to the public.

"You're a good boy, Adam," Kennedy began, "and we thank you for coming here. Now, tell us, do you know the governor's man Rolla?"

"I know Rolla. . . ."

"A little louder, Adam. Suppose you tell us when you first heard about the insurrection."

"About three months ago, sir. Rolla asked me to join with him in slaying the whites. . . ."

A clerk busily scratched pen on paper, trying to get the testimony down.

". . . When I asked Rolla what was to be done with the women and children, he said, 'When we have done with the fellows, we know what to do with the wenches.' He said there are many followers in the country. . . ."

240

"What can you tell us about the conspirators' meetings? Do you know where they were held?"

"I don't know, but I think 'twas in Bull Street, where Denmark Vesey lives."

Denmark Vesey again.

Mr. Axson, counsel for Governor Bennett, made an attempt to question Adam, but, being unable to identify Adam to Rolla and perhaps obtain relevant information, he found that an effective cross-examination was impossible.

The second witness against Rolla was George Wilson.

"This witness, as regards the concealment of his name," Kenneday said, "stands in precisely the same situation as the first witness. The divulging of his name publicly by anyone in this courtroom is expressly forbidden."

Channing stared at the justice.

The third witness was Major John Wilson. "What my servant has just said is substantially what he told me some days ago. He is a servant of the very best character, and every word he says may be relied on."

Of course, the major could not be identified to the accused, as that might lead to the indentification of George and Adam. His name, too, was ordered concealed by the court.

A fourth witness, to remain anonymous, was brought before the court. "Rolla asked me to join with the blacks to rise against the whites. . . ."

And a fifth. "About a month ago, Rolla advised me to join the blacks against the whites. . . ."

Channing listened incredulously. What could Jacob Axson do against such testimony? What could Rolla do, locked up as he was in another part of the workhouse, with no idea of who was accusing him? Five witnesses were produced on Rolla's behalf, but what could they do for him but say, "Rolla is honest and has never mentioned an insurrection to us, and therefore the witnesses against him must be lying"? It was not only an incredibly weak defense, it was hardly a defense at all.

Weak with fatigue, Channing forced himself to his feet. He had no wish to disrupt the court, no wish to involve himself in an imbroglio, but he realized that this first trial

241

would very likely set the standard for all those yet to come, and he had to do something. At least he had to try.

There was a lull in the courtroom, murmured conversations between the wardens, and a conference between the justices. Channing made his way to the front of the room and caught Kennedy's eye. He saw that Kennedy at once became wary, and all his tact, all his diplomacy, vanished.

"Lionel, for God's sake," he said in a low voice, "even if the man is guilty as hell, you're not going to convict on that kind of testimony, are you?"

"What's wrong with it?" Kennedy snapped.

"What's wrong with it! Four witnesses, five if you count the major, and every one of them anonymous? The accused doesn't get to face a single one of his accusers? Doesn't get a decent chance at cross-examination—"

The red-faced freeholder's fist came down on the table with a resounding thump. "Mr. Sabre," he said angrily, "with all respect, sir, why don't you just sit down and let this here court get on with its work?"

"But in all justice—"

"In all justice, sir, we all came here to hang us some niggers. And that, by God, sir, is just what we're gonna do!"

"Denmark Vesey," his father said. "There's no doubt about it in my mind or anyone else's. Denmark Vesey is the man behind the conspiracy. It started with him, it de-depends upon him, it will most likely end with him."

"But he ain't even been tried yet," Lew said. He had never seen his father look more tired than he did this evening: pouched eyes with heavy lids in a sagging face. Channing had had little sleep for several days, and the emotional scenes in the cramped, steaming courtroom had drained him.

"Tried!" His father laughed bitterly and shoved his empty soup bowl away from him on the dining table. "Do you think he's going to get a trial in that—that Star Chamber?"

"But if he ain't even been tried, how can you say—"

"A reasonable man can come to a reasonable conclusion on the basis of the available evidence. That's not the

242

same as hanging a man on the basis of a prejudice and without a fair trial. I may privately be convinced that Denmark Vesey is a murderous rogue, but I wouldn't harm a hair of his head until the fact was fairly established in a court of law. And I'd do my damnedest to keep my mind open to a reversal of opinion. But meanwhile," his father slumped deeper into his chair, "meanwhile, I am convinced that the man is guilty as hell."

Lew resisted the idea. He had no love for Denmark Vesey—that bullying voice, those threatening eyes—but it had occurred to him that he might have inadvertently aided in the escape.

"You don't really think he would have killed all the women and children like they're saying, do you?"

His father shrugged. "Insurrectionist armies aren't noted for their tender mercies toward their former masters, Lewis. Yes, I think that if the insurrection had succeeded, Charleston would have had a bloodbath. And Denmark knew it and probably even planned on it."

"Then . . . I reckon he ought to be hanged. If they catch him, that is."

"Oh, they'll catch him all right. But he's certainly done a good job of slipping away. From what we've learned, yesterday morning he was in plain sight, doing absolutely nothing to conceal himself. And then," his father snapped his fingers, "he was gone. He must have disappeared just about the same time the guard was on its way to arrest him. But there was no way in the world he could have known about that."

Lew's palms grew a little damper, and he rubbed them on his pants legs. "Maybe somebody overheard you all talking about it at City Hall. Those niggers overhear things, and then they talk—"

"Nobody overheard. And I wish you wouldn't use that word 'nigger' so freely. I know colored people use it among themselves, but coming out of a white mouth, there's something nasty about it. Something hurtful. Even if you don't mean it that way."

"Yes, sir."

"Christ, I remember when life was so pleasant. It was like I was living in a rosy dream, and then a few years ago

243

I somehow found myself waking up. To the real world. And ever since, I've been asking myself what the hell I managed to get myself born into." His father smiled, tried to laugh. "Now, that is a hell of a thing to tell a young man who's still got his whole adult life to look forward to."

"Things'll get better, daddy."

"Yes. Of course they will."

His father shoved back his chair and got up from the table, and Lew got up with him.

"You think they'll catch Denmark before long?"

"Lewis, starting tomorrow morning, troops are going to turn this city upside down and inside out and shake it till it rattles. If Denmark Vesey is anywhere near Charleston, they'll find him within thirty-six hours."

"And then lynch him, I reckon."

"Not if I have anything to say about it. And now I'm going up to bed."

His father started out of the room, then turned back.

"Oh, and Lewis . . ."

"Yes, sir?"

"You're getting a little old for me to tell you what to do all the time, but you have a disturbing habit of disappearing all night long. Now, there's some reason to believe that the insurrection threat isn't altogether past, and also there may be reprisals from Denmark's followers. I'd appreciate it if you would be home every night until this disturbance is over. Please indulge the whim of an aging father."

"Yes, sir. I'll come home."

"Thank you . . . and good night. . . ."

Probably just a coincidence he got away after I told Adaba, Lew thought, trying to wipe away the guilt. *Hell, it ain't my fault. It just happened that way. . . .*

The search for Denmark Vesey was well under way when Lew left the house the next morning. Looking about the city and asking questions, he found that the river- and harbor-fronts were so guarded that it was virtually impossible to leave the city without being seen and stopped. The wharves, of course, were particularly well guarded. Thus

244

the troops that were spread across the Neck and moving down on the city, searching every room of every house as they went, thumping every wall and looking under every floor, were rapidly reducing the area in which Denmark could hide.

The soldiers were fast, Lew observed, and they were brutal. They treated the blacks with contempt and the whites not much better. He watched with growing anger as he saw them needlessly shoving people about, abusing them, damaging their property. Old men were knocked down, young women were handled indecently, children were casually kicked out of the way—all in the name of the search.

He was there when the searchers arrived at Jovita's house. Benjamin had not welcomed him; the events of the last few days had turned black and white against each others as never before in Lew's memory, and he had a feeling that Benjamin would not welcome a white man for a long time to come. But he was more concerned with Jovita's welfare than with Benjamin's welcome, and he decided to stay as close to her as possible until the search was over and the troops were gone.

In a way, luck was with him—and with Jovita—when the searchers came. They were led by a young lieutenant of the Charleston Riflemen, straw-haired Hadden Hargrave. Lew knew him slightly through Adaba, and Hargrave knew who Lew was: the son of a city warden and therefore not the best person in the world to upset. Also Hargrave was not a bad fellow, and though he looked at Jovita hungrily, he merely gave Lew a knowing leer and departed with his men without causing any trouble. Lew sighed with relief and drew the laughing Jovita into his arms. The plain and simple truth was that, if he had had to, he would have killed for her.

Meanwhile, the trials continued. On the testimony of two witnesses, both anonymous, Batteau Bennett was found guilty of attempting to raise an insurrection of blacks against whites. Stephen, a Negro man belonging to Mr. Thomas R. Smith, was next brought before the court, but there being no testimony against him, he was immediately discharged. Peter Poyas was brought before the court, charged, and found guilty on the testimony of William Paul and the much lengthier and more detailed testimony of an anonymous witness.

Channing Sabre made enemies by pressing for fairer trial procedures, and Governor Bennett did the same, thus irrevocably damaging his political career. Actually, there was little they could do but express their views strongly among the city wardens and try to arouse at least some of them to protest to the court between the various trials.

But the court's attitude, self-righteous, vengeful, and defensive, was made clear by an incident that occurred early during the trials. On Friday, June 21, the second day of the massive search for Denmark Vesey, William Johnson, a brother-in-law of Governor Bennett and an associate justice of the U. S. Supreme Court, published in the Charleston *Courier* a letter entitled "Melancholy Effect of Popular Excitement." It attempted to warn against public hysteria by recounting how a dozen years earlier, during an insurrection scare, a slave had been dragged before a court and, on no valid evidence at all, had been condemned and hung. The court interpreted this as an assault upon itself (". . . an insinuation that the court, under the influence of popular prejudice, was capable of committing perjury and murder, and implied that the author of it possessed sounder judgment, deeper penetration, and firmer nerves, than the rest of his fellow citizens") and at once began pressing for a public apology.

The white public sided with the court. String the niggers up!

There would be no mercy in Charleston.

The hour was late, and the bed was warm but . . .

". . . Got to go home, Jo."

"Aw, no."

"Promised my old daddy . . . home every night . . ."

"Storming out there. Hear that thunder?"

"Don't matter . . . got to go. . ."

"Ain't going let you out of this bed. Ain't . . ."

"Aw, Jovita . . . "

246

"Ain't going let you go, Lewis. Not yet."

"Ah! . . . ah . . ."

"Now, you come closer here. Come on, one more time. You just bring it here to me. You give it to your Jovita. . . ."

And so they made love one more time, one last time, while the lightning flashed over their naked bodies and the thunder rumbled and the wind-swept rain came down in a deluge; made love until they struck their own lightning, making it explode and flash and burn in the darkness of the bed, and ended it all in soft laughter.

"Oh, God, Jovita, I do love you."

"Want to leave your Jovita now?"

"No, don't ever want to leave you . . . but . . ."

But had to, however reluctantly. Had to leave this place where he had no thoughts of bloody insurrections and hanging trials and the missing Denmark Vesey. Had to leave . . .

He held Jovita a little longer and kissed her before arising to dress.

"I'll see you in the morning, early."

"You ain't going to be here early, not after tonight."

"I'll be here early, you darling, and don't you go out on the streets without me, you hear? Aw, Jo . . ."

Even then he was tempted to stay just a little longer, but he had made a promise, and promises meant something to him. And his father would be worried. Lew held Jovita and kissed her a few last times, kissed her and stroked her, until she told him either to leave or to come back to bed.

"Good night, Jo. . . ."

The house was in darkness. There was no sound from Benjamin's and Delia's room across the hall. As quietly as possible, Lew felt his way down the stairs to the front door, opened it, and stepped out onto the piazza. There was still a light in the parlor of the house next door, shining past half-opened curtains. Lew stood on the piazza for a moment, hoping the rain might let up.

Lightning struck somewhere across the Ashley River. Thunder rumbled.

Denmark Vesey passed by the parlor window of the house next door.

Denmark Vesey.

Lew was stunned. He told himself that in that brief glimpse, at such a distance, he couldn't possibly have recognized Denmark. But he knew perfectly well that he had.

Denmark appeared in profile at the window once again. He stood there for a moment, almost as if to assure Lew that it was indeed he, and moved away.

Someone pulled the curtain closed.

For another moment Lew didn't move. What should he do now?

Gradually it came to him that there was only one thing he could do, only one conceivable right thing.

He no longer had any thought of the storm as he stepped out into the street. He plunged through it, ran through ankle-deep mud, through rain that pounded blindingly against his eyes. He knew only that he had to get the City Guard back here before Denmark got away.

Soaked through, muddy, bedraggled, he reached the guardhouse and raced past the miserable sentry who stood hunched against the storm in the entryway. Lamps were still burning in the office within, and a number of men were up and dressed, chatting and playing cards. Captain Dove was talking to a man Lew recognized as a city warden, but he broke off when he saw Lew, and his hard eyes got even harder. He knew who Lew was, and he hadn't much use for Channing Sabre these days. Not many people did.

"Denmark Vesey," Lew said quickly. "I know where he is!"

The captain stared at him for a moment. "Troops been looking for Vesey for three days. Guard's been looking for four and never laid an eye on him. And *you* know where he is."

"I saw him just a little while ago. I came right away. If you hurry, I can lead you to him."

Dove gave the warden a knowing look. "Where'd you see him, boy?"

"At his wife's house. He must have doubled back on you—"

248

"We've been through the house of every wife he ever had. You telling me you done what over two thousand troops and the City Guard couldn't do?"

"I just saw him, was all! By just plain luck. And I know Denmark Vesey's face better than I do yours. I saw him *twice* when he got too close to a window."

"Boy, there just ain't no way he could have got by them troops."

"Aw, captain," Lew said scornfully, "there ain't no troops out there to stop Denmark Vesey from going anywhere he damn well pleases! Coming here, I didn't see a single soldier or guard anywhere—they're all hiding someplace keeping their goddamn asses dry. All right, maybe Denmark won't be at his wife's house when you get there. Maybe he'll be on a ship, the way you're wasting time. But I know damn good and well I saw Denmark Vesey, and tomorrow the world's gonna know it too!"

It was, of course, a threat. The captain's eyes widened, and his strong jaw clamped tighter. If he had been alone with Lew, Lew might have had something to worry about.

"Look at it this way, captain," the warden said conciliatingly, "if the boy can take you to Vesey, fine. You'll get the credit for the capture. And if Vesey isn't there, nobody will be able to say you haven't followed up every lead."

The captain seemed to relax. "All right," he said. "All right, I'll get a few men, and we'll go take a look. But if Vesey ain't there . . ."

The captain's snarls brought a dozen sleepy men to their feet, cursing and grumbling, and they followed him out into Broad Street as he shoved Lew ahead of him. "You lead the way, boy. I ain't letting you out of my sight. . . ."

The rain, if anything, seemed to be coming down even harder as Lew led the men along the muddy streets. When they arrived in Vesey's wife's street, a light still showed in her house and in two or three others.

"All right, sergeant," the captain said to one of his men, "we'll surround the place. If Vesey's really in there, we don't want him going out no back window. Then you and me and a couple of others will go in and get him. You, boy, you just stay out of the way, and don't you dare go running off."

Lew backed into the muddy street directly in front of the house. Guards silently climbed over the yard fences and surrounded the house. Except when lightning struck, they were almost invisible in the night. The captain, the sergeant, and two other men climbed over the fence and disappeared into the darkness of the piazza.

The wind had stopped. The rain fell in a steady downpour.

A pistol went off inside the house.

Seconds later, lights appeared in the windows of a couple of other houses. Faces appeared in windows and at doorways. Lew found that he was holding his breath.

From this angle, he could see onto Jovita's piazza. In a flash of lightning he saw Benjamin and Delia appear on the piazza, followed by Jovita. Jovita then opened the piazza door to look out onto the street—to look at Lew.

The piazza door of Denmark's wife's house opened. Denmark appeared in the doorway, standing tall, with his arms bound behind him. Captain Dove and the sergeant, standing behind him, shoved him out into the street and the rain.

Denmark looked directly at Lew, looked at him unwaveringly through the downpour, his eyes fierce and accusing. Lew knew he would never forget that look, would never cease to be pierced by it.

"All right," Captain Dove yelled, "you all go back in your houses! That shot didn't mean nothing! Nothing's happening here, nobody got hurt!"

Denmark still looked directly into Lew's eyes, and Lew could not tear his eyes away.

The guards who had been surrounding the house reappeared. They fell in behind as Dove and the sergeant grabbed Denmark's arms and marched him off along the street.

Benjamin, Delia, and Jovita, without a word to Lew, vanished back into their house.

Other faces disappeared. Lights went out.

Lew continued to stand there in the rain, in the middle of the muddy street. Alone. For a long, long time.

Ten

What had he done?

The right thing. No more than that. Denmark was his enemy, quite ready to spill his blood—his, his sister's, his father's. And a man had a right to defend himself and his family, no matter what.

And yet Lew felt sick.

His father, exhausted by the past week, was asleep when Lew got home. He himself could barely sleep and managed only a fitful doze disturbed by vague, troubled dreams. When he heard his father getting up the next morning, he waited until coffee was on the table, then told him the news.

"Captain Dove captured Denmark Vesey last night. . . ."

Not *I captured*, or *I led the captain to Denmark*, but *Captain Dove captured* . . . For some reason Lew wanted no part of the credit.

When he thought Jovita might be awake, he hurried to her house. The rains had stopped, and the day sparkled, though the streets were thick with mud.

"She don't want to see you," Benjamin said flatly when he opened the street door. His eyes were angry, his lips twisted into a snarl. "Don't think we needs you 'round here no more, Mr. Lewis, *sir.*"

"Benjamin, what the hell!"

"You can just take your white ass—"

"It's all right, Benjamin," came Jovita's soft voice.

"It ain't all right with me!"

"But I want to see him."

Benjamin threw hard looks at both of them, then pounded back into the house, slamming the door behind him.

Lew stepped onto the piazza.

"What the hell's he mad at me for?"

"You got to understand, Lewis—Denmark is our friend."

"Well, he ain't no friend to me, and that's for sure."

Jovita's little smile vanished and returned. "He bring you to me, didn't he?"

"But, Jo, him and his goddamn insurrection—he would have *killed* me—"

"Lewis, you best go now—"

"Me and all my family! Goddamn crazy fool, he probably would have got you and yours all killed off too!"

"I don't know, Lewis. I s'pose you're right. And I don't want nothing bad ever to happen to you. But, Lewis, it's best you stay 'way from here for a while—"

"But why? Jovita, I love you, and I ain't gonna stay away from you—"

"Yes, you is."

She spoke very softly, and he knew she meant it, that no argument he could give her would change her mind. He stared at her, realizing that there was something different about her today. Everything about her was softer, her eyes, her smile, her voice, as if she had wept the entire night; and yet there was also a resolve that would not be bent or broken.

"Jovita, you sending me away?"

She nodded. "For a little while."

"I'll be back in a day or two."

"Best not so soon. I ain't feeling so good anyways, Lewis. I think I catch me a fever last night. Best wait till I'se feeling better."

"But I ain't gonna stay away long. I *can't* stay away long. Just a few days."

Jovita nodded again, and her gaze stayed on the floor of the piazza. She knew what Lewis wanted when he stepped toward her, and she raised her face to be kissed. But her eyes avoided his, and the kiss was awkward and fumbling, as if their lips had never touched before.

"I'll be back soon."

A third time she nodded.

As he left, he had a terrible feeling that things might never again be quite the same between them.

252

have pronounced you guilty. You have enjoyed the advantage of able counsel, and were also heard in your own defense, in which you endeavored with great art and plausibility to impress a belief of your innocence. After the most patient deliberation, however, the court were not only satisfied of your guilt, but that you were the author and original instigator of this diabolical plot. Your professed design was to trample on all laws, human and divine; to riot in blood, outrage, rapine, and conflagration; and to introduce anarchy and confusion in their most horrid forms. Your life has become, therefore, a just and necessary sacrifice at the shrine of indignant justice. . . ."

Channing thought he saw tears flowing down Denmark's cheek as the black man looked at Kennedy, but perhaps it was no more than sweat from the oppressive heat of the room. Still, he thought, why wouldn't Denmark weep, to see all his efforts come to this? For Channing remained morally certain that the man was guilty, whatever the faults of the court. And why, as Denmark himself had asked, should a man in his position risk all he had in the world, including his life, on a quixotic venture to help slaves?

"I sorry, master. I don't do it no more. Please, master, I'se good girl, I don't do it no more, master. . . . I'se good girl. Don't do this to your Gilly. Oh, please, master . . ."

It all came back to Channing in a rush, all the pain and the horror of it, and he nearly cried out. He remembered dragging the terrorized girl to Gore's office. The inspection the drugged girl had been put through, the desecration of her body at the hands of a stranger. And God only knows what the girl had been put through since.

Was that the meaning of Denmark Vesey?

Was it possible that the most decent man in Charleston, perhaps the only truly decent man, was a half-crazy old black (for surely in this world he had to be mad!) who preached human dignity, who stood up for defenseless Gillys, and who was now about to be hanged for his efforts?

"Your lamp of life is nearly extinguished," the judge intoned. "Your race is run, and you must shortly pass from time to eternity. . . ."

Channing wanted to stand up and scream, *"You've got to stop this! Stop this!"*

But he knew he never would.

The hanging was scheduled for Tuesday morning, July 2, between six and eight o'clock in the morning.

The word came up King Street, faster than the carriages that carried them, that the six condemned men were on their way.

Why was he here, Adaba wondered miserably. Why did he have to force himself to bear the unbearable? Did he wish a last look at his friend? Did he wish to gaze one last time into Denmark's eyes? And if he succeeded in that, would it help Denmark or only give him pain? Adaba had no idea. He only knew that it was abominable that a man was to be put to his death in this ugly manner as a public spectacle, no matter what his offense. Adaba felt a man should be allowed to die quietly, privately, alone.

At least Denmark would have his friends. And they would be here, not to be warned by his death, but to pay homage.

Long before dawn the crowds had begun to gather around the high gallows that had been constructed up above Boundary Street. The entire city, it seemed, black and white, was now here. In the early light, Adaba could see people watching from second- and third-storey windows, from high balconies, from rooftops: thousands of people gathered to watch one free black man and five slaves die.

The prisoners arrived. The guard had almost to fight its way through the crowd along King Street. Adaba could not get so much as a glimpse of Denmark.

But he did see Lew Sabre.

"Is it true, Lew," the voice said softly behind him, "that you're the one who turned Denmark in?"

Lew didn't have to turn around. He recognized Adaba's voice. "Captain Dove caught him," Lew said.

"But is it true that you led Captain Dove to him?"

256

Why was it so hard to say? "Yes. I did."

"Why, Lew? Why?"

"For God's sake! He was going to kill us all!"

"But he didn't, did he?"

"He sure as hell tried."

"And hadn't he the right to try, Lew?" Adaba sounded as if he were on the verge of weeping. "He was leading slaves. Innocent prisoners, Lew, a lot of them brought here from their homes thousands of miles across the ocean. Don't innocent prisoners always have the right to claim their freedom?"

"All right, maybe they do. But I sure as hell ain't gonna just stand there and let them kill me. I'm gonna defend myself."

"How? By executing hostages? Because that's what you're doing now, isn't it, Lew? 'See, nigger, this is what will happen to you if you dream of freedom. This is what will happen to you if you try to escape your bondage. This is what will happen to you if you try to assert your rights as a man.'"

Was that why he felt guilty? Lew wasn't sure. He only knew that once again in his life he had done "the right thing" and as a result felt like hell. That was why he was here. For some reason, he didn't have the stomach to claim the credit for turning Denmark in, but at least he intended to have the guts to see the results of his act.

"First Gilly, and now Denmark," Adaba said softly. "I never thought I'd ever be able to kill anyone, but with you, Lew, I just might be able to make an exception. So maybe you'd better turn me in and get me hanged too. Because one day, white boy . . ."

And now Denmark and the other five were on the scaffold, six men standing on the traps, their wrists bound behind them, their guards kneeling to tie their ankles.

Someone, Lew thought it was the intendant, said, "If you have any last words, any words of repentance, now is the time to say them."

One of the prisoners made a sound. Peter Poyas looked at him and the others and said quietly but distinctly, "Do not open your lips. Die silently, as you shall see me do."

Neither he nor Denmark nor any other said another

word. Denmark looked sternly, fiercely out over the crowd, aloof to it. Then the black hood was placed over his head.

All were hooded in black. The nooses were adjusted about their necks, the knot drawn tight under the ear.

The traps opened.

The bodies dropped.

Some claimed later that they had heard necks snap. But not all snapped. Some of the bodies twitched, and one danced wildly, while a moan of horror swept through the crowd, rising like the sound of a hurricane. Two guards leapt for the dancing man's legs and hung from them. The putrid stench of violent death filled the air, and Lew doubled over, suddenly ill, retching painfully.

When he looked up, Adaba was gone.

By evening, after supper, he could stay away from Jovita no longer. An hour in her arms would be an hour in which he could forget. An hour in her arms, and he would begin to heal.

People were up late that evening, and a light burned in almost every house as he walked along the street. He had a sense that the blacks of the city were in mourning, and as he approached Jovita's house, it seemed to him that he was being watched. The black people of the neighborhood had seen him often during the last ten months, and they knew him. Now he sensed their whispers: *There he go . . . that him . . . him that brought Captain Dove to Denmark Vesey. . . .*

From more than a block away and across the street he saw the lights burning in Jovita's house, and he stopped, suddenly hesitant. From the Sunday Jovita had sent him away, he had managed to leave her alone until last Thursday, when she had spoken to him briefly but had told him it was too soon. He had returned again on Saturday evening, but had been told by Delia that Jovita was sick in bed and couldn't be disturbed. It had been ten days since he had spent any real time with her. Ten days since that stormy Saturday night. Was it still too soon?

No, it couldn't be. This had been one of the worst days he had known in his entire life, the worst since his mother

258

had died, a day even worse than that one four years ago when his father had taken Gilly away. The hanging in the morning. Then the talk of it all through the day, Georgiana almost gloating, Norvin so pompous and self-righteous. The sickness he had seen on his father's face.

Perhaps Jovita had seen him coming. The door of her piazza opened as he stood there raising his hand to it, and she faced him.

"Jo . . ."

"Lewis," she said in little more than a whisper, "please go away."

It was one of the few times he had ever seen her without some semblance of a smile. Her face caught light from a window. Her eyes were very large.

"Please," she repeated, "please, Lewis, just go 'way."

He caught his breath. "Jo, I've got to see you!"

"No . . ."

"I won't stay long. Just an hour."

She shook her head. "No . . ."

"I don't mean, to go to bed. I mean, just to be with you. Just to hold your hand."

"No, Lewis."

"Not even that," he said desperately. "Just to be *with* you. Jo, *I need you!*"

"I'se sorry, Lewis."

"But you can't—can't . . . Jovita, I love you!"

He saw now that she was weeping. "Reckon I love you too, Lewis. But I can't let you in my house no more."

"For God's sake, Jo!"

"Been thinking and thinking 'bout it. I know you only done what you figure you got to do. I—"

"Then why—"

"'Cause he was one of *us,* Lewis. All he done, he done for us. And he died for us. Lewis, *he died for us!*"

She began to close the door. But surely she couldn't, not just like that, not so easily, not so soon.

"Jovita, please!"

"Best you go 'way now, Lewis. Best you don't come back no more. Good-bye, Lewis."

"Jovita!"

The door closed.

Lew stood there staring at it, incredulous.

He raised his hand to it again, this time to pound on it, to break it down, to tear his way through it.

He knew it was no use. There was another door closed to him, a door that would remain closed for as long as he lived.

"Good-bye, Lewis."

She was gone out of his life. As gone out of his life as Gilly was gone out of Adaba's. Gone forever.

He lowered his hand.

This time there was not even any reason to stand alone in the street.

He turned and walked away.

The total number arrested was one hundred thirty-one. Of sixty-seven convicted, thirty-five were executed. The remainder of the convicted, as well as a number not convicted but adjudged "morally guilty," were sentenced to be transported out of the state or out of the country.

On a single day, Friday, July 26, 1822, twenty-two slaves were hanged from the same gallows.

Eleven

He survived.

Not without pain, of course. In the months that followed Denmark Vesey's death, Lew learned two of the most difficult lessons of his life. One was simply that you don't always get what you want, no matter how vital it is to your life and happiness. No benevolent angel is going to guarantee you your heart's desire.

The other lesson was that, most of the time, at least, eventually you forget. The human heart is mercifully faithless, and the pain that seems ineradicable is the acid that is burning away memory. Something is always left, of course, like a faded picture that will forever be treasured, but one is freed of the past. One goes on.

The day of Denmark Vesey's death was not the last time Lew saw Jovita. At first he could not accept that she was gone from his life forever. He knew it was true, but he kept telling himself, give her a little time and she'll come back to me, she'll let me back into her life. Meanwhile, he couldn't stay away from her altogether, and he would find himself near her house and looking toward it in the darkness of evening. Sometimes he caught a fleeting glimpse of her, a glimpse that never seemed quite real.

One day, three weeks after the executions, Lew encountered Jovita on the street, headed for her house. He tried to talk to her, but she refused even to look at him, and she walked faster, hunching her shoulders as if a cold wind had suddenly struck her. She entered her house without a backward glance and closed the door in his face.

When he returned a month later, Delia told him that Jovita no longer lived there. Where, then? Was she still in Charleston? Had she taken another lover? Delia refused to say, and Lew knew he had seen Jovita for the last time.

And so he did as his father wished. He went north to college, to Princeton, in the state of New Jersey. He became a serious student for the first time in his life. And at Princeton, he committed his first infidelity to the memory of Jovita: an episode with a jolly blond barmaid and part-time whore named Hilda, who, if she liked you, would "go all the way" for a dollar. There was no memory of Jovita to be encountered in committing one's body to Hilda's deft ministrations. There was only forgetfulness.

By the time he returned to Charleston the next summer, Lew had to admit that the impossible had happened. He had survived the loss of Jovita. He thought of her little. His best memories of her seemed more romance than reality, and he never dwelt upon them. Even her features that he had so loved, the bright eyes, the softly dimpled cheeks, the hovering smile, were sometimes difficult to recall.

And yet, and yet . . .

Sometimes, he would be walking along a busy Charleston street when ahead of him he would see a young woman's back. He would see a familiar brown neck, long and graceful, above shoulders that moved with a familiar grace and rhythm. And suddenly his breath would stop, and his heart would seem to falter, and his mind would cry out, *Jovita! Jovita!*

"Jo! Wait! Jovita! . . ."

But of course it was never she.

What's the use? Why go on trying? . . .

Weeks passed. Months. The deadly season of August and September came and went, and the year 1822 drifted toward its end. And still Adaba's profound depression failed to pass.

Denmark was dead. Denmark and his comrades, and for what? Adaba tried to tell himself that the sacrifice had not been in vain, that the dead men would be an inspiration to him and to other blacks, but he could not make himself believe it. *"I shall die a happy man,"* Denmark had said, *"if only I can see my people marching through the streets of Charleston . . . and know that they are standing up before the world like free men and saying, I shall be a slave no longer!"* But Denmark had not died like that. He had not died leading his people on a march to freedom. He had died knowing he had failed.

Or so it seemed to Adaba, and that death was too painful for him to contemplate. When friends who knew how close he had been to Denmark tried to commiserate with him, he coolly shrugged off their words and acted as if he hardly remembered the name of Denmark Vesey. He refused to go through the rituals of grief, the sorrow was too deep.

Denmark had been right: Adaba's own efforts to help his people had been futile, a matter of taking a handful of blacks to freedom while the number in captivity increased faster than they could be freed. There was simply no hope, no way that the vast masses of blacks would be freed, until, as his father had said often, the nation exploded from the unbearable agony of its internal contradictions. In another hundred years.

And meanwhile, Adaba thought listlessly, how was he to spend that hundred years?

He could live well. He could go abroad, and his father would provide for him. He could give his full time to studies and perhaps even do something for his people one day —his father's dream for him. Or he could simply retire to plantation life. Enjoy the colored society of Charleston and marry a pretty young lady of color, and raise a few free handsome brown-skinned children. Why not? The prospect was not unpleasing.

And as for Gilly? . . .

He had long ago given up the illusion that he would ever again see the girl he had once loved.

All right, then. He didn't even have to inform Gavin Murdock of his decision. One day perhaps Murdock would come to Charleston looking for him. . . .

But of course that wasn't really so. He did have to inform Murdock, and besides he found the atmosphere of Charleston stifling. Fear of the black was everywhere— and fear of the white. Almost any excuse was good enough for stringing up another nigger, and there was talk of new laws to regulate both free black and slave. Slaves should not be allowed to hire out their own time, it was said, and all free blacks over fifteen years of age should be assigned white guardians. It was time once more to assume the identity of John Dove, free itinerant black carpenter, and smell the clean fresh air of the Carolina countryside.

And thus it came about that Adaba met Black Buck.

Adaba was with Gavin Murdock, in the same maroon camp to which Murdock had taken Adaba more than four years earlier. They ate stew from the same pot that evening, and it had been cooked by the same woman. And afterward they sat elbow to elbow against the same pine and watched the same stars, while Murdock puffed his pipe. He had accepted Adaba's decision with equanimity, considering it perfectly understandable, and Adaba had agreed to stay with him a few weeks to help move some people north. But now Adaba was thinking about returning home. He wanted to be with his family for Christmas.

There was a sound somewhere in the woods.

Adaba guessed it was less than a hundred yards away: a cracking of dry wood, such as some clumsy creature might make, a man more likely than an animal.

For a moment neither man moved. They were not particularly alarmed. This was an impoverished region; even the poor whites, dimly aware that there was an outliers' camp somewhere nearby, took care to avoid it. Guards were seldom posted, and the camp rarely had to scatter.

There was another sound, perhaps closer. Something in the echo told them of the approach.

"Maybe we'd better go take a look," Gavin Murdock said.

They had been together too long to have to confer. They got to their feet and went their separate ways, one to the left, the other to the right, Indian-silent. After fifty feet, Adaba took his hatchet from its sheath. The idea of killing a man was as abhorrent to him as ever, but there were other lives to be considered, and more than one white man had disappeared forever in these woods.

They soon found him: a young black in tattered clothes, stumbling through the woods on the verge of exhaustion. A runaway. Or so it seemed. To be sure he wasn't bait for a trap, they watched him for some minutes, until he had virtually walked into the camp. Then, as if on signal, they took him from both sides, Murdock clamping a hand over his mouth, and Adaba holding the glittering blade of his hatchet before the man's face. In an instant, they had dragged him through the trees and into some brush, where they held him, listening.

The young black's eyes were wide with terror.

But there was no sound.

They were, apparently, safe.

Adaba whispered soothingly. "It's all right. Ain't gonna hurt you. It's all right. You running away?"

The young black made no attempt to speak or nod, and his knees gave way under him.

"It's all right. Might be we can help you. It's all right. . . ."

They took him into one of the little cabins, and Gavin Murdock built up the fire. The young black wore only a torn shirt, pants, and boots, and Adaba perched him on a chair before the fire and wrapped a blanket over his shoulders. One of the women brought a bowl of stew and a spoon and put them into his hands, and he looked as if he could hardly believe it. After a moment, he began to weep and nearly dropped the bowl, but when Adaba tried to take it, he pulled it back and began wolfing down the food.

"It's all right. Take your time. There's plenty more. Minna always keeps the pot on, case somebody drops in for supper."

The young black finished the stew, sighed, and let the bowl and spoon slip from his fingers. For a moment Adaba thought the man had fallen asleep, but then he shook his head as if to clear it and looked up. He stared at Murdock.

"He ain't as white as he looks," Adaba said. "He's a Cherokee. You over being scared?"

The youth nodded and said "Yes" soundlessly.

"You can sleep now if you want, but first we got to know something. Anybody on your trail?"

"Don't think so." His voice was husky with fatigue. Adaba figured he was perhaps a year or so younger than himself. He was solidly built yet lean, and had the beginning of a mustache and beard: twin spikes at the corners of his mouth and another on his chin. They didn't keep him from looking very young.

"How long you been running?"

"Five, six days. Maybe a week. I don't know."

"Didn't find much help, did you?"

"No."

"What's your name?"

"Buckley."

"Where you come from, Buckley?"

"Redbird plantation. That's near Riverboro."

That meant little to Adaba, though he saw recognition on Murdock's face. They knew more or less where the village of Riverboro was, but their trails didn't run anywhere near it.

"Why'd you run away, Buckley?"

For a moment Adaba thought Buckley was not going to answer. Blank-faced, he stared at the floor. Then his shoulders began to shake and heave.

"They killed her," Buckley sobbed.

"Who, Buckley?" Adaba asked softly, gently. "Who'd they kill?"

"They killed her," he repeated.

"Why? Why'd they kill her?"

"For being with me. For loving me. They killed her."

"*Who'd* they kill?" Adaba asked again.

"Claramae," Buckley wept, hardly able to say the words. "Oh, Lord, they killed Claramae."

He collapsed from his chair and fell to the rough floor, rent by his sobs, in an agony that Adaba knew no one could help. So he didn't try. He waited, an anger rising in him he hadn't felt since before the death of Denmark Vesey.

He waited, waited a quarter of an hour or more, until Buckley began to calm and try to raise himself from the floor. Then Murdock picked Buckley up and almost roughly threw him back into his chair.

"When did they do that, Buckley?"

"The night I run away." Somehow the weeping had helped. Buckley's voice was stronger, steadier.

"I think you better tell us more," Adaba said, "so we can figure what best to do. Who is Claramae? your woman?"

"Vaych's wife. Vachel Skeet."

"White?"

Buckley nodded.

It was suddenly all too clear: an old story. Vachel Skeet's wife, Claramae, and this boy, Buckley, had been lovers. And they had been caught. The husband had taken revenge on his wife, but Buckley had somehow gotten away.

"He your master?"

"My friend." The word was bitter in Buckley's mouth. "My dear, good friend—till he went bad. My friend—and master."

"And he killed his wife, this Skeet?"

"Him and some others, a whole lot of them. Tag Bassett. Rolly Joe Macon. P. V. Tucker. Balbo Jeppson. Jeppson, he's the worst of the lot, 'cept for old Vaych. They was wearing masks, but I knew them all."

The names meant nothing to Adaba, though again he thought he saw recognition on Gavin Murdock's face.

266

"You sure she's dead? Did you see . . . ?"

"I didn't see it all, but I heard. I heard her screaming. . . ."

"Then you don't know." Adaba tried to hold out hope. "Maybe she's alive. Maybe she's all right now."

Buckley shook his head. "I try to think that, and maybe it's true, but somehow I know it ain't. Claramae is dead, and after what they done to her, maybe that's a blessing."

And Gilly, Adaba thought, what happened to her? Was she too better off dead?

"Where was you heading, Buckley?"

"Away. Anywhere, just to get away."

"Well," Gavin Murdock said, speaking for the first time, "maybe we can help you."

Buckley looked at him and then at Adaba as if deciding it was time to ask some questions of his own.

"Who you people?"

Adaba laughed. "Him, he's just a no-'count Indian, and I'm just a no-'count nigger. He don't even have a name, but you can call me Johnny Dove if you want."

"We may be no-'count," Gavin Murdock said, "but maybe we can get you north."

Buckley looked from one man to the other. "Where you come from?"

"That don't matter," Adaba said. "I'm a carpenter. I'm free, and I travel around looking for work. These people here, they don't like folks dropping in for supper unexpected till they're sure they're friendly, and that's why we grabbed you like we did, but you're more than welcome."

"This here is a maroon camp, ain't it? What's a free black carpenter and a white Cherokee doing in a maroon camp?"

Adaba shrugged. "There's a roof over our head, and—"

"And how come you took me so silent-like, like Indians?"

"Well, like I said, these people here—"

"A man called Dove, *Dove,* takes me into a maroon camp and sees me fed, and his friend and him offer to take me north. You know what I think?"

"What you think, Buckley?"

"I'm happy to meet you, Mr. Adaba."

Adaba was not surprised. Buckley struck him as a man who could put two and two together. But he grinned and said, "Lot of people by that name. Don't know as I'm one of them. What Adaba you talking about?"

"Big buck nigger, a slave-stealer they been talking about the last year or two or maybe longer. They say he takes slaves north—"

"Oh, him," Adaba said. "That's just talk. Ain't no such Adaba."

Buckley shrugged under his blanket. "Don't matter. Don't matter what you call yourself. Black folks with troubles talk about Adaba, and it gives them hope."

"Well, what about it?" Murdock asked. "You want us to take you north?"

Buckley gazed into the fire. After a long moment, he said, "No."

It was the last answer they expected, and Adaba and Murdock stared at Buckley.

"But you can't live down here," Murdock said.

"You do."

Adaba said, "But you don't know how—"

"I can learn. I lasted 'most a week without knowing how. Begged, stole, slept in trees, crawled in ditches, traveled by night—maybe I went in circles, for all I know, but I lasted. And I be goddamned if I'm gonna let any white men drive me north. I got business here." His gaze swung from the fire to Adaba. "You live here, and you can teach me, Adaba . . . or whatever you call yourself."

"I'd thank you not to use that name, Buckley," Adaba said. "Adaba is somebody no more folks sees than needs to."

"You teach me, Johnny Dove, and I'll stay here. And one day I'll go back to Redbird."

"But you can't for a long time," Mr. Murdock said. "If what you say is true—and I don't doubt you—they are gonna be looking for you at this Redbird place for years. You got to stay away—"

"I don't care. I'll outlast them. I'll stay here and help you steal slaves and take them north. I'll bide my time, I don't care if it takes ten years. And then one day, when he don't expect it, I'm going back and settle accounts with Vachel Skeet."

Adaba liked the resilience of this tough young black who had come stumbling into their camp. He seemed intelligent and resourceful. They could have used more like him.

"Mr. Murdock," Adaba said, "I think we got us a new partner."

Only after he had said it did Adaba realize he too had made a decision. But now it seemed to him that there had never been any real question of his quitting. He had to keep on—he owed it to Gilly, to Denmark, to himself. Gavin Murdock smiled at him as if he had known it would be this way all along.

June 1826

Somewhere downstairs, his sister wept. Lew was glad that she and Norvin had arrived at Jessamine in time, but he hoped his father couldn't hear her.

"He's awake again," the doctor said as they stood outside the bedroom door, "and he wants to speak to you. I've told him he should rest, he should sleep, but he insists."

Lew nodded and started through the bedroom door, but the doctor stopped him.

"Don't tire him. Make your visit as brief as possible. It's imperative—"

"I understand."

His father was so pale and still when Lew entered the room that he might have been dead already. But after a moment, he chuckled and spoke, his voice a dry rustle.

"I heard that. Don't tire me. As if it were necessary to cling to every last second of life."

"Maybe you should rest, father."

"Father. You've got so you talk like a Yankee. I'm your daddy, son."

"Yes, daddy."

"What time is it?"

"About four in the morning."

"And I'm supposed to get my rest," his father mocked.

"That old goat of a doctor must know that the next time I go to sleep I'm finished."

"No, daddy—"

"Yes. My heart's so tired it can hardly keep going. When I sleep, it'll sleep too. . . . Lewis, do you remember what I told you last night?"

"Yes, sir, daddy."

"What did I tell you?"

"Take care of our people. They come before anything else. Never separate them from each other. Don't sell them just for money or for my own convenience."

"That's right. You'll make a good master, Lewis."

"I'll do my best, daddy."

"There aren't many good ones, not by my lights, but you'll be one of them."

"I promise."

"And I thank you, son. Now tell Georgiana I want to talk to her. I'll talk to you again later."

"Yes, sir."

He left the room and went down to Georgiana and Norvin. He made Georgiana stifle her sobs before sending her upstairs.

When he heard her scream, he knew his father was dead.

Later he went out into the gray dawn that was just breaking. He had never in his life felt so desolate. He was the master of Jessamine now, but what did that mean to him? He supposed it would keep him in comfort for the rest of his life, but it would be a lonely responsibility. He had always been an independent sort of person with a scorn for conventions, and he had paid the price. After four years spent largely in the North, he had lost most of his old friends without making any permanent new ones. He had never been close to Georgiana and couldn't imagine that he ever would be. He had wistful memories of his boyhood friendship with John Guerard, but the Vesey affair, coming on top of the Gilly incident, had put an end to that forever.

He was alone.

Suddenly, he was deeply angry with his father for dying. How dare his father desert him! his father, the one person who still seemed to understand and love him, the one person he himself still loved! How dare he!

In the dawn, Lew Sabre wept.

John Guerard—nobody called him by that childhood name, Adaba, anymore—was said to be extremely reclusive. He spent almost all of his time on the family plantation, involved in his studies, and on his rare trips to Charleston, he avoided colored society. The latter was understandable. Why should he suffer its cruel snubs? The fact that legally he was a slave barred him from such exclusive organizations as the Brown Fellowship and the Humane Brotherhood, and his skin kept him out of the *café au lait* elite. Still, a number of light-skinned young ladies would gladly have overlooked both his legal status and the darkness of his complexion, considering the wealth he would have brought to them and to their children— and Marcus Guerard made no bones about that matter. But scorned by John, they were forced to set their sights on the younger—and really much more eligible—Phillip and David. John was doomed to become a lonely bachelor, living in virtual isolation.

But not entirely. An occasional traveler would stop by the plantation, and if John deigned to make one of his rare appearances, he would hear the latest news from the outside world. And sometimes he would hear the most fantastic tales about the notorious slave-stealer called Adaba and his friend and companion, Black Buck. . . .

Twelve

And then there was Rose.

How had he overlooked her! How had he failed to see her! He had, of course, been away at Princeton for most of the four years while she had been turning twelve to sixteen, but how had he managed to waste six whole months of his life by not noticing what had happened to her!

Lew discovered Rose during the Christmas season of 1826. There was at that time much party-giving and visiting back and forth between plantations, and Lew had, as always, been invited to the Guerards. The house was full that evening, mostly with white neighbors, and with a few respected people of color. John Guerard—or Adaba, as Lew sometimes still thought of him—put in one of his rare appearances, looking much older than his years. Lovely Diantha and her husband were down from Boston. Philip and David were there. But who was that young beauty who was gazing soulfully into the eyes of blond Hadden Hargrave, with his silly little-boy grin that the ladies could never resist?

Rose!

The sight of her that evening stunned him. He could do little more than pay her a polite good evening. But when he returned to Jessamine that night, he could not get her out of his mind.

Rose!

He couldn't have been right about her, he thought the next day. He knew he had been a little drunk, as befitted a gentleman at a joyous holiday celebration, and that could lead to errors in judgment. And lamplight was known to hide many a flaw and even to create a false beauty. He would drop by the Guerard plantation again, and then he would see.

Rose!

She was simply the most fetching, the most comely, the most beautiful, the most dazzling thing he had ever seen. Long auburn locks with a natural curl. A roseate complexion, faintly dusky, that made her name appropriate. Large clear brown eyes, sparkling with mischief. A large mouth of the kind called generous, a bright smile, a strong face, clean lined, with high cheekbones. A full, low, throaty voice, sensually charged. As far as he could tell—and he sought any glimpse of calf, any indication of breast—a fine, luxurious figure.

He had to have her.

At first, it didn't occur to him to wonder if he were in love with her, though if pressed he might have admitted the possibility. Nor did he think in terms of marriage,

272

though he wouldn't have let marriage, or the lack of it, stand in his way.

He simply had to have her.

He had quite forgotten the lesson that one does not always get what one wants. Lust had swept it from his mind. He was determined to have Rose, and he never let himself doubt that he would win her, even when she made it quite clear to him that she didn't take him seriously in the least. To her, he was just the lad from nearby Jessamine, the one-time friend of her older brother, John.

At the races in February, Rose had eyes only for Hadden Hargrave, of all the young men who thronged around her. And throng they did, causing a number of young white ladies to bristle with indignation that "that *darky* girl" was getting so much attention. But she soon ceased to get it from Lew. He rebelled. He started a spectacular flirtation with a distant cousin, a Miss Lucy Sabre, blond and beautiful, who immediately saw the game and cooperated by playing it to the hilt. Rose soon decided that there might be something to commend in Lew after all. Besides . . . she didn't like poachers.

She had to have *him*.

The next stage in this ritual took place in March and April. It involved long talks in the Guerard drawing room, where Rose's mammy was apt to appear at any instant, and long walks in the Guerard gardens, where they were never allowed to disappear into a gazebo for long.

Lew was a working planter, not one of those soft-palmed gentlemen who left everything in the hands of overseer and foremen, but he made the trip from Jessamine to the Guerard plantation as often as possible. He was almost always invited to Sunday dinner, which could not be said of Rose's other callers. It was a favorable sign. It meant that Marcus, as well as Rose, looked approvingly on him and would probably give his consent to a marriage.

But would Rose?

"I don't know that I *want* to get married," she said one Sunday afternoon. They were in a gazebo in the gardens, watching a gentle rain come down.

"You're joshing me, Rose. I can't see you as a lonely old maid."

"Oh, I didn't say I planned to be lonely. I don't plan to be lonely at all."

"Well, if you're not going to get married—"

"I'm considering becoming a courtesan."

"A *what?*"

"A courtesan. A courtesan is—"

"I *know* what a courtesan is!

"Daddy says if I'm a good girl, maybe he'll let me go to France—"

"And be a bad girl?"

"—and when I get there, I think I'll become some famous man's mistress. There's that poet, Victor Hugo—"

"He's happily married and has two children."

"That never stopped a Frenchman. And there's another new poet, *Count* Alfred de Vigny—"

"You have artistic tastes."

"And there's Monsieur de Chateaubriand—"

"He's too old for you. He must be sixty."

"Young, old, who cares? I don't want to be stuck with only one man, I want to sample them all. I want to be made love to by at least a hundred different men."

"Rose!" Lew was genuinely shocked.

"Ah, France! I can hardly wait!"

"Well, you'd better brush up on your French first, honey-child. I can tell you it's terrible."

"Oh, Lew!" She punched him in the ribs. "Are you really so naive as to think you have to know a man's language to be his mistress? Besides, I've heard that the best way to learn a foreign language is in bed with one of the natives."

"*Rose!*"

He understood her. She was the little girl who was never invited to the party. She was the little girl who was left alone outside the door when all the others were asked inside. She was a beautiful, intelligent young woman who, because of some small fraction of Negro blood, was forever marked as somehow different and to be excluded.

Very well, then, thought Rose defiantly, she would *be* different! She didn't want to go to their silly party! She would have fun that *they* never had! She would toss aside convention and say shocking things and take whatever this world had to offer. And at times that meant the sweetheart of every young woman who had ever looked down her nose at Rose Guerard!

But she knew that most of those sweethearts would never dream of marrying her. And it hurt.

Sometimes the pain made their meetings stormy.

"Why do you want to marry me, Lew?"

"What do you mean, why do I want to marry you? I love you."

"Nonsense. You just want to get my dress off and spread my legs, and you figure that's the only way to do it."

"Do you have to talk dirty?"

"What's dirty about it? It's the truth. Only *white* girls think the truth is dirty."

"For God's sake, Rose, you're a white—"

"I am a *nigger!*" she yelled in sudden anger. "Can't you accept that? I am a nigger, and I'll always be a nigger, and if you can't accept that, damn you, I don't want to marry you!"

"All right, goddammit, you're a nigger if you must insist, and I accept that! Now, can I join too, or is it some kind of exclusive club?"

She burst into tears, while he stood there wondering what the hell he could do for her. He would do anything, anything. . . .

Certainly there was one thing he really *wanted* to do for her, and heaven knows he tried.

"Oh, don't, Lewis!"

"Please, Rose!"

"Oh, no!"

"Just for a minute. I do love you so."

"If you had your way, I'd have *all* my clothes off!"

"Yes!"

"No!"

By the end of April they were meeting in secret regularly. It was easily enough arranged. Rose, something of a tomboy, had long had the run of the plantation and went wherever she wished, to swim, to pick berries, or simply to walk, and there were any number of shaded groves where they could rendezvous unseen. As long as Lew continued his usual visits to the big house, it was unlikely that anything would be suspected. Or at least so the lovers told themselves.

But these sweet love trysts were paid for in agony.

"Oh, my *God,* Rose!" Lew wailed on the first afternoon in May. He was lying on a blanket in the woods with Rose in the crook of his arm. They had been together for almost three hours, as long as they had ever met secretly, and far longer than was safe. "Oh, my *God!*"

"Oh, now, what's the matter, baby boy?" Rose lay half-naked beside him, a shoulder and a breast exposed and her drawers long gone.

"What's the *matter! Oh!* my—*God!"*

"But I don't understand, sweetheart!" Her eyes were bright with mirth.

"But you're *killing me,* woman! You're *killing me!"*

"Got your balls in an uproar?"

His agony was too great to allow for shock. "Listen, you've got to *let* me! I can't stand this any longer! Rose, you've got to *let* me!"

"Lew, honey," Rose mocked, "sometimes I think you only love me for my body."

"Well, it's a great place to start. If you'd only let me—"

"Oh, I couldn't do that, Lewis. It wouldn't be proper. And I know how you men are about taking a virgin to the altar."

"Oh, to hell with that!"

"Why, if I let you, you'd probably never look at me again. You would regard me as a fallen woman, a tarnished angel, a—"

"Oh . . . *shit!"*

"Why, Lewis . . ."

He relaxed, let the pain throb, tried to stop giving a damn. He lay on his back, let the blue sky fill his eyes, then closed them. He had about a week in which to seduce Rose before she returned to Charleston, where there would be little opportunity, and he had about given up hope.

"Lew," Rose said, a hint of worry in her voice, "are you all right, honey?"

"No," he said. "I'm shot. Busted. Permanently incapacitated."

"Lewis!"

"I mean it. I keep begging you to let me make love to you, and the practical fact of the matter is that if I tried to now, I wouldn't be worth a damn. To either of us."

"You wouldn't?" Rose sounded truly worried now.

"Hell, no. How much of this do you think a man can take? I don't know how it is for a woman, but for a man there comes a point of do or don't, and if you keep on don't-ing, you get worse and worse off. Until finally there just ain't anything worth having left."

"Lew, I'm sorry."

"It's all right. It's not really your fault. I won't die."

She giggled. "But when will you be all right again?"

"I don't know. Tomorrow. Probably this evening. I have great powers of recuperation, thank God."

Rose was quiet for a moment, as if considering something.

"Will you come see me tomorrow?"

"If I don't need crutches. How the hell I'm going to get back to Jessamine—"

"I love you, Lewis. I love you so much."

"I love you, Rose. When are you going to let me ask your father—"

"Meet me here tomorrow, Lew."

"Tomorrow, love."

And in that way it came about.

He knew what she had in mind even before he dismounted from his horse. He saw her standing there on the old blanket, wearing an old shift and a bonnet and sandals. He was sure she had nothing else on. It was the kind of thing she would have worn if she were going swimming with her favorite maids, but there were no other women with her. She was alone.

For a moment, as they stood there facing each other across the blanket, neither of them spoke. Rose's smile was tentative, and in the shade of the bonnet her large brown eyes had never been brighter.

Lew shook his head. "No," he said. "I know I've been pushing you, and I know I've got no right. I want to marry you, Rose, and you don't have to do this."

"I know I don't, but I want to," she said, taking a step toward him. "I've only been waiting for the right time."

"And this isn't it. You want what every other girl has. First you want a wedding like every other wedding, and you want to be a virgin bride—"

"No," she said softly but sharply, and she took another step toward him. "I don't want it to be the way it is for every other girl. I want to be different. I want to be like *you*. You're different, Lew, somehow you're different from all the rest of them, and you make it all right to be different. Maybe that's one reason I love you. For the first time in my life it's all right to be who I am and different from all the rest. It's *good* to be who I am! So unless you don't want me anymore . . ."

He reached for her shoulders. He brought her closer, and as she raised her head, he lowered his mouth to hers. Only in that way did they touch, his hands on her shoulders, and mouth to mouth; but he felt a quiver go through Rose, and his own body instantly sprang to hot life.

Their mouths parted, though their heads remained together. They both sighed. They looked down at themselves and at each other, and he saw that under the thin fabric of her shift her nipples had risen as firmly as his own flesh. As they kissed again, her hands went to her shoulders, brushing his hands aside. There was a faint soft renting sound of old cloth, and she let the shift slip from her shoulders, let it slip down over her breasts, baring them, and held it at her waist. He brought her closer again, brought her closer until this time they touched, and as he kissed her, he stroked each silk-smooth, cloud-soft breast, drew at each nipple, until she sank to the ground with him as if hardly knowing what was happening.

They kissed. They fondled. They murmured to each other.

"Tell me you love me, Lew."

"I love you . . . love you. . . ."

"There's nobody else in the world?"

"Nobody."

"And you want me?"

"More than I can ever tell you."

"Then show me . . . show me, . . ." she murmured, and she tugged at his shirt and his belt buckle.

A moment later he was more naked then she, and she sat beside him, her shift still about her hips.

"Ah, you do want me," she said, her mouth to his, knowing his passion through her exploring touch, though her eyes were closed.

"In that way and every other," he said, returning her touch.

"Ah, darling, you're driving me wild. . . ."

Gently, then, slowly, he did make love to her. He had long sought this hour for his own pleasure, but now he hardly thought of that. He thought only of hers, that this must be right for her, because it meant so much to her. He wasn't sure he could forgive himself if, in this their first time together, he failed her in any way.

The moment came when she was ready. As he kissed her breasts, as his mouth floated down over the softness of her belly, the cloth that was still about her thighs was kicked away, and she cried out as his tongue touched her open wanting flesh. Then, as if she could wait no longer, she seized his shoulders and tried to pull him up over her, and he answered her wish by kneeling between her thighs. For a moment he looked down on her. Looked down on her flushed, sweat-sparkling face with its drugged eyes, still within the bonnet. Looked down on that treasure of dusky cream flesh, thick nippled, deep naveled, auburn bushed, the skin darkening near the sex, over which his own dark sex speared so angrily. Looked until, with a little cry, she moved to offer herself, then moved the spearhead savagely into place and began to penetrate.

Carefully, carefully . . .

Heart thundering, he forced calmness.

Slowly, with great caution, he made them one, giving her less pain than he had feared. She cried out, and he stopped instantly. She lay breathless for a moment, her face pinched within the bonnet, her eyes closed.

She sighed, and smiled, and opened her eyes.

She looked down almost with satisfaction at what they had done.

She laughed.

Reaching for his hips she tugged at him, uptilting herself, to finish taking him.

"There," she said.

"There," he said, settling himself carefully over her, belly to belly, his chest grazing her breasts.

She tugged at a ribbon and pulled her bonnet away. Her face glistened.

"You have me she said."

"You have me, in case you hadn't noticed."

"And I feel so good."

"I'm glad." He closed his eyes and moved in her. "So do I."

"Do you think we'll ever be this happy again?"

"Rose, honey, this is only the beginning."

"Oh, I don't think I could bear more."

"You're just going to have to learn."

He began teaching her then, glad he had had some experience, but wishing to God he had had more for her sake, because for her sake he wanted to be the best.

He did everything in his power to bring her again and again to the highest precipice and then fling her over it, urging her higher with his whispers of promised delight, with his caresses, with his thrusting, pressing, plunging man-part. But in the end it was he as much as she who was flung through the heavens of burning delight. He as much as she . . .

On Sunday, May 6, 1827, Marcus Guerard was pleased to consent to the engagement of his daughter Rose to Mr. Lewis Sabre.

Lew expected to have trouble with Georgiana, and of course he was right.

"You are out of your *mind!*"

"No. I love Rose."

They were in the library of the Charleston house: he, Georgiana, and Norvin. After he had seated them and given Norvin an after-supper brandy, he had stood before them and made his announcement. Georgiana's eyes had widened and widened, and now she sprang from her chair.

"Love her! Why, it's ridiculous! My own brother, marry a—a *Nigress!*"

Lew had approached this moment with some nervousness, and he was surprised at how calm he was now. "Oh, for goodness sake, Georgiana, she's not a Negress. All right, she's got a touch of the tar brush—"

"*A touch!*"

"How do you know we Sabres don't have one too? Have you looked at the moons of your fingernails lately? Have you noticed that peculiar shade?"

"That is not funny! That is not even *remotely* amusing!"

Lew was inclined to agree. Judging from the way Georgiana was trembling, perhaps what he had said was not amusing. He regarded his sister as a fool, but he had no wish to be cruel to her.

"I'm sorry, Georgiana. Knowing how you feel, maybe I shouldn't have said that. But, please, no more nonsense about Negresses."

Georgiana turned away from him. "Norvin, *speak* to this boy!"

Norvin cleared his throat and shook his dewlaps. "Lewis, we've all known some mighty fine people of color, and I bow to no one in my respect for Mr. Marcus Guerard. You'll notice that I call him *mister*, because a mister is what he is, and a credit to his race."

"Which is mostly white." Knowing what was to come, Lew pulled a book down from a shelf and turned to a passage his father had marked.

"Mostly white, you say, *but!* And this is a mighty big but, Lewis. It is a sad fact that black pulls white down faster than white pulls black up, and—"

"Listen to this, Norvin." Lew read: " 'All nations of men have the same natural dignity, and we all know that very bright talents may be lodged under a very dark skin. The principle differences between one people and another proceed only from different opportunities of improvement.' That was William Byrd writing *The History of the Dividing Line* a hundred years ago, and it's as true today as it was then."

"Oh, a hundred years ago!" Georgiana said scornfully. "What did anybody know about anything a hundred years ago!"

"Sorry I can't agree with that, Lewis, truly sorry. Your William Byrd, whoever he was, would have mongrelized the white race, and then where would we be? But let's get down to brass tacks. Lewis, we're both men of the world, and we know it's one thing for a young buck to have a little fun with a nigger wench—"

"Better watch what you say, Norvin." Lew had been determined to keep his temper, but his face was beginning to burn.

"You're right! You're right!" Norvin held up his hands placatingly. "Lewis is perfectly right, Georgiana, and I apologize for speaking so frankly in front of a lady."

"Oh, I don't give a *spit!*" Georgiana said, still shaking. "You just tell this young fool off!"

"No, I won't do that. But since you give me permission, I'll be perfectly frank. Lewis, I'm a man of the world, and I don't think you ever heard *me* saying anything a few years back when you were, ah, spreading that little, what's her name, that Jobina nigger—"

"Norvin," Lew said, "I told you to watch your goddamn tongue."

"Don't you speak to my husband that way!"

Lew erupted. "Then tell your goddamn husband to watch how he speaks in my house!"

Georgiana looked stunned. "Your—! *Your* house! This is *our* house! And I will not have a nigger wench presiding over it as mistress!"

"This is *my* house, Georgiana. You're welcome to think of it as home, but you're only a guest in it if you don't remember your manners. And if you don't remember your manners, you won't be a guest in it for long!"

"Lewis Sabre—"

"Now, listen to me, both of you. I happen to love Rose Guerard. I'm going to marry her. *I* happen to think she comes from a damn fine family, but I wouldn't care if she came from sandhill trash, as long as she was Rose. I consider myself a goddamn lucky man that she agreed to marry me—"

282

"Leaped at the chance, I have no doubt! Probably seduced you and made you feel guilty. Appealed to your mistaken gentlemanly instincts."

Lew forced himself back toward calm. "No, Georgiana, she did not leap at the chance to marry me. I worked pretty damned hard and long to get her to say yes. Now, that's done, and it's not going to change, and you'd both better accept it."

The quiet in the room was palpable. Georgiana fell into a chair and pressed her fist to her mouth, refusing to look at either Lew or Norvin.

"You don't expect me to attend the wedding, do you?" she asked after a minute.

"You'll be invited. Whether or not you attend is up to you. You're my sister, and I'd like to see you there, helping to make it a happy occasion. But I won't grieve away our wedding night if you decide to stay away."

"I suppose you'll be married by some—some *African!*"

"The Guerards are Episcopalians, the same as us, as you know good and well."

"Well, I won't go to the wedding! I won't! And if you think you are going to make that—that *wench* the mistress of this house and of Jessamine plantation—"

His face had been hot. Now Lew thought he could feel the blood draining from it. "Georgiana, let's get this straight once and for all. That wench, as you call her, is more of a lady than you could ever hope to be. More of a lady and more of a woman—"

"Oh, I'm sure she's more of a woman, more of an *animal*—"

"Norvin, get your wife out of this house."

"Now, Lewis, old man—"

"Get her out, Norvin. Right now."

"You! You can't put me out of this house!"

"This is my house, Georgiana. You have your own, and you can damned well go to it. And unless, and until, you can accept Rose as my wife and your sister-in-law and treat her with every courtesy to which she is entitled, I do not wish to see you in this house or at Jessamine."

"Now, you know you don't mean that—"

"I damn well mean it! Both of you! You can damn well stay the hell out of my house and out of my life!"

The repercussions from the announcement of his engagement to Rose Guerard were far greater than Lew had anticipated. Certainly there had not been such a stir over Diantha Guerard's marriage; but then, her young sea captain had taken her north to Boston, and there had been no Georgiana to stir up trouble. Wasn't it scandalous, went the word from house to house, that Lew Sabre, the scion of a fine old family and the owner of one of South Carolina's finest plantations should marry a female of color, a darky girl, a wench with black buh-*lood!* No doubt there was in these mutterings a considerable amount of envy, deftly encouraged by Georgiana. "Oh, my dear," she told more than one female acquaintance, "I honestly thought that one day *you* would be the mistress of Jessamine plantation. I certainly never dreamed that we would see that —that colahed hussy . . ."

The few friends Lew had made in the last year seemed for the most part to be dropping away. When, three times in a row, he casually extended an invitation to the wedding and was politely told that the recipient would probably be away from Charleston at the time, he knew the way the wind was blowing. And twice a conversation on the street was interrupted by the other party's wife or fiancée who abruptly demanded to be taken home at once. The young ladies neither spoke to Lew nor looked at him.

If the Guerard family was aware of the stir the engagement was causing, they bore it cheerfully, imperturbably. In fact, they showed no sign of being aware of the commotion until after an incident that demonstrated to Lew his new status in the community.

At the end of May, about two weeks before the wedding, Lew was in the public room of the Planters Hotel with some young men, all of whom were pleasantly drunk. Hadden Hargrave was, perhaps, less pleasantly so. At any rate, he had been silent and sullen since Lew's arrival, and when Lew offered to buy a round for the party, he looked up and announced, "I don't drink with any man who'd marry a nigger."

284

The room went silent.

Lew was thunderstruck. Hadden was no friend, but he would never have expected such behavior from the man. Moreover, he happened to know that Hadden himself had asked Rose to marry him and had been turned down. It was not the kind of thing that Rose would ordinarily speak about or that Lew cared to mention now; they both had too much respect for the feelings of others. But it had slipped inadvertently from Rose's lips, and Lew knew it to be a fact.

Lew looked at Hadden and knew why the man was drunk and felt sorry for him—felt compassion well laced with contempt.

"Well, that's all right, Hadden," he laughed, "I don't know of any nigger who'd have you. Or care to drink with you."

Hadden got to his feet and, with clear intent to maim, lurched drunkenly toward him. Lew threw his drink in Hadden's face, sidestepped, and kicked his legs out from under him. Hadden fell heavily and sprawled over the floor.

"All right, get some goddamn pistols and sober him up," Lew said, coldly furious. "I'm going to blow this bastard's brains out."

Someone was helping Hadden to his feet, but Hadden shoved the man away. He suddenly seemed quite sober. "You ain't gonna blow nobody's brains out," he said. "There ain't a gentleman in Charleston that would fight a duel with a good-for-nothing goddamn nigger-lover like Lew Sabre."

"You'll fight me—"

"I'll be goddamned if I will. You ain't good enough. You ain't a gentleman. You ain't anything at all anymore but a goddamn nigger-fucker. Ain't that right, you men?"

Silence.

Lew could hardly believe this was happening. Ordinarily, if a man were refused a duel on the grounds that he was not a gentleman, a close friend would step forward and say, "If he's not good enough for you, I am! You'll hear from my seconds! Or are you refusing to fight because you're a coward?"

Now nothing of the sort happened. And Lew felt certain that it never would. The room remained silent.

Somebody muttered, "Aw, leave him alone, Hadden."

"Yeah, Hadden," Lew said slowly, "leave him alone. You ain't much, Hadden, but at least you're a gentleman, ain't that right? Never mind that you're a coward and a poor loser, you're a gentleman. Take comfort in that."

"Don't try to make me mad, Sabre."

"What's the difference if you're a coward and a poor loser and not very bright, Hadden? You're every inch a gentleman, in your half-assed way, so what the hell? Of course, you don't really have much of an idea of what a gentleman is, but you can call yourself that and run for cover whenever you see a real one coming, can't you, Hadden? So why worry about it? I apologize for suggesting a duel, Hadden. I don't know where I got the idea you were worth the powder to blow you to hell, Hadden, you being the half-assed sort of gentleman you are, but—" *Christ, when was he going to take the bait?* "—but—but, Hadden—"

"Let's get out of here, gentlemen," Hadden said, "I'm getting bored."

"That's right, Hadden, run for it. That's the kind of 'gentleman' you are, and I wouldn't lay a finger on you. Sabres don't fight Haddens, as all Charleston knows. They use them to wipe their asses."

Lew turned away.

And was spun back.

Half-blocked a big fist with his shoulder and felt his head explode.

Pounded a fist deep into Hadden's middle.

Hit again, again, again, hardly knowing what he was hitting, saw Hadden's red face falling back, saw him duck away and cling to a table to keep his feet, saw him pick up a chair and hurl it.

Ducked and heard the chair shatter against the wall behind him.

"Now, don't *do* that, Hadden! Sabres don't fight with the likes of you!"

Hadden rushed at Lew, his face screwed up like a little boy on the verge of tears. Lew felt himself pressed back

286

by blows harder than he had expected. He pounded a fist furiously into Hadden's throat. Hammered at Hadden's jaw, hammered at Hadden's gut. Hammered and hammered again, and saw Hadden falling back. Hammered. Hammered . . .

He stood back, gasping, to see Hadden standing there in the middle of the room, half-stooped, arms hanging down, blood running down his face. Sobbing.

"I don't want to hit you anymore, Hadden. Your kind of gentleman wouldn't understand this, but I find it demeaning. Why don't you go home and get sober and clean?"

Hadden made one more try, but it didn't mean anything. Lew left him lying on the floor, paid for his drinks, and went home. When he saw Rose the next day, her eyes seemed to sparkle more than ever. "Naughty, naughty boy," she said. "Beating my poor old Hadden that way!"

Adaba had thought that the years had healed the wound, but he found it ripped open and as raw and bleeding as ever.

"You can't marry him!"

Rose's eyes blazed. "Who are you to march into this house and tell me who I can or can't marry? Just who do you think you are?"

"I'm your brother, and I'm telling you—"

"You keep your hands off of me!"

"Rose, you can't marry him!" he repeated. "How can you even think of it!"

"Well, I'm going to!"

He had been away from the city and the plantation for over two months and had known nothing of Rose's engagement until, on his way to the Charleston house, he had encountered Hadden Hargrave on King Street. They stood talking within sight of the place where Denmark had been hanged.

"You all about ready for the wedding? Don't reckon I'm invited, am I?"

Adaba hadn't the faintest idea what Hadden was talking about. He had half expected Hadden to marry Rose. Could he be speaking of Philip? Suddenly, from Hadden's remarks, Adaba realized that he was speaking of Rose and Lew Sabre.

Rose and Lew Sabre.

Impossible. He felt a kind of insanity come over him, a grief he had thought assuaged becoming once again a savage pain. He knew that Lew was still friendly with the rest of the family, that he called occasionally. But not this. Not this. Adaba took a long look at the place where Denmark and his men had hanged. Then he all but ran to the house and burst in on Rose in the parlor.

"My God, Rose! The man who killed Denmark Vesey! How can you—"

"Oh, rubbish! Lew never killed anybody in his life! Denmark got himself killed by a court of law that had him hanged for trying to kill off the likes of us!"

The likes of us? Adaba looked at his sister in shock. Who the hell did she think she was? *The likes of us?*

"Rose, what are you talking about? Denmark—"

"If those niggers had got away with their insurrection, do you think we would have been spared? You might have, maybe, with your dark skin, but what about the rest of us? What about your own brothers and your father and your sister? We would have been killed."

"That's not true!"

"It's the truth and you know it! Your beloved Denmark never in his life did anything for us, and his niggers would have slaughtered us, right along with all the other whites and light-skinned people. It wasn't Denmark who worried about us and came here to warn us, it was Lew's father."

"Denmark did worry about you. He told me to warn you to leave, and I came here—"

"You see?" Rose was triumphant. "You see? You've got to admit that your damned Denmark Vesey would have got us all killed off! Don't tell me I owe *him* my fair white skin!"

"I tell you he stood up for black men!"

Rose's face twisted with rage. "And I tell you, to hell with your goddamn Denmark Vesey!"

He thought then that he really would strike her. She screamed as he went for her, taking her shoulders, shaking

288

her, drawing back a hand to hit her. But he found himself jerked around to look into his father's angry face.

"Just what do you think you're doing?"

"She's not going to marry him! She's not going to marry the man who caused the death of Denmark Vesey!"

"She is going to marry Lewis Sabre. She is going to marry him in three days' time. Now, get that through your head once and for all."

"You would let her—let her—"

"It's what I've wanted, what I've dreamed of. You know that. That she should have the security of the white world. The only thing better would be if she and Lewis went north, but I'm willing to settle for this."

"Your own daughter—married to the man who killed Denmark—"

"Oh, for God's sake," Rose cried, "he keeps saying that! He talks like Denmark Vesey was some kind of black Christ! Instead of just a crazy old nigger man who got himself and some slaves killed off and made trouble for all of us!"

"He was one of *us*, Rose," Adaba said, trying almost by an act of will to make her understand. "He was *for* us. He *died* for us!"

"No," his father said, "your sister is right. Denmark meant well, perhaps, but he did nothing but make life more difficult for us."

"I'll never accept that!"

"Then don't. But while Denmark and Gabriel Prosser and others like them were getting black people killed, the men in this family were working—working all their lives —to carve us a place in this white man's world. It's thanks to them, and not to Denmark Vesey, that you're not a slave toiling in the fields."

"Not a slave! But I am a slave!"

"Not like any other—"

"I am a slave! And do you call yourself a free man? when you're under the same laws and courts as any slave? when you can be hanged as easily as they hanged Denmark Vesey? when you're called Marcus and uncle by the same men you call mister?"

"I am nonetheless a respected member of this community."

"Well, I am a slave, and I stand up for slaves! I'll be a mean, evil nigger-stealing slave as long as there is one other slave in this country, and proud of it! And as for you . . ." So furious, so maddened that he hardly knew what he was saying, Adaba turned back to his sister. "As for you, if you marry Lew Sabre—I swear to God, Rose —I'll make you a widow before you're two hours a bride!"

Adaba had never thought himself to be a vengeful man. He had never thought he could kill except perhaps in self-defense. Did he really mean to kill Lew now? He hardly knew. He knew only that the idea of his sister marrying the man who had brought about the death of his friend and mentor was completely intolerable.

He bided his time, avoiding his sister, but learning all he could about her plans from his brothers and from various members of the household. The wedding would take place in the evening at the Guerard house, it seemed, and the bride and groom would spend the next two nights at the Sabre house, before departing by ship for a honeymoon in the north.

On the evening of the wedding, he was watching the house through the gathering dusk from a distance of several hundred feet. He observed guests arriving. He also noticed several members of the City Guard near the house. He had written himself a pass, because this was no time to be caught without one, but it wouldn't do him much good if they found the pistol he was carrying under his jacket. He moved away from the house. There would be time. Later.

John Guerard did not attend his sister Rose's wedding. The fact was noted and caused a few whispers, but no one said anything about it to the Guerards. No one wished to cause inadvertent embarrassment, and some privately thought that the dark-skinned youth showed good taste in staying away from this somewhat unconventional wedding.

They wondered if perhaps they shouldn't have done the same.

Still, the wedding went off very nicely, and this despite rumblings that there might be trouble. Marcus Guerard had alerted the City Guard and paid for special protection, and Lew had spoken privately to some friends. The house was crowded with guests, among them, at some political risk, the current intendant of Charleston. Even Governor John Taylor dared to send a message of congratulations and best wishes. Though the groom had only a few friends there, his sister and brother-in-law did attend, Georgiana subdued but on her better behavior. Somehow she had come to understand that her malice was beginning to redound to her discredit, and Georgiana Sabre Claiborne was a woman who cared a great deal about what other people thought of her.

Also in attendance were several distant Sabre cousins, notably Aaron and Joel Sabre and Aaron's daughter Lucy. Joel Sabre, a noted duelist, had heard about Lew's fight with Hadden Hargrave and, though he disapproved of this wedding, was quite enthusiastic about the prospect of trouble. "Wish I could have been there when you took that boy on," said the chunky, weathered older man. "I'da fought him for you! He sure as hell wouldn't have turned *me* down!" "Well, then I wouldn't have had the pleasure of giving him a spanking, Cousin Joel."

Rose and Lew were married. A buffet supper was given. A small orchestra played, and there was some dancing on the piazza under paper lanterns.

The bride threw her bouquet from the hall stairs and disappeared to change into street clothes. When she reappeared, a horse and carriage were waiting on the street.

Lew drove the carriage himself. Very discreetly, Joel Sabre and a couple of other men, all armed, went ahead of the carriage. Aaron Sabre and some friends followed behind. They accompanied the carriage all the way to the groom's home, and when the house was in sight, there had still been no trouble.

Adaba knew the route the carriage would almost certainly be using, and he waited in the shadows for it, right by the corner of the house. He waited, in fact, almost too long. He saw the carriage from some distance, little more than a slowly moving shadow among other shadows, darkness merging and separating in silver moonlight as it came down the street, and something about it alarmed him. Something about it, he had no idea what, was wrong. Then he heard something, sensed something, and he realized that men were coming ahead of the carriage on both sides of the street. Perhaps he should have expected that: an escort.

But he was certain he was still unseen; and keeping to the shadows, he made his way along the wall to the carriage gate. Just as he had done years before, when he had visited Gilly, he eased through the barely opened gate, which had been left unbarred for Lew and his new wife. Looking around the corner of the storehouse where Gilly had had her loft, he saw that the yard was lit up, and more lamps burned in the house than had been apparent from the street. Dorinda and Lucas had returned early from the wedding, and Dorinda was now chatting with a couple of maids, while Lucas chopped a few sticks of kindling. Adaba reached around the corner of the storehouse, and luck was still with him: the door was unlocked. When no one was looking his way, he quickly slipped inside. He left the door slightly ajar and, gun in hand, waited, watching through the slit.

There was male laughter outside the gate, and then the sound of the gate opening. There were "good nights," and Lew drove the carriage into view. The gate was swung shut again.

The carriage moved to the other end of the yard and came to a halt. Lew jumped down and reached out to help his bride. A couple of boys appeared from somewhere to take care of the carriage and the horse. There was chatter and gentle laughter. After a moment or two, Lew slipped his arm around Rose's waist and led her toward the house.

Now.

All he had to do was step out of the storehouse and do it.

Just cock and raise the pistol and say "Lew" and fire. They were at the door of the house. Lew pushed it

292

open. He picked up Rose, cradling her in his arms. *All I have to do is—*

It was too easy. There had to be more to it than this. And could he do it in front of Lucas and Dorinda and those maids and boys, those children, that were still in the yard?

He had time yet, plenty of time.

Lew and Rose disappeared into the house.

He realized then that if he had fired, the escort, which was still nearby, might very well have caught him.

"Oh, my Lord," she said, "what a bed!"

"Nine feet tall. Almost seven feet long and six feet wide. Reckon there isn't a bigger bed in Charleston."

"Lewis, I'll get lost in it!"

"I promise to find you."

They kissed again, and, oh, goddamn, wasn't he happy! He had beaten them all and won the greatest prize he could imagine in this life.

"All of this is yours now," he said, holding her close, as they stood at the side of the bed. "This house and the house at Jessamine and everything that's in them. The houses and the lands and the people. And they're going to love you just the same as I do."

She laughed. "I didn't know that houses and lands loved people."

"Oh, but they do. At least they do when people love them."

They had just spent half an hour going from room to room, exploring the house. If Rose had ever been in it before, it had been so long ago that she had forgotten, and seeing it with her, Lew felt as if he were rediscovering it. For the first time in years, he really *saw* the Sheraton furniture, the Chippendale mirrors, the oriental rugs, and the China Trade porcelain. And, yes, it was true that he felt that the house did somehow reflect back the love he had for it, and he supposed that that was what made it truly a home. And now it was to be Rose's home too.

"Well," she said, moving out of his arms.

She looked very pink in the lamplight, and he would have sworn she was blushing. It was an odd thing, but in spite of all her earlier boldness, in spite of her insistence that both she and he were "different" from others, from the moment her father had consented to their engagement she had suddenly become most maidenly and conventional. In fact, from then until this moment, they had hardly been alone together.

"I'm going to make you very happy," he said after a moment.

She smiled. "That's what I like—a confident man."

"You believe me, don't you?"

"If I didn't, would I be here?"

"Well, woman . . ."

He pulled off his coat and tossed it over a chair. He unbuckled his stock and dropped it on a table. Other than drawing a little farther away from him, while continuing to look at him, Rose made no move.

"What's the matter?" he asked softly.

"Nothing."

"Come here."

Obediently, still smiling, but now averting her eyes, she returned to his arms. When he lifted her chin and kissed her, he saw that her eyes were wet.

"Now, tell me!" he commanded.

"It's just that I love you so much, and I'm scared you'll be sorry you ever married the likes of me."

"Oh, Rose!" he began, but he realized that something was missing.

"The wine!" he said.

"The what?"

"The wine. I told Dorinda I wanted champagne in the bridal chamber, but she forgot. I'll go get it. It won't take a minute."

"You don't have to go outside, do you?"

"No, just down to the cellar. I'll be right back."

"Well, don't hurry. Take your time. If you don't hurry, when you get back, I'll . . ." Yes, he was sure of it: she was blushing. "I'll be ready."

Lighting a candle from a lamp, he left Rose to explore clothes press and cabinet and drawers, where Guerard maids, under the housekeeper's direction, had earlier put away her clothes. He had told Lucas that he wanted at least one light burning in each room, but he and Rose had extinguished them as they had explored the house. Now his candle's light, as he went down the stairs, barely pierced the darkness.

He was at the foot of the stairs before he saw Adaba.

He knew how Adaba had got in: the house was not locked. He knew the meaning of this visit even before he saw the glint of candlelight on the barrel that Adaba was raising.

He felt one instant of terrible fear before the fear became the most awful anger he had ever known in his life. His happiness and Rose's could not be allowed to end like this. He had often felt sorrow over Adaba's losses, and even, though he was not quite sure why, a certain amount of guilt. But whatever he might owe, he was not going to pay for it like this.

The barrel rose higher, until Lew was looking almost directly into it.

He threw the candle at Adaba's face, threw himself sideways. The candle instantly went out, and the pistol blazed in darkness. Lew thought he felt its hot breath.

As he scrambled to his feet, something, the pistol barrel, caught him a glancing blow on the head, and he nearly fell again. On the staircase, Rose screamed.

Lew thought he heard Adaba sob. The pistol barrel hit him again, this time on the left shoulder, and his arm went numb. He struck out blindly, a hammer blow with his right fist that landed solidly on a face, another hammer blow to an unseen wrist that sent the pistol flying.

A fist mashed his face, and he tasted blood. Another seemed to crush his ribs. Then he was caught by the shirt and flung against a wall. He let himself drop low and threw himself off the wall, all his weight behind a fist that drove deeply into a thick-muscled stomach. He heard Adaba fall to his knees, sucking air.

He opened the door to the carriage yard. Outside he saw Lucas trying to tear away from Dorinda to find out what was happening. Turning around again, he saw Adaba getting to his feet.

He said: "Get the hell out of my house."

But Adaba wasn't through. A taller, heavier, bigger

man than Lew, with five more years of bone and muscle, he came at Lew in a rush, his fists pounding like stones, and Lew found himself knocked back through the open door, thrown out of his own house, flying through the air from the steps and landing solidly on his back, all the air driven from his lungs.

For a moment he couldn't see. Then he rolled away as a boot caught him on his aching left shoulder.

Perhaps his anger saved him. He was *not* going to let Adaba do this to him! He was *not!*

He kept on rolling until his hand fell onto something: a piece of wood: a two-foot length of hard, well-seasoned firewood that Lucas had failed to stack. Then somehow he was on his feet again, not six feet from Adaba and advancing.

Out of the corner of his eye, he saw Lucas coming, hatchet in hand. "No, Lucas," he said, "get back from him."

Lucas backed away.

He saw Rose in the doorway.

"Rose, get back into the house."

Rose didn't move.

Lew stepped forward, guardedly, his club raised high over his head.

Adaba backed up two steps. Suddenly something glittered in his hand: nine inches of steel.

Lew took another step forward.

"Lew, don't make me use this."

"Why not? You came here to kill me, didn't you?"

Adaba knew how to handle a knife. He stepped back again, swayed and skipped from side to side, came forward to make a couple of dazzling passes that were meant to intimidate, then, left arm high to block a club blow, he lunged at Lew's belly.

But the club blow never came, and Lew was no longer where he had been. Slipping sideways into a fencer's stance, he delicately deflected Adaba's thrust with his club —and jammed the end of the club home to Adaba's forehead, a blow that could have crushed his skull.

Adaba reeled backward, and Lew followed for the kill. By some miracle Adaba found his footing, shook his head hard, and poised himself for a counterattack. Lew could have played with him then, but he didn't. His rage burned far too fiercely. He had about fifteen inches on Adaba, and he used them: a parry, a couple of feints, and a solid blow to Adaba's forearm sent the knife flying. Another couple of feints, and he clubbed the side of Adaba's head with a dazing blow. He then leaned down under Adaba's arms and with no difficulty cracked him behind a knee, and Adaba fell as if hamstrung—flat on his back.

Lew quickly stepped over him and stood astride his chest. Bending his knees, he again raised the club high over his head for the final blow. Adaba raised his arms over his own head in a futile effort to protect himself. Lew tensed every muscle to bring the club down.

"And now, you son of a bitch—"

Rose screamed again.

He never knew if he would have done it if Rose hadn't screamed. Afterward he hoped that he would not have. The very idea that he might have was enough to make him sick.

But at that moment he could only stand panting over Adaba, the club in his raised hand, ready to kill.

Until he knew he couldn't do it. Not to Adaba. Not to Rose's brother. Not on this of all nights, their wedding night.

He straightened. He lowered the club. He stepped away from Adaba, tossing the club away, and walked back into the house.

Adaba lay where he was, on his back. After a moment he rolled over, and very slowly and repeatedly he struck the earth with his fist. Tears rolled down his face.

I should have killed him, he wept. *I should have been able to. I should have. Why couldn't I? Why didn't I?*

But he knew the answer.

The answer was a thirteen-year-old boy with large dark eyes and an unruly mop of black hair who, while Adaba and Gilly had hid behind Denmark Vesey's shop, had stayed out on the street with the pursuing mob and yelled: *"Come on! They went up there, around the corner. Come on! Come on!"*

PART THREE

SHEBA

The Reckoning

One: November 1837

It was over: a dozen years as the master of Jessamine plantation. And all the years before that, the growing years, as an inhabitant of this great house and these vast acres. As he walked through the darkness and the downpour toward the house, the full reality of the fact struck Lew. All this was no longer his. It would never be his again.

When he entered the house, Rose was in the dimly lit passage, as if she had been there waiting for him the whole time he had been gone. She even had the same look in her eyes she'd had when he left—haunted, fearful, hopeful.

"Lew, darling . . ."

She hurried to him and gave him a quick warm kiss. "I've been so worried about you. You shouldn't have come back in this storm."

"I didn't think it would be so bad."

The truth was that though he knew he should find shelter and rest the horse, he kept right on going through the storm, abusing both the animal and himself. He had the feeling that if he didn't get to Rose as quickly as possible, he might die—not from any physical cause, but from simple failure of the spirit.

"Oh, Lew, you're dripping all over everything!"

"What's the difference? It isn't ours anymore."

Even as he said the words, he regretted them, knowing they were freighted with self-pity and could only give Rose pain. He tried to wipe them out with a quick smile and a question. "How are the children?"

"They're fine. In bed now, of course."

"Good. Let me get out of these wet clothes."

"Want me to help you?"

She had a wonderful voice, he thought, a rich contralto. So womanly. He sometimes wondered if it was her voice he had first learned to love. Hard to remember now.

300

"Lew? . . ."

He smiled at her again. He knew she was offering him more than assistance with his clothes. But he merely touched her cheek with a finger and her lips with his, and said, "Ask Dorinda if she has something I can eat. Hot, if possible."

Upstairs, he took a minute to look in on the sleeping children: Channing, named for his father, and Eleanor, named for Rose's mother. They would not be growing up at Jessamine, as he had done. No more Christmas parties at Jessamine for them, no fishing and swimming in its ponds and streams, no rambling its fields with their Guerard cousins. . . .

He took his time changing, and when he went back downstairs in sleeping shirt, robe, and slippers, he found hot biscuits and butter on the dining room table, and Dorinda brought in a large bowl of soup. Dorinda was white haired and growing old. It was so unfair to take her and Lucas away from Jessamine, but they and their family had said they wanted to stay with Lew and Rose.

He sat down at the head of the table. Rose sat on his right. He felt her tension, her need to know everything, but he had no real wish to discuss their situation. Somehow he had to hide how sick, how frightened, he really felt.

"Well, now," Rose said brightly after a moment, "tell me all about it. How did everything go?"

He shrugged and tried to look—satisfied? indifferent? He said: "As well as could be expected."

"Did you get what you wanted?"

"I got what I could."

"What does that mean?"

"It means we'll keep all those people who said they wanted to stay with us. The others will be able to stay here at Jessamine, and they won't be sold off. It means we'll keep all those personal possessions you wanted, and we'll have some horses, a carriage, and so forth."

"Well, that doesn't sound so bad. What else?"

"Under the circumstances, that's a great deal."

Rose was quiet for a moment, and Lew knew she was having difficulty restraining herself. She was not the kind of woman to leave business matters exclusively to her husband and follow him blindly. If catastrophe threatened, she would want to know.

"But you must have got some money as well, didn't you? Just on the crop alone, we have the profit coming to us, or at least a share of it. Surely we did better than just break even."

Lew closed his eyes. He thought he had made clear to her what they could expect, but perhaps she didn't want to understand.

"Rose," he said slowly, "I got a guarantee that the people we leave behind will always be allowed to live here, that they will never be sold, never separated."

Rose's voice shook. "And for that you had to take a cut in price?"

"Yes, I did. A considerable cut."

"For a guarantee that means nothing?"

"It's written into the sale agreement. A guarantee that—"

"Oh, a guarantee!" she said scornfully, all sympathy gone from her voice. "What does a guarantee mean? Once we're gone, how are you going to enforce it? How are you even going to know if anyone has been sold?"

Of course, she was right. For the most part, he could only depend on the buyer's honor in such a matter, and honor struck him as being in short supply these days. Since the bank panic had started, it had increasingly been every man for himself.

"Rose, I did the best I could."

"But if the new owner is going to sell the people, you might as well have done it yourself. If you'd sold a few families—"

He shook his head. Why couldn't she understand? "I promised my father I'd never do that. I promised him specifically, at least twice that I remember. That's one reason he felt he could safely leave Jessamine to me. But even if I hadn't promised him, Rose, I damned well wouldn't do it. What do you take me for, some kind of goddamn slave-trader?"

Rose's voice grew shrill. "I take you for a man whose

family is in desperate trouble! I take you for a man whose duty it is to provide—"

"Rose, for God's sake!" Lew's hand slammed down on the table. "For God's sake, I shall provide! One way or another, I shall provide!"

"Well, I'd like to know how!"

"We aren't penniless, Rose! We haven't much, but we do have a few dollars. We'll have a roof over our heads in Charleston, at least for a while, and if we sell the house in Charleston—"

"No," Rose said flatly. "I am not going to be without so much as my own house!"

"But it costs money to keep up a house. And what we have isn't going to last forever."

"I don't care, I'm going to keep my house!"

"Then we'll have to rent it—"

"No. I am not going to have strangers living in my house and using my things—"

"Rose, you have got to be reasonable! If we rent it out, we'll at least get an income to maintain it. We may even get a profit out of it. But if we don't do that, we'll have to sell it. I don't want to, I was raised in that house, but it's one or the other, Rose! There is just no way out of it!"

She hid her face in her hands, and he knew she was crying. Was this what misfortune did to people who loved each other? reduced them to bickering and angry shouting?

"I'm sorry, Rose."

She shook her head. "How did this happen to us? I don't understand. Everything was going so well, and then all of a sudden . . . How did this happen to us?"

Lew sighed. He had tried to explain it a dozen times—how thousands like himself had invested heavily in public lands, how President Jackson had ordered that only "hard money" be accepted as payment for those lands, how the demand for specie had started a bank panic. Of course, that was an over-simplification, but in any case, over five hundred banks had closed so far that year, and it looked as if the total would run over six hundred. Savings had been lost, other investments besides those in land had been lost, and thousands like Lew had been ruined.

"If only you hadn't tried to buy all that land—"

"I know, I know. My greed did it to us."

"I don't mean to blame you. I know it just *happened* to us, the way it did to everybody else. I'm just asking, why did it *have* to happen? We were so happy before."

"We will be again."

"But what are we going to do?"

She would never know how much hard thought he had given to that question. It was something he had put off discussing with her, but the problem had to be faced sometime, and he decided it might as well be now. Get all the unpleasantness over with as quickly as possible.

"Rose, do you remember when your brother was here a month ago? When I told him we were going to have to sell Jessamine? What he said?"

She remembered instantly, and under any other circumstances, Lew might have laughed at the look that came over her face. It was a look of consternation that almost amounted to horror.

"Well, Lew," Adaba had said mockingly, *"reckon you can always get a job as an overseer. Come to think of it, I heard they need an overseer at a place called Sabrehill. Ain't that owned by some kind of cousins of yours?"*

"You don't mean you would . . . ?"

Become an overseer. Cease to be a gentleman. Enter a class that was far beneath that of the Sabre family. Enter a class that many regarded as only a cut above that of the slave-trader.

Not that there weren't many admirable and respected men among overseers. Some were the younger sons of gentlemen. Others were, by virtue of personal quality, more entitled to the designation of gentlemen than were their masters. But to rise from the level of overseer to gentleman planter was virtually unheard of, and to descend from gentleman planter to overseer was a sad falling off.

"Rose, we have a lot of people dependent on us. Not only our children and ourselves, but our black people as well. Now, until we can find some opportunity to improve our position, we have got to find some place to light. Some place to make some money or, at the very least, to cut our losses. And yes, to do that I would take a job as overseer.

304

It's an honorable profession, in spite of some of the men who follow it, and I'd be better at it than most of them. So don't fight me on this, Rose. I can't expect you to like it, but you're going to have to live with it. And I hope you won't love me any the less."

Rose's face was calm again. "You fool, I'll never stop loving you."

"We're going to be all right, Rose. I promise you. My God, even as things stand, we are so much better off than most people. . . ."

Later, as they lay in bed together in the darkness, she in the curve of his arm, the questions crowded in on him.

Where was he to get a job as overseer, when all jobs were scarce? Had there really been such a job available at Sabrehill? Might it still be open?

Had he been a pride-cursed fool not to ask Rose's father for help? But Marcus Guerard had his own financial problems these days, and he would be doing them a great favor simply in taking care of Lucas and Dorinda and the others for the time being.

Rose felt he had been a fool to keep all those black people. So many of them! It had meant a reduction of thousands of dollars in the value of Jessamine, money he badly needed. And unless he could find a way to support his people, the others might live to regret ever having followed him and Rose away from Jessamine.

So this is the way it ends, he thought—the happiest ten years of his life.

For they had been happy years, happier than any of his childhood or his boyhood, happier even than those wonderful months before the Vesey affair. God knows, he could never have expected so much happiness from the way his marriage had started: the scorn of his sister and her husband, virtual ostracism by so many of his old friends, a murderous confrontation with his brother-in-law. But then something happened. He had realized that he was being observed with a certain amusement by one segment of the Charleston population that bore him no ill-will at all. *What do you think of that?* they said. *Young Lew Sabre. Got hisself a nigger wife. Well, then, the son of a bitch can't be all bad! . . .*

These were the eccentrics, the iconoclasts, the freethinkers of the city. They included the wise, the witty, and the simple good-hearted. They included men of artistic and intellectual bent, and drinkers and gamblers. They included the city's unconventional old reprobates and, less openly, a handful of *very* respectable citizens. They were a jolly band and the only kind that Lew could ever really be comfortable with. They, some with their wives and others with their mistresses of various complexions, had provided Lew and Rose with the happiest kind of society and companionship.

Now, if Lew and Rose had to leave Charleston to regain their fortunes, they would have to leave all that behind, and Lew was afraid they would never find anything like it again.

Rose sighed in the curve of his arm, and her fingertips moved over his chest. Instantly, Lew's thoughts broke off, and his body tensed. He knew what she wanted.

"Lew," Rose whispered.

He remained silent, pretending to be asleep.

Her fingertips drifted lightly down his chest, down to his thigh, then tugged up the hem of his sleeping shirt and felt beneath it.

Nothing.

He had never felt colder, never deader.

"Lew?"

He didn't answer. He could force himself to perform, but he knew it wouldn't be good. It hadn't been good for months. The last time, several weeks earlier, it had been like a solitary act that his body had wanted to end as quickly as possible, and he had come to the end of it before they were even completely together. Afterward, Rose had wept and had slapped his hand away as he had attempted to caress her. The night had been miserable in every way.

Tonight promised to be no better. Rose sobbed with frustration when he didn't respond. He suspected she knew he was awake.

"Oh, God," she whimpered, "God . . . *damn* you!" And releasing him, she turned away.

Christ, he thought, what was this doing to them?

Tearing them apart in spite of all the love they felt for each other. Eventually, it might even destroy their love.

He had to do something. Something to save them.

Tomorrow he would write.

To Sabrehill.

Two: December 1837

Sheba watched from the doorway of the fine new brick house Balbo Jeppson had built at Redbird plantation. The morning was chilly but beautifully sun drenched, and Redbird sparkled: the whitewashed kitchen house and office and storehouse and other outbuildings. Even the field quarters, every house in it, off in the distance, gleamed. Only one building in sight remained dark and somber, a reminder of suffering and mortality.

The jail, with the tall whipping gallows standing nearby.

At the moment, the jail had only one occupant; but over the last twenty years or more hundreds of men and women and sometimes even children had been forced to live in it, often a dozen or more bodies within a few square feet, until every board and brick stank of human waste and misery and death. For this was where rebellious blacks were sent to be "broken": to be deprived of any last shred of pride or dignity that might lead them to stand up against their masters. Redbird plantation.

Sheba stared at the jail, which was almost directly across the yard from the house, perhaps a couple of hundred feet away. It was a dark blot on the bright day, something that immediately caught the eye and held it. To Sheba, jail and whipping gallows were a constant reminder that no matter how privileged her position with Mr. Jeppson, others still grieved and suffered and died.

A sharp noise, the clattering of a pan in the kitchen, brought her back to awareness of other life about the big house. Saturday morning was always a cheerful time, as the leisure of Saturday night and Sunday approached.

Behind her, a couple of maids chattered and laughed as they went about their work, dusting and polishing. Outside, someone was whooping and hollering out by the barn. In the yard near the jail, Jeppson and the driver Sabin—gray now, and scarred from when he had been struck down three years ago on the Night of the Fires—stood waiting for a wagon that was approaching. The wagon, pulled by a pair of mules, carried a white man and a teamster on the bench seat. Something or someone lay on the bed behind them.

As the wagon got closer, Sheba saw that the white man was Mr. Buckridge, a planter from down the river.

And then she remembered.

Mr. Jeppson had talked about it: the two bad-acting slaves that Mr. Buckridge was considering bringing to Redbird for breaking. But Buckridge had never brought them, and Sheba hoped he had changed his mind.

Now she saw that there were two blacks tied together in the back on the wagon.

The wagon reached the yard. The black at the reins pulled it up beside Jeppson and Sabin. Sheba could clearly see the impassive faces of the bound men.

Oh, them poor boys, she thought. *Oh, them poor, poor boys . . .*

Money.

Cash money now seemed to Jeppson the most important thing in the world, the mainstay of existence, the blood that kept the true body of his fortunes alive. He wasn't used to such an idea. As a boy, he had seen little in the way of U.S. specie—not much had existed—or even much in the way of banknotes. All of his life he had been accustomed to thinking in terms of land and slaves and crops, and money notations had merely been symbols in his account books or those of his factor. Ink scratches on a piece of paper, rather than the coin or the banknote, had been the medium of exchange. But now all of that had changed. With the cry for specie and the closing of the banks, money had become real for him. And he had very little.

Born poor, he had become accustomed to thinking of himself as a wealthy man because he had accumulated land and slaves, not because he had money. He had worked hard all his life and risen in the world, and three years ago he had seized his greatest opportunity.

He had long coveted Redbird plantation, which lay next to his own. While Old Man Skeet, the owner, was drinking himself into senility, Jeppson had managed to buy a few acres cheap. But young Vachel Skeet was a different proposition. Vachel had hung onto the land tenaciously, building up the plantation in a way that made Jeppson yearn for it all the more.

Then had come Jeppson's opportunity. Three years ago, thirty-odd slaves from several plantations had rebelled, fired a number of buildings, and run off. Jeppson himself had lost three slaves that night—the Night of the Fires, as it was called—and both his and the Redbird big houses had been burned down. But more important to Jeppson's fortunes, Vachel Skeet had been killed.

An Alabama cousin of Vachel had inherited Redbird. He had been willing to sell, but with cotton at its highest price in years, he had been looking for high bids. And Major Kimbrough, the owner of the plantation on the other side of Redbird, had wanted the land as much as Jeppson had.

Well, perhaps not quite as much, because Jeppson had outbid him. He had sworn that Major Kimbrough, by God, was not going to have Redbird, not after he himself had waited all these years to get it. The market was beginning to boom, his credit was good, and he was going to have Redbird, no matter what the price.

That was his mistake. He had even been warned by the banks. The price of Redbird was so grossly inflated that he had had to mortgage much of his own plantation to cover it, and the bank terms had been exorbitant. He wasn't sure how he would ever pay such a mortgage off! But suddenly a Northern investor had appeared—he said he represented the Bluebell Company, and had drawn up what appeared to be a more reasonable mortgage contract. In his elation, and since he was no businessman, Jeppson

309

had hardly read it. He had signed it, had annexed Redbird, and with Bluebell's help had proceeded to build a fine new big-house on the site of Redbird's old one.

Jeppson felt that all of his dreams were being realized. When you were one of the biggest land- and slave-owners in the area, when you owned one of the longest stretches of land along the river, it was a little harder for the gentry to sneer down their noses. Balbo Jeppson was becoming a man to be reckoned with. The sandhiller upstart of years before was actually becoming respectable.

But now, this year, all he had worked for was on the verge of being swept away.

The panic had started, the banks were closing, the price of cotton was plummeting. It had taken Jeppson some time to realize he was in trouble. He had payments, steep payments, of interest and principal to meet, and the profit from his crop would be much smaller than he had anticipated. He couldn't sell any of the land or the slaves that were his security. Some said the state would pass new laws to protect mortgagees, but would the new laws come in time? And was it true, as a Charleston lawyer had told him, that his "reasonable" Bluebell mortgage contract anticipated almost any protective bill the legislature might pass?

Balbo Jeppson knew he was facing ruin.

But he wouldn't face it passively. He would fight. He would meet his payments to Bluebell, and within a few years he would say to hell with them and good-bye—Redbird would be all his. To that end, he would squeeze every last cent of profit out of the land and out of his slaves, he would squeeze them unmercifully. And he would do the same to every other slave he could get hold of.

That was what he saw when he looked at the two blacks lying bound in the back of Buckridge's wagon: Profit. Money. Payment to Bluebell.

But Buckridge, unfortunately, seemed to be having second thoughts.

"I don't know, Mr. Jeppson," he said, tugging at his long gray mustache, "I just don't know." He remained where he was, on the seat of the wagon, so that he could

310

avoid shaking hands. He was a thin-faced, slightly built man of about Jeppson's age, though he looked older.

Jeppson struggled to hide his eagerness. "Well, now, Mr. Buckridge, sir, it's purely up to you. But you been having trouble with these here two. You been talking a long time about bringing them to me. And now you're here. All you got to do is dump them off this wagon and put them out of mind and ride away. I guarantee you that in a month or two you'll have a couple of niggers that'll never give you trouble again." He wondered if he dared ask a fee for the two blacks' upkeep, and decided against it. "You say they back-sass you?"

"Too damn much."

"Once is too damn much. I guarantee you it's happened for the last time. You say they lazy?"

"Don't do a damn thing anymore."

"Any nigger is lazy if he ain't watched. Or if he don't know he's gonna get hurt if he don't finish his task. But if I train him, he's gonna be the liveliest nigger you ever saw, and no back-sass. You leave these critters here, and I'll put them right."

Buckridge looked dubious. "Mr. Jeppson, let me be frank. I've heard about some blacks being hurt awfully bad here. I've even heard of two or three that died."

"That's the chance you take, getting a nigger busted."

"Well, I don't want these boys killed or even badly hurt—no bad scars or broken bones. That's got to be understood."

Jeppson's first impulse was to curse the man for a fool, but then he saw that Buckridge's conditions had certain advantages. "Well, sir," he said slowly, "I reckon I could guarantee that. But it'll take a lot longer to break them that way." And he would have the free labor for his fields that much longer.

"I don't give a damn how long it takes," Buckridge said. "The way they are, they sure as hell aren't doing me any good."

"Then we're in agreement?" Jeppson held up his hand. Buckridge's handshake would mean something, whether he wanted to give it or not.

But Buckridge didn't extend his hand. "One more thing. You've got to guarantee me the full value of these boys. Now, Jonah here is a trained cooper."

Jeppson looked at Buckridge with astonishment. He had certainly never expected such a condition, and he saw himself losing the two slaves. "Mr. Buckridge, sir, they ain't worth *nothing* if they won't work!"

Buckridge shook his head. "They have a big potential value if you can break them, otherwise I wouldn't have brought them here. You tell me they won't be badly hurt, but—"

"My word ain't good enough for you?"

For a moment the two men stared with distaste at each other, all pretense of friendliness gone.

"Let's just say, Mr. Jeppson, that it's a matter of sound business practice."

Jeppson took time to spit at the mules' legs before looking up and answering. "Mr. Buckridge, sir, I always thought people like you looked down on business. But since you're a businessman after all, I'll put up fifty dollars on each of these boys and not a cent more."

Buckridge shook his head again. "Two hundred."

Buckridge was smiling, as if glad to find an excuse not to come to an agreement, or Jeppson would never have said it: "One hundred."

After a moment, Buckridge shrugged. "One hundred."

Jeppson told Sabin to put the two bound slaves into the jail. A handshake should have been enough to seal the agreement, but Buckridge suggested that they write it up so that there would be no misunderstanding, and they went to the nearby office to do so. They had no white witness to their agreement, but Jeppson had no doubt that Buckridge could make it stand up in a court of law: his word in such a matter would always be accepted. When Buckridge was back on his wagon and riding away, the two still had not shaken hands.

But what did Jeppson care? He had two more slaves he could put to work, slaves he would hang onto for months. There were moments when he burst out in a cold sweat with the fear—no, with the certain knowledge—that he was going to lose everything, that all his efforts were a flailing against the inevitable. But not today. Today was one of those when he felt that nothing in the world could defeat him, and he hurried to the big house to tell Sheba the good news.

He found her in the passage at the door. "You see that, Sheba? You see what Mr. Buckridge brought us?"

Sheba rarely criticized him aloud. Instead, she was apt to take on a kind of blankness, a silence that was almost obsidian. Now she stood before him, her arms crossed under her breasts, her head cocked back, and said nothing.

"Now, Miss Lady . . ."

She deigned to speak. "Mr. Jeppson, you too good for nigger-breaking, and you know it. Long ago you say you plan to give it up. Yet you go on and on."

How was it that she managed to make him, at his age, feel like a small boy? "Well, things change, Miss Lady," he said weakly. "Anyway, somebody always got to do the breaking, and the jail come with Redbird. And with these hard times come on us, we're lucky Redbird's known for breaking. It got us two more hands."

"Them hands ain't gonna do you no good, Mr. Jeppson, no more'n that boy you already got in the jail house. Sabin spend all his time watching them when he should be working the other hands. Ain't no profit in that—the good Lord gonna see to it!"

That riled Jeppson. "The *good Lord*, Sheba, is on my side!"

Sheba said nothing further. The blankness came over her again. It didn't judge him, it simply cut him off from whatever was going on inside of her, and he was forced to look at her as if she were a statue.

But what a statue! Odd, but at moments like this he saw more clearly and coldly than ever what a handsome woman she was. She was in her middle thirties now, if he figured correctly, and over the years her thin, prominent nose had grown nobler, her full mouth fuller, her dimpled chin stronger. Her skin, taut as a girl's, still had a rich, coppery sheen, and he thought that it wasn't true that she had white blood—it must be Indian. But he rarely thought of her in terms of race. He couldn't afford to. She was simply Sheba. *His* Sheba. His Miss Lady.

"Aw, now, Miss Lady . . ."

He stepped toward her, his hands out to take her elbows. She neither moved away nor showed any sign of yielding to him. She was impervious as stone, and somehow he had to bring her back to life again, back to life to *him*. Sometimes he thought, what if he had never found her? What if he had sat here on his plantation all these years with no other purpose in life than to add to his land- and slave-holdings and keep the blacks in line and hate the goddamn gentry? He probably would have ended up like Old Man Skeet after his wife died, drinking himself out of his head and into his grave. Gradually, in recent years, it had dawned on Jeppson how much meaning this woman had brought into his life—virtually the only positive, human meaning it had.

Suddenly moved, he touched Sheba's arms. "Sheba, you got to understand. Things is bad now, and we could lose Redbird, we could lose everything. But we ain't gonna lose it. And when things get better, I promise you there ain't gonna be no more nigger-breaking at Redbird. And no more riding with the patrol and the posses, none of that. Hell, I done my share of keeping the niggers in line— I'm getting sick and tired of it. Let somebody else do it."

Very faintly, he saw something come to life in her eyes. He couldn't tell if it were doubt or hope or pain. But at least it was something.

"I *promise* you, Sheba," he said softly. "I ain't never broke a promise to you if I could help it, have I?"

He leaned forward and kissed her cheek, and he didn't give much of a damn if any of the people did see. There were a lot of things he didn't care nearly so much about anymore.

Sheba favored him with a hint of a smile and said, "I got work to do, Mr. Jeppson," and went outside.

Jeppson watched her as she walked toward the kitchen house. No wonder the people had come to call her Miss Lady, he thought. She was more of a natural lady than

314

any white woman he had ever met. Maybe she didn't have white women's high-flown talk or their manners or airs, but she didn't have their damn chicken brains or their cold eyes or their poison tongues either. God, or somebody, had given her quality. Real quality.

What was going to happen to her when he was gone?

It was a question that occurred to him with increasing frequency. He wasn't old, he told himself, but he was a lot older than Sheba, and somehow he had to provide for her. It was unlikely that the state would give him permission to free her, but maybe he could arrange to have her sent to another state and freed and cared for. Of course, he didn't believe in freeing blacks, but Sheba was different. Nothing bad, he told himself, must ever happen to Sheba. Not ever again.

Them poor boys . . .

Somehow she had to help them, and there was only one way she knew to do it.

Fortunately, the people trusted her, even loved her. They had learned years ago that she was the one person in the world who could to some degree control Jeppson—could temper his discipline and modify his rages. No one who was old enough had ever forgotten how, after young Remus and the others had abused her, she had kept Jeppson from mutilating the boy. And in the years since, a thousand times she had mediated between Jeppson and his people.

So even though she was known to be close to Jeppson, it had not been difficult for her to get some glimmering of what was going on in the quarters. Apparently it had started in this region on the Night of the Fires. For some months thereafter nothing more had happened, and then it had resumed again: the disappearance of slaves at an alarming rate.

Five or six years earlier, in another part of the country, this phenomenon had been given a name: the Underground Railroad. It had not taken Sheba long to realize that at Redbird the Railroad's agent was a woman called Serena.

She was in her late twenties, this Serena, a woman once pretty who had been so badly treated that she now looked years older than she was. She had been the chief driver's woman, frequently shared with Redbird's master, until three years ago, when both driver and master had been killed. Since Mr. Jeppson had taken over Redbird, Sheba had done her best to restore Serena's spirit and some of her lost youth, and they had become close friends.

Now, as she had expected, she found Serena in the kitchen with Fenella and Abel, and it was almost an hour before they found a chance to talk alone. The opportunity came before dinner, when Fenella sent Serena to the root cellar. Sheba followed casually after her, down into the dark, cool room.

"You see them two boys Mr. Buckridge bring this morning?" she asked.

"Jonah and Moses," Serena said, picking through some potatoes.

"Oh, you know them?"

"Some. Brothers, from Virginia. Cooper and wheelwright. Mr. Buckridge buy them five, six year ago."

No matter how the masters tried to keep the slaves apart, and Jeppson was far stricter in that respect than most, somehow they met, and information was passed along. Sheba had heard masters complain that their slaves knew more about what was happening around the countryside than they themselves did.

"No wife here, no children?" she asked.

"Jonah had wife and children, they dead."

"Nothing to keep them here, then?"

"Nothing but that damn jail house!" Serena said in a sudden display of irritation. "Goddamn fools got to get theyself put in the jail house *now,* of all time!"

"What about that other in the jail house?"

"Nestor, from Breakline plantation. He got a family. He don't want to go nowhere."

Two, then. Two for the Underground Railroad. And it had been unnecessary for Sheba to speak to Serena. Sooner or later, Serena would have spoken to her.

"Been a long time since anybody break out of that jail house, Serena," she said. "Wonder when it happen again."

316

"When they get a chance, I reckon."

"Just hope it happen on a night when Mr. Jeppson sleep real good."

Serena, blank faced until now, but knowing what she meant, shot her a quick grin. "I hope so too, Sheba. And I hope it happen real soon." Ordinarily, Jeppson slept like a cat, awakening to any strange sound in or around the house. But Sheba knew how to deal with that.

"You just tell me when."

Sheba helped select some carrots and onions, putting them into the fold of Serena's apron. She was about to leave when a troubled look in Serena's eyes caught and held her.

"What is it, Serena?"

"Don't know I should tell you yet or not."

"Now, you know you can tell me."

"Maybe I go with them, Sheba."

Sheba made a little sound of pain before she could stop herself. Though she knew every black on the plantation, had nursed many of them in sickness, and had helped bring a number of them into the world, she was close to only a very few. Of those few, Serena was most like a younger sister to her.

"I got to go soon, Sheba. I think maybe Mr. Jeppson getting 'spicious 'bout me. He ain't no fool, you know."

"I know."

For a moment, the two women looked at each other. Then they embraced tightly, and the vegetables—potatoes, carrots, onions—spilled from Serena's apron and went rolling about the floor.

"You see your sister again, Serena!"

"Yes. See her and Tobe up there."

"You 'member me to them!"

"I surely do that."

"I going miss you so. . . ."

Serena's lips worked, and for a moment Sheba thought she was going to cry. Instead she burst out: "Sheba, you come too!"

The possibility had occurred to her more than once, and she didn't have to think about it now. She shook her head.

317

"Someday, maybe. But not yet. I got a life here, Serena. Ain't so bad for me."

"But Mr. Jeppson a lot older than you, and he ain't going last forever. You get too old to run away north, what happen to you then?"

Sheba sank down onto a bench in the shadows by the steps. "I don't know, Serena. I only know it ain't time for me to run away yet. I can still help our people here. And . . . and I can help Mr. Jeppson too."

Serena shook her head wonderingly. "Sometimes I think 'spite of everything you got love for that man."

"I s'pose I do, some."

"How can you . . . ?"

"He been good to me, Serena. All these years, I hear hardly a ill word from him."

"But he's bad, that man!"

" 'Course he's bad. First night I was here, he ruin a poor black boy's feet. And that same year, him and some others kill a white woman for bedding with a black man. And there's been all them others he's hurt so much. And if the people here'd followed Denmark Vesey, I . . . I'd . . ."

"What, Sheba? What you would done to him?"

"Never you mind." Sheba heard her voice growing bitter. "Yes, it's true I got a kind of love for Mr. Jeppson. I got more love for that evil man than I ever want to say. But when I think 'bout Denmark Vesey . . ."

Serena sat down and put her hand on Sheba's. "What 'bout when you think 'bout Denmark Vesey?"

"Ain't supposed to know 'bout Denmark no more. They hang him and his people to make examples, and then we supposed to forget like he never was. But I don't forget. Not ever." Sheba raised her eyes to Serena's. "I *knowed* Denmark Vesey!"

Serena stared at her. "You *knowed* him? Sheba, you never told me that!"

"Never told nobody till now. But I knowed him well. He taught my young man and me. Stand up strong, he said. Keep your head up. You act like a slave, you deserve to *be* a slave!"

318

She added after a moment, "And you best 'member that too, Serena."

"I learned from you, Sheba."

Sheba nodded. "Then it gets passed on. And even if they want to forget his name, Denmark Vesey is still alive. And we ain't never going to let him die."

Serena got up from the bench and gathered up the vegetables again. Sheba sat where she was in the dimness at the side of the steps, not wanting to move. Thoughts of Denmark sometimes stirred things best left quiet.

"What your young man's name, Sheba?"

That was one of them. There were no tears left in her, there hadn't been for years; the girl who had wept was dead. But still she hesitated to say the name that had once been so dear to her.

"John," she said instead, after a moment.

"John. That a nice name. . . ."

Serena finished picking up the vegetables. As she started up the steps, Sheba put out a hand to detain her.

"If you go, who take your place?"

Serena knew what she meant. "Leonie and Bishop."

Leonie and . . . Dear Lord, Sheba thought. A thirteen-year-old girl and her ten-year-old brother. Well, why not? At Redbird, children too knew the meaning of bondage.

"And when you know when you all go?"

"Got no idea." Serena shot her another quick grin, an impudent grin that made her battered, lined face look surprisingly childlike. "Maybe today, maybe tomorrow. Whenever I see that old Brown Dove again!"

. . . So Buckley Skeet had made good his vow to come back, Adaba thought, and had got himself killed, and here I am now, at Redbird. Odd how things worked out. If it hadn't been for Buck's stumbling into the maroon camp one night fifteen years earlier, Adaba might never have come anywhere near the area. He would never have hidden out at Sabrehill three years ago, when he and Buck were on the run, would never have met his Zulie, who lay at his side right now in a patch of woods. Lay watching the glistening white-painted big house that Balbo Jeppson had built and the whitewashed outbuildings and the dark brick jail. Did everything in life have a purpose, then, or was life just one shake of the dice after another?

Redbird looked deceptively beautiful in the late-afternoon sunlight. The light itself had a kind of antique glow about it, a blue clarity that conveyed a rosy stain from the drifting clouds, and which made the scene appear strangely timeless. Servants moved between the various outbuildings. A child chased a chicken about the yard. A heavy-set, barrel-chested man walked from the office to the kitchen. That would be Balbo Jeppson: Adaba had learned to identify him from a distance. The slim figure of Miss Lady, the housekeeper, appeared at the door of the big house for a moment and disappeared again. "She the only one can do anything with Mr. Jeppson," Zulie had told him more than once. "Been his housekeeper ever since I 'member. My momma and her was good friends. Momma teached her how to heal."

The light seemed to thicken with rose and blue, as the hour neared five and the sun touched the horizon. They had to be careful. Field hands, working later than usual for a Saturday, in order to get in the crop, would soon be returning to their quarters. Adaba's ears were alert to every sound around them.

No sign of Jonah and Moses as yet.

He and Zulie had watched as Buckridge delivered the two slaves that morning. Jeppson, of course, had lost little time in putting the pair to work in the fields.

Damn them anyway, Adaba thought again. The two slaves had had to make things complicated. He had promised them that he would return for them in a few weeks— in fact, by this very Saturday night. They were to be ready. They were to have bedrolls, food, and the stolen tools of survival hidden away. They were to behave themselves and take no unnecessary risks. But—a pair of bright, playful, don't-give-a-damn young blacks—they had sassed and teased Owen Buckridge one time too many, and he had fulfilled an old threat to turn them over to Balbo Jeppson for breaking. Adaba had half a notion to let them take their medicine.

But of course he would never really do that.

When he and Zulie had arrived at the Buckridge plantation last night, they had learned what had happened. Fortunately, the stolen supplies had not been discovered, and Adaba figured the situation could be salvaged. Early this morning they had come to Redbird and had been observing the main buildings ever since.

Adaba's stomach rumbled. Zulie handed him a piece of dried beef from a poke and took another for herself. By the time they had finished eating, it was quite dark.

"Reckon it 'bout time I have me a little talk with Serena," Zulie whispered.

"No. I'll go talk to her myself. You stay here."

"O-o-oh!" Zulie was disgusted. He knew she thought he was overly protective only because she was carrying his child, but he had other reasons as well.

"Don't argue with me, woman."

"Ain't going argue. You know I can get to Serena easier'n you. Maybe I talk to Miss Lady to this time. Been a long while since I talk to Miss Lady——"

"Zulie, you ain't going nowhere near that big house."

"Bet you I could walk right through it, and Mr. Jeppson never lay eyes on me!"

"Goddammit, that's just what I'm afraid of—that you'll try some such damn-fool stunt!"

In the past three years he had taught Zulie everything he knew about survival—every trick, every skill, everything he had learned from Gavin Murdock, and a great deal more. Now she could move through the woods and fields as silently as he, and as swiftly. The forests, the swamps, the pattyrollers held no terrors for her. She needed only her hatchet to survive in almost any situation. She also had a skill he lacked, an uncanny knack of disappearing, not only in the wilds, but in the midst of a crowd —she could wander into a group of a dozen or fewer blacks, and not even their own master would notice her. And if she were to walk through Jeppson's house and Jeppson saw her, the chances were: God help Jeppson. Adaba was forced to admit that, all in all, Zulie was an even better "Indian" than he or Gavin Murdock.

Except for one thing.

She was overconfident. She was like a person who suddenly discovered she had a genius for horseback riding and who insisted on taking every jump she encountered, no matter how many or how high or how difficult. She had to meet every challenge that came along, if only for the sheer joy of it. And if she persisted, she was going to get caught or hurt or perhaps killed.

He didn't think he could stand that. He wasn't sure he would want to go on living if anything happened to Zulie.

"Now, don't you fuss," she said, getting to her knees. "I ain't going do nothing foolish."

He sat up beside her. "You just stay away from that big house. Talk to Serena and get back here quick as you can."

She gave him a kiss. "You know I always do like my man say."

Like hell.

She stood up very slowly, keeping close to a tree, as he had taught her. She was a tall woman of about thirty years, with broad shoulders and a small head that made her look curiously doll-like in spite of her height. Dressed in pants and a jacket, with a slouch-brimmed hat over her closely cropped hair, she might have been taken for a boy. She was Erzulie, daughter of Erzulie, last of a line of conjurewomen and healers, and one of the thirty-two slaves he had led away from these parts on the Night of the Fires.

Now he watched her vanish into the darkness of the night. He had trained her well. She would be safe. She would return soon, as she always did.

"You stay 'wake tonight, Sheba Lady," Serena had said when they were alone together in her cabin. "You see Adaba yourself. Once Mr. Jeppson sleep, you come out to the jail house and talk to him—"

"No!" Sheba had said, too sharply.

Serena had looked surprised, puzzled. "You don't want to talk to Adaba?"

"Best not. Best you talk to him, you and Leonie and Bishop. I don't want Mr. Jeppson to think I ever anywhere near that man."

But of course that was not the real reason, or at any rate not the only one.

Adaba. The Brown Dove. With an identifying mark on his left cheek, some said, just as John Guerard had had. But she didn't want to believe it was true that they were one and the same, she didn't even want to think about the possibility. Gilly was long dead, and the past was dead with her. Let the past and all its pain stay dead and buried.

Anyway, she told herself, there must have been dozens of Adabas over the years, Adabas with and without marks on their cheeks. It was only a name and not uncommon. . . .

She had other things to worry about. Hard times, she thought, as she slowly made her way through the quarters back toward the big house. Hard times. Here Mr. Jeppson was with all this land and a new house and two quarters full of people and not even a full-time overseer to help him. Not even old Mr. Birnie, now long dead. Just occasional buckra from the village and the drivers—evil brutes, most of them, like Sabin. At least Mr. Jeppson did look after his people fairly well—kept them well clothed and fed and in sound cabins; but with hard times, how long would he keep that up? And if he decided to sell off any of his unmortgaged people, would she be able to stop him? No, she thought, it was no time for her to be thinking about leaving Redbird.

When she arrived back at the big house, she found that Mr. Tucker and Mr. Macon, who had stopped by, had departed. She was glad, because she didn't like the way they looked at her behind Mr. Jeppson's back—one of the reasons she had gone out to the quarters. Mr. Jeppson was in the parlor, reading the big volume of Shakespeare. Sheba smiled to herself. In all their years together, she had never been able to teach Mr. Jeppson to read very well. Not that he had tried hard, she had to admit; he much preferred to have her read to him, and at least he had been generous in providing her with books. She had dared salvage only the Shakespeare and a few other volumes when the old house had burned on the Night of the Fires, but her library had been replenished in the three years since. She could not have kept her sanity otherwise.

Going into the pantry, Sheba took two fresh glasses from a cabinet. From a drawer she took the small flask of laudanum which Mr. Jeppson had supplied her when she had complained of not being able to sleep. She poured a few drops into one of the glasses—not much, for she wanted Mr. Jeppson to awaken feeling that he had slept soundly, not that he had been drugged. Into both glasses she poured some of his finest brandy. He would have already had a drink or two with his friends, which would help cover the taste of the opiate.

She carried the two glasses to the parlor, where Mr. Jeppson was still reading the Shakespeare. He looked up at her and smiled, as she put the drugged drink into his hand.

" 'Age cannot wither her, nor custom stale her infinite variety,' " he quoted.

"Why, Mr. Jeppson, you sweet thing, you!"

Sheba leaned down and kissed him on the forehead.

And they drank.

"And now, Mr. Jeppson . . ."

She set the empty glasses and the Shakespeare aside. She took Mr. Jeppson's hand and pulled at it.

He grinned at her. "Now, Sheba Lady, what you want?"

"You know what I want. It's Saturday night, honey, and I got to pay you for that sweet compliment."

She took him upstairs to his bedroom and undressed him. She undressed before him, teasing him, playing with him until he could no longer wait, then straddled him and took him into herself and drained him, not forgetting her own pleasure. Then, with lip and tongue and many a soft caress, she brought him back to life again, until, maddened, he threw her onto her back and took her with all the force of an invited rape. She was holding him, gently tugging at him, trying to bring him to a third conclusion, when she saw his eyes close and heard him sigh.

Mr. Jeppson slept all through that night.

Jeppson awakened at dawn, as the first hint of light crept through the bedroom window. It was his custom to arise early even on Sunday, but he might have slept later that morning if someone hadn't been banging about downstairs building a fire.

He found that he was naked under the covers, and he smiled, remembering last night. My God, was it really possible that Sheba had given it to him that good? and he that good to her? The last thing he remembered was holding her in his arms, and . . .

He reached out for Sheba, wanting to hold her close, but she wasn't there. He was disappointed. She used to go to her own bed afterward, so that others wouldn't know, but since they'd moved into the new house they had both grown careless. He hardly cared who knew anymore—taking chances on being found out made him feel less like a goddamn hypocrite. Anyway, a white man putting it to a black woman wasn't nearly as bad as a white woman taking on a black man. A white man ought to be allowed a little sin or two, and with Sheba somehow it didn't seem like a sin.

And he didn't have any little nigger yardchildren running about like some of the fine gentry did, did he?

For a moment he felt troubled, remembering his recurrent dream of guilty coupling with Sheba, followed by a child—a child that in real life had aborted. But he shook the memory and the dream off and sat up.

He was a happy man. After last night, he knew that nothing too bad could happen. He was going to have a good crop this year even if prices did fall, and he was going to pay for Redbird in no time at all, and he was going to live another thirty years and—he swore it—have Sheba every night of his life.

He got out of bed and washed and dressed in the near darkness. His stomach felt hollow and his bladder full, and laughing to himself, he resisted the impulse to piss out the window. Miss Lady had broken him of the habit.

God, but he felt good!

Whistling between his teeth, he left the bedroom and went downstairs. A fire was burning in the passage fireplace, but it wasn't going to take off much chill with the door standing open.

Jeppson looked out the open door.

What the hell was happening? Fenella standing in the kitchen doorway, looking toward the jail. Sheba, Sabin, Abel, and some others standing near the jail.

The jail door open.

What the hell . . . !

He hurried out of the house, down the steps, across the yard. Sabin looked grimly toward him. Sheba's face was blank, but her eyes were wide. Abel looked frightened.

"What . . . what's going on here?"

No one had to answer. He knew. The two heavy beams that were supposed to bar the door had been cast aside. The heavy lock he himself had added to the door lay broken on the ground. Among the group standing around the door was the slave Nestor from the Breakline plantation, but Buckridge's Jonah and Moses were nowhere to be seen. And Jeppson knew they were gone.

The knowledge was like a physical blow, a crushing blow.

It wasn't a matter of having to pay Buckridge a couple of hundred dollars. He would manage that somehow. It was more as if the loss of the two slaves were a sign. All his hopes were childish illusions, and he had only one thing left to look forward to in this world, one thing that was as certain as death.

His ruin.

Three

Sheba knew her Mr. Jeppson so well. She saw the blow hit him, saw him reel under it. He seemed almost physically to shrink, and she understood exactly what was happening, that he was foreseeing his own destruction. But then, just as surely, she saw him deny fate, destiny, whatever it was—seize it and shake it and dare it to do its worst, because he was *not* going to be defeated. She supposed he was, in his way, heroic.

He turned on Nestor, the slave from the Breakline plantation. "You didn't go with them."

Nestor looked frightened. He was being "disciplined" for repeatedly protecting his wife from his master's sons, and he wanted only to get back to her. "No, sir, Mr. Jeppson," he said. "I got me a family. I ain't no runaway, sir."

"You didn't go with them, but you saw how they got away."

Nestor hesitated. "It so dark, Mr. Jeppson, sir, I don't hardly see nothing—"

"You didn't see or hear nothing at all? You was sleeping—"

"Oh, yes, sir," Nestor said quickly, seizing the idea, "I sleep all the time."

"Good," Mr. Jeppson purred, as he took a coiled blacksnake whip from Sabin's hand, and Sheba was frightened to see that he was actually smiling. "Good for you, Nestor —you're lying."

"Oh, no, sir!"

"You're lying, and I'm glad to see that, Nestor, because it means you know something that can help me. And you're gonna tell me."

"No, sir, master," Nestor said in a panic, "I don't know nothing!"

"You want to start running, Nestor? try to catch up with the others? I don't mind. My drivers enjoy getting the dogs out and having a good chase."

Nestor held his hands out, imploring. "Please, Mr. Jeppson, I don't know nothing! I tell you anything you want to know!"

"I think I'd rather have you run first, Nestor. Give the dogs a good workout. Give you plenty of head start while I go get me some friends, maybe Mr. Tucker and Mr. Macon and your master. You helping them others get away, we ought to get some sport out of running you down—"

"I ain't running 'way, Mr. Jeppson! Please! You listen to me, please!"

"All right, I'm listening, Nestor."

"Was—was one of your woman let them out, Mr. Jepp-

327

son. I don't know her name, but I see her, she work 'round the cook house—"

"Serena," Sabin said. "I ain't seen her 'round this morning. Never did trust that bitch."

"Serena," Jeppson said. He looked at Abel. "Go see if you can find her. And who else, Nestor?"

Sheba shut her eyes and thought hard: *You close your mouth, boy!* If Serena was gone, there was no need for him to mention anyone else. It was best to put the whole blame on Serena alone.

But Nestor had hesitated, and now Jeppson knew he had more to tell.

He smacked the butt of the whip against the leathery palm of his left hand. "Who, boy? Who else was there?"

Nestor's eyes were indecisive, but he knew he had hesitated too long. He said, "Was two of them."

"*Two* of them?"

You fool! Sheba thought. *You fool!*

"Was two. I can't hardly see in the dark."

"Two men. What they look like?"

"I can't hardly see—"

"You seen something, and I want to know what. And don't you lie to me."

"One was big, had a beard 'round his mouth. Other was maybe a boy, maybe a gal. I don't know."

"You don't know?"

"Mr. Jeppson, I can't tell—"

"What they call each other?"

"I . . ." Nestor made a futile gesture. "I don't know!"

"One called the other a name. Most always someone does. Now, what name did they say?"

"Mr. Jeppson, I don't 'member no name."

"The name, Nestor."

"Please, Mr. Jepp—"

One quick motion with a lot of shoulder behind it, and the butt of the whip cracked against the side of Nestor's head. He gave a short little scream, almost soundless, and fell to the ground. Jeppson gave him a kick in the hip that flipped him over onto his stomach. He snapped the whip as if to limber it up, then flicked it overhead and brought it

328

slashing down across Nestor's buttocks. This time Nestor's scream rent the air.

"The name, Nestor."

Jeppson brought the whip down again, and again Nestor screamed. The whip went up, came down. Went up, came down. Went up, came down. Screaming, Nestor tried to crawl away, tried to roll over and fend off the whip with his arms, but still the long blacksnake came down, mercilessly, inescapably. Within seconds Nestor's shirt and pants were soaked with blood.

Sheba realized before Jeppson did that Nestor was saying the name.

"A-a-ah!" he screamed. "A-a-ah! Ada-a-ah! Ah! Adaba!"

Adaba!

Jeppson lowered the whip. He was hardly breathing hard.

"Adaba? Is that what you said?"

"Adaba!" Nestor sobbed. "She call him that!"

"She? Serena?"

"No! The other one! She call him Adaba!"

She. Zulie, who was said to run with Adaba.

Adaba and Zulie.

Afterward they sat together in the kitchen house and had a cup of coffee. Jeppson sat with his eyes almost closed, as if he were half-asleep or perhaps thinking of something very far away, opening his eyes slightly only when he took a sip of coffee. He looked craggy, massive, monumental. Implacable was the word that came to Sheba's mind—a word she would never use aloud, of course, unless she wanted to be laughed at. Yes. Implacable.

Jeppson finally smiled. "I guess there really is some kind of goddamn nigger-stealing son of a bitch called Adaba," he said. "One particular nigger-stealing son of a bitch that goes by that name. For some reason, for a long time I never really thought so. But I was wrong. There is. And," he said, "I am gonna have to catch him."

Oh, no, you ain't, Sheba swore.

She did sometimes ask herself if she was doing right in

helping blacks escape. Escape meant more repression for those left behind, and agony for such as Nestor who, as a result, were punished. And if her acts helped lead to the ruin of Mr. Jeppson, that might ultimately mean selling the slaves of Redbird and scattering their families. She asked herself the question, because she was an intelligent woman and did not wish to take her responsibilities for granted. But she knew the answer.

"If you act like a slave, you deserve to be a slave!"

The first Sunday in December dawned gloriously clear, and at the inn in Riverboro, Lew awakened feeling magnificently alive and charged with energy. He had felt this way almost from the moment he had posted the letter to Justin Sabre at Sabrehill. Defeat was now in the past, and he was doing something positive about their fortunes. He was fighting for his family, and he believed he was going to win.

The reply to his letter had come quickly. He had written quite frankly about their situation: he had been forced to sell Jessamine, and he had a wife and two children and a number of black people to support. He had recently heard that Sabrehill was in need of an overseer, and he felt qualified for the job. He would appreciate being considered.

Rose was less optimistic than he. "You know what's going to keep you from getting that job? and maybe any other?"

"What?"

"Me. Your famous 'nigger wife.'"

"Oh, for God's sake, Rose."

"It's true, and you know it."

"Rose, there just happens to be some tarbrush in their family too. There was a scandal some years back—"

"That was Aaron's daughter, Dulcy, by his second wife." That was the kind of thing Rose would know about. "But Aaron and his wife are dead and the daughter went north, so there's no tarbrush left at Sabrehill now."

That was true enough. Aaron Sabre had been notably liberal, and apparently his second wife had had black

330

blood. But that generation was dead now, and Lucy Sabre had married another distant cousin, Justin Sabre, from Virginia. Lew had no idea of how Justin would regard Rose. But he refused to let her dampen his spirits.

The opening words of Justin's reply were enough to do that.

The reply was cordial but negative. While it was true that Sabrehill was in need of an overseer, Justin hoped to find one with several older sons, as more than one man was needed, and a good, experienced overseeing family struck him as being the best arrangement. Nevertheless . . .

As he read on, Lew's heart began to thump harder.

Nevertheless, why didn't Lew and Rose come visit them? Bring the children and whatever servants they cared to have with them, and stay over the holidays? A virtually new overseer's house had been built nearby, and they could occupy it. There was plenty of room for their servants. Justin might have to be in Charleston part of the time, but still a nice long visit would permit them to get acquainted, and . . .

"He's *not* turning us down!" Lew said, excited. "Hell, the man's no fool! He just doesn't want to buy a pig in a poke! He wants to take a look at us first!"

"Now, Lew," Rose said, "don't you get your expectations up!" But he could tell that she was as excited as he.

"Why, look, honey, he's even saying, Stay in the new overseer's house! See how you like it! He says he's looking for a new overseer, but he's putting *us* in the new house!"

"Now, Lew . . ."

Arrangements were quickly worked out. The children, Channing and Eleanor, would of course come with them—over their protests that they wished to spend the holidays with their cousins on the Guerard plantation. Lucas and Dorinda, and two maids and a houseboy would come. They would be traveling light. Clothes were selected, bags were packed.

"Didn't you *ever* meet him before, Lew?"

"Seems to me I might have, once about fifteen years ago when his family came down to Charleston. I remember talk about him and Cousin Lucy hitting it off. You remember her, don't you?"

Rose shook her head.

"Christ, honey, she was at the wedding! Her father and her Uncle Joel sort of escorted us back to the house afterward just in case there was trouble—"

"Oh, *her!*" Rose's eyes lit up. "That blond hussy! The one I took you away from!"

Lew suppressed a smile. "Yeah, the one you took me away from. But maybe you'd better not remind her of that."

"Lewis, dear, I am *not* without tact!"

They had decided it would be best not to arrive exhausted at Sabrehill. Instead, they had arranged to spend Saturday night at an inn in the nearby village of Riverboro in order to refresh themselves, and to arrive at Sabrehill in time for Sunday dinner. And so it was that on Sunday morning they started on the last stage of their journey— an impoverished family, Lew observed with some amusement, traveling with no more than one large overloaded carriage, a smaller phaeton, two children, and five servants traveling light.

Justin Sabre was a tall, rangy man in his late thirties, long faced, hard jawed, and, Jeppson supposed, handsome after a fashion. The face was full fleshed but with no hint of jowl, and the body was lean and narrow waisted—the body of a hard-working farmer, not a gentleman planter. The eyes were dark and deep set. They were angry eyes, but less angry than scornful, and even as they looked up at Jeppson on his horse, they seemed to be looking down on him. Even Justin's arms, crossed over his chest, seemed to express disdain.

Justin Sabre stood for everything Jeppson detested in the gentry that had held him in such contempt over the years. And sometimes it seemed to him that all of his troubles had started three years ago with Justin's coming to Sabrehill and with the Night of the Fires, which had followed soon after. To Jeppson's way of thinking, there just had to be a connection between the two. He remembered a conversation he had had with P. V. Tucker:

"You ever considered that the Sabres mighta had something to do with it?" Jeppson had asked. *"Otherwise, how come they only lost one slave that night? I lost three, and the Haining place lost six. And how come Sabrehill was the only place around here that didn't get burned?"*

And since that time, how many slaves had Sabrehill lost? Maybe a few, but nobody had heard Justin Sabre complaining. Jeppson, however, had lost more than a dozen—thousands of dollars worth of property, blacks he might just as well have sold to pay off Bluebell.

And now, with the bank panic, he was being ruined. Ruined, while the Sabres—the goddamn snotty abolitionist Sabres, who had always looked down their noses at the likes of him—apparently prospered.

It was too much. Nothing could ever wipe out the loathing Jeppson felt.

"We followed them to Sabrehill. All three of them together, it seems like. We got to that broad creek to the west of here that meanders down to the river. Must have spent more than two hours going up and down that creek."

"And what did you find?" Justin asked, as if he didn't really care what the answer might be.

"Hounds picked up a couple of scents upstream."

"So you're going upstream."

"Went. Didn't find nothing more."

"Ain't the first time a scent led to Sabrehill and disappeared," one of the half-dozen other riders said bitterly.

"That's right," another agreed. "Happened two or three times since the Night of the Fires. And that night, they all ran off from here, right from Sabrehill. Goddamn trail, just when you think you got it, it ain't there anywhere. Leads here to Sabrehill and then just plain disappears."

"Trails have 'just plain disappeared' from a lot of places besides Sabrehill," Justin reminded them. "What do you want?"

"Got to search your outbuildings and quarters," Jeppson said.

Once they wouldn't have come to the big house first. They simply would have searched, and to hell with any objections the Sabres might have. Justin had changed that.

"You've never found anything here in the past," he said.

"The trail came this way, and now it's daylight, they're likely in hiding. We got to do it."

Justin shrugged. "All right, do it. But Jeppson . . ."

"Yes, sir, Mr. Sabre, sir?" Jeppson tried to get a mocking tone into his voice, but Justin didn't seem to notice it. He was smiling slightly.

"Jeppson, I don't want a whip laid on any of my people."

"We got a right by law to use a whip if—"

"I don't want any of my people touched. If there's any punishment to be handed out, I'm here to do it. I don't want them hurt in any way, not even 'by accident.' I don't want any property damaged or any wenches bothered or any other low-life behavior. You're leading this posse, and I'm holding you personally responsible. Remember that. Personally, Jeppson."

He was smiling. Probably hoping that Jeppson would be goaded into doing something violent. Looking for an excuse to drag him down off of his horse and give him what at one time or another he had given Tag Bassett and Rolly Joe Macon, who, with P. V. Tucker, were now at the rear of the posse, as if hoping to avoid Justin's notice. They had learned from experience that even if they all came down on Justin, they would damn well have to kill him (and perhaps hang for it) or he would just naturally wind up eating them alive.

That's what Justin had done, made cowards of Jeppson's friends. Or revealed them for the cowards that they were.

It was too much, and for a moment Jeppson was on the verge of saying, *To hell with it,* and settling with Justin once and for all. But he had a feeling that that was exactly what Justin wanted, and he wasn't at all sure that every man with him would back him up. For the moment, all he could do was shrug off Justin's warning, turn away with the bile still in his throat, and start the search.

But of course, they found nothing. They never did.

Afterward, as Jeppson led his posse down the long gently sloping road that ran from the big-house courtyard to the main road, Tucker and Macon at his sides, he paused to look back. "It ain't fair," Jeppson said. He didn't have to tell the others what he meant.

"So goddamn high and mighty," Tucker said.

"Untouched," Macon said. "That's what they is, untouched. Like they never learned a goddamn thing."

"But they will," Jeppson said after a moment. "They will."

The other two looked at him.

"They're gonna learn," Jeppson said. "I don't know when, but I'm gonna live to see this place burn, same as mine did. I'm gonna live to see Justin Sabre in the goddamn ashes."

"It could happen," Tucker said wonderingly.

"You understand, I ain't threatening. I'm just saying that the good Lord works in mysterious ways. And I'm gonna live to see it."

"Balbo," Macon said, "when it happens, old P.V. and me gonna be right there with you watching. You can count on it."

"You can count on it," Tucker said.

Though Lew had never been there before, Sabrehill was easy enough to find, and when they arrived, their reception was beyond anything they could have hoped. They had not circled the courtyard before three children ran out of the house and stood jumping up and down with excitement. Two boys and a girl, aged nine through twelve, Lew guessed, and if that was a bit old for Eleanor and Chan, who were eight and six, the kids didn't seem to know it. They were already yelling from the carriage at their new cousins.

As Lew followed the kids from the carriage and helped Rose down, Cousin Lucy came out of the house. She was as blond and beautiful as Lew remembered—except for a scar down the right side of her face, a present, Lew had heard, from her late, first husband. She and Rose were immediately in each other's arms, kissing and laughing, as if they were long-lost friends. Lew remembered Lucy as being rather cool, icy eyed, and aloof, though with an impish sense of humor; but there was nothing cool or aloof

335

about her now, and Lew realized, with a pang, that she understood just what this visit meant to them.

Justin was next out of the house, and again Lew had the feeling of being greeted as an old friend rather than as a stranger who happened to be distantly related. His arm was pumped, his back was slapped. Then Justin turned to Rose and embraced her. "Why, Cousin Rose, look at you, all grown up! You wouldn't remember, but we met years ago in Charleston. We were down from Virginia, and Lew's daddy took my daddy and me to your house to meet *your* daddy. I seem to recall that you had two, no, three brothers—am I right?—and an older sister. . . ." Justin greeted Dorinda and Lucas and the three black youngsters with smiling courtesy that made them feel right at home, and issued orders to some of his own people for the disposition of bags and horses and carriages. "My God, it's good to see you all! . . ."

They were swept into the house. They were introduced to Mark and Catherine Anne and Beau, Justin's children by an earlier marriage. And of course, they had to meet Macy Aaron, Justin's and Lucy's first together, a year-and-a-half-old toddler. "Lucy, he's ador-r-rable!" "He's a rascal." "But just seeing him makes me want another! When I think it's been six years since I had Chan!" "Well, you're not too old, after all. I'm older than you." Voices lowered; men not to hear: "And I think I've got another on the way, Rose." "Oh, I'd love to be you! I really ought to tell that man of mine he's got to do his duty more often!" "Well, tell him," Lucy said, all big-eyed seriousness. "That's what I do. I just tell him!"

Lew felt his face reddening. Christ, how long did women have to be together before getting intimate?

Dinner would be ready soon. Later they would be shown the new house where they were staying, but for now perhaps they would like to freshen up upstairs. They were shown to a room. "Chan, Eleanor, come here! Chan stop that shouting!" "Beau, mind your manners!" "Chan*ning-g-g!* Elea*nor-r-r!*" "Oh, let them go, Rose." "They have got to learn manners. . . ."

A little warm water to get the road dust off, and then downstairs again. More greetings, charged with energy,

336

especially on Justin's part. Plans. They would have to meet the Kimbroughs and the Buckridges and the Petti-grews, and of course there would be a party next week-end. . . .

". . . In the last few years, Lew, there must have been fifty or sixty runaways from around these parts. The god-damn fools can't see that by getting more repressive they're just *driving* their people off, *driving* them away from the very homes and families and friends that might otherwise keep them here. And then we have people like Jeppson and Tucker and Macon, riding around in posses and patrols, raising hell with our people, giving them still more cause to turn mean on us. . . ."

Dinner was served. A big family dinner, four adults and five children, everybody at the table but little Macy Aaron. Eleanor on her best behavior, but Chan looking around to see what he could get away with. Little Beau Sabre acting up.

Dessert. Coffee. Cigars. Strolling around the house to settle it all down.

". . . posse led here by Vachel Skeet and Jeppson and some others. And it got out of hand. By the time they were through, a child had been killed, and another had had an arm broken, and several of the women had been raped. And when they didn't find what they wanted, damned if they didn't beat the hell out of *me!* Skeet and the others, with Jeppson standing by. And it was that same Balbo Jeppson that came by this morning. . . ."

Lew at last understood Justin's display of energy. His greeting would undoubtedly have been cordial under any circumstances, but he had been keyed up this morning by his meeting with this Jeppson, whoever he was. Justin was an angry man, so deeply angry that hours after the meeting with Jeppson, he was still letting off steam.

". . . And then I heard that this man Macon has been telling people that I've been preaching abolition, which I had not, though I've never hidden my views from anyone who asked. But he was just trying to make trouble for me with my neighbors. So I loosened up his teeth. Tucker has been crossing the street and ducking around corners when he sees me coming ever since. But I still haven't really settled with him and Jeppson. . . ."

Lew also understood that he had arrived at Sabrehill at exactly the right time. Anger had taken Justin off his guard. He wanted to confide in someone, another man, and he was assuming, perhaps because of their shared name, that Lew was sympathetic. That gave Lew an idea of the kind of answers Justin would want from a would-be overseer.

". . . but I sure as hell don't want to have trouble with them now. I suspect that more than one bale of black wool has passed through the quarters here, and I haven't worried unduly about it. I've seen too many blacks abused, and any man has a natural right to save his hide, no matter what his color. But with those three running away from Redbird last night, Jeppson and the patrol are going to be mean as hell for a long time to come, and I don't want to give them any excuse for hurting my people. I don't want another child killed at Sabrehill or another woman raped. So I'll tell you frankly, Lew, any overseer I hire has got to keep those traveling parcels out of the quarters until things simmer down. And I mean absolutely, or I tear up the contract. . . ."

The day could not possibly have passed more pleasantly. In the afternoon, the children napped. Dorinda and Lucas went out to the kitchen house and gossiped with some of the house servants. Justin and Lucy took Lew and Rose to a grove a few hundred yards to the east to show them the new house. It was, of course, much smaller than the big house, but it had its own kitchen and well and servants' quarters, and was quite comfortable. It was a frame structure of common design, a central passage with three rooms off of it downstairs and three more above. "Why, it's lovely!" Rose said.

"Well, it's not even completely furnished yet, but of course you'll have your own things—" Lucy broke off, realizing that she was saying too much too soon. Lew and Rose pretended not to notice.

Justin and Lew left the women in the house and went to inspect more of the plantation—the two service lanes with their numerous outbuildings, the field quarters, and a

338

few of the fields. Then back to the house, with its formal gardens and its eight-pillared piazza and the broad green parkland that sloped down to Sabre's Landing and the river. "We have far more land than we can cultivate," Justin said as they stood on the landing. "We have tenants on some of it, but a lot of it is just lying fallow. Now, if our new overseer had a few hands of his own, there'd be no reason in the world why he couldn't put some of that land to work for him. . . ."

Lew held his breath. It was, it seemed to him, practically an offer.

Getting closer to each other, always closer. And feeling good about it. Lew explained why he had had to take such a beating in selling Jessamine, and Justin understood. And approved.

At supper, this time without the children, the four of them told stories and laughed and acted as if they had known each other for years. Surely Justin and Lucy felt the same, Lew thought. Surely they couldn't be this kind, this cordial, this warm unless they felt the same.

Justin led them through the darkness back to the little house. Someone, perhaps Lucas, had put lights in the windows, and there were fires burning, both upstairs and down. The little house was already as warm as home. . . .

"Lew, I can't believe it! Did you *hear* what she *said?*"

"He was telling me what he wanted of an overseer. Now, why would he do that, unless—"

"She said, 'You'll have your own things!' *Your own things*, Lew!"

"He said, if his overseer had a few hands—which he knows we do—he could put them to work. It was as if he were trying to persuade *me* to take the job! And us here less than a day!"

"Oh, Lew!"

They were alone at last in the master bedroom of the little house. The children were asleep across the passage, and a bottle of chilled champagne stood open on a bedside table. They took off their clothes with all possible speed. The day seemed centuries long, and yet it had passed like a matter of seconds.

"I tell you, Rose, it's a fresh start. Of course, we aren't going to be here forever. We're going to stay here long enough to raise a stake, and then we're heading west—"

"But, Lew, do you think they really like us?" Rose asked, kicking off her drawers. "They seem to, but do you think they *really* do?"

"Honey," Lew said, looking approvingly at her, "nobody in his right mind could help but like you."

"I love Lucy, I really do. And it's not just that we need this place so much—"

"But one thing, honey. I do wish you wouldn't talk so freely, if you know what I mean. I mean, it's one thing to talk like that in your own bedroom—"

"Oh, don't be silly, Lew. I couldn't shock that woman in a million years."

Yes, indeed, he did view her approvingly, as she lifted a thin silk gown over her head and let it slither down over her fine body. When she turned toward him, seated naked before her, her eyes widened with counterfeit alarm.

"Why, Lewis, what in the world has happened to you!"

"I think that's quite obvious, madam."

"But what do you intend to do with that—that *thing?*"

"Has madam any suggestion?"

"Well, Lewis . . ." Rose put a fingertip to her mouth, rolled her eyes, and thought about it. Her nipples grew visibly firmer under the silk, and her face took on a sly look. "Well . . ." She looked down at her mound, dark under the silk, and moved it invitingly.

And he proceeded to make love to her as he had not done in weeks, in months, or even in years.

And when he had wrung the last gasp, sob, gurgle, and coo from her, when he had finally thrown his seed into her and they still lay linked together in the warmth of their fires, he whispered promises to her, promises that she would never again have to be afraid, that he would keep her safe, that the best times of their lives still lay ahead.

340

And from down below in the dark house came the sound of soft mocking laughter.

Four

He recognized Zulie's voice instantly.

And he was furious.

Goddammitgoddammitgoddammit, he had thought they would be free of that goddamn pair by coming here!

For years Adaba had been passing his runaways through the quarters at Jessamine. It had made Lew nervous as hell, but there had been little he could do about it. He had little social standing except among his friends; he was the notorious Sabre who had taken a "nigger wife," and to implicate Adaba in the Underground Railroad would have been like implicating himself. Besides, he had no real desire to get his wife's brother into hanging trouble, even if he was a pain in the ass—a man just didn't do that kind of thing. And truth to tell, being the kind of self-centered, asocial, irresponsible soul he was, Lew just purely didn't give a damn about another man's troubles with runaway slaves. Let the poor bastards run, and more power to them.

But not through Sabrehill!

Dorinda and Lucas had unpacked and put everything away, and Lew had to paw through drawers, looking for a robe. *Shitshitshitshitshit!* Ever since his wedding, Lew and Adaba had been at an armed truce. If they had both been on the verge of killing each other that night, the plain fact was that neither had been able to go through with it. But now . . .

A showdown between them was long overdue. Lew had a feeling that it was going to happen at Sabrehill.

At last he found a robe and pulled it on. He picked up a lamp and started downstairs. Rose, her gown back in place and a robe over it, followed him.

Their visitors were sitting in the dark in the parlor,

warming themselves by the last embers in the fireplace.

"All right, John," Lew said, "what the hell are you doing here?"

Adaba laughed. "Why, Lewis, old son, is that any way to greet your brother-in-law and his woman?"

"You find the wine we put in your bedroom, Lewis?" Zulie asked, grinning at him. "Irish, the butler, stole it and passed it on to my brother Zagreus, and he gave it to me to give to you."

"Oh, my," Adaba said. "Didn't I ever mention that Zulie's a Sabrehill nigger? I stole her from here almost three years ago to the day. Naturally she likes to come back here and visit her brothers from time to time."

Lew set down the lamp. "I asked you what you were doing here."

But of course he knew. It was quite plain to him now. Adaba's suggestion that Lew apply for the job of overseer at Sabrehill had not been casual mockery. It had been calculated. If he was losing a station like Jessamine, why not try to get his man into another place where he would be useful? Adaba had used him in the past and intended to do so in the future.

"Goddamn, Zulie," Adaba said, "but he do continue to sound unfriendly."

"He just tired," Zulie said. "Had him a long day."

"I send him here to get work, and he sound plain ungrateful."

"Oh, Lewis is grateful. He going show us how grateful he is."

"No," Lew said firmly. "Not here. This isn't my plantation. And if I get the job of overseer, you're not going to run one goddamn slave through here."

"Oh, my *my!*" Adaba said. "This is strong talk from the man who killed Denmark Vesey!"

"And I am sick and tired of hearing about how I killed Denmark Vesey—"

Adaba started rising from his chair. "You figure you paid for that by now, son? You figure you'll ever finish paying—"

"I'm not paying, because I didn't kill him. It was a court that had him hanged—"

342

"It was *you* that turned him in, *you* that betrayed him—"

"Shut up, both of you!" Rose's quiet voice cut like a whiplash. "John, this is our house as long as we're in it. You're my brother, and you have certain privileges in my home, but you will keep a goddamn civil tongue in your head!"

Adaba, holding his breath, stared at his sister.

Zulie, looking a little startled, muttered, "Lord Almighty!"

Adaba released his breath with a little laugh and sank back down on his chair. "You're right, Rose. I was being rude in your house, and I apologize. And I was a damned fool to get Lew's dander up when I need his help."

"I'm sorry, John," Lew said, "but I couldn't give it to you even if I wanted to."

"Will you listen to me for just a minute?" Adaba asked. "Please, will you just listen to me?"

Lew shrugged and sat down.

"Let me tell you a little story. I was never anywhere near this place until three years ago. It was right after the one and only time I ever met Justin Sabre."

"He told Rose he was at your house in Charleston years ago."

Adaba looked surprised. He thought about it a minute, then shook his head. "I don't remember. Be funny if it was true.

"Anyway, things were bad for black folks around here—you know how they got after the Nat Turner insurrection—and a hell of a lot of them wanted to get free. So Zulie and me, we took about half of them away in one night, and I promised to come back for the others. And that's what we've been doing ever since. Stealing them away."

"Except from Sabrehill, I'm told."

Adaba grinned. "This old dove ain't no fool—he don't foul his own nest. Justin Sabre once did some conducting of his own, if you want to know—he once helped *me* get away, me and old Black Buck. But you hit a man in his account books, and maybe he says to hell with right and wrong and all that liberty and justice business. Anyway,

343

the Sabrehill people ain't bad off these days, so I leave them alone, and Justin looks the other way, same as you did at Jessamine."

"Not that I had much choice."

"Aw, Lew, admit it. If it had been anybody but me doing it, it wouldn'ta burned your ass half so much."

Which was true.

But not to the point now.

"John, now you listen to me for a change."

Adaba gestured expansively. "I'm listening."

"I think I've got the job."

"I'm happy for you, Lew. Not just for us and our plans, but for you and Rose too."

"But Justin Sabre laid down the law to me. You're right, he has been looking the other way. But because he's a known abolitionist and hasn't lost many slaves and hasn't had his placed burned by runaways, everybody around here is suspicious of him. And the patrols and posses around here are as mean as anywhere else, and once they came here and killed a child and raped some women—"

Adaba glanced at Zulie. "I know. I was here at the time."

A suspicion dawned in Lew's mind. "Was it you they were looking for that time?"

"Not exactly. More it was Buck. You remember Buck."

"So you've brought trouble to Sabrehill before," Lew said.

"We ain't the trouble, son. We ain't keeping people slaves."

"No, but somebody got killed just the same. And Justin doesn't want it happening again. So for now, with everybody riled up over the slaves you stole last night— they say it was you—he doesn't want even one runaway passed through his quarters. Not one, John, for a long time to come. And he says that if his overseer can't see to that, he'll tear up the contract. And he means it."

Adaba turned away. He stared at the dying fire.

"He doesn't have to know, and neither do you, Lew. All you have to do is turn your head."

344

"But I do know, and I'm not turning my head. You got those three here at Sabrehill?"

"Not yet. They're downriver with an old Indian friend of ours."

"Well, keep them away from here. I mean that."

Suddenly Adaba swung back from the fire to Lew, and his voice was hard again, his eyes hot with anger. "Lew, you got something wrong. You think *you're* the goddamn overseer here? *I* am the goddamn overseer here! And you don't work with me, then I don't work with you! And the work ain't gonna get done, and Sabrehill goes all to hell. You got a crop to get in, maybe you'd like to see it ruined."

Lew found he still had the strength to lift the bigger man from his chair, still had the strength to slam him back against the fireplace. He did it before he even thought about it, and then the knife appeared in Zulie's hand, the eight-inch blade that she always carried. Lew grabbed her wrist and swung her past Adaba, pulling the knife from her hand and flinging her to the floor.

"Now, listen, you!"

The point of the knife was at Adaba's throat, a little to the right, where a single thrust would kill in seconds. Adaba stood perfectly still, his arms out from his sides. Zulie lay unmoving.

"You listen, you bastard! I lost most of what I own. And I've got a family and a lot of people to provide for. And I'm damned well going to do it—feed my kids and my wife and all those people. Now, I've put up with a hell of a lot from you for a long time, Adaba, because you're my wife's brother, but I'm fighting for them now, Adaba, fighting for their lives and well-being, and if I have to kill you for them, I'll damn well do it! You make me lose this job, and I won't see you hanged—I'll hunt you down, Adaba, and wipe you out myself! Remember that! I'll kill you!"

Panting, he backed away from Adaba.

Adaba still didn't move.

Lew looked down at Zulie.

"Get up off my floor."

Zulie got up slowly.

Just as slowly, Adaba straightened up from the fireplace.

For a moment, they all simply stood there, as if embarrassed by the outburst.

Adaba smiled. "Well, Lew, we'll see."

"Yeah, we'll see. See that you stay the hell away from this place."

"Mind if we stay the night? Like I said, Zulie's got family here to visit, and she *is* from Sabrehill, after all. I mean, this is *home* to her, Lew——"

"Oh, shit," Lew said disgustedly. He handed Zulie her knife. "Don't cut yourself, honey-child. Everybody sit down. Have a drink. Is there any of that champagne left, Rose?"

And so they all sat down and had a drink, and Adaba asked how daddy was, and Rose said, "Getting grayer, and worried about you." And little Chan came downstairs and curled up in Uncle John's lap and promptly fell asleep again. The quarrel over, they had a perfectly ordinary, tranquil, domestic evening, and there was peace at Sabrehill.

But Lew knew it couldn't last.

Later, Adaba and Zulie went silently through the darkness to the coach house, which stood on the nearest service lane. Candlelight showed through a high window. Inside, they went up a flight of stairs and through a trap door into a neat, comfortable room, occupied by Zulie's older brother, Zagreus, and his white-skinned wife, Binnie. Zagreus and Binnie were already in bed but still awake, so they exchanged a few words and said good night. Adaba closed and barred the trap door and, taking the candle, followed Zulie into the next room, where old, dusty harness had been pushed back to make space for a bed and a table and a couple of chairs. More than one runaway had passed through this room.

Adaba watched pensively while Zulie undressed until she wore nothing but her sheathed knife on a leather thong around her waist. She had carried it for years, and it was always the last thing she took off. She poured water into a bowl and threw it on her face, then looked at Adaba.

"Why ain't you getting ready for bed?"

"I don't know. Thinking about Lew."

She laughed. "Wasn't he something *fierce* tonight?"

"He was pretty good there. Maybe there's hope for the son of a bitch yet." He reached for Zulie and drew her to him, fondling and kissing her. "You know something, I envy Lew."

"Now, that ain't a nice thing to say."

"I envy him 'cause he had ten years with a woman he loves, and I only had three."

Zulie grinned at him. "Now, that *is* a nice thing to say. You get them clothes off, and we'll make up for lost time."

She untied her knife and stuck it under a pillow, then climbed into the bed. Adaba undressed and washed, taking his time though the room was cold, then blew out the candle and slid into the bed with her. She rolled shivering into his arms, and immediately they began to create warmth.

"There, now," Zulie whispered as she caressed him, "ain't that nice?"

"Mm," he agreed, returning her touch. After a moment, he moved his hand up to her belly. "Still can't feel nothing."

"Oh, he ain't hardly started yet! Don't even show, 'cept maybe to a woman's eye."

"I don't want him born down here, Zulie. I want him born in freedom country and with a proper doctor."

"Maybe, but we ain't going argue 'bout that now."

"But having a baby is the hardest thing a woman can do. It's a lot more dangerous than leading slaves north."

"All the more reason to have it right here. Ain't nobody in the world better at helping with babies than Momma Lucinda, the cook here, and Reba, that I teached myself, and me."

"Thought we wasn't gonna argue."

"We ain't." Still pleasuring him, she giggled. "Why, Adaba, honey," she said, "what we got here? This here mean you wanna . . . you wanna . . . ?"

He laughed with her.

"Oh," she said soon after, as he took her in that now-warm darkness, "I guess you truly do. . . ."

Later, while Zulie slept, Adaba reviewed his plans. By tomorrow the area would have been fairly well searched, and in the evening it would be safe to relieve Gavin Murdock of the three fugitives and bring them back to Sabrehill. The fugitives would rest here for two or three days, and by then everyone would assume that they were long gone. He would take them to the next station and be back in a week. And Zulie, whether she liked it or not, would wait for him here. After that, the sooner he got her north to some place where she could live safely and have her baby, the better. Her years on the trail were all but over, even if his were not. The thought of long weeks, perhaps even months, of separation from his wife pained Adaba, but the thought that anything might happen to her was far worse.

Where, then, should he take her? He was beginning to think she was dead serious about staying down here. The trouble was that she, like Adaba himself, had little sense of herself as a slave. An accomplished healer, she had always had a privileged position at Sabrehill, living and doing pretty much as she pleased. She knew that no truly good master—and if there were such a thing, Justin Sabre was the best—would ever punish a runaway slave, or sell him away, for returning home voluntarily. Furthermore, Justin Sabre owed her a debt that could never be repaid. Years earlier, when Justin had been wounded in a duel, Zulie and her mother had saved his life, a fact he would never forget. As far as Adaba had been able to determine, Justin had never made any real effort to find Zulie after she had run off, and occasionally Sabres had even allowed favored slaves to go north. Thus it was perhaps only natural that Zulie felt that she could come and go from Sabrehill as she pleased. To her, it was home.

And undoubtedly, it was *not* the worst place in the world for her to have her child.

But still he was determined that both mother and child should live on free soil. As long as they were in the

348

South, even at Sabrehill, there was always the chance that they would suffer the same fate as Gilly.

And if that happened, he thought, he would either go mad or die.

There was simply no point in worrying, Lew decided the next morning. Even if Adaba ignored his warning and hid his fugitives at Sabrehill for a few days, the chances were that they wouldn't be caught; Adaba did know what he was doing. As for the future, it could look out for itself. He would take one day at a time.

The second day was as pleasant as the first. Out of habit, Lew and Rose awakened before dawn, in spite of the previous night's late visit, and found the plantation bustling with activity. Lights burned in the big house and in the office and kitchen buildings that flanked it and along the service lanes, and children, black and white, were already at play in the courtyard.

After breakfast, Lucy whisked Rose away on some mysterious female business, and Justin asked Lew if he would like to look over the plantation. Lew, of course, very much wanted to do that.

"We've had help from some of our tenants in running the place," Justin said, as they rode along the fields of cotton, "but they've had their own work to look after. I've tried hiring white men from around here, mostly to appease neighbors who thought we needed more white help, but most of them haven't been worth a damn. Gave more trouble than help. We do better with black foremen."

"Always did at Jessamine too," Lew agreed. "Black drivers, the good ones, take pride in being leaders without lording it over the others. And they aren't so fast with a whip as the goddamn buckra."

Lew thought that Justin's people appeared reasonably happy and energetic, and the plantation seemed to be flourishing.

In the early afternoon they returned to the big house for dinner. After leaving their horses at the stable, they started walking to the house, when a stranger suddenly confronted them in the courtyard. He could have been as young as forty, though a hard life made him look older.

349

His face was skeletal in its thinness, and he was ragged, unshaved, unkempt. The bundle he carried tied to the end of a stick probably contained all he possessed in this world.

"Mr. Sabre," he said anxiously, his eyes going back and forth uncertainly between the two men, "Mr. Sabre, sir? I been waiting for Mr. Sabre—"

"I'm Justin Sabre."

"My name's Pickett, sir, Wilbur Pickett. I just came up the river, came up this morning, looking for work."

"I'm sorry," Justin said, "but I don't have anything for you."

"Man downriver—Mr. Buckridge I think he's called—he told me you ain't got no overseer."

"Mr. Buckridge was wrong. I'm making arrangements for an overseer."

The stranger, Pickett, hesitated, his eyes again going back and forth between the other two men. "But . . . Mr. Buckridge . . . he told me . . ."

"I'm sorry you've had to come here for nothing," Justin said gently.

"But if you still making arrangements . . . I got good references, Mr. Sabre."

"I'm sorry, Mr. Pickett—"

The man wouldn't give up. The desperation in his eyes growing, he spoke quickly. "I worked for some of the best plantations 'round Charleston, worked for Charles Beaufort till he sold out this year. And I used to work for the City Guard in Charleston, and in the workhouse, and I know how to handle niggers, Mr. Sabre, ain't *no* black bastard I can't make stand in fear!"

"Mr. Pickett—"

"I *got* to find work, Mr. Sabre, and Mr. Buckridge said you ain't hardly got no white people here at all, and that ain't right, sir, you know that ain't right. If you already got an overseer, I can work for him. I'm a good worker—"

"My new overseer will pick his own men, Mr. Pickett."

Pickett's eyes fixed on Lew. "You're him, ain't you?" he said after a moment.

"This gentleman is my guest," Justin said quickly.

"Now, if you'd care to go to the kitchen house across the courtyard there—"

"Don't I know you from somewhere?" Pickett asked Lew. His voice was grim, suspicious, resentful.

"Possibly," Lew said, "if you're from Charleston."

"I know you." Pickett turned to Justin again. "It's him you're hiring, ain't it?"

"Mr. Pickett," Justin said with strained patience, "I have told you that this man is my guest. Anything more is none of your business. Now, you are my guest too, and I'm offering you a meal. If you don't want it, I want you to be on your way."

Pickett seemed slowly to deflate. He was obviously caught between his angry frustration and his hunger. Finally he nodded. "I 'preciate that. I need a meal. But I'm willing to work for it."

"That won't be necessary. Tell the cook I said to feed you and to see if she has a little something extra for you to take with you. And I wish you luck, Mr. Pickett, in finding work."

Pickett nodded sullenly and looked at the ground.

Justin turned toward the big house. As Lew started to turn with him, Pickett looked up, and once again their eyes met. Pickett's were hurt and resentful.

He was a threat. Lew felt it. First Adaba, he thought, and now this stranger.

He followed Justin into the big house. When he looked back from the doorway, Wilbur Pickett was still in the courtyard, staring.

It was dark as Jeppson returned to Redbird and wearily dismounted. How many useless miles had he ridden with patrols and posses over the years? How many miles had he ridden in search of Adaba and returned home empty-handed?

"Man here to see you," Sabin said, and Jeppson turned to see a skull-like face by the light of the stable lamp. The washed-out eyes held a mixture of anxiety and resentment. *Trash*, Jeppson thought.

"Well?"

"Looking for work, Mr. Jeppson, sir," the man said. "Come up the river looking for work, is all."

There was a whine in the man's voice, as if he expected to be refused. Jeppson said, "You've come to the wrong place."

"I been asking everywhere, and Mr. Buckridge, down the river, said you ain't got no overseer right now, and that Major Kimbrough, he said the same thing. And I'm the best damn overseer you ever seen, Mr. Jeppson, the best damn nigger-ass-busting—"

"No, you ain't. *I* am."

As Jeppson looked the man up and down, an idea occurred to him. The man wasn't much, but Jeppson still needed all the help he could get, and he needed it cheap.

"What's your name?"

"Pickett, sir. Wilbur Pickett. I was overseer for Mr. Charles Beaufort till he sold out, and 'fore that Mr. Henry St. Julian, and I worked on the Charleston City Guard, so I know how to handle—"

"What do you want for your time, Pickett?"

Pickett seemed to be holding his breath. His answer came in a rush. "My keep and fifty dollars a month."

Jeppson laughed with genuine amusement. "Six hundred a year? for a man I don't even know? in these hard times?"

Pickett's eyes widened with alarm as he saw a possible job vanishing. "Four hundred, Mr. Jeppson—"

Jeppson continued laughing.

"—even three hundred."

"No, not even one hundred," Jeppson said in sudden anger. "What kind of fool do you take me for?"

Pickett looked as if he were on the verge of tears. "Mr. Jeppson, I need work! I got to eat! I had one meal in two days! Please, Mr. Jeppson—"

"All right. I'll give you a meal, and you'll work for it. That's what you'll get, Pickett, your food and a roof over your head, and you can stay on a few days if you want. After that, if I decided I can use you, maybe we'll talk about something more."

Pickett's face actually became radiant with pleasure in

the lamplight. "Oh, Mr. Jeppson, I do thank you, I'll work real hard——"

"Sabin, give him some food and a place to sleep. Pickett, you'll do what Sabin tells you till I say otherwise."

The pleasure vanished from Pickett's face. "I got to do what a *nigger* says?"

"I think you heard me, Mr. Pickett. But if that bothers you——"

"No, no," Pickett said quickly. "Reckon old Sabin here knows better'n me what you want done."

"You reckon right."

Without another word, Jeppson headed for the big house.

Sheba was waiting for him in the doorway of the dining room. She had her arms crossed and her head cocked back in that judgmental way of hers, and her eyes were disapproving.

"Been a man here asking for you. Said his name was Pickett."

"I talked to him," Jeppson said uneasily. "He's gonna stay awhile."

The eyes hardened. "Mr. Jeppson, I don't like that man."

Jeppson held up his hands placatingly. "Now, Miss Lady, he's willing to work for his keep, and we need all the help we can get."

"I don't like that man," Sheba repeated.

"Well, it's only for a few days, and then we'll see how he works out. Now, I've got to get me some supper, 'cause I'm expecting them people to come."

"I still don't like him," Sheba muttered.

Jeppson had invited all of the more prominent planters of the region—all but Justin Sabre—to a meeting to discuss how to deal with the problem of fugitive slaves. Early that morning, he had sent out invitations, penned by Sheba. And with two or three exceptions, who sent polite excuses, they were all accepted.

First to arrive were Buckridge, Kimbrough, Devereau, and Haining, all in a group. Then came Harmon and

Breakline, and soon after, Pettigrew and McClintock. Jeppson felt that it proved these men were beginning to accept him as respectable.

Or that they were desperate.

Sheba had set out coffee and brandy in the parlor. A few of the guests sampled it. They socialized among themselves, saying little to their host, and that was all right with Jeppson. He was suddenly sweaty palmed and speechless and conscious that his new house was terribly underfurnished. He had no wish to talk to any of his guests until they got down to business.

"I don't see Justin Sabre," McClintock said.

"No, sir," Jeppson said. "Him and me don't have much to say to each other."

"He's too damn abolitionist anyway," Harmon said, and it was music to Jeppson's ears. He had thought of inviting Justin Sabre, if only to see how these other men would handle him, but somehow he had been afraid to do it. These others might disapprove of Justin in some ways, but still they were all cut from the same cloth.

Somebody complained that it was late and that he had a long way to go home, and they finally got to the matters at hand.

"You all know why I asked you here," Jeppson said, and his voice shook as it never did when he addressed his peers. He cleared his throat and spoke more forcefully in order to steady himself. "You all heard, I guess, how I took two of Mr. Buckridge's niggers to break and how night before last Adaba stole them away."

Yes, they had heard, all right. They looked at Buckridge with sympathy and at Jeppson with something less.

"Now, we got to do something about this," Jeppson went on. "I figure he musta stole some fifty or sixty from around here just in the last three years."

"Depends on how big an area you count," Buckridge said. "I wouldn't be surprised if it was more like seventy."

"I personally am very skeptical about this talk of an Adaba, a Brown Dove," Major Kimbrough said, "or even of an Underground Railroad." He was a military man, with a ramrod back and a straight bar of a mustache. "A rebellious slave doesn't need any Brown Dove or Underground Railroad to carry him off. I think that generally these blacks just run off on their own."

Jeppson felt himself heating up. "Major Kimbrough, sir, you may be right. Maybe a lot of them niggers did run off on their own, and I was the last person to be convinced there was a Brown Dove, as anybody that knows me can tell you. Still, the fact is that on the Night of the Fires more than thirty slaves disappeared all at once."

"Or they ran away over a period of several nights, more likely," the major said. "I am not convinced—"

"No, sir, in a single night, even if we don't like to admit that such a thing could happen. The thing is," he went on, "I don't think that thirty-some could disappear all at the same time like that without help from the Underground Railroad. And we've been hearing more and more around here about this Adaba ever since."

"I'm afraid I've got to agree with Mr. Jeppson," Pettigrew said. "Runaways never used to disappear the way they've been doing the last few years. My God, it's like if you get your slave mad at you, he just ups and walks off and you never see him again. Some of us have lost five or six slaves, and Mr. Jeppson has lost even more. Now, gentlemen, that's a hell of a lot of valuable property, and in the aggregate it represents a considerable fortune. I've been forced to the conclusion that we're being systematically robbed by a single organization. The Underground Railroad is as good a name for it as any, and whoever is directing it around here seems to go by the name of Adaba."

"It's Adaba, all right," Jeppson said. "Adaba and his woman, Zulie—likely Zulie that run off from Sabrehill."

"I don't know about that," Pettigrew said, "but I first heard of this Adaba a good many years before he was said to come around these parts."

"*If* it's the same one," McClintock said. "I'm inclined to go along with the major—Adaba is just a name the niggers use for some kind of imaginary savior."

"But if there *is* an Adaba," Jeppson said, exasperated, "and if there *is* a Zulie, you want to catch 'em, don't you? And if there *is* an Underground Railroad, you want it stopped!"

"Certainly," Pettigrew said.

Paul Devereau, a lawyer planter, held up both hands for attention. "I think it's time we asked Mr. Jeppson what his scheme is. He wrote me a note saying he wanted to discuss a plan for catching Adaba, and I for one want to know what he has in mind."

Smiling, Jeppson told them: "We're going to get that Adaba, and his Zulie too, by offering rewards for them."

The disappointment in the room was palpable. Some of the men looked as if they were about to stand up and walk out.

"Mr. Jeppson," McClintock said wearily, "there's been rewards out for this Adaba for years. But they never done one damn bit of good, which is one reason I'm disinclined to believe there even *is* an Adaba—"

"Now, listen to me, goddammit," Jeppson interrupted angrily, "you all don't even know what I'm talking about yet! I know no reward has got Adaba. I know that with hard times some people are even withdrawing the rewards they posted. Me, I'll even admit I ain't got a hell of a lot of money to put up for a reward these days, and I don't reckon you do either. But maybe we won't have to."

"We're still listening, Mr. Jeppson," Pettigrew said. "What do you have in mind?"

"I have in mind Denmark Vesey," Jeppson said.

Once again he had their full attention. Even after fifteen years, the name of Denmark Vesey would still do that.

"I been studying the lessons of history," Jeppson went on, "and I want to ask you, who was it that got Denmark Vesey?"

"As I recall," the major said, "it was a captain in the Charleston Guard."

"No," Jeppson said. "All the guard done was pick him up. It was a pair of nigger slaves called Peter Prioleau and George Wilson that caused the downfall of Denmark Vesey. And I want to ask you, who turned in George Boxley when he tried to start a rebellion? It was a nigger slave woman. And who turned in them Camden rebels? It was one of Colonel Chestnut's people."

"I think I'm beginning to understand," Devereau said.

"The lessons of history. In all those cases it wasn't white men caught them niggers out. It was other niggers, turning on their own kind. And all those rewards for Adaba don't do any good, 'cause they don't do any good for niggers. If a nigger helps catch Adaba, his master is gonna take the reward for hisself, and the nigger knows it."

"Which is only right," McClintock said.

"You're suggesting," the major said, "that we reward the blacks?"

"After Peter Prioleau and George Wilson told about the Denmark Vesey conspiracy, the legislature give their owners permission to free them, and each slave got fifty dollars a year for life from the state, and no taxes, as I recollect."

"But those people didn't know they were going to be rewarded," the major said. "They acted out of the goodness of their hearts."

"Irrelevant, I think, major," said Devereau.

"What you're telling us," Pettigrew said, "is that we should offer rewards to the blacks, rather than to the whites."

"That's exactly right! Whoever gives information leading to the capture of Adaba gets his freedom and, say, a thousand dollars. Whoever gets Zulie captured gets his freedom and five hundred. Them rewards that's already out, they'll go to the master of the slave that gets Adaba or to any free black that does it."

"Off hand," the major said, "I can't think of a single instance since the Vesey affair when the legislature has authorized manumission."

"Not for *you* to free a slave, maybe, not for me, maybe, and maybe not for any single one of us. But on request of *all* of you gentlemen? Why, you all are some of the richest and most influential men in South Carolina. Some of you are in politics. Do you mean to tell me you can't get the state to free the slaves that get two of the most notorious nigger-stealers in the South, and compensate the owners, and pay off the reward?"

"It's just possible," Pettigrew said.

"We might have to start our own reward fund," Buckridge said, "but I suppose that's possible too."

"It can be done," Devereau said positively. "There's enough political influence in this room to do it."

"Well, I'm still skeptical," the major said, "but I'll go along with you gentlemen. After all, what can I lose?"

He had done it, Jeppson realized. He had sold all these fine gentlemen on his plan. They were going to put it into action.

Pettigrew got up from his chair and walked toward Jeppson, smiling and extending his hand. It was the first time he had ever done such a thing.

"Mr. Jeppson," he said, "if your plan works, we're all going to owe you a great deal."

"Mr. Pettigrew," Jeppson said fervently, as they shook hands, "I'll be glad that I been of service."

From the passage, where she sat in case she was needed, Sheba heard it all: the enthusiasm, the determination, the planning. There was no need to wait for the legislature's approval; every man would spread the word among his blacks at once. Whoever caused Adaba to be caught would be freed. He would be rich. He would be a hero among white men. Jeppson had figured it all out, and Adaba, the Brown Dove, would be captured and slain at last.

Finally, the meeting broke up. Two or three at a time, Jeppson's new friends went to the door of the passage and shook his hand, giving him a hearty good night, as if they had all been boon companions for years. Sheba went into the parlor and began clearing up the coffee cups and the brandy glasses.

"Was you listening, Miss Lady?"

"I heard some, Mr. Jeppson."

Jeppson jerked his head toward the door. "They ain't so bad, some of them. Once you get to know them."

His eyes were bright. He was flushed with success.

"We gonna get him, Miss Lady," he said, smacking a fist into a palm. "Gonna get him at last. And I reckon we got as much chance of catching him right here at Redbird as any of them other places. I mean, he's stole as many

358

niggers from me as from any of them others, and there ain't no reason to think he won't be back for more. And when he comes here . . ."

The cups and glasses tinkled as Sheba, trembling, put them on a tray. She thought of the pistol in the tall mahogany secretary that stood only a few feet away.

Jeppson laughed. "If I'm right about Adaba, there must be somebody on just about every farm and plantation around here that knows him, somebody that don't run away but that maybe helps him. Serena. Wouldn't be surprised if she was helping him all along, all these years. And now it's somebody else right here on Redbird."

The pistol, loaded, its charge changed regularly, because Mr. Jeppson liked to keep his weapons ready at all times . . . if only she had used it on Saturday night, if only she had used the pistol instead of love and laudanum, Mr. Jeppson would never have been able to do this. . . .

"But we're gonna get him, Miss Lady, because one of them people is gonna talk. He's gonna talk to get his freedom and all that money. To get his freedom without having to run away and starve for it. It don't have to be an enemy of Adaba. It could even be somebody real close to him, somebody he trusts most of all.

"Maybe that's what makes your true nigger, Sheba—the way they'll turn on their own kind. Maybe that's the difference between them and us."

How could she help but stare at him? Between them and *us*, Mr. Jeppson?

Perhaps he noticed her look. He returned it peculiarly, as if a thought had occurred to him for the first time. "Would *you* turn him in for all that money and your freedom, Sheba?"

Her laugh was broken, and it was all she could do to keep her voice steady. "Why, Mr. Jeppson, what a strange thing to ask! I already live free with you, and you give me anything I ask for!"

He took her hand, and his eyes were suddenly as moist as hers. "Oh, Sheba, you are a grand lady."

"Why, I do thank you, Mr. Jeppson."

"Now! You just let that tray be. Let's go upstairs and

celebrate. We really got something to celebrate, you and me."

"I should clean up first. . . ."

"Aw, let it go!"

"You go on up without me, and I'll follow in a few minutes. I just want to take these things out to the kitchen and—and get a breath of fresh air."

"Well, you hurry, now."

"I'll hurry, Mr. Jeppson."

She hardly felt the chill of the night as she walked through the darkness. After putting the tray in the kitchen and relocking the door, she hurried toward the quarters.

There was only one thing she could think to do. Adaba had to be warned. From now on, he and Zulie must be more careful than ever before. They must trust no one. They must leave South Carolina as soon as possible, perhaps leave the South altogether and stay away until those who would betray them had tired of the search. Perhaps it would never be safe for them to return again.

She stopped at a cabin door and tapped lightly and repeatedly until someone asked, "Who that?"

"Sheba. Send Leonie out."

A moment later, a yawning, blinking thirteen-year-old girl slipped out through the doorway.

"Leonie, Serena said from now on you get messages to Adaba."

The girl suddenly came awake. "Don't know where he be now. But I tell Zagreus at Sabrehill, he tell Adaba when next he can."

"Good. You got to go to Sabrehill tonight, Leonie, and don't get caught. You tell Zagreus that Adaba and Zulie in great danger. Tell him they mustn't trust no one. Tell him—tell him—"

But how could she entrust a message of such importance to a child? She wouldn't even have entrusted it to Serena, had that young woman still been here.

"What else I tell him, Miss Lady?"

"Tell him—tell him, *Miss Lady must see Adaba!*"

360

the name, Nestor."

Jeppson brought the whip down again, and again Nestor screamed. The whip went up, came down. Went up, came down, came down. Screaming, Nestor tried to

Five

Breakfast was on the table, and the air was rich with the aroma of crisp bacon and strong coffee and steaming grits. Jeppson hadn't felt so good in months, no, he thought, not in years. It was hard for him to believe that only forty-eight hours earlier he had been close to despair. Why in the world had he been so worried, he wondered. It was true that he had debts, it was true that he had problems, but he, by God, was a man who could mold the world to his liking. When he had beckoned the gentry, hadn't they come flocking? And when he had presented his plan to them, it certainly hadn't taken them long to accept it. And they were accepting him too. Hell, he was more than accepted by them—last night he had been their leader!

"You know, Miss Lady," he said as he sat down to breakfast, "I feel lucky. Like I said last night, I reckon we got as much chance of catching that Adaba right here at Redbird as at any other place, and then we'll collect all them other rewards they got out on him. Wouldn't be surprised if they came to ten thousand dollars or more. And I won't pretend that we can't use the money."

"Would you free the slave that got him caught? if the legislature let you?"

Jeppson gave a careless wave. "Oh, hell, yes. Likely couldn't get away with not doing it, the kinda nigger-lovers we got for neighbors. Anyway, I reckon the state'll pay me compensation. But what I told 'em last night, that ain't all my plans, Sheba."

"No, Mr. Jeppson?"

"No, ma'am. If the plan I told 'em don't get Adaba pretty quick, I got other things in mind, lots of other things."

Sheba sat down with him and poured herself a cup of

coffee. "Well, now I'd kinda expect that, Mr. Jeppson—you being a mighty clever man."

Jeppson grinned, pleased. "Sheba, tell me something. If you was trying to find this Adaba yourself, how would you go about it?"

"Why, I don't know. I never give it any thought."

"That's the trouble, nobody gives it any thought, not much. Least not the way I do. Now tell me what we know 'bout Adaba."

"Don't know nothing 'bout him."

"Maybe we know more than you think. He's said to be tall, and dark, but not as dark as some, and he wears a beard to cover a birdlike mark on the left side of his chin."

"That sounds like some kind of tale, Mr. Jeppson."

"No, it ain't. You may recollect hearing 'bout how he was once caught and identified by that mark. He got away that time, but he still got that mark on him. Let's guess his age between thirty and forty or so. Now, what do you suppose his real name is?"

"I don't know. Don't nobody know."

"That's right. But I heard long ago he was somebody called John Dove, and another time that he was John Edisto. Ain't likely Dove or Edisto is his real name, but what does it tell you?"

"Don't tell me nothing, Mr. Jeppson."

"It sounds to me like he's fond of that name John, like it might be real. And with names like that—Dove, and Adaba meaning Dove, and Edisto—it sounds like he was from somewhere along the coast, Gullah country. Somewhere, say, between Georgetown and Brunswick. Maybe from Edisto, if he really uses that name, maybe even Charleston."

"But some people say he come from up north—Maryland or Delaware—"

"No," Jeppson said positively. "If he was northern, he wouldn't be coming way down here to do his nigger-stealing. There's plenty to be stole up there, and a lot easier. And he wouldn't be using a Gullah name. I tell you Adaba is a Carolina or a Georgia nigger from the coast, maybe from the Sea Islands."

362

"Mr. Jeppson, a thousand people must have thought every one of these things before."

"Maybe they did. But how many of them went to Charleston and Georgetown and all 'round and put in the newspapers, 'I want to know 'bout a young nigger 'bout fifteen or twenty years ago had a birdlike mark on the left side of his chin and was called Adaba and maybe John. You got a nigger knew a boy like that? Reward for you and for him if you find him for me.' It's so goddamn simple, and yet I can pretty near guarantee you it's never been done, Miss Lady. Just advertise for him like he was any other runaway, but look for him the way he was years back. Somewhere there's a nigger field hand or maybe a white man who's gonna remember him."

"But Mr. Jeppson, this is all *if* and *maybe* and *might!* And there got to be a hundred Adabas, and some called John, and even some with this mark or that!"

He did not like her resistance, could not understand it. His logic seemed so solid to him. "Sheba, 'course it's all *if* and *maybe* and *might!* But you find three ifs or maybes or mights together, and the chance is it ain't coincidence. The chance is you've found what you're looking for."

"But even if somebody remembers this boy you looking for, he is long gone now, Mr. Jeppson. He is somewhere out in the maroon camps. He ain't just standing 'round waiting for you to grab him."

Jeppson grinned. "That's so. But maybe that don't matter as much as you think." He wondered if Sheba were feeling poorly. She didn't look at all well this morning.

"What you mean, Mr. Jeppson?"

"How do you think Adaba come into this world, Sheba? He didn't just crawl out from under a rock. Most likely, he's got family somewhere. Maybe a daddy, a momma, brothers and sisters. And if I can find someone who remembers that Adaba, I just bet you I can find his family."

"You mean you'd use them. . . ."

"That's right. One way or another, I'd lay my hands on them. Buy 'em if I had to. And then . . ." Jeppson thrust a large hand, palm up, out over the table. Slowly he

363

closed the fingers. "I'd grab 'em by the balls, Miss Lady. And then I'd squeeze . . . and squeeze . . . and I'd make them niggers scream. . . ."

"What good that do, Mr. Jeppson?" No, Sheba was not well this morning. Her voice was thin and weak.

"Oh, I'd let it be known what I was doing. And I reckon he'd hear about it sooner or later. And being a nigger-stealer, he just might try to do something about it. Nigger families are a lot closer than some folks realize.

"And when he made his move, I'd make mine. . . .

"Sheba, you sure you all right? Sheba?"

Lew awakened in the cool dawn to find Rose nuzzling him and to hear the children already up and running around somewhere downstairs. Dorinda's voice pursued them: "You get dressed now, you hear me? 'Fore you catch your death of cold!" Fine familiar domestic sounds, he thought, and what a nice way to be awakened. He returned Rose's nuzzlings, remembering last night, and thinking how the world had changed for the better. They exchanged good mornings, as Lew got out of bed and tossed cold water on his face.

"Lew, are you *sure* you don't remember anybody named Wilbur Pickett?" Rose asked.

Now, why did she have to do that? when the morning was so nice, and she looked so beautiful, sitting there half-awake on the bed, with her gown down off one shoulder? It was at least the fourth or fifth time she had asked since he had told her about Pickett.

"Rose, I haven't the slightest idea who he was. All I know is that he said he worked in the City Guard and the workhouse, and he was overseer at a couple of places. I've known a few people in the guard over the years, but I don't remember him there or anywhere else."

"But you said he looked right at you and told you he knew you."

Lew shrugged. "He didn't seem to know my name."

"It wouldn't take him long to find out, if he stayed around here."

"Well, he's probably far up the river by now, still looking for work."

364

"He wouldn't have to know you personally, Lew. In Charleston a lot of people know who you are, even if you don't know them, just because you owned Jessamine."

"Yeah. Owned."

It was still impossible not to feel some bitterness, even though everything was now looking so much better. Lew threw more cold water on his face, as if that might wash the bitterness away.

"Rose, honey, please don't worry so much."

"But if he knows about *me* . . . and if he starts talking about me around here . . ."

"Honey, most likely people around here already know about you. You're Marcus Guerard's daughter, and I'm Lewis Sabre, and ten years ago a lot of people had their fun being scandalized by our marriage. And most of them still haven't forgotten it. But that hasn't kept us from having ten damned good years, has it?"

"Just the same, I get scared when I think about that man. I wish you hadn't told me about him."

"Well, I thought you might remember him. Might have some idea of who he could be."

"All I know is, he's somebody who could start talk about us around here. I'll bet you nobody comes to the party Lucy is giving for us next Saturday night."

He went to her on the bed. "Honey, that is no way to talk. I've taken a goddamn vow I'm not going to let anything bad happen to you ever again."

"Why, Lew . . ." She looked surprised by his vehemence.

"Mr. Wilbur Pickett, whoever he may be, is long gone and far away, and I doubt very much that we'll ever see or hear from him again. And meanwhile, you are sitting here on this bed, half-naked, and looking so beautiful. . . ."

He threw off his nightshirt and took her into his arms.

"Why, *Lew!*"

"It's been a long time since we've done it in the morning."

"But breakfast—"

"Too hell with breakfast."

"The children—"

"Never mind the children or breakfast or Pickett. I'm going to make us both forget everything but this . . . and this . . . and this. . . ."

And for a little while they did forget.

But afterward he remembered again: that wasted skull-like face, staring at him in the courtyard.

"Why, them dirty devils!" Adaba chortled.

The news had arrived at Sabrehill with amazing swiftness: passed by a Redbird slave to a Kimbrough Hall slave and thence to a number of Sabrehill people. Zulie's two younger brothers had picked it up in the stables and passed it on to Zagreus, who had passed it on to Adaba and Zulie. There was to be a wonderful reward for any slave who brought about the capture of Adaba or Zulie: freedom and money.

"Them dirty, dirty devils!" Adaba laughed again after Zagreus had left. They were alone in their upstairs room in the coach house.

"It ain't nothing to laugh at," Zulie said, looking worried. "Ain't every black man in the world is our friend, you know it. There's people right here at Sabrehill would give us to Jeppson for two dollars and a wench."

"Who you got in mind?" Adaba stretched out on the bed, trying to appear at ease.

"People like that Hayden and Luther—them two you took away from here that time, and they come running back like cowards. They turn you over to Jeppson just for meanness."

"Only they don't know we're here."

"How you *know* they don't know?"

" 'Cause they ain't turned us over."

Adaba joked, but only to calm Zulie and to hide his own unease. What she said was true enough. Aside from those who had to know, such as Zagreus and Binnie, there might well be others who suspected their presence and that they had the three fugitives with them—Moses and Jonah were across the service lane in the blacksmith's shop, and Serena in a cabin out in the field quarters. They had to be fed, and the observant might notice strange comings and goings. It was easy enough for Adaba and Zulie to hide at

Sabrehill when they were alone, but for five to hide was considerably more difficult.

"Well," Adaba said, "don't you worry, honey. I figure on leaving tomorrow night. And once I get them three out on the trail, you'll be a lot safer here—"

"Me!" Zulie looked shocked. "You ain't going nowhere without me!"

Adaba had expected her protest and ignored it. "I'm gonna take them three fast and far—"

"I never slowed you down!"

"The fewer of us, the better. The less chance of getting caught."

"That time you took thirty-two people away from here—"

"Six of them got killed. I ain't taking no chance on our baby being killed."

Zulie shook her fists with frustration. For a moment, Adaba thought she was actually going to stamp her feet.

"I wish I hadn't told you 'bout that baby! Wish I hadn't told you for months and months!"

Adaba laughed and pulled her down to the bed. "I think I woulda noticed sooner or later," he said.

"Should keep my dumb mouth shut!"

Adaba put his arms around her and held her still. "Zulie, honey, don't take on so. You're gonna stay here and keep hidden till I come back, and then we can decide where you'll have the baby." Then, to soothe her: "You know, you used to tell me how you dreamed of living in Charleston. And I been thinking and scheming and planning, and maybe, for a little while before we take you north . . ."

"Don't want to live nowhere, north or south, without you."

"You got to live somewhere while you're bringing up our baby, honey, and I'm out doing my work."

Zulie was silent. She knew it was true.

And I'll be so glad to know you're safe, Adaba thought. There was always danger when they were out on a trail, even though he could provide them with false papers, but of course the danger was greatest when they were transporting fugitives, and Zulie did tend to be reckless. But once he had her settled down . . . perhaps he could arrange for her purchase by his father . . . she would be safer then . . . and he didn't think his father would refuse him this time, not when Zulie was bearing his grandchild. . . .

"You going stay out there till they kill you," Zulie said softly.

Adaba laughed again. "I heard that before. No, honey, they had their shot at this old dove and missed. Ain't nobody gonna kill me." Sometimes he really believed it.

" 'Sides, I got to stay alive now to help take care of my *little* Brown Dove."

"You die, I want to be there and die with you."

"No, you gonna live forever." He drew her closer to him. "And now we got some time to pass 'fore tonight—what sweet way we gonna spend it?"

Arranging the meeting had been simple enough. After Leonie delivered Miss Lady's message, Zagreus sent her down to Sabre's Landing. He walked about the big house and some of the outbuildings for a few minutes to see if there were any signs that she had been followed—a simple precaution, probably unnecessary, but wise. Then he returned to the coach house and woke Adaba. Quickly they devised a simple plan. Zagreus went down to the landing and sent Leonie home with the message that Miss Lady should be ready the next evening for someone to fetch her.

That evening he watched with some nervousness as Binnie climbed into a cabriolet and started off in the evening darkness for Redbird. Adaba could hardly blame him: Zag and Binnie both had reasons to hate and fear Jeppson, as did a great many other blacks of that region. But Binnie carried a pass written by Adaba and sighed with Miss Lucy's name, and the chances were that no harm would come to her.

She was to inform anyone who cared to know that a slave wench named Vidette was giving birth—that happened to be true—and having difficulties with which the midwives of Sabrehill could not cope—which was not true. Anyway, Miss Lady's famous skills would be ap-

368

preciated. Fortunately, Jeppson was known to bed down early, especially on weekday evenings. As it happened, Binnie reported later, Jeppson was sound asleep, and Miss Lady was at the door awaiting her.

Adaba and Zulie watched from a darkened upstairs window of the coach house as the cabriolet came to a halt in front of Zagreus and two dimly seen figures stepped out.

"Evening to you, Miss Lady." Zag's voice could barely be heard.

"Binnie say you got a sick wench," Miss Lady said for the benefit of anyone who might be listening. "What's the matter? Can't Lucinda or Reba help her?"

"They ain't done nothing for her yet."

"Well, I better go look at her. She in the sick house?"

"No, I think they got Vidette in the big-house servant quarters." Zagreus pointed along the service lane and across the courtyard. There another service lane led past various outbuildings to the servants' quarters.

"I'll just walk over there," Miss Lady said.

She walked the distance slowly, and the whole time she was observed by Zulie's younger brothers, Orion and Paris. Again, it was a simple precaution. But nothing suspicious was seen. Apparently she and Binnie had not been followed.

Moments later she returned to the coach house, and Adaba heard her murmur something to Zagreus about Vidette not having been in the servants' quarters.

"I'm sorry, Miss Lady. Must be they took her to the sick house in the field quarters. You want to ride out there?"

"No, I'll walk."

Miss Lady spent some ten minutes with Vidette in the sick house, giving her a genuine examination and advice, and then came out again. Adaba stood some fifty feet away in the darkness, watching as Paris approached her and told her where she was to go next. Miss Lady nodded and walked away.

At one corner of the quarters, somewhat separated from the other cabins, stood the cabin Zulie had once occupied. No one had taken it over since Zulie had run away: it had for generations been a conjurewoman's home and thus a voodoo temple and a place of awe. Adaba and Zulie occasionally made use of it in conducting fugitives, and until tonight Serena had been hidden there. For the time being, she had been put in one of the rooms over the coach house.

Zulie and Adaba walked to the cabin. Zulie opened the door and went in, and Adaba followed her, quickly closing the door again. The only light came from a small fire that Orion had built in the fireplace, and Miss Lady stood facing it.

"Miss Lady!" Zulie said. "Sheba!"

Miss Lady turned. Adaba saw a high forehead, a thin, noble nose, a cleft chin. The eyes were faintly slanted, the mouth generous. In the firelight, her skin seemed to have a coppery tone. She smiled at Zulie.

"Why, good evening, Zulie," she said. "My, it's been a long time since we see each other."

Zulie laughed and went forward to embrace Miss Lady. "I see you more than you know, Sheba—but from way off!"

The two women laughed together. Then Miss Lady backed away from Zulie and turned toward Adaba. "I guess it's 'bout time you and me meet," she said. "Good evening, Mr. Adaba."

"Gilly," Adaba said.

Those few seconds seemed to go on forever, and the flash of light and the searing pain were endless.

Adaba saw Zulie move, saw her whip around and look at him in astonishment. "Gilly!" she said. *"Gilly?"*

And still the moment went on.

"No," Miss Lady said softly, "not Gilly. Sheba. Gilly died a long time ago. She had to die, for me to go on living."

"Gilly," Adaba said again.

"Sheba," Miss Lady repeated patiently.

Time began to move again, and it was not the painful thing he might have expected. Not yet. It brought a terrible numbness, a feeling of having been shattered.

370

"I looked for you," he said, after what seemed like hours.

"You looked for your Gilly. I knew you would."

"This?" Zulie asked incredulously. "This here is your Gilly that you tell me 'bout?"

Sheba closed her eyes and shook her head.

"Sheba Lady, I thought you was with Mr. Jeppson always!"

"You was young when he brought me here," Miss Lady said. "Only 'bout ten."

Adaba seemed to see overlapping images. He saw the girl he had lost, but this was a woman. The cheekbones seemed higher, the cleft in the chin deeper. The voice was lower and richer, and had lost its Charleston lilt. But this was undeniably his Gilly—this woman who called herself Sheba.

"I looked for you," he said again, "I looked for years. I asked everywhere. A new slave. A girl. A beautiful girl named Gilly."

"Mr. Jeppson changed my name before we even got here. First night out of Charleston."

Adaba sank down on the edge of the bed. Miss Lady continued to stand by the fireplace, smiling at him slightly.

"*He* bought you," he said. "Of all the people in the world. Him. Jeppson."

"He been kind to me, Adaba."

Adaba looked up at her, unable to believe what she said.

"Yes, it's true. In all these years, that man had hardly one bad word for me. He been kind and gentle and loving. Always. Only one time he ever did strike me, and I guess you remember that."

"No." Adaba shook his head. "I don't know what you mean, Gilly . . . Sheba."

"In Charleston, at the market. You and little Lew and—and me. I bumped into a white man on the street, and he hit me. And you pulled me away and grabbed him and started hitting him, putting bad-mouth on him—"

Adaba saw a large, weathered white face, a face in shock; that was all he remembered of it: the ruddiness of that face and the shock. "—and we all run away, and you and me hid in the courtyard behind Denmark Vesey's shop, while little Lew led all them white people away from us."

"He bought you? That was Jeppson? . . ."

"He bought me to make me lead him to you. But I told him I didn't know who you was, and he come to believe me. And to love me."

"What I've heard about that man, I never thought he could love anybody."

"Well . . ." Miss Lady sat down on a chair and stared into the fire. "Well, everything you heard is likely right. Mr. Jeppson ain't always bad, but he can be evil. I remember a time a few years back when some bandits burned Mr. Buckridge's house and carried away his little girl. Everybody thought they was maroons, though they wasn't, least not all of them. Mr. Jeppson and his friends, they caught a black man out after dark, and that man had a pistol. So they said he was one of the maroons, and even if he wasn't, they was going to make an example of him for carrying a gun. So they whipped him and set him on fire and hanged him. To make him an example for the other niggers." She paused and shuddered.

"Denmark Vesey was right," Adaba said after a moment. "I should have been with him. Even if I hanged for it."

"Denmark Vesey," Miss Lady mused. "I never forgot Denmark Vesey and what he preached to us, and even way out here we heard about what he done." She smiled. " 'Course, that spring most black folks out here was mostly interested in the question, was Mr. Justin spreading Miss Lucy or was he not? He was." She and Zulie laughed softly. Miss Lady's smile faded. "But Denmark Vesey . . . Adaba, I always remembered him, and no matter how good Mr. Jeppson was to me, and no matter how much I come to care for him . . . I always kept my heart with our people. And if the people out here had riz up to follow Denmark, I would have been with them." She closed her eyes. "I would have murdered that man in his bed. And maybe I ought to yet."

"And you say a man like that can love you."

Miss Lady nodded. "And I got a sort of love for him."

372

"I don't understand. I don't understand how it can be."

Miss Lady was silent for a moment. She looked into the fire as if she too were trying to understand how such a thing could be.

"There's something that nobody 'round here seems much to realize," she said. "And that is that Mr. Justin Sabre and Mr. Balbo Jeppson is a lot alike. They both got their lights, and they both try to live by their lights more than just about anybody else you ever meet. And sometimes that makes just plain living awful hard for them."

"But Mr. Jeppson's lights," Zulie said, "is evil lights!"

"Yes," Sheba Lady agreed, "his lights is evil, but he don't know that, and he still believe in them. And loving me goes 'gainst all of them. Sometimes it tears him apart, loving me, and he got to forget I'm black, or go crazy. I remember when he give me that baby. He near went crazy then. What he supposed to do? Keep that child, his own child, for a slave? Or sell his own child away so he don't have to look at it? When I lost it, I reckon he was relieved, but still he cried, long and hard and in secret. 'Cause he knew then he wasn't never gonna have no son to be proud of or little girl to love. Not by me, and likely not by any other. And he didn't touch me again for almost a year. Torn apart, that man . . . After that, I was lucky, or what Zulie's momma taught me worked, 'cause I ain't had no more babies."

For a moment, the only sound was the crackle of the fire.

"Gilly . . . Sheba . . . Sheba, we can take you north."

"No." Sheba, still looking into the fire, shook her head. "No, ain't no reason for me to go north, least not yet. Not while Mr. Jeppson is alive. I live good with him, and lots of times I keep him from hurting people. I hadn't been here, I couldn't help you and Zulie and Serena—make sure he sleeps and the dogs don't rouse him up when you come 'round. No, best I stay here."

"For now. But someday . . ."

"Maybe so. Someday." Sheba Lady turned away from the fire. "Adaba, I made sure Mr. Jeppson is sleeping good tonight, but I best not stay too long. He'll surely make a fuss if he wake up and find me gone. I just come here 'cause I figure I best tell you myself 'bout the scheme Mr. Jeppson got to free the slave that helps catch you."

"We know about that," Adaba said. "We heard all about that this morning."

"Reckon I should have knowed you would." Sheba Lady smiled. "You know, I been hearing about this Adaba man for years, and sometimes I said to myself, 'I'll just bet that's my . . . I'll bet that's Gilly's Adaba!' And then when you come 'round here, I thought, 'I'd surely like to see that man!' And then, 'No. Best not. Might turn out to really *be* Adaba! And what's finished is finished, and it ain't nothing but pain, prying 'round in the past.' So I stayed out of your way. But last night . . . maybe something in me was looking for an excuse to talk to this Adaba I been hearing 'bout for so long. Maybe there's a little bit of Gilly alive in me still."

"Is she feeling pain?"

"A little. So I guess she's still alive some, and she's surely glad you got her friend Zulie to take care of you. But never mind Gilly. There's something else I got to tell you. This morning Mr. Jeppson dreamed up another scheme. . . ."

She told him of Mr. Jeppson's plan to find someone who remembered a young Adaba from years ago and then to find that Adaba's family. Adaba listened with growing unease.

"It's crazy," he said. "Nobody close to me has called me Adaba for years—except Zulie and sometimes someone in my family. I guess I musta told somebody I was called Adaba, 'cause they started calling me that in the maroon camps. Hard to stop them. And after a while I found out that when runaways knew I was Adaba, they trusted me. Well, they had to call me something, and Adaba seemed good enough. Not very smart of me, I'm afraid."

"Do you think his plan will work?" Zulie asked worriedly.

"It just might. Or more likely, he'll find the family of some other Adaba and make life hell for them, and they won't have the slightest idea of who or where I am."

374

"Then somehow we got to stop him."

"We will. I got to think about it."

"He'll be stopped," Miss Lady said quietly. "I promise you. If he try anything like that . . . he'll be stopped."

"No, Sheba," Adaba said, "no, we don't want you getting hurt. You leave Mr. Jeppson to me."

Sheba, he said. But no matter what he called her, he still saw Gilly sitting in front of the fire . . . the girl he had loved so much, the only other girl he had ever loved. . . .

For a little time, they talked. Though Sheba still refused to be called Gilly, they talked of the old days, of Denmark Vesey and of Lew Sabre, who might soon be the overseer of Sabrehill. When she heard that, Sheba's face turned ashen for a moment. They talked of Jessamine and of Dorinda and Lucas and of Adaba's brothers and sisters. They even laughed together.

But afterward, Adaba wept. After Sheba had kissed his cheek and slipped back into the night to return to Redbird, the pain of that loss so many years earlier came back to him, and quietly, achingly, he wept for himself, for Gilly, for all that might have been. Zulie, who had suffered losses of her own and who understood, tried to comfort him.

"She said Jeppson bought her in order to get at me," he said bitterly as he wiped the last tear from his face. "Just to get at me."

"Yes," Zulie said, with a faint smile, "and it do sound like he still trying."

"Let him. Zulie, I got to do something. I can't just sit here tonight. I got to do something."

"All right, sugar, what you want to do?"

Adaba thought about it. "I wonder . . . I wonder how much cotton one man with a scythe can ruin in a single night."

"Not one man. Two. You and me."

"No. Just me—"

"*And* me," Zulie insisted, grinning, "*and* Zagreus *and* Orion *and* Paris and, lessee, who else? . . ."

As if in a dream, Jeppson looked out over the devastated fields.

They seemed to stretch endlessly in every direction. It was a sight beyond his worst nightmares, and he wanted to howl with rage and despair. Yesterday, everything had been so wonderful. He had new friends among the gentry. They were going to help him catch Adaba. He was going to pay his debts and be wealthy again and live in happiness and peace with his Miss Lady. But today he found his crop, acres of it, cut down and trampled into the dirt, bringing him that much closer to ruination.

Who could have done this to him? What curse had been laid on him? Was there no end to his misfortunes?

No. No end. And he was being driven into madness . . . madness. . . .

Six

Adaba was ready to leave Sabrehill. He had slept until well after nightfall and awakened refreshed, after last night's hard work. Binnie brought him some supper, and he ate it quickly, eager to be on his way. He had his boots on, his blanket roll was made up, and his hatchet hung from his right side, his knife from his left. As he kissed Zulie good-bye, Zagreus came into the room, laughing and shaking his head.

"Been thinking 'bout that Mr. Jeppson," he said. "Binnie tell you 'bout him?"

No, she hadn't.

"Well, he been acting like he was out of his mind. Come riding over here all by hisself, said he was looking for them niggers that tore up his fields. Mr. Justin didn't take nothing from him, though. 'How you know it was Negroes, Jeppson?' he say. 'How you know it wasn't some of them trash friends of yours, playing their little joke on you? How you know, Jeppson? Or maybe your own Negroes done it—they got any reason to love you, Jeppson?

How many your own Nee-groes love to see you ruined?'
And Jeppson, he ride out of here so mad, oh my!"

They all laughed together.

"The others ready, Zag?"

"They all out at the house in the quarters—Zulie's old house. Just waiting for you."

Adaba put his arms back around Zulie. "Then all I got to do is finish saying good-bye to my woman."

Zagreus took the hint and left the room.

"I oughta be going with you," Zulie complained. "I know I oughta be going with you."

"No, you shouldn't. I'm gonna be traveling fast. I'll be back in a week, ten days at the most. And while I'm away, I want you to stay hidden here and grow fat."

"But, sugar, I'll go plain crazy doing nothing here!"

"Have Binnie borrow some books from the big house. You ain't practiced your reading in a long time. I've got to teach you to talk right, make you fit for Northern society, and reading's a good way to start."

She wiggled impatiently in his arms. "But, Adaba, I could be getting some more people ready to steal away—"

"No! Godammit, Zulie, if I leave here thinking you might do something like that, I'm gonna be scared the whole time I'm gone. And when a man is scared and thinking about the wrong things, that's when he makes mistakes. That's when he's most likely to get himself caught or killed. Now, if you want me to keep safe, you've got to promise me you'll keep yourself safe—and make me believe it!"

Zulie slipped from his arms and sat disconsolately on the bed. "All right," she said after a moment. "I still wish I was going with you, but I'll stay hid here and get fat and lazy, and Binnie can get me some books. Maybe I can borrow some from Sheba—"

"No, I want you to stay away from Redbird."

"All right, I stay 'way! I know that place like my own hand, but I stay 'way! I want you to believe me and not worry!"

He drew her up from the bed, and again they embraced, and he was off into the night.

He loved this life, he thought, as he hurried through the

darkness toward the field quarters. He told himself that he lived it because he hated slavery and loved freedom, because he cared for his people, because he owed it to Denmark to help keep alive the spirit of rebellion. All of that was true. But he also loved the danger, the adventure, the living by his wits and his woodsman's skills, for its own sake.

Did he have the right to continue this life, when soon he would have a child to care for?

Did he have the right to leave it, as long as there was still a man anywhere in bondage?

He didn't know. He only knew that he would never willingly quit, but that he was glad that Zulie would soon be safely out of it. And once she was settled down with their child, he would have a place to come home to. He liked that thought.

Contrary to Rose's fears, the party on Saturday evening could hardly have gone better. At that time of year, people were usually on their plantations, so all the neighbors were in attendance, and the house, holiday bright, was crowded. An orchestra played in the ballroom. Irish, the young butler, served drinks in one of the parlors, while Leila, the housekeeper, presided over a buffet in the dining room. Cousin Lucy said that they seldom entertained at Sabrehill, but when they did, nobody enjoyed her parties more than she.

In the course of the evening, Lew and Rose were introduced to every guest, and Lew saw that Rose was tensely waiting for a hint of recognition. But it never came. If any guest knew of Rose's origins, he gave no sign of it. But then even among those who might know and disapprove of Rose's bloodlines, there was some ability to observe the common decencies.

There were, however, a few less-than-genteel people at the party, which led to some touchy moments. Midway through the evening, Mr. Owen Buckridge managed to corner Lew in the library.

"I suppose, sir," he said, "that, as a Sabre, you share your cousin Justin's abolitionist opinions."

"Mr. Buckridge, sir," Lew said, "my cousin Justin and I

378

share a name more than a relationship, proud though I am of both. And since I regard abolition as neither a threat nor a realizable dream at this time, I can't say I have any *useful* opinions on the subject at all. I'm not much of a philosopher."

"But you must have some opinion on the inferiority of the Nigra race."

"Ah, the inferiority of the Nigra race. Sir, far better minds than mine have proclaimed it, so how can I doubt it?" Mr. Buckridge looked pleased. *"But,"* Lew added quickly, "on the other hand, how can I believe in it?"

"Why, Mr. Sabre, you just said that far better minds than yours——"

"Exactly. Not having a great mind, Mr. Buckridge, any belief I might entertain in the inferiority of another race would necessarily be suspect. It would almost certainly be self-serving, self-justifying, a rationalization of my own good fortune in being a slave-owner rather than a slave. No, Mr. Buckridge, I must leave the belief in the inferiority of the Nigra race to far better minds than mine."

Mr. Buckridge looked confused, as if he were not sure whether his leg were being pulled or not.

The evening passed, the little crises were surmounted, and Rose showed every sign of relaxing and enjoying herself. The guests began to depart, family by family, and those few who were staying the night were shown to their rooms.

Justin summoned Lew into the library. For another drink, he said, looking grim, and Lew wondered what was wrong. Had he failed some important test?

"I don't know how you do it," Justin said, when he had poured two brandies.

"What's that, Justin?"

"Handle people like Owen Buckridge the way you do. I overheard you talking to him in here earlier."

"He doesn't seem like a bad old boy."

"He's not. But when he gets onto that 'natural inferiority of the Nigra' business . . . mostly I manage to stay calm, but sometimes my hands start trembling, and I want to throttle the old bastard. I first met him right here at Sabrehill at a party like this, and he had the nerve to ask me if I was a nigger-lover."

Lew laughed.

"You see, you're laughing! And I'm slopping brandy all over the place! Thinking about it, I'm madder now than I was three years ago when he said it to me!"

"Well, I'm an easygoing kind of fellow, Cousin Justin. I've had a fight or two with people like Buckridge, but mostly they amuse me more than make me mad. I am sorry for the suffering they cause, and I do what I can about it. But it ain't my fault that that ain't much, and I try not to lose a lot of sleep over it. I need all my energy to take care of my own family, white and black both. Not that I've done such a hell of good job of it."

Justin threw himself down into a chair. "Now, you see, that's the difference between you and me. I used to tell Lucy that I could never live in the South. Not the way it is today, with slavery tightening its grip and people calling it a positive good. What am I supposed to do, stand there listening, biting my tongue, when everything in me tells me I should be beating heads until somebody chops me down?"

"You're a good man, Cousin Justin. If you'll pardon my saying so, maybe just a little too good for this imperfect world."

Justin gave him a hard look and a hard, choked laugh. "Ha! I'll tell you something. If goodness is what I've got, the more a man's got, the greater his chances of becoming corrupt. And I often feel that that's what's happening to me. Just by living in the South, I'm becoming corrupt."

"I can hardly believe that."

"Let me give you an example. Right now, you know, some of our neighbors want to get the legislature to permit the manumission of any slave who'll betray Adaba. Naturally, they want me to join with them, all the more so because they have an idea of my sentiments in such matters. Well, everything in me says to tell them to go to hell. But I'll probably wind up going along with them, just to keep peace with my neighbors. And to keep them from bothering my people."

380

"Unless you plan to be a saint, you have to make compromises, Justin."

The thought did not noticeably soothe Justin. He took a large swallow from his glass, the latest of a good many during the evening, and Lew wondered if the liquor were loosening his tongue.

"Have some more," Justin said, and Lew poured for both of them. "I'll tell you something, Lew. I know you well enough by now, I'll tell you something I never told anybody else around here. Nobody but Lucy. I once helped that damned rogue, Adaba, to escape."

Lew hoped his face showed nothing. "You did?"

"He and another, Black Buck, had been caught by a couple of ragtag and bobtail who were bringing them down the river to collect the rewards on them. Frankly, I didn't know at the time who Adaba and Buck were—I just knew that those two drunken whites were beating them to death. Literally killing them. So I let them go. And goddammit, I'd do it again!"

"Reckon I might myself."

Justin nodded. "Yes. You would. Because you're the kind of man that treats other men like human beings."

"Well, I'm pleased you thinks so. . . ." Lew wandered about the library, looking at book spines. Where the hell was all this leading to, he wondered.

"I don't suppose you and I agree on everything, Lew, not by a damn sight. But we agree on enough, and we get along. Obviously you know how to handle people like Buckridge a lot better than I do, and that could be mighty handy to me. I did worry about the kind of hell some people around here might raise when they found out about Cousin Rose, if you'll pardon my mentioning it, but I figure now that that wouldn't be anything we couldn't handle." Justin hunched forward in his chair, elbows on knees. "What I'm getting at, Lew—why don't you sit down?—what I'm getting at . . ."

Lew had been expecting it, and yet it put him into a kind of shock. He heard himself talking calmly, joking, laughing, but as if he were listening to another person. They settled the details and shook hands. "You might as well take over Monday. I'm leaving then for Charleston, be back Saturday or Sunday. . . ." They went out into the passage, where Lucy awaited them. "I gave Rose some champagne and sent her home. I thought you'd like to be alone with her when you tell her. But of course she may have guessed. . . ."

Lew walked to the overseer's house in a daze. When he went upstairs, he took a moment to look in on the sleeping children. *Safe*, he thought. *I've made them safe again.*

And now Rose . . .

She looked radiant, standing by the bed in her prettiest gown. She held up the bottle of wine and said softly, not to disturb the children, "This time it's not stolen!"

He said, "I guess you know I've got some great news for you."

She put down the bottle. Her eyes glistened. She held out her arms and said, "Come to me."

And he did.

Find Adaba. Find the black or the blacks—for surely they had been black, and there must have been many of them—who had destroyed so much of his crop. Had Adaba led them? Did Adaba inspire them? And what was Adaba—a man or a curse?

Each day Jeppson rode out, either with the patrol or alone, searching. Trying to find a trace, a clue, something that would lead him to Adaba. He had no time for his plantation. Let Pickett and Sabin and the drivers take care of it. He had to search for Adaba. Anyway, what was the use of caring for crops that might be destroyed on any dark night? What was the use of tending to a plantation he was on the verge of losing?

No, he would not lose it. Not if he found Adaba. And to that end, he would question anybody, everybody, black and white alike, threaten them, beat them, abuse them. Mr. Pettigrew, who had once shaken his hand, told him to stay the hell away from his niggers. Major Kimbrough, who had been skeptical all along, asked him to his face who could have faith in the plan of a madman. His new friends were falling away from him, and he knew it, but he couldn't stop what he was doing. He was not going to lose everything. Sooner or later, he would have Adaba.

382

In the evenings, when he came home, he would look into a mirror and wonder: who was that swiftly aging stranger?

On Friday evening, nine days after Jeppson had looked out at those devastated acres, he came home to find Pickett had news for him.

He left his horse at the stable and, without bothering to wash, went directly to the kitchen house. There he ate, sitting on the steps, his plate balanced on his knees. He was hungry after the long day, and the food was good, but it might as well have been sand for all he tasted it.

Pickett came hurrying out of the shadows to the light of the kitchen door. "Mr. Jeppson! Mr. Jeppson! I been waiting for you to get back! I got some news for you!"

Jeppson continued eating without looking up. He was weary. He wanted to hear nothing about his plantation, whether good or bad.

"Mr. Jeppson, I got *news!*"

"Yes, Mr. Pickett," Jeppson said heavily.

"That Sabrehill plantation! It got itself a new overseer!"

"That ain't news, Mr. Pickett. He's been there about two weeks. Started work this week, I heard."

"Yes! But do you know who that overseer *is?*"

Jeppson wished Pickett would go away and leave him alone, but he hardly had the energy to tell him so. "I know. It's a man named Lewis Sabre. Said to be some kind of cousin to them others."

"That's right! And do you know who Lewis Sabre is?"

Jeppson finally raised his eyes from his plate and looked at Pickett. The man's eyes, deep in the skull-like face, gleamed with excitement.

"Mr. Pickett, you got something to say, why the hell don't you say it?"

"Mr. Jeppson, I know you been wondering why it was that every place around here had troubles with burnings and niggers running off and all kinds of nigger mischief—every place, that is, but Sabrehill."

"What's that got to do with Lewis Sabre?"

"Well, sir, when I came to these parts a couple of weeks ago, I stopped by Sabrehill to look for work. And what I *saw* was this man, I was sure I knowed him from somewhere, but I couldn't remember. Then today Mr. Tucker stopped by here to see you, and you wasn't here, and we got to talking. And he said the new overseer was called Lew Sabre, and the name sorta clicked in my mind, and then it all come back to me!"

Some of Jeppson's weariness faded, as he got the feeling that Pickett might be onto something, however long it might take him to say it. He forced himself to be patient.

"*What* come back to you, Pickett?"

"Mr. Jeppson, first off, you ever heard of Jessamine?"

The name had a vaguely familiar ring. "Plantation? Near Charleston?"

"That's right," Pickett said with satisfaction, "a fine one, owned by Mr. Lewis Sabre."

"And *he's* working as an overseer? Ha!"

"Oh, I don't know, Mr. Jeppson, I don't know. Lots of people in bad trouble these days, losing their plantations. Could be he's one of them."

That was true enough. Jeppson wasn't the only planter in trouble.

"Well, what about this Lewis Sabre?"

"Ever hear of the Guerard plantation? Marcus Guerard?"

"I heard of him," Jeppson said sourly.

"Well, maybe you don't know that he had a passle of children of various hues and colors and that some of them could pass for white. And maybe you don't remember or never heard that there was a big scandal about ten years ago, when Lewis Sabre married none other than one of old Marcus's nigger daughters—"

"Wait a minute." Jeppson felt a sudden excitement. "You telling me that this Lewis Sabre got a *nigger wife?*"

"You'd hardly notice till it was pointed out to you. Then you might notice something about the skin, and I reckon if you was to look real close . . ."

Jeppson had heard enough. It was possible. It made sense. Sabres: nigger-lovers, all of them. There had been another scandal, only a few years ago, when it had come out that one of the Sabres actually had black blood. Yes, black blood did seem to run in the family, and that might

384

be the reason why Sabrehill hadn't had the troubles that other plantations had had.

Jeppson stood up. As he turned and flung his plate and spoon onto the kitchen floor, he saw Sheba standing in the doorway.

"You hear that, Miss Lady?"

"I heard—"

"I'm going to Sabrehill."

Sheba looked concerned. "Tomorrow, Mr. Jeppson. You had a long day, and you're tired—"

"No, now. I'm going to talk to Mr. Lewis Sabre. Tonight."

He went alone, on horseback. Pickett wanted to go with him, but Jeppson told him to tend to his own business and see that the people were in their cabins for the night. He didn't need any help facing Lewis Sabre.

It was late when he arrived at Sabrehill, but there were still lights in the big house and a number of other buildings. Jeppson turned off the road, went through the open gate, and rode up the gentle slope toward the house, taking his time. He made sure that the pistol in the pocket of his coat would come free easily if he should need it.

Someone must have seen him coming. As he got closer, he saw them waiting for him in the scattered light from the big house and the kitchen. He had run across Lewis Sabre two or three times lately, and he recognized the man at once. As arrogant, as disdainful as any other Sabre, he stood in the courtyard in his shirtsleeves in spite of the chill, his feet apart and his arms crossed over his chest, precisely as Justin Sabre might have stood. In the fingers of his right hand glowed a cigar. The door of the house was open, and in its light Jeppson saw Miss Lucy. He could even make out the scar on the right side of her face.

The road made a circle around the courtyard. Jeppson didn't follow the circle but rode directly across it on the grass. He drew his horse to a halt beside Lewis Sabre, so that he could look down on the man.

"Jeppson, isn't it? What can I do for you?" The voice was indifferent even if the words were friendly.

"I come here to ask questions."

"It's late, and Mr. Justin isn't here."

"You'll do."

Lewis Sabre tasted his cigar. "I can give you a minute."

"That's about all I'll need. What do you know about Adaba?"

Sabre smiled and shrugged. "I don't speak Gullah the way I did as a boy, but as I recall—"

"I don't have time for any of your shit, Mr. Sabre. Just tell me what you know about Adaba. Who is he and where do I find him?"

"Sorry, Jeppson, but at the moment I haven't the slightest idea."

Jeppson returned Lewis Sabre's smile. He savored the man's resistance. He liked it, he liked it very much. This wasn't Justin Sabre, after all, this was a terribly vulnerable man, and he was going to enjoy watching the bastard break.

"I think you're lying," he purred.

Sabre's smile faded. "Careful, Jeppson."

"Maybe you don't know where he is right this minute, but I think you do know something about him. And I think you're gonna tell me."

"Mr. Jeppson, even if I did know something about Adaba, *I* think you are just about the last person in the world I'd tell."

Jeppson laughed. "Oh, you are so wrong, Mr. Sabre. You see, you ain't got much choice."

"Your minute is up, Jeppson."

Jeppson waved the words aside. "You see, I know all about you. From what I hear, it sounds like there's black blood running all through the goddamn Sabre family—"

"I said, your minute is up."

"—and I figure that's why Sabrehill don't have all the troubles the rest of us do. I figure you must know something about Adaba, and you are gonna tell me. From now on, you are gonna cooperate with me, 'cause—"

Lewis Sabre threw his cigar to the ground. As he stepped closer to Jeppson, his eyes looked glazed. "Get off of Sabrehill. Right now."

Jeppson ignored the order. While his right hand dug

386

into his pocket, he leaned down toward Lewis Sabre and curled his left hand. " 'Cause I have got you where you live. You see, Mr. Sabre, sir, I know a lot of people 'round here who don't like the kind of white man that would marry a nigger woman. And when I tell them you got a nigger wife and a couple of pickaninnies with nigger blood, somebody's gonna be mighty unhappy. Most of all, likely you, or that woman of yours, or even those little pick—"

Maybe he wanted Lewis Sabre to come at him. Because he was already drawing the pistol from his pocket, was already pulling back the cock. Maybe what he had really come for all the time was simply to kill one of these sons of bitches—just give him an excuse, any excuse at all—in order to turn his luck.

But he was too slow. He didn't dream that Lewis Sabre would come at him the way he did, like a springing cat, to seize his coat front and pull him from the saddle. Jeppson heard the woman in the doorway scream. He found himself falling through the air, somersaulting, to land with sickening force. The air was driven from his lungs. Shoulders, back, buttocks slid grinding through the gravel. For an instant he lost consciousness, yet somehow he clung to the pistol, and it didn't go off. Breath burned back into his lungs, and by sheer force of will he managed to fling himself over onto his belly. He struggled to get to his knees, at the same time seeking a target for his pistol. But something struck him between his shoulder blades, and he was flat again, and as a boot heel came down painfully on his hand, the pistol went off.

Then something went around his neck—a leather belt? A pressure on his lower back, perhaps from a knee, held him down, while the belt lifted his head from the ground, and over him a voice, ugly and unfamiliar, said, "Jeppson, don't you ever threaten my family again. Don't you ever threaten my children. Don't you ever threaten my wife. Because if you do, I'll have your head on a pike. Do you understand me, Jeppson?"

Jeppson couldn't answer. His breath was almost completely cut off, and he was strangling. A horrible sound came from his throat

"Do you understand me, Jeppson?"

Jeppson's lungs were in agony. The lights of Sabrehill were a fading blur.

"Lew, stop!" came the woman's voice from a great distance. "Stop! You're killing him!"

"On a pike, Jeppson, and I mean that! I'll have your head on a pike!"

The pressure left his back. The belt slipped away from his throat. For a moment, Jeppson could only lie there, sucking air back into his tortured lungs. He felt himself being lifted to his feet but found that he could hardly stand. His hat was jammed back onto his head. Something was being shoved at his coat, and he realized that the discharged pistol was being put back into his pocket. Tears and pain nearly blinded him, but he could see the glow of a cigar, once again jutting from Lewis Sabre's jaw.

"Now I'm telling you again. Get back on that horse and ride off Sabrehill. And stay off."

The injustice was immeasurable, the humiliation unforgiveable. He had come here thinking he had the upper hand, had come here with right on his side. And no nigger-loving Sabre—

"Kill you," he sobbed. "I'll kill you."

"No, you won't, Jeppson." Hands shoved him against his horse. "You'd like to think you will, but once you cool off, you'll be too afraid of hanging."

"Won't hang . . . call you out . . . my seconds . . ."

Lewis Sabre laughed. "To hell with your seconds. Even if I did duel, which I don't, do you think I'd ever accept a challenge from the likes of you?"

Of course he would not. Not a Sabre. And Jeppson knew that nobody would ever blame the man. Not even those new friends who were so swiftly proving false.

"I say I'll kill you, I'll kill every goddamn Sabre," he swore in frustration. "I'll kill you, I'll burn you out."

"What was that?"

Arson: one of the most terrible of threats. Feared as massacre and murder and slave conspiracy were feared.

"I'll burn you out and—"

Then again Jeppson felt his coat being grabbed, and a

388

hard flat hand struck across his face, struck back and forth like a rawhide paddle, while the woman cried, "Lew! Please! No more! Please let him go! Please!

The blows stopped. Hands shoved him away.

"Only because she asked me to, Jeppson," Lewis Sabre said, panting, the ugliness back in his voice. "Only because she asked me. I ought to bury you here and now, but we don't even want your damn carcass at Sabrehill. Now, *git!*"

And so he was allowed to go. Was boosted back into his saddle and allowed to go. Like a whipped cur.

He slumped in the saddle. His head and shoulders seemed to carry the weight of years of struggle, the long struggle to fight his way out of near-poverty and to make something of himself in his own eyes and the eyes of the world. Years of scratching a meager living from wasted land, of expanding and bettering his holdings . . . and for what? To see it all vanish in the sixth decade of his life. To find that the long struggle had been for nothing. To find that he was still scorned by men who had never felt a rope-burned palm or chopped a row of cotton along side their slaves.

The lights of Redbird at last came into sight, and his horse increased its gait. Jeppson let it have its way, carrying him into the yard. Pickett and Sabin came hurrying to meet him, and he wondered vaguely what they were doing up at this late hour.

"Mr. Jeppson!" Pickett cried out. "Mr. Jeppson, we got somebody! You gotta come see!"

"Was *me* catch her, *me!*" Sabin said excitedly. "Catch her out at that old slave graveyard, Mr. Jeppson!"

"We got her, Mr. Jeppson! Come take a look at her!"

Jeppson turned his face away from them, fearing what it might reveal.

"Wasn't hardly any time after you left!" Sabin said. "I follow her out there to that old graveyard——"

"I was right with you!"

But it was *me* grab her!"

"But *I* was the one that got the knife away from her!"

Painfully, Jeppson slid down from the saddle. For the

first time, he realized that torches had been lit, and a number of blacks stood in the area between the big house and the jail. Sheba was there, wringing her hands and looking worried—or perhaps scared.

"Mr. Pickett, it ain't Saturday night—why ain't these niggers in bed?"

"Mr. Jeppson, something happened—"

"Mr. Jeppson, it was me—"

"What the hell are you two jabbering about?"

"We caught us a nigger," Pickett said. "Thought it was a man at first. Come look, Mr. Jeppson."

He followed them to the jail. Sabin unbarred the door, and Pickett thrust a torch inside. At first Jeppson saw only the Breakline slave, Nestor, sitting on the floor, a blanket wrapped around him. Then, looking farther, he saw the second black, crouched in a corner as if trying to hide. Her eyes were wide with fright. She was dressed as a man, but undoubtedly she was a woman.

For the first time in days, just when everything seemed to be lost, Jeppson's heart began to sing. God was in His heaven still—or rather, He was right here at Redbird. Let his fine new friends desert him, let the Sabres think he was cowed and defeated. There was still justice on this earth. And vengeance belonged to Balbo Jeppson.

He knew the wench.

Zulie.

Seven

Zulie of Sabrehill. Zulie who had disappeared on the Night of the Fires and who was said to run with Adaba. To have her in his grasp now, immediately after his humiliation at Sabrehill, was a pleasure so acute that it was almost like love.

"Look at them big eyes roll," Pickett said. "Look at 'em glisten!"

"It was *me* caught her," Sabin continued to insist, "and

390

I know her right away. Remember her from Sabrehill—"

"Why, if I hadn't been with you, she'da stabbed you dead with that knife of hers. It was *me* grabbed her arm and took that knife away from her!"

"Shut up, both of you," Jeppson said. In spite of the deep aching of his body, he found himself grinning. "You'll both get what you deserve. How did you catch her?"

"It was me," Sabin said. "I see her, I see somebody right near here, and somehow it don't look right, and I follow her—"

"And I followed along too," Pickett said.

"And I *know* it ain't right, she go so quiet and in the shadows so she near vanish. And I ask, what a nigger man doing so far 'way from the quarters so late at night?"

"Oh, we knew she wasn't up to no good, Mr. Jeppson."

"She go right to that old graveyard, and she kneel down by a tree, and she got some candles and cornmeal—"

"And that's when we grabbed her and found out she was a wench. Reckon I saved this nigger's life, when she pulled out that knife. But what's she doing out there with candles and cornmeal?"

Jeppson's grin widened at the sight of the frightened face. "Why, she was making a spell. Ain't that right, Zulie? Our Zulie here is a witch, Mr. Pickett! She's a sorceress, a conjurewoman, and she thought she come over here and put a curse on her old friend Balbo Jeppson. Ain't that right, wench?"

Zulie didn't answer, didn't move.

"She ain't said a goddamn word since we caught her, Mr. Jeppson," Pickett said. "Not a goddam word."

"That's all right. We'll teach her to talk. Sabin, drag her out of there, and you, Mr. Pickett, get me a whip."

The Breakline slave rolled out of the way as Sabin rushed into the jail. Zulie struggled, but Sabin managed to pull her arms behind her and drag her out through the open doorway.

"Now you know what to do with her, Sabin. The same as with any other wench that needs punishing bad."

Sabin tried but it wasn't easy, and he needed the help of two other drivers. Zulie fought them silently every minute, kicking out at them, shouldering them away, teeth flashing at them.

"Mr. Jeppson . . ." Jeppson felt a touch on his arm and turned to look into Sheba's pained eyes. "Mr. Jeppson, maybe you don't have to do this. And she ain't even ours. Maybe if you wait—"

"You got too soft a heart, Miss Lady. This here is nothing but a criminal nigger wench, and she can get Adaba for us. And there ain't no point in putting off what's got to be done. We got her, and we might as well get started tonight."

And so they dragged her to the whipping gallows. And piece by piece, ripped off her clothes, stripping her naked.

If anyone from the quarters had not known of the capture of Zulie, he did now. Every slave was present. When a black was punished, for whatever reason, Jeppson liked to have the others watch, as a warning. More torches were lit, and he looked around to see black faces frightened, sullen, angry—and a few excited.

"All right, get her up there."

The gallows was built tall so all could see. The drivers tied ropes to Zulie's wrists and threw the free ends over the cross beam. As they began pulling her up, angry tears flowed down her cheeks, but she still had not uttered a sound.

"All you got to do, Zulie," Jeppson said, "is tell us where Adaba is. And how to get him."

She hardly struggled as her ankles were tied to the two side posts of the gallows. Jeppson stepped behind her, working his shoulders to loosen them up. They still hurt badly, but this was one whipping he intended to administer himself.

"By God!" Pickett said, awed, as he stood before Zulie, looking up at her torchlit body. "By God, she is something, ain't she? That's as handsome a breeding wench as I ever seen. I wouldn't mind having me some of this when you're through—"

"Keep your hands off her," Jeppson snarled, as Pickett reached for her. "You put a hand on her, and I'll take that hand off you!"

Startled, Pickett snatched his hand away. "Mr. Jeppson, I wasn't gonna hurt her none!"

"You got no cause to touch her. Just stay away from her."

As Jeppson uncoiled the long blacksnake whip, it seemed to come alive in his hand.

"One last chance, wench," he said. "Tell us about Adaba. Talk."

Zulie said nothing.

And Jeppson was glad.

He snapped the whip once, twice, three times, as if limbering it up, knowing how frightening the shotlike sounds could be. He could see the ripple of muscles in Zulie's back, the clenching of her buttocks, as she braced herself for the first blow.

He brought the whip back and shook it. Not too hard, he reminded himself. He didn't want her passing out. He wanted her to feel every stripe.

He brought the whip forward, a good cutting blow that sliced across her on a diagonal just below the shoulders. Her body arched forward, her head snapped back, her mouth opened in a silent scream. A thin trickle of blood ran down her back.

There was no hurry. He flexed his arms. He resettled his feet. When he felt ready, he drew back the whip, took aim, and delivered a stripe across the buttocks that drew blood. The was no sound from Zulie, but a moan from the crowd.

"Talk!"

He whipped her again.

He felt better every moment. He wasn't simply whipping a woman. He was whipping the whole foul world that had turned against him. He was whipping Sabrehill He was whipping Lewis Sabre. He was whipping Miss Lucy, and Justin Sabre, the abolitionist, and Adaba, the slave-stealer. He was getting back at them all, and every blow of the whip got harder.

"Talk!"

Again, the whip cut across Zulie's buttocks.

"Talk!"

Across her shoulders.

"Talk!"
Across her back.
"Talk! . . ."

Adaba arrived back at Sabrehill before dawn but later than he would have wished. Fortunately, it was the darkest part of the year, and the workday on the plantations began much later than it did in the spring. Still, he lingered in a grove north of the field quarters for a few minutes to be sure he was safe. When he saw no one, he swiftly crossed the open ground to Zulie's cabin. He looked into it on the off chance that she might be there, and not finding her, hurried away from the quarters and back into the woods, then on in the general direction of the big house.

When he came to the overseer's house, he saw light in the kitchen and the passage, and smiling to himself, he resisted the temptation to pay Lew a call, worry him a little, and beg some coffee. He had promised Zulie that he would be gone only a week, ten days at the most, and ten days were almost up. She would be as worried about him as he was eager to see her.

Quickly, he entered the coach house, closing the door behind him. He found the stairs in the dark and felt his way up them. He started to tap on the door, which Zagreus almost always barred at night, then, on impulse, tried opening it. To his surprise, it gave way to the pressure of his hand. He pushed up the door and went up a couple more steps.

"Who that?" It was Zagreus's worried voice.

"Only me."

Adaba went the last few steps up into the room and shut the door. Zagreus slid out of bed and, a shadow in the dawn gloom, began to dress. Binnie, in bed, lay still, and Adaba kept his voice low in order not to disturb her.

"How you been, Zag?"

"Oh, I been all right." The note of worry was still in his voice. "You get them people away safe?"

"Oh, yes, they're safe. Honest to Moses, Zag, sometimes I don't see why black people don't just walk off the plantations and go north in *droves,* it seems so easy. Then

394

I remember, they not only don't know the tracks and stations and signals the way I do, most of them don't have any clear idea of the lay of the country at all."

Adaba started for the next room.

Zagreus's voice shook: "She ain't there."

Adaba froze.

". . . Where is she?"

"I don't *know!*" The note of worry turned into something closer to anger. "That sister of mine! She say she going crazy in here, nothing to do but read them books Binnie sneaked out of the big house. Last night she say she has to *do* something, she has to *see* something 'sides these here walls!"

"Where did she go?"

"She say . . . she say she was going to Redbird."

Adaba had a suffocating sensation. "Why? What . . . ? Did she go to see Gil—Sheba?"

"No. She say she was just going put a spell on Mr. Jeppson, and she be back soon as she can."

Adaba sat down on a chair. Keep calm, he told himself.

He tried to keep his voice steady and confident. "Well, Zag, it still ain't quite light yet, and she has time to get here. Most likely, she'll be back any minute now. Could be too that she didn't feel like coming all the way back after all that spell-making, and she just curled up in the cabin of somebody she knows. Or she might even have curled up in the woods. She's a real fox when it comes to making her own warm little burrow that nobody can find."

That was true enough. And yet he knew he was speaking only to reassure himself. He didn't really believe that Zulie would let anything keep her away from the comfort and safety of her own room and bed at Sabrehill if she could help it. And with every passing minute, he felt himself growing a little sicker with fright. *Zulie, come back!*

Come for her! Sheba prayed desperately, as the sun, like a silver moon, climbed higher in a leaden sky. From the doorway of the house, she looked out beyond the yard and the jail and the whipping gallows, beyond fields and streams and woods, to a point where the road leading to the house disappeared in a grove of persimmon trees. *Come for your Zulie! Someone, please, please come for her!*

Sheba had done her best to stop Mr. Jeppson. "You shouldn't ought to whip her like that! She ain't our property!" "She's a runaway, and I got as much right to whip her as any patrol." "But you're cutting her bad! You get in trouble, cutting 'nother man's property!" "She's an Underground Railroader, and the property of a goddamn abolitionist, and ain't nobody gonna stop me from doing anything I want to her!"

And later: "Ain't no use whipping her more, Mr. Jeppson. She done passed out. She ain't feeling nothing now." "She's pretending. She ain't passed out, no more'n you. She's hearing every word we say. Ain't that right, Zulie?" "No, Mr. Jeppson, no, she ain't! Please . . ."

Something must have happened to him earlier at Sabrehill, Sheba thought, something bad, because even in his wildest angers, she had never seen him quite as he had been last night. It was as if something vital had come loose in him; he had a peculiar wildness in his eyes. But finally it had become apparent even to Mr. Jeppson that he was going to get no information from the captured woman that night. She was unconscious and could say nothing even if she wanted to. He had had her untied, wrapped in an old blanket, and dragged back into the jail. Sheba had attended to her wounds, trying to minimize any scars the whipping might cause, and had surreptitiously drugged her to reduce the pain. This morning Sheba had fed broth to the half-conscious woman and had again treated her whip marks and drugged her.

Why, Sheba asked herself now, oh, why hadn't she sent a messenger to Sabrehill? But there had seemed to be no need. Once the people were at work this morning, the news of Zulie's capture should have reached Sabrehill swiftly, and she had thought that Mr. Justin or perhaps Lewis Sabre would surely come at once. Miss Lucy herself had been known to come, pistol in hand, when someone was holding one of her people. Yes, Sheba had told herself, someone would surely come soon, and meanwhile, Jeppson would sleep long and deeply—as she had insured last night—and Zulie would lie undisturbed. But hours had passed, and still no one appeared.

Lord, please, she continued to pray with all the strength of her soul, *please send someone before it's too late! before he wakes up and puts her on that gallows again and kills her! Please!*

As if in answer to her prayers, a carriage emerged from the persimmon trees. With a feeling of relief, she stepped out of the house and squinted toward the carriage, trying to see who was in it. The broken lock on the jail door hadn't been replaced, and it wouldn't do to let the visitor simply remove the bars and take Zulie away. The Lord only knew what that would do to Mr. Jeppson, after his recent losses. No, Mr. Justin, or whoever was coming, would have to speak to Mr. Jeppson and make him see reason. He would have to show at least that much respect. And perhaps she had best awaken Mr. Jeppson right now, but first . . .

As the carriage approached, she saw with dismay that it brought neither Mr. Justin nor some other person who might be Mr. Lewis Sabre grown twenty years older. It brought Mr. Tucker and Mr. Macon, two of the people she wished least to see in all the world.

"Sheba!" Tucker called out as he reined up the horses. "It true what we been hearing this morning?"

"Don't know what you been hearing this morning, Mr. Tucker," Sheba said with no pretense of friendliness.

Tucker laughed. "Then I reckon it ain't true, or you'd know. Or maybe Sheba Lady is just funning Mr. Macon and me."

Sheba remained silent, hating the way the two men, and especially Tucker, looked at her as they got out of the carriage and came toward the door.

"Mr. Jeppson 'round?" Tucker asked.

"He still sleeping. He was up real late last night."

"Well, you just wake that lazy bastard up and tell him—"

"Hell, P.V.," Macon said, "let him sleep. If he got that Zulie here, he got her in the jail house, and we can go look for ourself."

"Yeah, that's right." Grinning, Tucker raked his eyes

397

over Sheba. "Heard he whipped her good and flung her in there naked. And me, I always did 'preciate seeing a handsome wench naked—as Sheba here knows."

"Seeing, hell," Macon said, turning toward the jail. "I like spreading 'em. And I remember that Zulie—them goddamn long legs and them tits."

"Oh, yeah, I remember too. But she sure ain't got what Sheba here got. Ain't that right, Sheba?"

"Old Vachel Skeet once told me he spread Zulie," Macon said. "Told me it was the best satisfaction he ever got from a wench. I think I'll just go out there to the jail house and find out what he was talking 'bout."

"Rolly Joe, I think I'll just join you."

With a last grin at Sheba, Tucker followed Macon toward the jail. Sheba's face was hot with anger and disgust, but she had no time to think about that. Only Zulie mattered now. There was no telling what assaults, what indignities, the two white men might inflict on the helpless woman. But would they be any worse than the continued whipping, and perhaps other tortures, Mr. Jeppson would give her? Possibly not, Sheba thought; but if the choice were Zulie's, she would almost certainly prefer the whipping.

Sheba hurried back into the house and up the stairs to awaken Mr. Jeppson. There was only one thing to do, she decided as she shook the groggy man in his bed. The morning was almost over, and before long Zulie would be back on the gallows. Time and again, Sheba had told herself that by now—by now, at last—someone was surely on the way from Sabrehill. But she could no longer trust in that probability. She had to assume that no one in authority there—no white person—had yet learned of Zulie's capture. Therefore someone had to be informed. Somehow she had to get word to Sabrehill.

What could he do? The question was like a scream, echoing unceasingly in Adaba's mind.

They knew now. After the long, painful waiting, their fears had been confirmed. By sheer chance, it had taken this long for word to be passed from one black to another until it reached Zagreus; and immediately thereafter, the

398

boy Bishop had arrived with his message from Sheba: "Miss Lady say tell Mr. Justin and Mr. Lewis that Mr. Jeppson got Sabrehill's Zulie. . . ."

Adaba sat on the edge of his bed in the room over the coach house, feeling sick and scared. Never before, not even when he had suffered gunshot wounds, had he felt such terrible dread.

"What we going *do?*" Zagreus asked. "Mr. Justin ain't back home yet! And Mr. Lewis, old Jeppson likely kill him if he go there after what happen last night! What we going *do?*"

"I don't know," Adaba said, "I don't know yet, let me *think!*"

Why had it taken so long for the news to reach Sabre-hill? Why had Zulie had to endure so much, and what kind of hell was she going through at this moment?

". . . And then this morning," Bishop had said, "Mr. Tucker and Mr. Macon come, and they doing things to her, when Mr. Jeppson come out all mad. And he cuss them out, but he let them watch when he tie her up on the whipping gallows again. . . ."

The panic, the fear for Zulie, the sickness in his gut made clear thought almost impossible. All he knew was that somehow he had to get Zulie away from Jeppson before he killed her. But he hadn't a chance in hell of stealing her from the Redbird jail as he had stolen the two Buckridge slaves. They would be waiting for him. Indeed, according to Bishop, Jeppson's highest hope was that Adaba might try to rescue Zulie. "He just waiting for that old Brown Dove. . . ."

"Miss Lucy," Adaba said. "Didn't you tell me she once went to Redbird and brought back a slave they were holding—"

Zagreus shook his head angrily. "That was long time ago. And Skeet was at Redbird then, not Jeppson. Jeppson ain't going do *nothing* for Miss Lucy, 'specially after last night!"

"Then, goddammit, you've just got to tell Lew. You've got to tell him to get some law out here, to send for the constable, and . . ."

Adaba broke off, shaking his head. No, that wasn't the

answer. It would take hours, perhaps even days, to get the law to Redbird, to get due process, to get the whole matter straightened out, and in that time Zulie could die. Besides, as a reputed Underground Railroader, she very well might wind up in the jail at Riverboro, and then at the end of a rope, rather than safely back at Sabrehill.

But he had to do *something,* he had to do it *now.* He could not stay hidden in this upstairs room, sending messages by Zagreus, trying to get other people to do what had to be done. Somehow, he himself had to act.

And why not? Who here knew him as Adaba? Not Miss Lucy or any of her neighbors. Even Justin Sabre, had he been here, might not have recognized him. He could go to Miss Lucy, put on his best face, apologize for his rough appearance, since he was traveling on foot. Try to disarm her suspicions and hope that Lew would play along. Tell her something close to the truth—that he was John Guerard of the Charleston Guerards, and that knowing his sister and his brother-in-law were here, he had stopped by to see them. And on arriving, he had learned that one of Sabrehill's people was being held by a certain Mr. Jeppson. He thought she should know at once.

Of course, under the circumstances, he would be taking a huge risk. From what Zagreus had said, Jeppson already had some accurate suspicions, and he wouldn't be slow to noise them about. But what did that matter? At the moment, Adaba didn't give a damn about his own safety or the good of the Underground Railroad or anything else other than Zulie. Perhaps Denmark Vesey had been capable of sacrificing others to a cause, but there, Adaba now realized, the two of them parted ways. To Adaba nothing else in the world mattered if personal loyalty and love didn't come first.

"What we going *do?*" Zagreus asked.

Adaba told him.

The lady was no fool, he saw at once. The large blue eyes were turned on him as if he were some kind of exotic. And not simply because he was a black man with a white sister—his half-sister, he tactfully emphasized. And not because he spoke like an educated white gentleman. And

400

not because he was a rich man's son with the appearance of a woodsman and traveling on foot—he had given her a cock-and-bull story about his horse going lame. Even if Lucy accepted all of that, she had sensed almost at once that she was not being told everything. She had glimpsed Lew's anger when Adaba and Zagreus had appeared at the door of the plantation office; she had seen Adaba defy that anger; she had felt Lew's anger turning into something quite different as Zagreus reported Zulie's capture.

"My husband might return at any moment, and I wish he were here right now. But we can't wait for him, not if Mr. Jeppson is abusing that poor woman. I'll just have to go after her myself."

"Cousin Lucy," Lew said, "from all I've heard and seen of that man, he's not about to give up your Zulie to you."

"He won't be the first to have had that idea."

Adaba might have smiled at another woman as she reached for the six-shot pepperbox pistol that lay before her on her desk. But something in those cold blue eyes told him she was quite capable of using it without hesitation or remorse.

"Mrs. Sabre," Adaba said quickly, "there must be another way to get the woman back. Surely you have neighbors who will go to this Redbird plantation for you, friends who will see to it that Mr. Jeppson behaves properly."

"Some of them might, yes. But I'm afraid they would prefer to see Zulie jailed rather than returned to Sabre-hill." Lucy's eyes held Adaba's, searching for a reaction. "Perhaps you don't know, John, that Zulie is a runaway and supposedly a part of the Underground Railroad. Some say she's a member of a group responsible for a great number of slaves escaping around here in recent years. They say she's one of Adaba's people. Have you heard that, John?"

The blue eyes were blinking and unwavering.

'Why, no, ma'am, Mrs. Sabre," Adaba said carefully. "I just arrived here, of course, and I can't say I've heard anything about that in Charleston. Perhaps you're not altogether unhappy that your Zulie has been caught."

Adaba saw the slightest tightening about Lucy's eyes, a

401

kind of wince—an instant, he was sure, in which she suspected mockery; and when in anger and frustration, she was tempted to slap out at him. He began to like her.

"John," Lew said, "we don't wish anybody into Jeppson's hands. Not black or white. Not slave or free or runaway. Saying that to Miss Lucy is almost like insulting her."

"Then I apologize to Miss Lucy."

"That's quite all right." Rising from the desk, Lucy turned to Zagreus, who stood in the doorway. "If you'll get me a carriage, Zagreus. The cabriolet should do—"

"No." Lew took the pistol from Lucy's hand. "You're not going. I am."

"I'll go with you," Adaba said quickly, but they both ignored him.

"You can't, Lew," Lucy said, "not after last night. If you so much as set foot on Redbird, that man will kill you. But he won't dare touch me."

"He's not going to kill me." Lew examined the pistol. "Not while I have this."

"But it's very unreliable—"

"They all are. I wish I had one of those newfangled Colt pistols, they're supposed to be better. But at least if the first load in this thing doesn't fire, I'll have five more."

Lucy hesitated. "Lew, I wish you wouldn't. I wish you'd let me—"

"Cousin Lucy, I kind of have to, don't I? Not just because I'm the overseer here. I'm a Sabre, and while Justin is away, I'm the man on the place." Still speaking to Lucy, Lew looked at Adaba. "You might say, it's a family matter."

"Well . . . at least let me send for one or two people who might stand by you—"

"There isn't time for that."

"You could stop by Kimbrough Hall and ask the major—"

"Who'd prefer to see the woman in jail in Riverboro. I think I'd better just go get her myself."

"I told you I'd go with you," Adaba said tensely.

"No. I'm not taking any strange black man to Redbird.

The way Jeppson's been acting these days, that would be asking for trouble. But I will take Zagreus with me."

Zagreus was sent to hitch up a carriage that would take two and bring back three. Lucy told Lew to try to placate Jeppson by offering him a reward of five hundred dollars —"Oh, God, offer him more, if you have to! Offer him anything he wants! Just bring Zulie and yourselves back safely!"

The sky had darkened, and as they left the office, lightning struck in the distance, and thunder rumbled ominously. A steady drizzle had begun to fall. Miss Lucy was called to the kitchen house for some minor emergency, and Adaba followed Lew along the east lane toward the coach house.

The carriage was not ready yet: one horse had a bad hoof and another had thrown a shoe. Such delays were inevitable, but every moment seemed to Adaba to stretch into an age, an age in which Zulie might be suffering, and not in years had he felt so close to complete panic. He almost threw Zagreus and his brothers aside to do the job himself.

"Goddamn, Zag, that's my woman at Redbird—"

"That's our *sister!* Mr. Lew, make him get his ass away, and let us do what we got to do!"

Lew drew Adaba into the shelter of the coach house.

"Simmer down, now."

"How can I simmer down? thinking about Zulie hanging there—"

"She'll be all right. You know how these things get exaggerated."

"Lew, I have *seen* that whipping gallows! I have *seen* men hanging on it!"

"But not Zulie. All you've got is a tale—"

"I'm going with you," Adaba said again. "Goddammit, I'm going—"

"Don't be a damn fool. Jeppson's just waiting and hoping you'll come for her. He's certain I know who and where Adaba is, and you're just asking me to deliver you into his hands. And if I do that, you'll be as dead as—as your old Denmark Vesey."

Adaba stared at Lew, and for the moment, thoughts of

Zulie faded. Not in fifteen years had he heard Lew voluntarily speak of Denmark.

"You think about Denmark?"

"Think about him?" Lew said irritably. "Of course I think about him. I must have tried a thousand times to puzzle out the rights and wrongs of old Denmark and why I felt so bad that night, just doing what I had to do."

"And you regret—"

"No," Lew said sharply, "I don't regret a goddamn thing. You say I'm the man that killed Denmark. Well, maybe you're right. I knew that, innocent or guilty, he didn't have a prayer in that court, so maybe I do have his blood on my hands. But let me tell you this, John. I concluded a long time ago that a man who's worth his salt can't get through life without getting some blood and muck and dirt on his hands. Not Denmark or you or me. So I *don't* regret what I did to Denmark, and I don't apologize for it, not one bit."

"But he was a good man, a great man, and he had the right—"

"I don't give a damn how good or great or right he might have been. He was a threat to my family. He was a threat even to you, whether you know it or not. And anybody who threatens me or mine damn well better be ready to answer for it. If he makes so much as a move against them, I'm ready to kill the son of a bitch myself, and to hell with all great and holy causes."

And that, Adaba realized, was the real reason Lew was going after Zulie. Not because he was the overseer or even, as he had told Miss Lucy, because he was a Sabre and, in Justin's absence, the man on the place. Zulie was his brother-in-law's woman, his old friend's wife. And the bitterness that had come between Lew and Adaba over the years was irrelevant. In the office, Lew had looked directly at Adaba and stated his reason, his creed, the principle of his honor: *"You might say, it's a family matter."*

And was he so different from Lew?

"Yes," he heard himself saying, "I understand. I understand. . . ."

Zagreus gave a call that the carriage was ready. Instantly, Lew was out of the coach house and springing up

404

onto the seat beside Zagreus. He called back to tell Rose that he would return as soon as possible, and taking the reins, he drove away.

And now it was Adaba's turn to stand in the rain for a long time without moving.

The drizzling rain had all but stopped by the time they reached Redbird, but the sky was quite dark except for an occasional flash of lightning. There was light in the slave quarters, but no sound of music, no sign of festivities, even though it was Saturday evening. Redbird was quiet, brooding, waiting.

As they emerged from a grove of persimmon trees, Lew saw the lights of the big house and the kitchen, and Zagreus pointed out the dark bulk of the jail. "The place no slave want to go," he said. "Long as I remember, the place they go to get broke."

"I don't see the whipping gallows you've been telling me about."

"On the far side of the jail, Mr. Lew. You see it soon."

Lew took the pepperbox pistol from his coat pocket and stuck its unwieldy bulk into his belt, fastening one coat button over it.

They had been seen. Even in this dismal weather, a few people were out and about, and near the big house and the kitchen, dark figures moved, paused to look toward them, moved again. Lew felt his nerves sharpening, and he wondered if he were a fool to have come here with only Zagreus. He had no worries about handling Jeppson, and he figured he could bull down the other two he had heard about, the white man Pickett and the driver Sabin. But if Jeppson had some of his other friends about, it might not be so easy.

As they rounded the jail they saw the tall gallows and, hanging stretched within its frame, a woman. A flash of lightning revealed her to be Zulie, unclothed, rain-drenched, still as death.

Zagreus gave a cry of pain and jumped out of the carriage. Lew reined up and followed him. Zagreus cried out again as he circled Zulie and saw the whip marks on her body. He reached up and lifted her face.

"She dead, Mr. Lew!" he sobbed. "I think she dead!"

Lew pressed his fingertips into the side of Zulie's throat. He found a pulse, weak but steady.

"No, she isn't. But we've got to get her down from here and get her warm." He leaned down and began untying one of Zulie's ankles. "We'll wrap her up in our coats and take her back to Sabrehill. Your sister is going to be all right, Zagreus."

"And her carrying Adaba's baby! You know she got a baby in her, Mr. Lew?"

"No, I didn't, but—"

They were interrupted by a laugh, a single triumphant syllable, and Lew looked around to see Jeppson standing twenty feet away, pistol in hand.

"So you come to Redbird, did you, Mr. Nigger-Lover," he said, grinning.

Any faint illusion Lew might have had that he could be conciliatory with Jeppson vanished. He saw he would have to be as hard and as threatening as the man himself.

"Yes, I've come to Redbird," he said angrily, "and you know why. What the hell kind of man are you, Jeppson, to hang up a woman like this and whip her and leave her hanging in the rain? And who gave you the right to whip her anyway?"

"*She* gave me the right! When her and that Adaba stole from me—"

"You're in trouble, Jeppson, bad trouble. You're holding a Sabrehill slave, and you know it. And you know there's laws against that."

"I know there's laws against slave-stealing, and this here wench is a thief—"

"There's only one thief here, and that's you. I can have you jailed, fined, maybe even hung for holding Sabrehill property, and I'd like nothing better. Now, I'm taking this woman with me—"

Jeppson came forward a couple of paces, his pistol held at ready. "You're doing nothing of the kind, Mr. Nigger-Lover."

"I'm taking her with me," Lew repeated, "but I've got orders to treat you fairly—though I personally don't think

406

the Sabres owe you one damn thing. So if you don't want to hear me out, just say so."

For an instant, Jeppson looked uncertain. "What the hell are you talking about?"

"The wench is a fugitive, a runaway. The Sabres will pay you for your trouble in catching and holding her. Damned if I know why, after the way you've treated her. But Miss Lucy says there's a five-hundred-dollar reward for her, and it's yours if you want to claim it. Otherwise, you get nothing but trouble with the law and a lot of it. Take your choice."

Jeppson stared at him. And then began laughing again. Lew saw from the light in the man's eyes that there would be no dealing rationally with him. Balbo Jeppson was beyond reason now, a creature of his own half-mad passions.

Lew's hand was on the one fastened button of his coat. He eased the coat open.

"Well, Jeppson?"

Jeppson tried to subdue his laughter. "You said something about burying me at Sabrehill, Mr. Nigger-Lover. But if you don't get away from that wench and move out fast, maybe I'll just bury you at Redbird. You and your nigger boy. I could do it, and nobody would ever know."

Someone, a woman, was running from the big house toward Jeppson.

"You're not that big a fool, Jeppson. You know you'd hang."

"Who'd testify against me? Ain't a white man in sight 'cept you and me, and black can't testify against white."

Lew feigned impatience. "Jeppson, the offer still stands. Five hundred dollars. But if that woman hangs there much longer, she's going to fever and die, and you'll be accountable. Now, do you want the reward or not?"

Jeppson only laughed again. He flourished his pistol. Suddenly his eyes widened as he saw the butt of the pepperbox under Lew's hand.

Lew had had no intention of drawing the pepperbox if he could avoid it. But Jeppson didn't know that and probably didn't want to know it. As he saw the weapon, he roared and brought his own pistol down level.

But by that time Lew had the pepperbox out and aimed. "Mr. Jeppson, don't! Oh, my God," the woman screamed, "don't!"

Adaba had not told Lew. There had been little opportunity and no thought of telling him. In the short time they had been together that afternoon, their sole concern had been Zulie.

Now Lew saw her, the face out of his guilty dreams, the face of his first, betrayed love, the face so long forgotten and yet unforgettable. After twenty years, the same face.

Gilly!

All thought of Jeppson was swept from his mind in that instant. There was only Gilly before him after all this time, and he was trying to cry out her name.

Gilly!

He never heard Jeppson's pistol go off. It was as if lightning had struck. It seemed to strike into his skull, smashing it into a thousand burning pieces. He had time only for one last angry thought, the thought that he had failed. Failed Adaba. Failed Zulie and Zagreus. Failed Rose and his children, and Cousin Lucy, and Gilly so long ago, failed one and all. Failed.

Eight

Sheba blamed herself. By trying to save Lew, she had distracted him, and in horror, she saw the blaze of fire from the pistol barrel, saw Lew's head kick back and throw blood, saw him fall. The pepperbox flew away from his hand as if he had flung it. Zagreus cried out, but stood frozen as Jeppson scooped the pepperbox up from the ground and aimed it at him.

"He dead?" Jeppson asked almost gleefully.

Sheba couldn't answer. She could only stare down at the half-familiar face, dimly visible in the night. It was easier to see the boy he had once been, the thirteen-year-old who had been both friend and betrayer to Adaba and her.

"He dead?" Jeppson repeated.

"I don't know." And she knelt down beside Lew.

Blood flowed freely from a long gash through the flesh, and she thought there might be a furrow through the bone. That, she knew, would probably be fatal. When she held Lew's wrist, she could barely discern a pulse, and she could detect no breathing at all.

"I think he's dying, Mr. Jeppson. I think the ball break his head. I don't know if I can help him or not."

"Well, to hell with him. Let him die." Jeppson's eyes were the brightest things in the night.

"Mr. Jeppson, you can't kill a white man like that! They hang you—"

"Ain't nobody gonna hang me. He come here armed and pulled a pistol on me, and ain't nobody gonna say otherwise. Not about a nigger-thieving, abolitionist Sabre."

"Let me try to help him, Mr. Jeppson. Then can't nobody say you just let him die. You got truth on your side."

Even Jeppson liked to have truth on his side. He shrugged. "Suit yourself. But keep him in the jail. First chance I get, if he lives, I'll turn him over to the constable." Jeppson looked at Zagreus. "I know you, don't I, boy."

Zagreus looked both grieved and terrified.

"Well, speak up!"

"Yes, sir, Mr. Jeppson. You know me."

"Zagreus, brother to Zulie, here. You see, I never forget. Zagreus, married to a wench with a whiter skin than my own. Nearly got you lynched a few years back, when people thought she really was white, didn't it?"

"Yes, sir, Mr. Jeppson—"

"But you lived through it. Now let's see if you can live through this. 'Cause I'm gonna take your sister down off that whipping gallows, Zagreus, and I'm gonna put you up. I figure if your sister knows about Adaba, likely you do too. And you're gonna tell me, Zagreus, you're gonna tell me all you know."

No, Sheba thought. *No, you ain't, Zagreus. You mustn't! You be like your sister. If you can hold out for just a little while, maybe Adaba . . .*

She banished the thought. If there was any one thing in the world that Adaba must not do, it was to come to Redbird and attempt to rescue the captives. The one hope, the only hope, was that Zulie and Zagreus could hold out until Mr. Justin arrived—as Sheba was certain he inevitably would. Mr. Jeppson had shot Lewis Sabre, but Mr. Justin would be forewarned by Lewis's failure to return home. Mr. Jeppson would surely not succeed in doing such a thing twice.

Pickett and Sabin and a couple of other drivers, drawn by the shot, had come running. Jeppson gave them their orders. Sheba wished there were some way she could drug Zagreus as she had drugged Zulie, and thereby save him pain, but she foresaw no opportunity.

"You got a long night ahead of you if you don't talk, boy," Jeppson promised, as the other men dragged Zagreus toward the gallows. "And after that, you got a long day ahead, and it's gonna go on and on and on. . . ."

Zagreus, be silent!

"Miss Lucy, I can't stand this waiting any longer. I'm going to Redbird."

"No, John, you mustn't!"

Adaba felt caged. Night had fallen, the hours continued to slip by, and still Lew had not returned. There could be only one reason. He had failed. He and Zagreus—God only knew what Jeppson had done to them, as well as to Zulie.

Rose was on the verge of hysterics. Only the need not to frighten the children gave her some semblance of calm. Lucy had told her to bring the children to the big house and spend the night, and she was upstairs with them at this moment. Adaba paced the library, pretending to inspect the books, while Lucy stared at him with an open curiosity that he found disconcerting. Leila, the housekeeper, had entered the room uninvited and plunked herself down in a chair. She appeared to ignore the other two, but she wore an angry frown on her pretty face, and her knitting needles clicked furiously.

Oddly enough, under the circumstances, the afternoon and early evening had, on the surface, passed quite

410

pleasantly. Adaba had bathed and allowed Lucas to barber him. Lucy had produced some old but clean clothes for him. He had eaten supper with Rose in the overseer's house and played with the children of both families. Later, he had gone to the big house and talked about Charleston and "the old days" with Lucy. She had known more about him and his anomalous position in life than he would have guessed. But all the time he had felt as if a scream were welling up inside him, until now he could hardly hear Lucy's next words.

"John, I can understand your concern for your brother-in-law, but your going to Redbird would do absolutely no good. And you don't know how bad that man Jeppson can be. I myself have seen him lynch a free black man for carrying a pistol—"

"I've heard about that."

"Then surely you understand that you must not take such a risk!"

"But, Miss Lucy, I've got to *know*—"

At the look of puzzlement in Lucy's eyes, Adaba broke off and turned away. He knew what she was seeing, what he could no longer hide. Deep concern, even desperate worry, for a brother-in-law was one thing. But this was more like fear for a loved one. It seemed to ooze from the very surface of his skin.

"John, my husband could be back at any time now—"

"With all respect, Miss Lucy, you've been saying that since this afternoon."

"But it's still true. And I've sent for the constable. As soon as he gets here, either my husband or I will go with him to Redbird."

"Miss Lucy, it's Saturday night, and you aren't going to see that constable until Monday, I'd bet on it. And you yourself have said that if Jeppson is abusing Zulie, we can't wait! So, if you'll allow me to leave now . . ."

For a moment, Lucy didn't answer. She merely stared at him as if considering a new and surprising set of possibilities. Then she came to him and put her hand on his.

"John, please. If you must go to Redbird, I can hardly stop you. But don't go there with the intention of confronting Mr. Jeppson."

Adaba shook his head vigorously. "Ma'am, I have *no* intention of confronting Mr. Jeppson. I want only to determine if our people are in that jail of his, and how well he's got it guarded, and how I can get our people out."

"Then you do that. But don't go yet. Wait so that you'll arrive a little before dawn. That's when you'll be safest."

Reluctantly, Adaba agreed. He knew that what she said was only common sense—he would have given the same advice to another. But he was beyond common sense. He would leave for Redbird, he decided, as soon as he could get away from the house.

"Now, if you'll excuse me, I want to speak to cook about some coffee. . . ."

Aside from the clicking of her needles, Leila, the housekeeper, had been so quiet that Adaba had almost forgotten her, but Lucy was hardly out of the room when she was on her feet and facing him.

"Boy," she said, "you gonna do just like Miss Lucy say!"

"*Boy?*" Even at this moment, Adaba could be amused by the small woman's anger.

Leila shook her knitting in Adaba's face. "You may think you fooling her, and maybe you are—though she knows more about what goes on out in the quarters than she lets on. But you ain't fooling *me!* Just 'cause I'm a house servant don't mean I don't know. Now, Miss Lucy had her full share of trouble, and you and that Black Buck and your damn Underground Railroad ain't the least cause. So you steal away all the niggers you want, Mr. John *Adaba* Guerard, but if you cause more trouble and sorrow for Miss Lucy, you gonna answer to *me!*"

Leila strode out of the library looking a full six inches taller, while Adaba stared after her.

It was as if the sound of the whip told Sheba—the sound of the whip as it cut across Zagreus's back. And it was in Zagreus's screams and in the moans of the slaves as they stood watching. Sheba had heard those sounds too many times in the past twenty years, and now an ending had been reached, an ending as inevitable as the last tick of a clock whose time has run out. Sheba didn't

412

even have to make a decision. It had been made for her long ago, and its moment had now arrived.

Zagreus's last scream was like a dying sigh. His head fell forward, and his body went slack. But Jeppson was not done yet. He laid the whip across Zagreus's back three more times in rapid succession before Sheba could step forward and put a hand on his arm. In the past, Jeppson had always administered punishment systematically, with a kind of cold, narrow-eyed anger. Now his eyes were wild, his laughter uncontrolled, his movements erratic.

"No more, Mr. Jeppson."

"He ain't told us nothing yet." Jeppson's voice was hoarse and weak.

"No more. Not tonight. It won't do no good."

Jeppson stood staring at Zagreus and panting from his exertions. After a moment, he reluctantly nodded. "No, I don't reckon it will. But in the morning . . ."

"Shall I take him down, Mr. Jeppson?" Pickett asked.

"Take him down, Pickett." Jeppson turned to the slaves who had been watching. "Now, you all listen to me, you niggers! I want you to spread the word I got Adaba's woman! Spread the word I got her brother too! Let everybody know!"

"How come you want them to do that, Mr. Jeppson?" Pickett asked, as the slaves moved back toward the quarters. "When that Mr. Justin Sabre finds out—"

"He ain't gonna find out," Jeppson said, grinning. "I heard he was in Charleston."

So Mr. Justin would not soon be coming for his people after all. But that didn't matter, now that Sheba knew what she was going to do.

"But what if that old Adaba hears you got his woman—"

"I hope he does hear, Mr. Pickett. That's my bait! Miss Lady, do you remember how Vachel Skeet caught Black Buck just before the Night of the Fires?"

"I 'member."

"He knew Buck was skulking 'round somewhere, just trying to get at him, Mr. Pickett. So he put his biggest and meanest hands out on patrol 'round this place. He promised that the one that caught Buck would get a week off work, all the food and whiskey he wanted, and three or four of the best wenches on the place to pleasure that whole time. And that did it. That's how he got Black Buck."

Sheba's voice shook. "But don't you 'member, Mr. Jeppson? He didn't get Adaba, Adaba got away! And Redbird was burned to the ground!"

Mr. Jeppson stared at her for a moment, then grinned. "But not this time, Miss Lady. Don't you worry none. This time I'm gonna get him." He turned to Pickett. "Mr. Pickett, it's likely Adaba already heard about Zulie, so we're gonna get them patrols out tonight. And I want you to see to it that there's two guards looking after the jail house all night, and I want you to check on 'em yourself from time to time."

"It's cold and wet, Mr. Jeppson," Sheba said quickly. "If you're gonna keep them boys out all hours, you surely better give them a little whiskey to keep them warm, or they all gonna come down sick."

"You're right, Sheba. You see to it. And see that Mr. Pickett and Sabin each gets an extra measure, 'cause they done so good, catching Zulie last night." Jeppson gave Pickett a hardy slap on the shoulder. "Who knows, maybe tonight you'll capture Adaba. He could be here anytime."

Yes, he could be. And she would have to act quickly, quickly!

In Mr. Jeppson's bedroom, the cedar logs in the fireplace gave off a spicy perfume, while the flames cast a flickering light and banished the damp chill. The bed was turned down, the whiskey and the glasses were on the tray, and all was in readiness—except Sheba.

Returning to her own room, she opened a large jewelry box that stood on a chest of drawers. The box contained a variety of adornments, most of them silver, with a semi-precious stone here and there. Except for some earrings and an occasional necklace, Sheba had worn none of it for several years.

Tonight she would wear a great deal of it. She would wear it for the last time.

414

Quickly, because she heard Mr. Jeppson entering the house, she stripped off her clothes. She selected a pair of ornate silver earrings and, standing before a wall mirror, put them on. She picked out a silver necklace to dangle between her breasts. Bracelets and bangles went on wrists, an upper arm, an ankle. Odd, she thought, that Mr. Jeppson so much liked to see her like this. But this was the way he had first seen her, in the slave-trader's office, and he had never forgotten.

Nor had she.

She heard Mr. Jeppson's footsteps on the stairs, and in spite of her sense of inevitability, she wondered how she could go through with this. Zagreus's screams were still fresh in her ears. She didn't really mind the jewelry, at times had even rather liked wearing it, but she'd rarely in her life felt as cold as she did at this moment. The very thought of pleasuring repelled her, sickened her, so that for a few minutes she had to sit in a chair with her head down between her knees.

Never mind. She would do what she had to do.

She got up from the chair. From a wardrobe she took out a negligee of white silk and slipped it on, lightly tying its sash. Mr. Jeppson was not much for pretty things, but he liked to please her, and this was one of the nicest gifts he had ever given her.

Without giving herself any further chance to think of what was to come, she left the room, crossed the upstairs passage, and stepped through Mr. Jeppson's doorway.

He stood by the bed, barefoot and bare chested, a glass of whiskey in his hand. The massive body was as lean and hard as a boy's, but the face was ravaged beyond its years. It seemed to Sheba that Mr. Jeppson had aged greatly in only a few weeks, and yet he still had some of the rough handsomeness of twenty years earlier.

She stood by the door, letting him look at her and understand why she was here.

"Why, Miss Lady," he said softly after a moment, "I thought you was angry with me."

"No, Mr. Jeppson, I ain't angry. But it always saddens me to see some poor boy or woman up on the whipping gallows. You know that."

"Gotta be done, Miss Lady."

"I understand that, Mr. Jeppson. Anyway, I ain't angry."

Mr. Jeppson's gaze, gentle now, all wildness gone, moved slowly down her silk- and silver-clad body and back up again. "No, I reckon you ain't. Been a long while since you fixed yourself up like that for me, Sheba."

"Then it's 'bout time."

Mr. Jeppson set his glass aside. "Whyn't you come over here to me?"

Still repelled by the thought of sex, still sickened by the sound of the whip and the smell of blood, she went to him and allowed him to draw her into his arms. His big, calloused hands moved gently over her as she had taught him, gently over curve of shoulder and back and breast, as if warming her.

"You know, Sheba Lady," he said huskily, "I never been much of a loving man. Except with you and maybe Redbird. With you, I forget all about right and wrong and everything else but the loving. I even find myself wondering why I got to have a jail house and a whipping gallows. Just want to sit in the sun with my Sheba, and let the people be, and listen to them sing. You soften a man, Sheba Lady. But I don't care. I got a real love for you."

Sheba found her throat tightening and tears coming to her eyes. Everything in the world seemed so wrong, so twisted, so wasted.

"And I got a real love for you, Mr. Jeppson," she said. "I want you to know that. I don't want you ever to forget that. No matter what."

"I ain't gonna forget it. Sometimes I feel like my whole life was nothing, till you come along, Sheba Lady. So I ain't never gonna forget it."

At last, a saving lust came to her, and she was able to do what she'd planned. Under Mr. Jeppson's touch, her nipples tingled and rose. Heat flooded her loins, and her mind blurred. Quickly, she fumbled at buckle and buttons and pulled his clothing away. The silk slid from her shoulders, and she found herself being lifted and carried to the bed. Kisses were exchanged, wet kisses, hungry kisses, on

416

every part of the body, until they could wait no longer. Spread wide, she parted the lips, and he entered.

"Oh, Mr. Jeppson . . ."

"Sheba . . ."

"Never forget."

"Ain't never gonna forget. Never . . ."

Mr. Jeppson slept.

For a time, she sat beside him on the bed, waiting to be sure, though there could hardly be a doubt. Pleasure and whiskey and laudanum had taken their toll as never before, and Mr. Jeppson lay like a fallen giant, his flesh shrunken and exhausted.

Once again, one last time, she had betrayed him. She wondered if it might not be kinder to cut his throat.

But there was no time for such thoughts. She had taken her last look at Mr. Jeppson, had given him her last kiss. From now on, she must be resolute, never looking back. And so, with hardly a glance at Mr. Jeppson, she drew the covers up over him, blew out the light, and left the room.

In her own room, she quickly took off the negligee and the bracelets and bangles. For some reason, it seemed wrong to take them with her, though she could have used the value they represented. She started to take off the earrings and the necklace then hesitated. Those, at least, she would keep.

She dressed warmly. She hurried downstairs to a cellar storeroom and brought back a large bag. She had no idea of what Adaba would advise her to take on a trip north, but she decided to take a few blankets, all the clothes she could carry, and her herbs and medicines. If necessary, she could always abandon some things later. She also picked out some clothes for Zulie.

When she was ready, she took the bag and the lamp from her room and hurried downstairs again, forcing herself to pass Mr. Jeppson's room without hesitating. *Never look back.*

She found Zulie's knife and sheath and the pepperbox pistol on a table in the passage, and she dropped them both into her large reticule. It seemed important that they be returned, and besides, she might need weapons before the night was over. Then she remembered the loaded pistol in the secretary in the parlor, and she got that and put it into her reticule too. Mr. Jeppson kept little money in the house, but she took the few dollars she could find.

In the passage again, she glanced around. What had she overlooked? *Never look back.*

But it was not, after all, that easy not to look back. She had come to Mr. Jeppson's plantation as little more than a child. She had spent almost twenty years with him, more than half of her life. Years of caring for him in sickness and in health. Years of toiling to make a good home for both of them. Years of mediating between him and his people. *Her* people . . .

Bearing his poor, lost child, laughing with him, weeping with him . . .

Loving him, hating him . . .

With a small cry of pain, she threw herself through the open doorway and out into the night.

After that, it was easy.

The two guards sitting on the bench in front of the jail were asleep—or passed out. The jug she had given them —more whiskey than Mr. Jeppson would have wished— lay empty on the ground. One of the guards moaned and shook his head. Sheba remembered that he had complained that he would have less chance than the patrollers of catching Adaba, and she showed no mercy. With all her strength, she brought the heavy barrel of Mr. Jeppson's pistol smashing down on his head. He fell from the bench and lay still.

Leonie and Bishop, following her instructions, had hitched the horses to the Sabrehill carriage again. Both children were tired and frightened but game, and Sheba praised them for being good Railroaders. With their help, she got some clothes onto Zulie—she had dressed Zagreus after treating his whip wounds—and loaded all three victims into the carriage. She bade Leonie and Bishop goodbye, climbed onto the driver's seat up front, and started off.

Now came the part that worried her the most. She didn't particularly fear Mr. Pickett or Sabin. She had

418

made sure that they, like the two guards, had received their full share of the drugged whiskey and that they had drunk it. But her supply of hoarded laudanum was limited, and there was no way of knowing that each and every patroller had received enough. It was far more likely that some of them were still walking their beats. One or another of them might easily see her and realize what she was up to.

She kept the pepperbox handy.

But once she was through the persimmon grove, she began to breathe easier. And with every step the horses took, she felt a growing exhilaration. It was a feeling so heady that at first she could not understand it. But at last the meaning came to her.

For almost twenty years she had lived a good life, as women's lives in this time and place went. She had been well fed, well clothed, and cherished. She had been allowed to do more or less as she pleased. She had had her books and a handful of friends like Serena and the power to do good. She had traveled somewhat—to Columbia, to Charleston (though that had frightened her), and a couple of times to Savannah. For almost twenty years she had led a life that any but the richer white women of the region might have envied.

But something had been missing. It had been missing for her entire life, until now.

Now she was rebelling. Rebelling as a slave, as a black, as a woman. For the first time in her life, she was truly setting her own course and going her own way, no matter what the consequences.

For the first time in her life, she felt truly free.

Dry-throated, nauseous, his head throbbing, Jeppson stared at the open door of the jail and tried to understand the enormity of what had happened.

Except for the Breakline slave, Nestor, who crouched in fright in a corner, the jail was empty. Zulie, Zagreus, Lewis Sabre—they were all gone.

And Sheba was gone with them.

"Mr. Jeppson," Pickett said, his voice shrill with panic, "I tried to wake you up, I tried for hours! The minute I seen what happened, I come to get you, but I couldn't get you up till now!"

"Shut up, Pickett."

"It was like you was sick on bad liquor. Like we was all sick, but you most of all."

Not sick, Jeppson thought. Drugged.

"You sure Sheba ain't around here somewhere?"

"She ain't nowhere, Mr. Jeppson. And Nestor swears it was her and a couple others that stole them three away. Sheba, Mr. Jeppson, I bet it's that goddamn Sheba been helping steal away the niggers all along!"

If Pickett had been within reach, Jeppson might have struck him. But he knew the man was probably right. Just two weeks ago, the Buckridge slaves had been stolen from the jail, with the help of Serena. And not only of Serena. He had slept that night as he but rarely slept, hearing nothing, never rousing up. He remembered that night with Sheba all too well.

And now, like a recurrent nightmare, exactly the same thing had happened, but this time he had slept all the morning away and had awakened feeling half-poisoned. And this time Sheba too was gone.

Sheba, the one person in the world he loved. Sheba, who was not black or white to him, but simply woman, his woman, the nearest thing he had to a wife, a family, a cherished mate. *Why?* he asked himself, as he stared at the open door of the jail.

But he knew why.

She had been corrupted. Corrupted by his enemies. Corrupted by their abolitionist talk, corrupted by tales of Adaba and the Underground Railroad, corrupted into thinking of herself not as *his* Sheba but as one of *them.* As one of the *niggers!*

"We're gonna get 'em back, Mr. Pickett," Jeppson said after a moment.

Some of the panic went out of Pickett's eyes. He was not about to be punished. Someone else was going to be punished.

"How, Mr. Jeppson? How we gonna get 'em back?"

"We know where they went. To Sabrehill."

Pickett's eyes lit up with excitement. "To Sabrehill, Mr.

Jeppson? Why'd they go there? Don't you reckon they hiding out in the woods somewhere—"

"That Lewis Sabre is half-dead, if he ain't dead already. Miss Lady would take him home—ain't no place else in the world she woulda took him. And them others, Zulie and Zagreus, ain't fit to travel, and they're Sabrehill niggers, so she woulda took them back there. That's where they are, and that's where we're gonna find 'em. And likely Adaba too."

"We going after 'em, Mr. Jeppson?"

"After Sheba and Zulie and Adaba. I don't give a damn about Mr. Lewis Sabre or Zagreus, though they're likely Underground Railroad. But Sheba is mine, and Zulie is mine since I caught her, and if Adaba is there, I'm gonna have him too. I'm gonna have 'em all, dead or alive, and then . . ."

And then vengeance—vengeance. Vengeance at last.

Nine

Vengeance—the word was honey on the tongue. The very thought that he would strike a blow against the Sabres was cleansing and healing, and it gave Jeppson new life. Saliva formed in his dry mouth, his sick stomach began to ease, and the throbbing in his head began to fade away.

Maybe they thought they had him beaten, those pretentious, holier-than-thou, hypocritical, nigger-loving aristocrats, but they were going to learn different. He had suffered their scorn too long. And the Sabres were the worst of all. Now at last he was going to claim his due.

He looked about the yard. Sabin stood a few feet away, still as stone, waiting to see where his master's fury would turn. Fenella and Abel stood in the kitchen door, big-eyed and staring. A few other blacks stood watching from a distance, curious, but hoping not to be observed. Jeppson grinned.

"Sabin, you got some niggers 'round here that ain't got nothing to do. I don't care if it is Sunday, if they just standing 'round the yard, put 'em to work."

The blacks instantly turned away and disappeared. Jeppson laughed, and Pickett laughed weakly with him.

"We got work to do too, Mr. Pickett."

Pickett brightened. "We going to Sabrehill today, Mr. Jeppson? You want me to go with you?"

"Not just you and me, Mr. Pickett. We got to find our friends right fast. First of all, we got to find P. V. Tucker and Tag Bassett and Rolly Joe Macon, and then they got to help us get our friends together. The right kind of friends, Mr. Pickett. No Buckridges or Kimbroughs or Pettigrews or their likes gonna do us any good now. We got to have friends that know how to handle niggers. And nigger-lovers like the goddamn Sabres."

Confidence began to flow back into Jeppson, confidence that came in the form of great surges of anger. He was not defeated yet, and nothing in the world could defeat the anger that he felt. It had served him well before—sometimes it seemed to him that he had built his life on it. Anger against those who controlled the wealth and the power of this world that he lived in, anger against those black inferiors who had to be driven into serving him, anger against anyone, black or white, who stood in his way. Only Sheba had been able to temper that anger. And now she was gone.

But he would have her back.

And what would he do with her when he had her back?

Blacks—slaves—had to be disciplined. He had always known that. They had to be punished for every transgression, for every mistake. They had to be kept in their place, always. And that was as true of Sheba as of any other . . . nigger.

She had to be taught.

As he turned looking about the yard, Jeppson's gaze fell on the whipping gallows.

In all the time he had had Sheba, it had never once occurred to him that he might someday put her up on that gallows. As the thought struck him now, he felt an instant of shock, and he was appalled by the idea. But a fresh

422

rush of anger came to him, and he knew he could do it. He would strip her naked, the same as any other errant wench, he would have her hauled up and spread-eagled, and before the entire population of Redbird, he himself would whip her. She would learn that, however privileged she might be on his plantation and in his house, she was still a nigger and a slave. *His* nigger and *his* slave.

He took a deep breath.

"Yes, sir, we got work to do, Mr. Pickett."

Pickett was fairly jumping with excitement. "We'll do it, Mr. Jeppson! When you figure we gonna ride on Sabre-hill?"

"Tonight, Mr. Pickett. Tonight."

The memory was vivid. The only time, as far as Adaba knew, that he had met Justin Sabre, he and Black Buck had been chained to opposite sides of a "cotton box," floating down the river . . . he wounded in his side and leg, and feverish . . . the whips of their drunken captors coming down on them again and again, putting them in such an agony that they hardly knew who else was on the box or what was happening . . . and then that night a quietly angry white man had poured more liquor down the men's throats, loosened the chains that held him and Buck, and sent them on their way. In the flickering torch-light of the river landing, they had hardly been able to see each other's face, but Adaba remembered Justin's voice clearly. *"I'm going to talk to the guard a minute or two, try to distract him. . . ."*

He recognized the voice now: a baritone with a mellow timbre, full but not musical. Standing by the passage door, Adaba could not quite make out what Justin was saying, but the sound carried from the carriage in the courtyard, where Justin stood talking to Lucy in the last light of dusk.

At last the two turned and started walking slowly toward the house, Justin's arm around Lucy's shoulders. Adaba backed away from the door, wondering again if he were doing the wisest thing by remaining here. Justin, if he recognized this strange black man in his house, knew him only as Adaba. But Adaba had identified himself to Lucy

423

as John Guerard, and there was no way to change that now.

Well, at least he knew where Justin Sabre's sympathies lay.

The instant that Justin and Lucy stepped through the door, Justin stopped, a half-frown frozen on his face. Lucy looked worriedly from one man to the other.

"Justin, dear, this is John—John Guerard, Rose's brother."

Justin didn't move, didn't speak, didn't blink.

"My sister," Adaba said, "tells me we might have met some years ago in Charleston, Mr. Sabre."

Justin continued to stare. The lamplight was warm on Adaba's face.

"Yes," Justin said after a moment, "I think we might have met before. But I'm not sure it was in Charleston."

"I can't think where else it might have been, sir. But in any case, I'm happy to renew the acquaintance."

Justin came slowly forward. His eyes never left Adaba's face, and Adaba remembered that on the cotton box Justin had had better opportunities to see him than he had had to see the white man.

"My wife tells me you wanted to go to Redbird last night to get some of our people back from Balbo Jeppson."

Lucy's laugh was uneven. "I kept John up all night drinking coffee. I didn't dare leave him alone for a minute for fear he'd go there. When I couldn't hold him back any longer, when he was saddling a horse to ride to Redbird —that was when Miss Lady came in the carriage with the others."

Justin sounded almost angry. "My God, John, how could you even think of doing such a thing—you, a black, and a slave at that, to go to that madman's place!"

"You seem to know something about me, sir."

"You're damn right I do. And I know what Jeppson would have done if he'd caught you."

"Well, Mr. Sabre, sir," Adaba drawled softly, "I had other plans than being caught."

At last Justin did something other than stare unblinkingly. He shook his head as if in disbelief. "You're either a mighty brave man," he said, "or a goddamn fool. But I want you to know something. One of those people you were going after, the woman Zulie, hasn't got much use for us whites, and I can't think of a reason in the world why she should. But she means a lot to us. About fifteen years ago, when I was damn near killed in a duel, she and her mother saved my life. I owe her my life, John. And I'm obliged to anybody who looks out for her or even tries. Do you understand me?"

"I'm sure that's something anybody can understand, Mr. Sabre."

Justin's laugh was a sharp, skeptical bark. "Not in the world I live in." He turned to Lucy. "Where are they? Lew and the others?"

"Lew is in your old room upstairs. Rose and Leila are with him now. I put Zulie in the downstairs bed chamber, where I can look after her. Zagreus insisted that he wanted to be in his own bed, out over the coach house with Binnie."

"And Miss Lady?"

Lucy glanced at Adaba.

"Gone," Adaba said.

The frown returned to Justin's face. "What do you mean? Gone where? Surely she didn't go back to Redbird."

Adaba shrugged. "Could be she did. She's just gone. I don't know where she is, and neither does Miss Lucy. She brought Lew and your two people back, and she left."

"I see," Justin said dryly. "Well, it's nice to know that when Jeppson comes looking for her I'm not going to have to lie to him."

Adaba nodded. "It's always nice to be able to tell the truth."

"Or to have somebody else," Lucy said, "to do your lying for you."

Perhaps it was a private joke, because Justin looked at her and grinned.

"John," he said, thrusting out a hand, "I don't remember you from Charleston, but I remember your family well. And if my wife hasn't already said it—welcome to Sabrehill!"

425

If Justin was worried about Jeppson coming to Sabrehill in search of Miss Lady, he didn't show it. "He probably had trouble getting a posse together today, on a Sunday. But if Miss Lady is missing, he'll have one riding all over the countryside tomorrow, searching all the quarters and annoying the people and generally raising hell."

"Isn't there anything we can do to stop him?" Lucy asked.

"There certainly is. The minute he shows up here, I'm going to rope and hog-tie that son of a bitch and take him to jail myself. And I'm going to raise hell with the constable for not getting out here when you sent for him."

"But what about Zulie, Justin? Aren't they likely to arrest her and take her to jail too?"

"Why should they? Because of some wild tales about her being part of the Underground Railroad? Nonsense. She's just a runaway wench who was on her way home when Jeppson picked her up and abused her. And now we've got her home again, and nobody is going to take her away from us." Justin's face grew stormy, and he flourished the pepperbox pistol he had been examining. "Nobody touches Zulie or any other of our people except over my dead body!"

Lucy smiled. "Yes, my love."

When it was fully dark, Adaba slipped out to the rooms over the coach house. There he found Sheba applying fresh salves to the half-conscious Zagreus's whip wounds, while Binnie, more white-faced than ever, looked on. When Sheba had finished, Adaba took her into the next room, the same one he and Zulie had occupied, and showed her the hiding place in the hollow wall.

"It's just big enough for a man my size," he said, "and plenty big for you. These boards here, they're a kind of door. You can pull them out. . . ." He demonstrated. "Then step into the hollow. Pull the door closed, and you'll find bolts inside so it can't come loose. The harness hanging over the wall will help keep the door hidden. Nobody will be able to see you, but you'll be able to see out through the cracks in the wall. When Jeppson comes looking for you, you get in there fast and stay there till Binnie or I tell you you can come out. You'll be safe. Nobody has been discovered in there yet."

"It been used much?"

"Enough. Zagreus and Zulie were hiding fugitive slaves long before I first came to Sabrehill."

"I know."

Adaba smiled and gave Sheba's shoulder a reassuring pat. "You got a new life ahead of you, Sheba Lady. As soon as the search for you dies down, I'll take you north. You're gonna have new friends and a new home, and you're never again gonna see a nigger jail or a whipping gallows."

Sheba sank down on the edge of the bed. Instead of looking pleased, as Adaba had expected, an almost hopeless look came over her face.

"You really think I like it in the North, Ad—John?" she asked.

"Well, I'll be honest with you, Sheba. It ain't the Promised Land, and life ain't always easy up there, no more than it is here. But I never heard of black folks up north trying to escape *south*. And I never heard of a poor starving free black up there petitioning to be taken into slavery in order to get fed. That only happens down here."

He wasn't sure Sheba had been listening. She continued to sit perfectly still, gazing into space.

"John, I been thinking. . . ."

"What you been thinking, Sheba?" Odd, how easily that name came to his lips. But then, that just proved that this truly was Sheba and not Gilly. Adaba sat down on the bed beside her.

"I been thinking . . . I'm glad I brought Zulie and Zagreus and Mr. Lewis back here. I'm glad I done what I knowed was right—and right for Mr. Jeppson too, if only he understood. And I'm glad I run off from him. It made me feel free like I never was before. Free in my heart."

Adaba took her hand. "That's where it matters most, Sheba. We both learned that, long ago."

"But I been thinking . . . Mr. Jeppson is going hurt an awful lot of niggers 'count of me."

He patted her hand. "Now, don't you even think about that. Whenever I steal off some people, some others get

427

hurt. But do you think they grudge my runaways their freedom?"

"But this time it be worse, John. I know my Mr. Jeppson, and he'll make it so much worse. But if I was to go back to Redbird . . ."

For a moment, Adaba wasn't sure he understood her. She couldn't possibly mean what she seemed to be saying.

"Sheba, you *can't* do that!"

"Oh, I know he be mean to me. Mean like he never was before. But he mean *only* to me and not anybody else. And even the meanness won't go on forever."

"He'll kill you! You know he'll kill you."

"Oh, I don't think he'll do that. Maybe things can't never be just the same 'tween us no more, but I don't think he'll kill me. And 'sides . . . 'sides . . ."

" 'Sides what, Sheba?"

A tremor passed through Sheba's body, and she seemed to collapse. Her face became the little-girl-Gilly face, and her eyes flooded.

"Oh, Lord God, I swore I wouldn't never look back! But I can't help it, not after twenty years! He ain't old, but he's getting old so fast, and he needs me, John! He's losing Redbird, and he be lucky if he save a few acres of dirt farm and hands enough to work them. I know he's going beat me bad if'n I go back, but he's going need me to weep on too!"

Suddenly Adaba found himself shaking with anger, and he sprang up from the bed. "For God's sake, woman, you're talking about Balbo Jeppson! He's evil, he's wicked, you've said so yourself. He's the scum of the earth. He's a nigger-killer, an animal, filth! You've seen my woman hanging from his whipping gallows, and you know what he is! You're the most blessed woman in the world to be free of him, and I say, please, God, damn Balbo Jeppson to hell for all of his sins!"

Sheba sat utterly still, tears stopped, numb cheeked, as if she had been slapped repeatedly across the face.

"I'm sorry," Adaba said hoarsely after a moment.

Sheba nodded. "You right. I know you right. And I meant it when I said that if the people had riz up with Denmark, I woulda killed him myself. The first night I got to his plantation, he tore the toenails off a poor boy that didn't want nothing but to be free, and I ain't never forgot nor forgiven. But Adaba . . . John . . ." The tears threatened to return, and Sheba shook her head. "For twenty years that man been so good to me, and maybe I growed to love him even more than I knowed. 'Cause trying to cut myself away from him now . . . oh, it's hard, hard, hard!"

"I'm sorry," Adaba said again, and his throat felt clogged with pain. "I reckon I ain't got the right, talking about him to you like that."

"You got the right. 'Cause it's true. Every word you say 'bout him is true."

Adaba returned to the bed, sitting close to Sheba, and for the first time in years drew her into his arms. "Gilly . . . Sheba . . . I know it ain't easy . . . it wouldn't be, even if you didn't care for Jeppson. But you ain't old, Sheba, you're still young, with lots of good years ahead of you. You're gonna have a new life, a good life, and you're never gonna regret leaving Redbird and Mr. Jeppson, I promise you."

Sheba nodded.

After Adaba had left her, to return to the big house, she sat for a long time without moving.

How could he make such a promise to her, she wondered. How could he know what Mr. Jeppson meant to her, however much she tried to tell him? What could he know of the strange mixture of love and hatred for their men that tore so many woman apart. . . .

Where was Mr. Jeppson right now, she wondered. How could she stop him from hurting more people? Adaba thought he understood Jeppson, but he really had no idea of the depths of the man's fury and the lengths to which he would go. He would demand payment for last night's losses as he had never demanded payment before.

Unless she could stop him.

She reached for her reticule, which lay on a nearby table. Opening it, she took out the loaded pistol she had taken from the secretary at Redbird. She stared at it.

Would she really have killed Mr. Jeppson in his sleep, as she had told Adaba? Could she really kill him now?

She didn't know. But looking at the deadly reality of the pistol, she doubted it.

He did love her. Of that she had not the slightest doubt. Then wasn't it possible, just barely possible, that she might calm the worst of his fury? teach him that happiness was preferable to vengeance? persuade him that their fortunes did not depend on this mad pursuit of Adaba?

It was possible. She truly believed it was possible.

She had to.

Jeppson wanted to laugh aloud, he wanted to sing. Now at last he was about to settle accounts with the Sabres, and he knew that after tonight his luck would turn and he would be saved. So they thought they could take his Sheba away from him, did they? Well, tonight they would learn differently. They would learn in flames and fury—and tomorrow a new day would dawn for Balbo Jeppson. Never again would Adaba steal from him, never again would his crops be destroyed. Come February, his factor would pay him the highest prices ever, he would cover his mortgage, and Redbird would be saved.

And Sabrehill would be no more.

He wheeled his horse around to face the others. He had almost two dozen men with him, more than enough.

"Now, you all listen to me," he said, his voice like a low rumble of thunder in the darkness. "Anybody here don't know what we're gonna do?"

"Burn 'em," came Rolly Joe Macon's voice from the darkness at his side. "Burn 'em out."

"That's right. Burn out Sabrehill—the only place 'round here that didn't get burned on the Night of the Fires. And you all know why it didn't. 'Cause it's a house of abolitionists and nigger-lovers and most likely Underground Railroaders as well. They ain't deserving of no mercy—"

"And they ain't gonna get none," said P. V. Tucker.

"No more than any nigger insurrectionist," Jeppson confirmed. "Now, anybody got any questions?"

"What if they're just sitting there waiting for us, Balbo?" came a worried voice from among the riders.

"They ain't waiting for us, Daitch."

430

"But they could be. I heard 'bout a case down in Georgia, they was after some abolitionist, but him and his neighbors heard 'bout it, and they had 'bout fifty armed niggers in the house. And they just purely blew hell out of them poor white boys."

"Now, you listen to me!" Jeppson roared angrily. "They ain't waiting for us with armed niggers nor nobody else, but even if they was, we got nothing to worry about. I told you before, when you hear Rolly Joe blow his bugle the third time, that means it's all over, and you hightail it, no matter what! And the way I got it planned, if there's any trouble, it won't come till you hear Rolly Joe blowing his bugle the third time! . . . Now, any more questions?"

"We all gonna burn the field quarters together?" Tag Bassett asked.

"That's right. We'll fire our torches in them woods just north of the field quarters. Then, when Rolly Joe starts blowing his bugle loud and hard to scare the niggers out, we all ride in and start burning, burn every goddamn shack and cabin we can set afire. You and your men, Tag, you hold the hostages in case we need 'em."

"We know what to do."

"Then, when you hear Rolly Joe start blowing his bugle a second time, the rest of us ride like hell to the big house and start burning all the outbuildings. And I tell Justin Sabre what we want of him. But don't you all go shooting at him unless he shoots first, 'cause we want to get them niggers back—Sheba and Zulie and Adaba— and God only knows where they got 'em hid."

"And you all keep your bandannas up," Tucker said. "Don't nobody show his face. Then they can't truly say they saw who it was, and we can all alibi each other."

"Can't nobody say who it was if they dead," came Daitch's voice from the darkness.

"Yes," Jeppson said with satisfaction, "that surely is true."

"Once we get them niggers," another voice asked, "whyn't we just take care of Justin Sabre and them others for good?"

"Once we got the niggers, and I see Sabrehill burning to the ground," Jeppson said, "I don't give a damn what

431

you do to the Sabres. Until you hear that bugle blow the third time, you do anything you damn please."

"*Anything*, Balbo?"

"Anything." The hot, rich anger flowed through Jeppson like the physical sensations of love, and he said more than he had ever expected to say. "When we got what we want and Sabrehill is burning, you do any damn thing you want to Justin Sabre. Whip him, geld him, cut his guts out—whatever you think he deserves. You can do the same to Lewis Sabre—he's no better than Justin. You can spread Miss Lucy, every damn one of you, for all I care, and carry off Lewis Sabre's white-skin nigger wife. They're all Sabres, and you know what that means. Until you hear that bugle blow the third time, you give 'em what they deserve, men and women alike."

"I'm for that," Bassett said, "I'm for that!"

"All right, then. Let's ride."

They were in the library when they heard the bugle the first time. It was a dim and distant sound, tuneless, braying, and urgent. Lucy paused for a moment, listening, then laughed and said, "My goodness!" Evidently something was going on in the field quarters, some kind of celebration. The bugle was not a normal Sunday-evening sound, but Christmas was only eight days away, and the mood in the quarters was buoyant and festive.

They went on talking, the three of them, discussing Balbo Jeppson's history, his probable reaction to the loss of his three captives, and what had best be done about him. "He's gone too far this time," Justin said. "He belongs in jail. And if Lew dies, God forbid, I'll see that man hang for it!"

But they all knew it was not that simple. The shooting had taken place on Jeppson's property, and evidently there had been no white witnesses to it. Whatever Jeppson's story might be, it would be one man's word against the other's. And however disliked Jeppson might be by the powerful planters of the region, there were plenty who disliked "those damned abolitionist Sabres" just as much. It very well might be impossible to get justice.

432

"Something's wrong," Lucy said suddenly. "I thought I heard the fire bell out in the quarters."

"I didn't hear anything," Justin said. "It's not ringing now."

"It was cut short. Something's wrong, Justin—I feel it. Something's happening—"

The second sounding of the bugle cut her off. It sounded closer now, and it was, if anything, wilder and more urgent than ever. Again and again it sounded, with hardly a pause between calls, growing ever louder. It had hardly stopped, when they heard a thumping on a door and then a voice in the passage.

"Mr. Justin! Mr. Justin, Miss Lucy!"

Justin snatched up the pepperbox pistol and hurried out of the library, through the dining room, and into the passage. Lucy and Adaba followed him. They found Cheney, the chief driver, a big scarred bull of a man, standing in the open doorway. Blood was flowing from a long cut in his bald head.

"I come soon as I got 'way from them," he said, panting, as he staggered into the passage. "I come fast as I can!"

"Cheney," Lucy said, "what is it?"

"They burning—burning—"

"Oh, my God!" Lucy said, as she stepped to the doorway and looked out. *"Justin!"*

Now, for a moment, they heard the fire bell clearly, and Adaba saw flames lighting up the sky to the northeast.

"Oh, my God, Justin, they're burning the quarters!"

"And not only that, Miss Lucy," Cheney said. "They taking prisoners! They got 'em there with a rope 'round their neck, maybe ten, twelve our people. And they abusing the wenches!"

"Who, Cheney?" Justin asked. "Is it Balbo Jeppson?"

"They all wearing bandannas over their face, Mr. Justin, but I think it him all right. And I heard Mr. Bassett's voice, and that's Mr. Macon blowing the horn—"

"Justin!" Lucy cried again, pointing through the open doorway to where fire was blooming along the east service lane.

It was moving toward the coach house, where Sheba was hidden. Adaba had to get her out of there.

But before he could leave the house, half a dozen riders, each carrying a torch, came galloping out of the lane. While most of them crossed the courtyard and entered the west service lane, two reined up in front of the big house. One, a tub-gutted man, held a bugle as well as a torch. The other, a big barrel-chested man, spoke with the voice of Balbo Jeppson, and even at a distance Adaba could see the madness in his torchlit eyes.

"Justin Sabre, you come out here!"

Justin unhesitatingly stepped out through the door and raised the pepperbox, aiming it carefully.

"Go ahead, shoot!" Jeppson shouted. "Shoot me dead, and your niggers gonna die with me. They already got the nooses 'round their necks, and we gonna hang them on every road that leads from Sabrehill as a warning to niggers and nigger-thieves and abolitionists like Justin Sabre. So go ahead and shoot!"

Justin slowly lowered the gun.

Flames began to rise from the west service lane.

"You know what we're here for, Justin Sabre?"

Justin didn't answer.

"You got a runaway nigger named Sheba. And that's one runaway your Underground Railroad ain't gonna take north. We're here to take her back, Justin Sabre."

"I don't know where your Sheba is, Jeppson," Justin said, "and I wouldn't tell you if I did."

"Well, that's too bad, Sabre. 'Cause if we don't get her back, some of your niggers is gonna die. And I'll tell you something else. You got that Railroader, Zulie, and we want her too. And Adaba. If he ain't here, you or Zulie or somebody better be able to lead us to him. 'Cause niggers gonna die for him too."

"Jeppson, you can't—"

"We can, Sabre, and we gonna! We're through having our niggers stole from us! We're through having abolitionist troublemakers in South Carolina! We're through putting up with you, Mr. Justin Sabre! I got more'n twenty men with me, and we're gonna keep right on burning till

434

you hand over them three niggers. And I tell you again—for every one we don't get, a lot of others is gonna die!"

Without waiting for an answer, Jeppson wheeled his horse around and headed for the west lane. The tub-gutted bugler followed him.

Justin stepped back into the passage. He slumped against the wall. His face was pale, his expression one of despair. It was a look Adaba had never thought to see on this man's face.

"Justin," Lucy said, "what are we going to do?"

"I . . . I don't know," Justin mumbled.

"We can't just hand those people over to him!"

"But . . . he said he'd kill . . . and he meant it."

Adaba said softly, "It's your choice, Mr. Abolitionist."

For a moment Justin didn't move. Then something happened to him. His pale face began to darken and reform itself before Adaba's eyes. A tide of anger seemed to be rising in him that could match anything Jeppson had to offer.

"God damn that man to hell!" he said, raising the pepperbox pistol.

"We've got to stop him," Lucy said frantically, "but how?"

"He said he only had twenty-some men with him," Justin said, turning toward the door.

"Justin, no!"

"Twenty men! Well, I, by God, am good for at least ten of them!"

Lucy cried out again, but Justin was already out the door. "Take the west lane, Justin!" Adaba shouted after him. "You take the west, and I'll take the east!"

But he didn't follow Justin out the door. Instead, he ran to the other end of the passage. There he opened the door a slit and peered out across the piazza. He saw no one. Slipping out of the house, he closed the door behind him and ran east, through the garden and up some steps into a gazebo. Hidden there, he looked about. He saw no one, but he did confirm that the flames in the east lane were coming from the carriage and coach houses.

He heard pistol shots, apparently from the west lane. Justin was at work.

Crouching, Adaba ran toward the burning coach house. The instant he entered the firelit lane, he ran into a horseman, backed up by two others. As the first horse reared, with a screaming whinny, Adaba threw himself up at the rider and dragged him from the saddle. The rider's pistol went off, and his torch flew through the air. He pulled a knife and brandished it, but by that time Adaba was behind him, with one arm around the man's head. The man screamed horribly as Adaba twisted his head, but the scream ended abruptly with a snapping sound, and Adaba tossed the body aside.

By then, the second rider was coming at him, bringing down a pistol barrel to fire. Adaba picked up the first man's knife and leapt aside as the pistol went off. He dodged again as the rider tried to ride him down, managed to grab the man's coat and drag him from the saddle, then stabbed him repeatedly as he fell. The rider was dead before he hit the ground.

The third rider got off a shot that missed and turned to flee. With all his strength, Adaba threw the knife. He was lucky. He saw the man rise in the saddle and stiffen, then fall to the ground and lie still.

Adaba ran for the door of the coach house.

In the room at the head of the stairs, Binnie, wide-eyed and frightened, was trying to get Zagreus out of bed and dressed. Adaba ran into the second room. The hiding place was open and empty.

He returned to the first room. "Where is she? Did they find her? Where did she go?"

"I don't know! She left here just a few minutes ago!"

"But why?"

"She said—she said she had to stop Mr. Jeppson!"

"Oh, sweet Jesus!"

He all but threw himself back down the stairs. He ran along the lane toward the courtyard, hardly seeing the three men he had killed. As he neared the yard, he saw that he was too late. Jeppson was once again in the yard, his torch held high, and Sheba was approaching him. Adaba came to a halt, frozen, at the head of the lane, unable to decide what he should do next.

At last he was showing them, these so-called aristocrats, these nigger-loving Sabres! Sabrehill was burning, as if in the flame of Jeppson's wrath, and Sheba was his again. Sitting high in the saddle, he looked down at her as she approached; a small defenseless figure, her reticule clutched before her, a pleading look on her face.

"Miss Lady," he said in the voice of God, "I have come for you!"

A few feet away, she came to a halt and looked up at him. "Mr. Jeppson," she said, "please don't do this!"

"Miss Lady, you done wrong to me. I took you into my house. I let you use it like it was your own. I gave you everything you ever asked for. For twenty years I cared for you like no other nigger was ever cared for. And in return for that, you betrayed me to my enemies."

"Mr. Jeppson, I had to do it—"

"That's why I'm here tonight, Miss Lady—on account of you. I'm taking you back, and I'm gonna punish you. Never again are you gonna soften me, Miss Lady. Never again are you gonna make me forget who's the master and who's the slave—"

"Oh, Mr. Jeppson, I go back with you! I *want* to go back with you! But I heard what you told Mr. Justin 'bout killing all them black people—"

Jeppson felt powerful, implacable, merciless. Justice was his, justice untempered, to mete out like an Old Testament god. Truly, he was Yahweh.

"They gonna die, Sheba. They gonna die if we don't get Zulie and Adaba."

Sheba's hands twisted her reticule. "But they ain't done nothing, them poor people!"

"Likely they're hiding Zulie and Adaba somewhere in the quarters right now. That's why we're burning 'em. They got to be taught a lesson—white and black alike at Sabrehill, they got to be taught!"

"Mr. Jeppson, I'm begging you!"

Jeppson watched with satisfaction as the tears ran down Sheba's face. "It ain't no use begging, Sheba. We got you, so we'll spare some. But every nigger that hangs, you can count yourself the cause. *You* done it, Sheba, *you* done it when you stole away them niggers."

Sheba dipped one hand into her reticule.

Jeppson didn't know, couldn't believe, what she was going to do with the pistol she was taking out.

"Please, I'm begging you, Mr. Jeppson!"

He stared as the barrel swung up toward him. Light from his torch glinted on the metal. The muzzle was a huge black hole, dark as death.

"Oh, dear God," Sheba said, her face a tear-stained mask of pain, "oh, please, Mr. Jeppson!"

Using both hands, she cocked the gun.

She was going to kill him, he realized with horror. His own Sheba, his beloved Sheba, was about to kill him.

Two shots were fired.

Sheba staggered back, her pistol swaying away from Jeppson, a look of astonishment on her face.

Another shot, and she spun around.

A fourth shot knocked her to the ground.

"Sheba!"

Jeppson flung his torch away and leapt from his horse. He raced toward Sheba, every step taking an eternity. Crying her name, he threw himself to his knees and gathered her into his arms.

"Please, Mr. Jeppson, please," she murmured. Her body was slack in his arms, as if all strength were draining out of it.

"Sheba, what they done?"

"Oh, Mr. Jeppson . . ." And then, her eyes were empty.

"Sheba, you ain't hurt bad, you can't be!" The unthinkable was happening, the one possibility he had never considered, the one thing in the world he could not bear.

"Mr. Jeppson, please . . ."

"You gonna be all right!"

"Please . . ."

"Don't you leave me, Sheba!"

"Ain't never . . . ain't never going leave you, Mr. Jeppson. . . ."

"I'll take you home and make you well! Don't leave me, Sheba!"

Sheba's voice seemed to come from an ever-greater distance. "Take me home now, Mr. Jeppson. Take me home. . . ."

"I'll take you home, and everything will be just like it was. Like you always wanted it to be. Won't it, Sheba? Won't it?"

Sheba didn't answer. And rocking her in his arms, Jeppson knew she would never answer him again.

"Blow your bugle, Rolly Joe," he cried out, sobbing. "Blow your bugle. It's all over now. I'm taking Miss Lady home."

Ten

He lived.

Lew wasn't quite sure how it could be, but somehow he had been pulled back out of the darkness, back through the pain, back into life again.

At first there were isolated moments of consciousness. He heard Rose weeping on his shoulder and begging him not to die. He saw the doctor's face and heard him mutter: "Not much I can do . . . but he *might* live . . . he's a mighty game cock." He felt the bandage on his head being replaced.

Then there were longer periods of consciousness, periods when his head hurt so much that he longed for oblivion. He found himself sitting up against pillows, with Rose or Zulie or another spooning broth into his mouth. He saw Cousin Lucy looking into the dimly lit room, heard her asking how he seemed to be. He saw Adaba standing over him, felt him patting a shoulder, heard him saying, "Don't you worry . . . you're gonna be all right, old son. . . . Zulie is up and looking after you now . . . saved old Justin once, and saved me a few years back, and now she's gonna take care of you . . . so don't you worry. . . ."

And then one day Lew found himself quite awake, and most of the ache was gone, and he knew, finally, he was going to live.

"Hell of a thing," he heard himself murmur.

Rose looked around at him, as if surprised to find him awake. "What's that, Lewis?" she asked.

"Hell of a thing, getting shot just before Christmas."

"Yes, you did pick a lovely time."

"Got to be up for Christmas."

Rose laughed. "Why, dear, Christmas is long past. So's the New Year. It's the middle of January, Lew. 1838."

"Goddamn . . ."

Struggling to sit up in bed, he found that he was skeleton thin and almost too weak to move. Rose helped him, tucking pillows behind him.

"Where's Zulie?" he asked.

"Lewis Sabre, the way you keep asking for that woman, you're going to make me plum jealous."

Lew had no memory of having asked for her. "Where is she?"

"Gone to Charleston, with John. With all the talk going around about her and the Underground Railroad, Justin thought it would be best to get her away from here, at least for now."

"Jeppson hasn't got her?"

"No, of course not. Are you still having trouble remembering, Lew?"

Suddenly he did remember. The woman running toward Jeppson. *"Mr. Jeppson, don't! Oh, my God, don't!"* The face out of guilty dreams. And then the pistol shot that had burst his skull and sent him into oblivion.

"Gilly . . ."

Rose looked worried. "Do you really think you should be sitting up, dear?"

"Gilly, she . . . I saw her, and . . . what happened?"

"Dear, I really do think you should rest—"

"But I saw Gilly! What happened! Tell me!"

When he insisted, she told him the whole story—how Sheba had drugged Jeppson and the guards, how she had brought the three captives back to Sabrehill, how she had been shot down by Jeppson's men in the courtyard—and of the long night that followed, fighting the fires at Sabrehill.

"Oh, my God . . ." Lew covered his face.

440

"But I've told you all this before, Lew," Rose said gently.

"I don't remember. What have they done to Jeppson?"

"Well . . . nothing yet, dear."

"Nothing?"

"All of his friends swear he was nowhere near this place that night. None of them was anywhere near here—none but those few John and Justin killed, and dead men tell no tales."

"And I don't suppose the constable is trying very hard to prove any different, is he?" Lew asked.

"Now, don't get upset, Lew."

"Don't get upset?" Lew wanted to weep. "Why should I get upset? What have I ever done to get upset about? Except lose my plantation, and botch up the overseer's job, and go to Redbird and get myself shot like a damn fool and poor Zagreus whipped half to death—"

"Lewis, you stop that!"

"First I got Gilly sold, and then marched back into her life and fixed things so she got herself killed! Killed trying to protect Zulie and John! Trying to do the job I wasn't man enough to do—"

"Lewis, you stop!"

"I failed you, Rose, and I'm sorry. I failed you and the children and our people and Zulie and Gilly and Justin and Lucy and—"

"You stop!"

Rose's eyes blazed, and she drew back her hand to slap him. But the blow never landed. Instead she burst into tears.

"I'm sorry, Rose."

"Oh, you damn fool! It wasn't your fault that crazy man shot you. Sheba . . . Gilly . . . she told us all about it. And you're a brave, good man, Lewis Sabre, and we're all proud of you. Zulie thinks you're the best white man in the world. And the children are proud of you—they've got a hero for a daddy!"

Lew pulled Rose down to him. She buried her face against his shoulder.

Well, not a hero, he thought, stroking Rose's hair. But a very lucky man. A loved man.

Suddenly he was very happy.

"I'll tell you something, Rose," he said, still stroking her hair. "I've said it before, and I'll say it again. This is going to be a fresh start for us, here at Sabrehill. A fresh, new start. And I've got a feeling that the best times of our lives still lay ahead."

This time there was no mocking laughter.

Jeppson slept late.

He had been doing that a great deal lately this last couple of months. He sat up late drinking most nights, always alone, and when he awakened in the morning, he wanted only to stay where he was, unmoving, nursing his aching head and cotton-filled mouth.

Finally, one February morning, he forced himself to get up. The sooner he got plenty of hot coffee down his throat, the sooner he would feel better. Staggering from a bed that hadn't been made in days, he poured water into a bowl and splashed it over a face that hadn't been shaved for a week.

The room was cold. Someone had built a fire but had done it badly, and it had soon gone out.

Sheba would never have allowed that.

Jeppson dressed. Dirty clothes. As he went down the stairs, he observed that there was dust in every corner. The place was getting to look more and more like his old house, the way it had been before Sheba had taken charge of it.

Fenella, hard eyed, arms crossed over her chest, was standing in the dining room as he entered. She looked as if she had been waiting for him, angrily, for hours. As he went toward the table, she whirled around and stomped out of the room, slamming the door behind her.

Jeppson sat down at the table.

A few minutes later, Fenella returned, carrying a tray. She dropped it noisily on the table. She slammed a plate of fatback and grits in front of Jeppson. It looked greasy and cold. She slopped some coffee from a pot into a cup.

Jeppson saucered and tasted the coffee. It was tepid.

"Can't a man even get a hot meal in this house anymore?" he complained.

"Well, if you was up and at work like decent people," Fenella said angrily, "it'd *be* hot!"

Slut!

Once Jeppson would have beaten the woman to her knees for such an impertinence. Now it hardly seemed worthwhile. He struck out with a clumsy arm, and she easily jumped out of the way, leaving the room with sounds of anger in her wake.

Somehow, he managed to get through most of the breakfast. What was going to do today, he wondered vaguely as he finished. How was he going to get through the day?

What did it matter?

He had been to Charleston. He had sold his crop. The price of rice was up a little, but as he had expected, the price of cotton was way down. Now there was no longer any doubt in his mind that he was going to lose Redbird, or most of it. He would be lucky if he could salvage a few acres of land and a few hands to help him work it. He was right back where he had been so many years earlier.

And he was too old to start over again. Another man might have, but Jeppson was old, old far beyond his years, and he felt it and knew it.

Well, he would at least go through the motions of working. He would oversee his hands at their tasks. The habit of work would carry him through the day. But first . . .

He went to the mahogany secretary in the parlor and got out the loaded pistol—the same pistol Sheba had stolen and had used to threaten him. He had brought it back from Sabrehill. Sometimes he looked at it and wondered . . . would she actually have pulled the trigger? would she really have killed him?

He stuck the pistol into his belt.

He picked up a bullwhip that lay across a chair, coiled it, and went out into the yard. He had to squint in the bright morning sunshine. No one was in the jail, and the door was off one of its hinges. The whipping gallows too was in need of repair. It had begun to sag and stagger to one side like a drunken man.

Jeppson saw that Pickett was talking to several slaves. Not working them, not ordering them, not driving them,

443

just talking to them. Chatting and laughing. Some of the old anger boiled up.

"Mr. Pickett, goddammit, are you gonna put them niggers to work or not?"

Pickett looked startled. "Oh, yes, sir, Mr. Jeppson, we was just—"

"You was just talking 'bout the wenches you want to spread. Well, I want to see some work getting done, goddammit! Why you got these hands standing here when the jail house door got to be fixed and the gallows set up straight?"

"Yes, sir, Mr. Jeppson, I—"

"I want to see that door fixed this morning. And I want to see that gallows up straight and strong by afternoon. And by evening I want to see a lazy nigger hanging from that gallows, and I want to see him in the jail house tonight." Jeppson looked around at the little group. Uncoiling his whip, he drew it back and cracked it hard and loud. "Now, which one of you black bastards is it gonna be? Which one of you lazy sons of bitches gonna feel the bite of my whip?"

"I'm putting 'em to work right now, Mr. Jeppson!"

"See you do it, Mr. Pickett. There's gonna be discipline on this plantation, if I got to see raw meat on a nigger's back every night of the year!"

He coiled the whip again and walked off, feeling the hatred in the stares that burned into his back. Hatred so strong that he had taken to carrying a pistol.

And now what was he to do?

He didn't know.

He simply walked. And walked. Until he became aware that once again he was heading for Redbird's slave graveyard. For a time, he had avoided going there, but now he found himself visiting it almost every day.

He wished he had some flowers.

The tall black man with the broad shoulders and the black muzzle of beard moved soundlessly through the shadows of the woods. He wore a broad-brimmed hat, a bandanna was tied around his throat, and he carried a rifle. He moved Indian-like, sometimes swiftly, sometimes

444

very slowly, but he paused to look about between every move, and he saw everything.

He saw the hands at work in the fields. He saw their drivers and overseers. But they didn't see him.

Today, Adaba thought. Today, with any luck, he would do it. He had thought about it for a long time, and he had decided to do it in broad daylight and at a particular place. He would do it cleanly and as painlessly as possible, with a rifle, but he wanted to see Jeppson clearly first. And he wanted Jeppson to see him clearly and to know why it was happening.

He reached the slave graveyard. Located in a clearing in the woods, it was fairly typical. The graves were decorated with colorful bits of broken glass and pottery, whatever could be found. Wooden images, snakelike and phallic, reminiscent of Danbhalah, spirit of life, were scattered throughout the yard. A number of them were as tall as Adaba. Some of the graves had old quilts and blankets over them. A blanket lay over Sheba's grave, and he saw that someone had recently washed it.

Sheba had been loved.

Ever since he had returned from Charleston, Adaba had been watching Jeppson from a distance, and he knew something of the man's habits. But perhaps he would not come to the graveyard today. Very well, then, Adaba would return tomorrow. He would return as many times as necessary. He wanted it to happen here, if at all possible.

He was not to be disappointed. Crossing the graveyard and looking out between trees, he saw Jeppson coming. The man trudged along, head down, as if he could barely carry his own weight. Adaba swiftly stepped behind a tree.

Jeppson, whip in hand, pistol in his belt, entered the graveyard.

As usual, Jeppson went to Sheba's grave; there, as usual, he stood perfectly still, silently looking down. Now was the time. Even in the cool air, Adaba's hands felt damp on the rifle. Aiming it at Jeppson, he stepped out from behind the tree.

Jeppson heard nothing.

Now speak. Say his name. Let him look up and see you. Let him know why.

445

But Jeppson did something different today. Usually, he simply stood by the grave a few minutes, then turned and walked away. Today, the whip dropped from his fingers. His knees seemed to buckle, and he fell to the ground by Sheba's grave, bending over it as if in pain.

He made a sound.

After a moment, as the sounds grew louder, Adaba realized that the man was weeping. And he was weeping, not easily, not gently, but in great tortured sobs that seemed to be torn out of his soul. Adaba hadn't heard a man weep like that since the night he had met Black Buck.

All right! Don't say a thing! Just fire! Put the son of a bitch out of his misery!

But Adaba did not fire.

He continued to stand there, perfectly still. Only when Jeppson's weeping had entirely subsided did he slowly pull back the cock of his gun.

Jeppson heard it. And, just as slowly, he looked up.

Adaba knew the face.

For twenty years, it had been a blank to him, a mere impression of shock and anger. Whenever he had seen Jeppson since, it had always been at a distance or in darkness. But now he recognized that face, and what was more—

—Jeppson remembered!

The black girl stumbling against him, her foot coming down painfully on his ankle . . . the girl laughing, *"Oh, I sorry! Oh, master, I sorry!"* . . . his own rising anger . . . striking the girl, shaking her . . .

And then that angry young black face, those black hands that had dared to seize him—to seize *him*—and those angry black curses: *"You—you goddamn—you bastard! You ignorant swamprat bastard, you touch her, I'll kill you! You hear me, you buckra bastard, I'll kill you!"*

Jeppson had often bragged that he never forgot a black face. And he had not forgotten this one. Not even twenty years and a mask of beard could hide this one from him.

He remembered being cursed, he remembered being struck, he remembered being thrown sprawling in the dirty street.

And that was not all he remembered.

He remembered the girl crying out in alarm, crying out a warning, crying out words that had meant nothing to him at the time.

"Adaba!" she had cried out. *"Adaba!"*

That was what she had screamed! And *that* was why he had so hated that name over all the years!

Adaba!

Sheba *had* known who the boy was. All these years she had lied to him. All these years she had protected the young buck who had assaulted him on the street, who had cursed and threatened him, who had treated him like a nigger.

What was he to think, then? That his Sheba had never really cared for him? That her allegiance had always been to this slave-stealing black Railroader? Had she cared nothing at all for him.

No! He could not believe that!

"I got a real love for you, Mr. Jeppson," she had said that last night together. *"I want you to know that. I don't want you ever to forget that. No matter what."*

He had to believe that she had loved him even as she had raised the pistol to end his life. He had to cling to that—

"So you remember me, do you, Jeppson?"

The shock of recognition remained on Jeppson's face, but he didn't move, didn't say a word.

"Maybe you remember that I swore if you hurt Gilly I'd kill you?"

And still Jeppson was silent, though a tremor passed over his face.

"Nothing to say?" Adaba lowered the barrel of the rifle slightly. "Well, don't worry, Jeppson. I reckon I ain't gonna kill you after all. Not this time."

Adaba's voice shook. "Oh, I came here to kill you all right. To kill you for what you done to Zulie and Zagreus. For what you done to Lew Sabre, who was only trying to take them back where they belonged. For what you helped do to Black Buck's Claramae all them years back. For what you've done to a thousand niggers, Jeppson, and for what you caused to happen to Gilly. To Sheba.

"But I ain't gonna kill you. And the only reason is that I reckon you musta loved her too, in your way. And maybe she had a kind of love for you."

"She did," Jeppson said. "She loved me . . . loved me."

"Maybe. Just maybe. So I'm letting you go. But I'm warning you, Jeppson. Sheba told me how you planned to get me by tracking down my family. And if I ever hear of you doing such a thing, if you ever get near anybody dear to me, if you dare lay a finger on anybody in the world to get at me, I'm coming back for you. And I'm gonna give you a worse death than you ever gave any slave. So take heed, Jeppson. Or you're gonna learn to die."

Jeppson stared unblinkingly at Adaba, as if hardly hearing or comprehending the warning. Then an odd sound began to come from his throat. It was a low growl, purely animal.

As it rose in volume, Jeppson got up from his knees. Suddenly he plunged toward Adaba, tearing the pistol from his belt.

The sound became a word: *"NIGGER-R-R-R—"*

Adaba raise the barrel of his rifle.

"—R-R-R-R—"

The shot's echo racketed across fields and through woods. Birds arose from the trees around the graveyard in a flurry of wings.

Jeppson staggered back. He dropped his pistol and fell, not far from Sheba's grave.

Adaba waited for a moment. Jeppson didn't move.

When he went closer, he saw that Jeppson's eyes were open and blank.

"Well," Adaba said softly after a moment, "I reckon you wanted it that way."

He stood by the grave and the dead man for a few minutes longer. Then, unhurriedly, he turned and made his way into the concealing woods.

The birds began to return to the trees. A squirrel ran across the graveyard.

The gentlest of breezes swept across Redbird and Sabrehill, hinting at spring.

448